Wild Sage wanted to turn away from him, to tear herself from his embrace. This man was her enemy. He'd fought in the battles that had taken her parents' lives, he'd brought her here to an alien land and people, yet all that was forgotten in the blaze of fire he'd ignited within her. Her arms went about his neck, and she felt the unyielding breadth of his shoulders, his muscular back. Her aching breasts were crushed against his hard chest. Then his hands cupped her soft flesh, his thumbs brushed against her sensitive nipples, and unnamed desires swept through her. The barrier of innocence melted beneath his touch, and she pressed against him. . . .

WILD
SAGE

Peggy Hanchar

FAWCETT GOLD MEDAL • NEW YORK

A Fawcett Gold Medal Book
Published by Ballantine Books
Copyright © 1994 by Peggy Hanchar

Library of Congress Catalog Card Number: 94-94403

ISBN 0-449-14771-1

Manufactured in the United States of America

First Edition: November 1994

10 9 8 7 6 5 4 3 2 1

Chapter 1

"*C*OMANCHE!" CALEB HUNTER uttered the one word like a curse and spat between his teeth, a further indication of his loathing for the line of horsemen silhouetted on a distant ridge. Capt. John Wright glanced at his tracker.

"Could be Kiowa," he said. "They're too far away to see their markings."

"I can smell them." Caleb slouched in his saddle, one hand resting easily on the pommel, the other gripping the reins. His tall, whipcord-lean body seemed at ease, but Captain Wright wasn't fooled by Caleb's stance. He knew from experience that Caleb was a coiled spring capable of striking faster than a mad sidewinder. He also knew he could rely on Caleb's information about the menacing line on the horizon. Caleb Hunter was the best damn tracker around, better even than the half-breeds the army usually employed—and a damn sight more reliable. Once they'd earned enough for whiskey, the Indian scouts would often disappear into the mountains for a few months, returning only when they were broke, hung over, and half starving.

Caleb never seemed to need a rest. No one knew

much about him, except that he hated Indians, all Indians, but the Comanche most of all. No one knew why exactly, although rumors abounded. No one had ever found the courage to question him about his past. The secrets lay sealed behind weather-beaten features seemingly carved of stone and flinty gray eyes that could look at a man in such a way it made his blood run cold. Captain Wright had seen more than one man back down from a fight with Caleb, intimidated by his rock-hard demeanor. Those who hadn't backed down learned the hard way and never came back for a repeat lesson.

In a land of tough, hard men, Caleb Hunter stood out as the toughest and meanest, yet Wright had never seen him pick a fight with anyone or shoot a man in the back. If anyone had asked him who were Caleb's friends, he guessed he would have had to say he was the one and only man close to him, yet even he didn't really know anything about the loner. And Caleb Hunter was a loner. He had no family. Sometimes Captain Wright imagined he had been fashioned of Texas clay and mountain granite, receiving the breath of life from a hot prairie wind.

Rumor had it he was only fifteen when he killed his first redskin and was in turn wounded and left for dead among the mutilated bodies of his family and the charred remains of their ranch. There were a lot of rumors about, true or not, but one rumor everyone trusted was the one about the mechanical skill with which he killed the redskins. With unemotional detachment he sought out their haunts, running the Comanche to ground even in the Cross timbers, where they believed themselves to be safe. Caleb found them and killed them. Only once had Captain Wright looked in Caleb's face on such an expedition—and the hell he'd seen mirrored in his eyes had caused him to look away. If ever a man lived in torment, Caleb Hunter was that man.

Now Captain Wright turned his attention back to the line of warriors on the distant bluff. In the blink of an eye, they'd disappeared, drawing back down the hill on the opposite side.

"Let's go after them," Wright said, signaling to his men to prepare to ride.

"Wait," Caleb said, and, leaning forward, flicked a match head against his boot and lit a cheroot.

"They're on the run. They must think they're outnumbered," Wright persisted.

Caleb shook his head and pulled his sweat-stained, broad-brimmed hat lower over his eyes. "They didn't run," he said in a low, flat voice. "They'll play with you and your men awhile, tiring out your horses, making you careless, then they'll attack."

"How do you know?" Wright demanded.

"I know." Caleb drew the smoke deep into his chest and slowly let it out. His eyes were keen beneath his hat brim. Trail dust lay in the creases of his cheeks and near his eyes. His jaws were unshaven, containing several days growth. There was a tense anticipation about him, yet he smiled, a savage grimace that boded no good for anyone.

Reluctantly Captain Wright lowered his hand and gazed at the empty horizon, where dust still hung in the air like a curtain, testifying to the passing of their enemy.

"We'll do it at our time and pace," Caleb said. "Turn

your men and ride toward that distant ridge back there. That's where you'll find your Comanche."

"Are you sure about that, Hunter?"

Caleb's glance was derisive. He turned his horse with a sharp prod and set it to cantering toward the ridge they'd just left. Captain Wright sat warring between his choices; his men watched silently. How they all longed to dash over that hill in full-out pursuit of the Indians, but if what Caleb said was so, the Comanche wouldn't be there. They'd be at the regiment's back. Wright nodded to his assistant, and the order was given. Wheeling his horse he followed Caleb Hunter.

The men sat in a neat line, their horses turned to their rear, their weapons unsheathed and ready. The foothills had gone silent, as if the hills and prairie held their breath, waiting for what was about to happen. The Indians came silently. They were closer here; Wright and his men could pick out details in their dress.

Their lances could be seen first, poking out along the ridge like stiff barren stalks drying in the wind, then came the heads of the Comanche, some of them wearing their war headdress. Their painted buckskin shields reflected the sun. Bits of cloth and hawk feathers, deer hooves, and eagle feathers decorated the rounded disks in various symbols and meanings. Even the manes and tails of their mounts had been woven with bits of cloth and feathers. They came forward stealthily.

"Son of a bitch!" Caleb Hunter said under his breath, and his knuckles grew white on his rifle butt.

"What is it?" Captain Wright asked, then felt the hair at the back of his neck tingle.

"It's our old friend, Two Wolves," Caleb said, without taking his gaze off the head Indian.

The Indians came on as if they hadn't yet caught a glimpse of the line of soldiers, then a war chief wearing the honored buffalo scalp headdress came to an abrupt halt and held up his hand. As if connected, the line of warriors obeyed him instantly. For a full minute the leader known as Two Wolves glared down at the soldiers, then with a wild, savage cry he led the line of screaming Comanche down the ridge toward Captain Wright's regiment.

Army horses snorted with terror at the sudden rush of noise and animals, but the men brought them under control with an impatient jerk of the reins. They were brave men, experienced in Indian fighting and not easily routed.

"Fire when ready," Wright cried, and a volley of shots echoed across the valley.

Caleb Hunter took little notice of Wright or his men. He waited until the mad dash brought the savages closer, his rifle cocked and aimed at the leader known as Two Wolves. Closer the warrior came, his lance raised high, the whites of his eyes fierce and menacing in his painted face. As the war chief stood up in his saddle to throw his lance, Caleb's finger tightened on the trigger. His shot nearly spun the warrior out of his saddle. Caleb aimed again, but Two Wolves was no longer in his saddle. Caleb wasted no time looking back on the ground. He knew the wounded Indian lay in a sling against the side of his horse, only a heel holding him in his saddle.

The battle raged around them. Comanche horsemen

reached the line of soldiers and engaged in a bitter fight. Caleb paid little attention to the sound of mortal combat, the cries of men dying. He thought only of the Comanche leader streaking away from him. He sighted along the barrel of his rifle and fired again. The tough little Indian pony stumbled, then regained its feet and ran toward the open prairie. Caleb prepared to fire again. This time the little pony went down, and the Comanche clinging to its side flung himself clear of the floundering beast. Taking shelter behind his horse, Two Wolves lay studying the battle behind him. Caleb drew a bead on him again and fired. The bullet kicked up dirt near the warrior. He drew back, his fierce dark eyes glaring at Caleb. The gaze of the two men locked in deadly combat. Pinned behind his dead pony, the Comanche war chief could do little. He was used to fighting from horseback and now he'd been dismounted, but his hate-filled glare promised vengeance.

Some silent signal had been given. The Comanche rallied their men and galloped away. Distracted, Caleb fired at their departing backs, taking down three men in as many seconds. When he glanced back at the dead Indian pony, Two Wolves was no longer there.

The gunfire died away, followed by an instant of silence before the soldiers sent up a cheer. "They're on the run. We ran the bastards off, sir," they cried jubilantly.

Captain Wright grinned and holstered his gun, looking around to find Caleb. "You were right, Hunter," he called. "How'd you know they would double back?"

"Like I said, Captain, you can smell a Comanche.

When I couldn't smell them anymore, I knew they'd moved downwind."

Caleb's gaze never wavered from the backs of the fleeing Indians. Two Wolves, mounted on a fresh pony, was leading his warriors up a ridge. When he reached the top he whirled his pony and glared back down at the white men. Raising his lance over his head, he let out a bloodcurdling shriek that brought shivers to the bloodied men below. Caleb knew the wild cry was meant for him. Raising his rifle, he sighted along its barrel and pulled the trigger. The lance splintered in Two Wolves's hand. In a cloud of dust, he whirled his pony and disappeared over the ridge.

"Shame you missed him, sir." Nye Garrett wiped his sweat-stained face and peered at the horizon.

"I didn't," Caleb said, and sheathed his rifle.

"Why didn't you kill him when you had the chance?" Captain Wright snapped. "He was their leader."

"This wasn't the time," Caleb said. "I want to look into Two Wolves's eyes when I kill him."

"How come you hate this Comanche so bad?" Nye asked, remounting. He was still a young man, but years in the army, riding the trails and fighting, had prematurely aged him. His brown hair had long since turned gray at the temples. Only the lithe spryness of his trail-hardened body gave some clue to his true age.

The men around Caleb grew quiet, silenced by the hard-bitten gaze of the tracker. Most doubted he'd answer Nye. They were surprised when he pushed back the rim of his hat.

"A few years back when I rode with Murray's Rangers, a band of renegades started attacking homesteads south of here. They were a bunch of rebellious young Comanche bucks out to make a name for themselves. I saw the evidence of their handiwork. Men disemboweled, women raped and left cut in a way that—" He stopped talking. "They took no prisoners, not even children, but they scalped 'em. Have you ever held a baby that was scalped and left to die in his own blood?" Caleb gathered up his reins and looked around at the circle of stark faces.

"Comanche take scalps, but there's no real honor in it. It's just a symbol of the battles they've fought. Taking the scalp of a baby wasn't necessary for him to make a name for himself, but he did it anyway. Someday, I'm going to take *his* scalp—and I want him alive when I do it."

Their moment of jubilation was ended. Caleb's stark narration had brought them back to the reality of the foe they sought. If the Comanche had ridden away from them this day—after only a short skirmish—they'd had a reason. Some of the men counted themselves lucky; some longed to ride back to the safety of the fort. Only the wounded would be sent back. The rest would go on. Silently they waited for Caleb Hunter, not their captain, to give them new orders.

"Now we go after them," Caleb said. "We follow them far enough back, so they don't suspect we're there. We're goin' all the way to their village."

"Into the Cross timbers?" a man cried, whether in dread or disbelief Captain Wright wasn't sure, nor did he care. His gaze was locked with the bleak, fierce gaze of Caleb Hunter. Slowly Wright nodded in agreement.

"See to the wounded," Wright called. "Assign a detail to take them back to the fort. The rest of you, prepare to mount up and ride."

Exhilaration over razing the Comanche was gone. Each man thought about the Cross timbers, the desolate wooded area of West Texas that was a hiding place for Comanche and Mexican bandits alike. If one didn't get you, the other surely would.

Wild Sage raised her head and looked back toward the Comanche village. A spiral of dust had been spotted out on the plains and a messenger sent to the village to warn them of the return of the war party. She should be down there, preparing food for the warriors, for they would have ridden long and hard and would surely be hungry. Instead, she'd crept up here to this high, secret place she'd found and kept as her own special place. Here she could look down on the conical shapes of the village tepees and see the people moving among them.

Their village was very small now. Once it had been great, with hundreds of tepees, but the white soldiers had hounded the Comanche people, destroying their villages and taking captives. Many of their leaders had been imprisoned and their women and children put on reservations. There were only a few separate bands living deep in the Cross timbers, vowing never to give up their freedom for the white man's ways. Wild Sage sat down on the grass, near a tiny brook that tripped over multicolored rocks, and thought of all that had occurred.

Her father, Ten Bears, was a very brave man, well respected among his people, as were all ancient ones. His wisdom had kept them from the blazing guns of the white soldiers. His warriors were still intact, leaving the

Cross timbers only to hunt buffalo and raid the white
settlements for goods. Once the Comanche had traded
with other Indian tribes, the Kiowa and Pueblo, and
even some of the white settlers, but the constant stream
of settlers into the land of the Comancheria had ended
all that. Now the Comanche were mortal enemies with
the white men.

Wild Sage sighed, glancing down at her arms and
legs. They were slender and brown, but not with the
same duskiness of the people. Beneath her clothes, her
skin was as pale and white as the hated soldiers who
had driven her people away. Fiercely, she wished this
were not so. Ten Bears and his wife, White Weasel, had
adopted her as their daughter many years ago, when she
was a small child. She had been treated as a true Comanche ever since, but she wished she carried the blood
of her people in her veins instead of that of their enemy.
Still, it did not matter to Ten Bears or White Weasel,
who loved her, or to Two Wolves, who would take her
as his wife now that he had returned from his raid.

Wild Sage lay back in the grass thinking of the fierce
warrior who'd wooed her, showing off his prowess on
his favorite war-horse, demonstrating his superior
strength. He was a war chief, an honor for one so
young, but Two Wolves had earned that honor by
meeting with the white men and fighting them while
still a young untried boy. He and his band had brought
back many gifts to the village—horses and metal pots
and, best of all, the white man's guns, which were hard
to come by and highly prized. Two Wolves had also
brought back many scalps, and they hung in his tepee.
Wild Sage had trouble looking at his scalps, for they re-

minded her of the people he'd killed. Sometimes she was afraid of Two Wolves, though she tried hard not to show it.

When Two Wolves looked at her with his bold, unblinking gaze, she was proud he had chosen her from all the young maidens, but still she felt frightened. Would he one day turn his savage strength against her? Wild Sage knew that some warriors misused their wives. Would Two Wolves? Or would he be like Ten Bears and treat her with the same respect and gentleness her adopted father showed White Weasel?

She frowned, pondering these mysteries and many others she knew existed between men and women. Would Two Wolves be pleased with her ripening body? And what of the pale skin hidden beneath her elk dress? Two Wolves hated the whites. Would he see her skin and hate her as well?

"Wild Sage! Are you here?" A familiar voice interrupted her troubling thoughts.

"White Weasel. I am here," Wild Sage answered, and leapt to her feet as her mother climbed into the shaded nook.

"Ah, here you can fly with eagles," White Weasel said, gazing at the valley below. She was a tall, dignified woman, nearly as tall as Ten Bears. Her slim figure was clad in a fine dress of elkskin. Elk teeth had been sewn in a thick pattern over the bosom and at the hem. White Weasel looked very elegant, her long dark hair combed smooth and flowing around her shoulders. She'd painted her part and the inside of her ears a bright vermilion and adorned her earlobes with bits of fur, beads, and feathers.

"This is a good place," she said, smiling at Wild Sage.

"How did you know where I was?" Wild Sage asked, not in the least displeased that White Weasel had found her. She loved the Indian woman fiercely.

"When I was a girl, I, too, found my own place to sit and think." White Weasel smiled, and her long plain face lit up with beauty. As the wife of an honored peace chief, White Weasel possessed much dignity and prestige among the other women, and her demeanor reflected that, but when she was alone with Wild Sage and her husband, her lively eyes reflected a wicked humor that often set them laughing. Now White Weasel sat down beside the mountain stream and gazed at the valley below. Her face was somber as she continued.

"Two Wolves and his men return. Why do you not come down to greet him?"

"I have been watching their approach," Wild Sage said guiltily, "but I had a wish to be alone." She seated herself beside White Weasel, grateful she'd come to offer her advice.

"Soon you will become Two Wolves's wife," White Weasel said. "Does this not please you?"

"I am much honored," Wild Sage said, and hung her head.

"Then why do you not smile?" White Weasel asked. Her touch was gentle as she cupped her daughter's chin and raised her face, so she might meet her gaze.

Wild Sage sighed and lowered her lashes. "I'm frightened," she whispered, and blinked back tears. She would never be a good Comanche. No other woman would admit to such fears, yet here she was, near tears.

She bit the inside of her lips and clenched her hands into fists to still this weakness.

White Weasel watched her daughter struggle with her emotions and once again reached out a gentle hand to her. "It is not unnatural to have such fears, little one," she murmured. "Once, I, too, felt fear that Ten Bears would not find me comely enough, or that he would not show me kindness on our marriage pallet. But such fears were groundless."

"Two Wolves is not Ten Bears," Wild Sage whispered.

White Weasel glanced at her daughter sharply. "That is true." She sighed. "Two Wolves is not Ten Bears. You must teach him how to be gentle."

"But how?" Wild Sage wailed, bringing her gaze up to meet White Weasel's. "How do I begin?"

"Your beauty and virtue will show him," White Weasel answered. "You are the daughter of Ten Bears and not to be ill used. Two Wolves will know this and will respect you for it. You are beautiful and with virtue; this will win his heart to you for all time. Do not be afraid, little one. Tomorrow you will wed Two Wolves—and afterward, you will laugh at your fears."

Wild Sage smiled tremulously, her eyes bright behind their unshed tears. "Thank you, Mother. You have eased my fears," she said, and caught White Weasel's hand and brought it to her cheek.

White Weasel watched the changing expressions on her daughter's face. How she had come to love this strange girl. When Ten Bears had traded for the child, thin and bruised from her ill-treatment among the Kiowa, White Weasel had felt disappointment. She'd wanted to adopt a strong boy who would one day hunt and fight for his people. Instead she'd been given a small scrap of humanity she wasn't even sure would live past the summer. But Wild Sage had clung to life tenaciously, gaining weight and health and even impudence, often bringing White Weasel to laughter with her independence and rebellion.

Ah, but how quickly such rebellion could be deflected with just a gentle touch of a hand. It had been easy to cherish a child as quick and bright, as courageous and giving, as this one. Now she sat before White Weasel, her gaze trusting, her rounded cheek soft beneath her mother's hand, her beauty a shining light. No wonder Two Wolves and many of the other warriors wanted Wild Sage as a wife. She was a hard worker and fearless in her own way. Her heart was kind, so that she rushed in to protect those weaker than she. And she was beautiful, her hair neatly braided behind each ear and her soft gray eyes shining with love. White Weasel felt the sting of tears behind her own eyes at the thought of losing this daughter she valued so highly. She knew Ten Bears felt the same.

"Come, we must go down. Two Wolves will want to see you there, ready to greet him." Taking Wild Sage's hand, she led the way down to the village.

They reached the village square just as the warriors rode in amid a cloud of dust. Two Wolves rode at the front of the raiding party, but Big Elk rode close beside him, holding Two Wolves in his saddle. The Warriors rode around the square, their cries shrill and triumphant.

Wild Sage could see their raid had been successful, for the warriors drove many extra horses ahead of them and their parfleches were fat with loot. The villagers set up a welcoming cry, rushing forward to touch the warriors. But Wild Sage's gaze was pinned on the tall warrior who sat rigidly in his saddle. As if feeling her glance he turned and met her gaze, his black eyes fierce and filled with anger. Toward her? Wild Sage cast her thoughts backward to see what she might have done to offend Two Wolves. Big Elk spoke to him, and he turned back to the revelry in the square. Only when the warriors had finished their display of bravery and their parfleches were opened to the villagers did Two Wolves dismount. With Big Elk by his side, he limped toward the tepee of the medicine man.

Wild Sage felt her heart beat rapidly. Two Wolves had been wounded. She gripped White Weasel's arm, and the Indian woman smiled reassuringly.

"Do not weep or show distress, little one," she advised. "Two Wolves is a proud warrior. He did not wish the people to know he is wounded."

Wild Sage nodded in acquiescence, then watched silently as the last of the warriors rode into the square—leading horses over which bodies had been draped. Two men had been lost in the raids, and now their families came forward, the women raising their voices in a high-pitched wail of grief.

Wild Sage felt a shiver run up her back. Warriors had been killed and Two Wolves wounded. She might have been one of these grieving women and be required to tear at her skin and hair in anguish and even to cut away a finger joint. Her fingers curled into her fist and she wondered if she would have felt such anguish if Two Wolves had been among the dead.

"Come," White Weasel said. "We will wait outside the medicine man's lodge." Wild Sage went with her willingly.

Silently they waited, barred by tradition from entering the lodge. No sound came from within save that of the medicine man's chant and the rattle of his medicine stick.

"Do not fear, Wild Sage. Two Wolves is a strong warrior. His wound isn't fatal," White Weasel reassured her.

"I was wondering if this will delay our wedding day," Wild Sage said. White Weasel looked at her daughter and wondered if that had been her wish.

They waited until shadows gathered among the tepees and along the riverbank. Then Ten Bears came to them. He was a squat man of medium height and the years had bowed his shoulders, but he held his head proudly and his eyes bespoke an intelligence and wisdom that drew men to trust him. Now he stood before his wife and daughter.

"He Who Fights With A Feather has tended Two Wolves's wounds and sent the evil spirits from his body. Two Wolves will live and the wedding will continue tomorrow as planned."

"Thank you, my father, for this news," Wild Sage whispered. "I give thanks to the spirits for their forbearance."

Ten Bears smiled at his daughter and clamped her on the shoulder in approval, then he turned to his wife. "Come, White Weasel. I am hungry!" The twinkle in his eyes bespoke a hunger far different than White Weasel's meat pot would fulfill. Silently White Weasel followed her husband back to their tepee.

Wild Sage stood in the shadows, watching them go. She wouldn't follow right away. She would give them time alone, for she knew from the nights shared in her parents' tepee that their mating would be lusty. She would go instead to the square and share the celebration there. Before she could turn away, the flap of the medicine lodge was flung back, and Two Wolves stepped out. When he saw her waiting, he grunted in approval and stalked over to her.

"I see you wait for me, Wild Sage," he said, and his voice was harsh, as if he were ignorant of a softer way to speak.

"I—I wished to see if you were well," she stammered, trying to meet his gaze.

"You will make a good wife," he grunted, already staring over her head at the mass of figures in the square.

"Are you well, Two Wolves?" Wild Sage asked, and felt him pulling his thoughts back to her. "Was your wound very bad?"

He scowled at the mention of his wound. One hand went to his thigh, wrapped now in herbs and a soft piece of deerskin. "It is nothing," he said dismissively.

"Did you kill many enemies?" Wild Sage persisted, trying to find some subject that would reach him and make him really look at her.

His scowl only deepened. "We took many scalps in our raids," he said.

"Then you have taken the scalp of the one who wounded you?" Her voice was light. She wanted to share his triumph with him, but his hand shot out and clasped her arm in a painful grip.

"Do not ask so many questions, Wild Sage," he berated her. "It is not seemly in a wife." He flung her away from him and stalked away.

Wild Sage bit her lips to keep from crying out and stood rubbing her wrist, watching his departing back. A sound made her whirl and face the warrior who'd stayed beside Two Wolves since their arrival.

"Big Elk," she said, and strove to compose herself.

"Two Wolves feels much anger now," Big Elk said by way of explaining his friend's abrupt behavior. "He has an enemy among the white eyes who seeks him out."

"Who?" Wild Sage asked, knowing Big Elk would not rebuke her as Two Wolves had done.

"The man known as The Hunter."

"I have heard the warriors speak of him. Is he as evil as they say?"

"Like the wolf, he tracks the Comanche to their homes here in the Cross timbers. Like the coyote, he slinks in quietly and makes his kill. Today, he stood on two legs like a man and aimed for Two Wolves alone. His bullets took the life of Fire In The Sky, his warhorse."

"I am sorry to hear this," Wild Sage answered. "Two Wolves has much reason for being angry."

Big Elk nodded, and with a final farewell walked toward the village square to seek out his friend.

Thoughtfully Wild Sage followed and stood in the shadows, watching as the two warriors joined the other men. They would celebrate far into the night, distributing their gifts, partaking of the feast of dog meat, and bragging of their exploits. Two Wolves would not share the information of how he was wounded, as Big Elk had explained it to her. Tomorrow she would become the wife of Two Wolves, but she felt no elation. Sighing, she turned toward Ten Bear's tepee. Who was this enemy known as The Hunter? Would he lead the white soldiers here to this village as he had to others? He must be a great warrior, indeed, to best Two Wolves. Wild Sage prayed silently that the Great Spirit would keep her from the path of The Hunter.

Chapter 2

THE MORNING DAWNED warm and promising. Wild Sage heard the discreet rustling of her parents' bed robes and quickly rose and set about her chores, gathering wood for the fires and taking the water bag, made of a dried buffalo stomach, to the river.

Lingering shadows of the passing night lay over the river, turning its still surface to a mirror shine. Wild Sage shivered in the damp chill before pulling her buckskin dress over her head and stepping into the water. It curled around her slender brown legs. Steeling herself for the first shock of cold water, she dived headlong beneath its bright, placid surface and swam with quick, sure strokes to the middle of the river. When she resurfaced, her hair lay sleek and dark against her head, giving her the appearance of an otter or beaver. Wild Sage flipped on her back and lay back in the water, staring at the gray dawn sky.

Today was her wedding day. Two Wolves's wounds were recovered enough to proceed as planned. Already he seemed impatient to be done with the wedding and all the attendant ceremonies and feasts, so he might gather the other young men and set out to find the man

who had wounded him. Wild Sage had crept to the edge
of the crowd of villagers listening to the warriors recite
their tales of the raids and the battle with the white soldiers. She'd seen how Two Wolves's face twisted with
hatred as he spoke of the white eyes and their guide, the
man called The Hunter by her people. The Hunter had
counted coup against Two Wolves, and the warrior
seemed unable to forget the humiliation of it. He'd paid
little attention to his future wife.

Now Wild Sage wondered if Two Wolves would be
able to put aside his anger and his need for vengeance
long enough to claim her as his wife. Would he be as
gentle with her as Ten Bears was with White Weasel?
Would their mating be mingled with as much mutual
satisfaction? White Weasel had said she must not dwell
on these things, but how could she not?

Wild Sage turned her thoughts to the lodge covering
White Weasel had helped her sew. Wild Sage had
tanned the great buffalo hides herself, rubbing the ash
and brain mixture into the hides to soften them, scrap-
ing and working the skins until they were supple. Once
the skins had been cut into the proper shapes, she'd
sewn them with great care, so they would be strong and
withstand the winter winds of the prairies and mountains. Furthermore, Wild Sage had tanned hides for several parfleches, in which she would store the food she
would gather for her new husband and the meat he
would hunt and bring to their tepee. She would be a dil-
igent, hardworking wife, and Two Wolves would see
what a good choice he had made.

But what about her? Had she made a good choice in

accepting his courtship? She flipped onto her stomach
and swam upstream with long, lazy strokes.

White Weasel had made her a beautiful wedding
dress of buckskin, which had been bleached nearly
white by the sun and decorated with beading and
fringes. Even her moccasins were of the softest
buckskin—dyed yellow and heavily adorned with beading and silver buttons—carefully saved from the days
when the Comanche traded with the Mexicans. She
would be very beautiful for Two Wolves. But he was so
consumed with hatred, would he even notice?

Wild Sage sighed. It wasn't his fault, she reminded
herself. If not for the war chief and his warriors, their
village might be even now on the white men's hated
reservation, instead of still roaming the vast territory of
the Comancheria. For the tribes who had already been
forced onto reservations, the white eyes' promises had
proven false. Unable to roam and hunt the dwindling
herds of buffalo, the people had no food to eat, save
that given by the Great White Father in the East. When
he had failed to send food, the people had killed their
mules and horses to keep from starving. Wild Sage and
all her village knew of this because some of the people
who had gone to the reservation had left it and returned
to those tribes still free. They had warned the Quahadi
and Kotsoteka factions of the Comanche that as bad as
things were now for the people on the Comancheria,
they were far better off than those on the reservations.

Unhappy with her thoughts, Wild Sage waded back to
shore. The water sluiced away from her skin, falling
back to the river in bright droplets. Quickly she re-

dressed, and, taking up the water bags, returned to the village.

White Weasel was seated beside the outdoor cooking fire, a kettle heating on the red coals. The sides of the tepee had been rolled up to allow a cooling river breeze to flow through the dwelling. White Weasel's face was serene and content—as it always was after a night on Ten Bear's pallet. Now she raised her dark head and glanced at Wild Sage.

"You rose early, daughter," she observed. "You seem eager to greet the day."

"It is my wedding day," Wild Sage said, sinking to her knees beside her mother.

"You are ready for it now?" White Weasel's hands were quick and sure as she cut away hunks of dried meat and added them to the pot of roots and herbs.

Wild Sage nodded. "I feel honored that Two Wolves has chosen me. I will be a good wife for him. When he sees the lodge covering we have sewn and the parfleches I have decorated, he will feel proud of his new wife. He is a good hunter. He will provide much meat for our pots, and I shall be happy to share our bounty with my mother and father."

White Weasel smiled, but wisely said nothing. Once she, too, had been a young wife and had taken such pride in the wealth of her young husband's skills.

The sound of riders approaching the village brought both women to their feet. Ten Bears stepped from his lodge and joined the other men who were gathering in the village square, their weapons at the ready. The riders called out a greeting before entering the village, and the men relaxed, recognizing the voice of Red Otter, a warrior from a distant village. Wild Sage and her mother hurried to the village square.

"Welcome, Red Otter," Ten Bears called as the rider and his men skidded to a halt in a flurry of stones.

"Greetings, Ten Bears," the squat Indian warrior answered, dismounting. "I have brought news from Ishatai."

"Come to my lodge," Ten Bears said graciously. "We will smoke the pipe." The men of the council followed as he led the way back to his lodge and indicated the place of honor to his guests. As war chief, Two Wolves was also present. White Weasel motioned to Wild Sage and quickly filled bowls with meat and roots from her cooking kettle. Wild Sage carried them to her father and his guests, then returned to the fire with White Weasel. The men didn't talk until their bowls were emptied and the pipe brought out and lit. When it had been passed so that each man had drawn on it, Ten Bears turned to Red Otter.

"What news do you bring of Ishatai?" he asked. Although the Indian leader, Ishatai, was a chief of the Quahadi Comanche, his words would be given respect.

"Ishatai has called for all the Comanche people to unite, Quahadi and Kotsoteka, and all the other tribes who have not been sent to the reservation, for Ishatai has been given a message from the Great Spirit himself. He knows how to restore Comanche land to its people."

"This is a good thing," Ten Bears said, shaking his head solemnly. "Has Ishatai said how this is to be done?"

"The Great Spirit has told Ishatai to gather the Comanche and lead them in the sun dance. This will make us invincible against the white man's bullets, so we may drive them from our lands. Then the buffalo will return and we will know the plentiful times of our past."

Ten Bears was silent as he contemplated Red Otter's words. Sitting by the fire with her mother, Wild Sage listened to the warrior's message and her heart beat wildly. But before she could leap to her feet and spread the word, White Weasel's hand was strong on her arm, her glance warning the girl to silence. Wild Sage bit her lips and lowered her eyes. Still, she couldn't hide the wild elation that swept through her, for the people had lived with such dread of the white soldier coming and the steady disappearance of the buffalo. Now, all that was behind them.

"The Comanche have never practiced the sun dance," Ten Bears was saying. "Why would the Great Spirit ask this of us?"

Red Otter shrugged. "I do not know," he confessed, "but Ishatai says it is so."

"If the Great Spirit bids us to do this thing, I say we go at once to Ishatai and perform the sun dance," Two Wolves said from his place in the lodge.

"We have only Ishatai's word that the sun dance will earn the favor of the Great Spirit," Ten Bears said. "Afterward, what are we to do?"

"We will fight!" Two Wolves said, raising his fist.

"We will be granted the power to overcome the white soldiers," Red Otter said. "Their bullets will not penetrate our shields. Ishatai has said this is so."

"I say we go at once!" Two Wolves cried, leaping to his feet. The other members of the council looked to Ten Bears.

"What if Ishatai's powers fail and our men are killed?" the old peace chief asked. "Our women and children will be left alone in the villages. They will have nowhere to go except to the reservations, where they must eat their own horseflesh in order to live."

"It will not happen that way," Red Otter said. "Our men, even now, dance the war dance."

"Now is not the time to be afraid," Two Wolves cried. "If the Great Spirit has sent us this message, then we must heed it. If we do not, the white men will take all the Comancheria for their forts and houses. We have no choice. We must fight as warriors rather than sit here like old women waiting to be sent to the reservations."

The members of the tribal council seemed swayed by Two Wolves's eloquent words. They nodded their heads in silent agreement. Still, they looked to their peace chief, for he had gained much loyalty and respect from them.

"I was born upon the prairie," Ten Bears said, his dim old eyes fixed on a memory, "where the wind blew free and there was nothing to break the light of the sun. I was born where there were no enclosures and where everything drew a free breath." He paused and drew a deep breath, as if to show them how it was. His final words were said softly, almost sadly. "I want to die there and not remain within walls."

The men of the council let out a collective breath. Wild Sage glanced at White Weasel and gave a start when she saw tears in her mother's eyes. The voices of the men in the lodge mingled in shouted opinions regarding all that had been said, but Wild Sage no longer listened.

"Why do you weep, Mother?" she asked softly.

White Weasel's silent tears rolled down her cheeks unchecked, frightening Wild Sage more than wails would have done. White Weasel's hands rested against her lap, the palms up in a strangely defenseless motion. Wild Sage took hold of one brown hand and carried it to her hot cheek.

"Mother, why do you weep?" she whispered tearfully.

"Our men will fight," White Weasel said in a voice so low that Wild Sage had to strain to hear it. "They will die on the open prairies, with their dead eyes gazing at the sun, but we"—she turned her tragic eyes to Wild Sage—"we will go to the reservations and grieve the loss of our men."

"No! It won't be like that," Wild Sage cried. "The Great Spirit has sent a message to Ishatai to show us a way."

Behind them, the buzz of voices had quieted; now the council and the chief left the lodge. Wild Sage gazed at her mother a moment longer, then rose and hurried after the men. Two Wolves had already captured his horse, which had been tied near his tepee.

"Two Wolves!" Wild Sage cried, and ran to him. When he faced her, she saw the wild exhilaration in his eyes. And she saw his impatience with her.

"Go back, Wild Sage," he said hoarsely, and turned to tie his saddle more securely. "I have no time to speak with you."

"But where are you going? What of our wedding?"

He whirled to face her, his strong hands flashing out to grasp her shoulders.

"You must wait for me," he said sternly. "Today, I go

to join Ishatai, to perform the sun dance and drive our enemies from our land. When I return, I will take you as my wife."

He released her as abruptly as he'd grabbed her. There had been no tenderness in his touch and he didn't look back as he leapt into his saddle and let out a war cry. Wild Sage stood watching as he prodded his horse with his heels, causing it to rear and trumpet a cry. Two Wolves's black braids flew out, his lips drew back in a snarl, then he galloped forward to join the other warriors.

All was confusion and motion. The men formed themselves into two columns and galloped out of the village. Wild Sage stood watching them go until they disappeared over a ridge. When she turned back to the village, she saw other women standing alone, uncertain of all that had transpired, so quickly had it happened. Only old men and young boys had been left to guard the village. Wild Sage thought of White Weasel's words and shivered with premonition. She wished she could call the men back. Wildly she looked around, but even Ten Bears had gone. Slowly Wild Sage made her way back to the fire. White Weasel had not moved; the tears had dried from her cheeks.

Dirty and exhausted, the Seventh Cavalry followed Caleb Hunter and Captain Wright into the clearing at Adobe Walls. The small trading post, composed of several buildings of adobe and sod, rested beside the Canadian River, and the soldiers quickly dismounted, grateful for a surcease from the hot, dusty prairie they'd diligently covered. Caleb had lost track of Two Wolves and his warriors, a fact that had made him even more difficult to live with the past few days. They'd still be out there, searching out every ravine, every stand of timber, if Caleb had his way, but Captain Wright had called for a return to Fort Sill to replenish supplies. Night had caught them here at Adobe Walls. Now men left the sod buildings and ambled out to meet Captain Wright.

"Buffalo hunters," Caleb grunted, and turned his back.

"Howdy, Captain," one of them said, holding out a hand and scratching his scrawny, bewhiskered chin with the other. His clothes were trail-worn and filthy, his whole personage giving off the foul odor of his trade. "Welcome to Adobe Walls. I'm Hank Radburn, and this here's Max Lowell."

"Howdy," Captain Wright said, briefly clasping the man's hand. His blue eyes scanned the buildings. "Where's Rudd?"

Radburn shrugged his shoulders. "I don't rightly know, Captain. We just pulled in here ourselves a few nights ago. We figured the place had been deserted." His glance turned to the tall man who'd just appeared around the ring of horses and his smile disappeared. Nervously he glanced back at the captain. "We ain't caused no trouble here, Capt'n," he whined, "and we ain't lookin' for none."

Caleb had joined them now and his flinty eyes studied Hank Radburn without pity. "What are you doing here, Radburn?" he demanded. "You buffalo hunters aren't allowed south of the Arkansas River."

"We ain't allowed to hunt buffalo *south* of the Arkansas River," Hank Radburn said snidely. "Ain't nothin' said about how far west we kin go. Besides, maybe we're huntin' somethin' other'n buffalo."

"We don't want you men to cause trouble with the Comanche," Captain Wright said, his jaw grim. "Things are stirred up enough as it is."

Hank Radburn laughed, revealing tobacco-stained teeth. "Like I said, we ain't fixin' to cause trouble, Capt'n. 'Sides, we heard that Indian, Ishatai, is going around preaching to his people 'bout how the Great Spirit showed him a way to make his men invincible and all that."

"Where'd you hear that, Radburn?" Captain Wright demanded.

Radburn snickered, enjoying himself. "We got our ways of knowin' such things. That's how we stay alive. We just go reconnoiterin', you might say."

"Reconnoitering what?" Caleb asked flatly.

Hank Radburn threw back his head and laughed again. "Why possums, Caleb, possums. Come on around and join us. The other men and me was just fixin' to have some supper. We been workin' on the roof over the storage shed. It leaks like a sieve."

"What need do you have to fix the roof, if you're moving on in a few days?" Caleb demanded. His eyes were flinty and his nostrils quivered as if he didn't like the smell of the buffalo hunter.

"We aim to leave the place in better shape than it was when we come here. Come on in and eat with us. Rudd's wife is here and she's been cookin' for us." Radburn turned toward the largest of the adobe buildings. "Time to eat," he called to the men on the roof.

Caleb exchanged a quick glance with Wright.

"Can't be anything wrong if Rudd left his wife here," the captain observed.

"Maybe," Caleb said. "This'll give us a chance to ask her." They followed Radburn inside.

A flushed middle-aged woman scurried between stove and table. When she saw Caleb and the captain, relief flooded her features.

"Howdy, Miz Rudd," Caleb said, crossing the room to her.

"Howdy, Caleb," Margaret Rudd said. Her greeting was affable, but her eyes held a wariness.

"How're you doing?" Caleb asked in a low voice.

"As well as might be expected," she answered. "Rudd was due back two days ago and he ain't here. I been kept busy feedin' this lot of men."

"Have you had any trouble with them?"

"Not yet, but it's been like settin' on a pot that's about to boil over." Her plain face lit up with a smile. "I'm glad you're here."

"Everything'll be all right," Caleb reassured her, gripping her arm briefly before turning back to the rough wooden table.

Seating himself across from Hank Radburn, he leveled a steely gaze at the buffalo hunter. Radburn tried to brazen his way, affecting an attitude of nonchalance, but Caleb's unrelenting gaze caused the hunter to glance away first.

"So what are you hunting down here, Radburn?" Caleb asked.

"I ain't sayin' we're huntin' anythin'." Radburn sat, and, picking up a spoon, attacked the bowl of stew Mar-

garet Rudd set before him. His manners were as foul as
his smell. Runnels of soup ran into his coarse, unkempt
beard. He wiped at his thick lips with the back of a
dirty hand and grinned at Caleb and Wright.

"The boys and me are fixin' t'move on just as soon
as we get that roof finished."

"My men will help you after supper," John Wright
said. "You can be finished that much sooner."

"And on our way that much sooner, eh, Capt'n?"
Radburn laughed, a gusty belly sound that held little
real humor. His brown eyes glittered. "Maybe we'll just
be on our way without finishin' the roof, since our presence is so disturbin' to all of you." His gaze moved
around the table and settled on Margaret Rudd, who had
filled all the cups and now stood with the metal coffeepot in her hand. Without looking at him, she turned to
the stove and carefully replaced the pot on its heated
surface. Radburn laughed again and finished off his coffee, sloshing the dark brew onto his shirtfront. Banging
the tin cup down on the table so that Margaret Rudd
and the captain jumped, he got to his feet. Caleb had remained unmoved by Radburn's words and action. Now
he rose, his arms hanging easy, his hands near his gun
belt. Radburn glanced at Caleb and snickered.

"You won't get no trouble outa me, Hunter," he said.
"No, sirree—not with a whole regiment of soldiers
camped out there." He nodded to the door. "I ain't that
much a fool. No, sir! I'll just get me my gear and head
out." He reached for his gun belt, hanging over a peg
near the door. In the flicker of an eye, Caleb's gun was
in his broad hand, its barrel pointed at the buffalo
hunter.

"Whoa!" said Radburn, raising his empty hands and spreading them to show he was unarmed. "I meant what I said, Hunter. But you got to let me have my gun. Ain't no tellin' what I'm liable to run into out there."

Caleb stared at the fawning man a moment longer, then nodded and relaxed his stance, slowly holstering his gun. Without wasting another moment, Radburn grabbed up his holster and moved toward the door.

"Ben, Charley!" he called. "Come on. We're goin'."

"Goin'?" one of the men yelled back. "I thought you said we was usin' this as our headquarters."

Radburn glanced back over his shoulder at Caleb, his expression sheepish. "I changed my mind," he hollered back. "Saddle up."

In short order the men were saddled and riding out of the clearing. Standing in the doorway, twisting a dishrag in her hands, Margaret Rudd heaved a sigh of relief. "I tell you, Caleb, I ain't ever been so worried. I was afeared Ned would come back and there'd be gunplay."

"They're gone now, Miz Rudd," Caleb said. "What was all this talk about a leaking roof?"

"I do have a leak over the storage house, but it ain't that bad. That Radburn fella just picked up on it as an excuse to stick around here. I told him Rudd would fix it when he come back."

"You said he was due back a day or two ago."

"Something like that," Margaret said, and her voice was sharp-edged. "The dang fool prob'ly got himself all liquored up and had to lay over a day or two to sober up."

"Could be," Caleb said to ease her fear.

"In the meantime, I'll set some men to mending that

roof for you if you'll provide us with supplies," Wright offered.

"Seems like a fair enough trade to me, Captain," Margaret said. "I'd be much obliged."

Dark was falling rapidly now. "Soon as it's daylight, we'll start work on it." The captain tipped his hat and went off to join his men.

Margaret turned to Caleb. Something about the hard-bitten man made her want to comfort him. She'd heard the rumors and knew how close to the truth they were. Caleb had been about fifteen when his family had been wiped out in an Indian attack. He'd been left for dead, but he'd taken down the war chief before passing out from his wounds. She and Rudd had taken care of the boy until he'd gotten well enough to walk. After that, he'd been like a madman, forcing himself to walk to gather strength, practicing his marksmanship till he could hit a nail head a hundred yards away without hardly looking. His chest was still bandaged when he went out with his first posse to search for Comanche.

"When're you goin' to stop this warrin' against the Indians and settle down, Caleb? A man needs a family, a wife and some kids, to keep him grounded. You ain't gettin' any younger."

"Some men are meant to have a family and some aren't," he said gruffly.

"Pshaw. I never knew a man who wasn't better for havin' a family," Margaret said. "Someday you're goin' to look around and find it's too late. Then you'll live a lonely old life."

"I reckon that's my lot, Miz Rudd," he said quietly.

"There aren't many women who'd want a man like me."

"Ain't nothin' wrong with you, Caleb Hunter."

"Ain't much right," he said, mimicking her tone and words. His smile was brief and weary, a rare occurrence, she guessed. "I've got too much blood on my hands, Margaret," he said, staring off at the black shadows.

"Indian blood," she scoffed.

He brought his gaze back to her. "But humans, nonetheless."

"This is strange talk comin' from you, Caleb. Could it be you're ready to put your anger to rest and take up a normal life?"

"This is a normal life for me, Margaret. I won't consider any other until every Comanche is dead or on a reservation." His voice was harsh with anger.

"I'm sorry I brought it up, son," she said softly. "I didn't figure you was still carryin' that much hurt around with you."

He glanced away. "I'm the one who's sorry, ma'am," he said in a low voice. "Guess I forgot how to have a regular conversation with normal folks. I'll be bidding you good night, Margaret."

"Good night, Caleb." He stepped off the front porch and headed toward the corral. Like as not, he'd bed down with the horses rather than the other men. He seemed like a stray mutt and was fearful he didn't belong anywhere. Yet she remembered the look on his face when he'd confronted Radburn. There had been a feral joy in his eyes.

"He's comin' to like killin' and such," she said, shaking her head with worry. Cleaning up the supper dishes she wondered who she was worrying about the most, Ned or that hard-faced young man out there. When she was finished, she set a lamp in the window before turning in, just in case Ned came home during the night.

At the first rays of light, Captain Wright had his men at work on the roof. Margaret Rudd was up brewing coffee and frying up a good portion of salt pork and beans. She'd extinguished the lantern she'd left for Ned. Maybe tonight, she thought as she worked, but it was getting harder and harder to have hope.

"Sir," one of the soldiers up on the roof called out sharply.

Everything seemed to happen at once after that. Coming up from the creek, Caleb caught a glimpse of a rider bearing down on him. Drawing his gun, he aimed and shot instinctively. The rider fell at his feet, and any second thoughts he might have had were ended. He ran up the riverbank toward the trading post. He could hear Margaret Rudd screaming and couldn't know that Hank Radburn had just ducked into her kitchen with her husband's lifeless body used as a shield. Ned's bloody head lolled, a raw wound where his scalp once had been. Radburn dropped his body and slammed the heavy wooden door closed before taking up a stance at the window. Margaret Rudd knelt and cradled her husband's bloody head against her bosom, quietly sobbing.

"He's dead, woman. There ain't no use you wailing over him now," Radburn said between firing out the window.

Margaret glanced at him and slowly wiped her eyes. Then gently straightening her husband's body, she rose and crossed to the fireplace, where a rifle hung above the mantel.

Radburn glanced around in surprise when he heard the sound of gunfire beside him. Without any squeamishness, Margaret Rudd was firing out the second small window.

When Caleb ran into the clearing, he expected to see a post under siege and in much trouble. Mounted Comanche warriors did indeed circle the buildings, whooping and firing. Caleb fired at a warrior nearest him. He fell from his saddle; his foot caught in the stirrup and was dragged away by his crazed horse. Another warrior, this one clad in a buffalo war headpiece that Caleb recognized, galloped toward him. Caleb squatted, took aim, and fired, rolling away as the horse charged past him. Caleb grabbed a quick glance, saw Two Wolves pulling himself back into his saddle, then glanced around. He had little doubt the war chief would come after him.

He thought of Margaret Rudd; images of his dead mother came to him and all fear for himself disappeared. Running in a zigzag pattern, he made his way to the sod house and crashed against the heavy door. Bullets and arrows thudded into the wood beside him and he thought he would surely be hit. He could hear the pounding of animal hooves coming nearer and knew it was Two Wolves, still astride his horse. Caleb turned to take aim, but suddenly the locked door gave, and he tumbled inside. Two Wolves's tomahawk entered the cabin and buried itself in the opposite wall. Margaret Rudd slammed the door shut and picked up her rifle.

Caleb was staring at Ned Rudd's scalped head, fury growing in him.

"Get down," he ordered when Margaret took up her stand again at the window. He leapt forward and tried to take the rifle from her.

"Caleb Hunter, if you want to stand here at this window and shoot at them devils, you're welcome to, but don't you try to stop me from killin' a few of 'em myself." Her voice broke, and Caleb stared at her grief-stricken face.

Slowly he turned back to the window, and, taking out his pistol, began to fire at the howling mounted figures galloping past. Radburn was using his buffalo gun, a powerful and accurate rifle. The impact of such a gun left a bloody, fatal wound.

"Guess Ishatai's powers aren't good enough to defeat old Betsy here," Radburn cackled. For the first time, Caleb found himself happy to side with the disreputable buffalo hunter. "Looks like they're runnin'."

"They'll be back," Caleb said, and sure enough, after regrouping the warriors were back, slipping below their horses' bellies to deliver their shots.

But their arrows and bullets were harmless, thudding into the thick adobe walls, and the rifle fire of the soldiers and the buffalo hunters soon took its toll. By late afternoon, the survivors had galloped away, leaving some of their dead behind.

"Reckon they're gone for good?" Radburn asked as the men stood in the post yard and looked around.

"They won't be back," Caleb said.

"Guess they lost faith in Ishatai and his promises," Radburn said gleefully. He danced around like a malevolent spirit himself, then seeing the body of a dead Comanche slumped against a building, he pulled his buffalo knife and began scalping him.

"Radburn!" Captain Wright shouted. "Leave him be."

The hunter looked up, his eyes narrowing. "They'd do it to us, Capt'n," he said, and kept cutting a thin line around the dead Indian's scalp. In a quick movement, he jerked the scalp free. Margaret Rudd moaned and turned aside, deep sobs shaking her body.

"Radburn!" Caleb shouted, reaching for his gun. He felt sick and helpless inside.

"Ooh, I made the missus feel bad. She ought to be happy I took his scalp. An eye for an eye, a scalp for a scalp, I allus say. Here, ma'am. You kin have it if you want." He held the bloodied scalp out to the sobbing woman, who flinched from the gruesome sight.

Caleb's fist stopped Radburn dead in his tracks and sent him to the ground. He lay in the dirt, his ugly trophy beside him, and stared up at the man with blazing eyes. For a moment he was sure Caleb Hunter's wrathful face was the last thing he'd see of life.

"No, leave him be, Caleb," Margaret Rudd said, stepping forward. "The likes of him don't know no better."

Caleb stepped back and unclenched his fists. "Get up and get out of here, Radburn," he ordered.

"You mean"—Radburn's gaze slid around the circle of faces—"you mean leave the post? My men got killed out there by them devils. If I leave here, they'll get me, too."

"Not if you head north," Caleb said unrelentingly. "Get going."

"Capt'n?" Radburn called desperately.

Captain Wright shook his head. "That's good advice, Radburn," he said. "Unless you intend to stay here alone."

"Wh-What d'you mean?" Radburn got to his feet and looked around. His dirty fist still gripped his bloody prize.

"Both your men are dead, and we're leaving," Captain Wright said. "We're going after the Comanche. You can choose to go with us, or you can stay here by yourself, or you can head north like Caleb suggested."

Radburn rubbed his chin with a bloody hand. His gaze wavered as he considered his options. None of them appealed to him. Finally catching sight of Caleb's scowl, Radburn made up his mind. He gathered up his rifle and caught his horse and pack mule. Climbing into the saddle, he glared back at the group of people gathered in the yard, then, with a defiant whoop, he raised the bloody scalp above his head in a victory salute and galloped out of the clearing. Before he'd gone very far, he abandoned the scalp, hanging it in a tree, so the hair trailed in ghostly wisps. Then, cursing Caleb Hunter and the whole Comanche Nation, he turned his horse and pack mule on a northerly trail.

Chapter 3

*B*ACK AT ADOBE Walls, Captain Wright ordered his men to begin a burial detail. Caleb crossed to Margaret Rudd.

"We'll take you to Fort Sill," he said softly. "I'm sorry about Ned. He was a good man."

"Yes, he was a good man," Margaret said fiercely. "But this land is hard on good men." She glanced at Caleb and felt like weeping all over again. She could read his thoughts. As hard as this land was on a man, it was twice as bad for a woman.

"Do you have any family you can go to?" he asked.

Dully, she nodded. I got a sister up in Kansas. Reckon I'll head up there." She turned away then, for the soldiers were carrying Ned's body to his grave. Slowly she walked down to the riverbank, where her husband would be put to rest. This was fitting, she thought, staring at the river. Ned had loved this land and had never once thought of going back East. Her lips tightened as she thought of the lost dreams.

The funeral was brief, with one of the soldiers reading from the Bible over the mounded grave and Margaret laying a bouquet of wilted wildflowers near the

41

rough stick cross. Then they were mounted, the mules loaded with the last of the supplies in the supply shed and Margaret Rudd seated astride one of the Indian ponies. In three days' time they arrived at the junction of Cache and Medicine Bluff Creeks, where Fort Sill was located. The Wichita Mountains rose in the west. When they arrived they went straight to Colonel Grierson's headquarters.

"Continue in your pursuit of this war chief, Two Wolves," Colonel Grierson said. He was a tall, imposing man with white hair and a penetrating blue gaze. Grierson had been in charge of the initial construction of the fort, which had become a base of operation against the plains Indians. Right now the concentration was on the last holdouts of the Comanche Nations. Grierson's eyes gleamed at the thought of finally bringing the recalcitrant warriors to their knees.

"Orders have come down that we're to drive the Comanche onto reservations or kill them." He glanced at Caleb. "I hardly need tell you that, Hunter, since that's been your policy from the beginning."

"Yes, sir," Caleb said quietly. He was slouched in a chair set against the wall. In contrast, Captain Wright and his officers stood at full attention before the colonel's desk.

Grierson smiled to hide his irritation at the quiet man. "Well, now. You'll be doing it with your government's blessings. That must make you feel better."

Caleb slapped his hat against his boots and glanced up at the colonel. "Nope," he said quietly. "It makes me no nevermind."

"I see." Grierson's smile faded. Caleb was a civilian

and not under Grierson's command. The colonel longed to give the tracker the boot, but his skills were necessary to defeat the Comanche. Now Grierson forced his smile back and continued giving orders to his officers. Captain Wright nodded sharply and saluted before turning to the door. The interview was over. Caleb stayed seated until the room was emptied save for him and the colonel.

"You wanted something?" Grierson asked.

Slowly Caleb got to his feet. His eyes were level with Grierson's, something the colonel noted with further irritation. "What's on your mind, Hunter?" the colonel asked, shuffling papers on his desk as if suddenly busy.

"Has word come down about just how the Comanche will be treated once they're on the reservations?"

Grierson glanced up. Caleb's expression was closed, his eyes unreadable.

"I'm surprised you care, Hunter," Grierson said. "I thought you hated the Comanche and wanted them all dead."

"I don't cotton to having the younkers starve to death on a reservation. I've been hearing some of the agents have cut food rations, so the Comanche are eating their horses and mules to stay alive. It'd be better if we killed them all in their villages."

"Younkers?" Grierson questioned blandly.

"Children," Caleb snapped. His eyes flashed with dislike for this man who'd spent several years in this country and hadn't yet learned its idioms.

"So you think we should just shoot the women and children when we find them."

"It would be more humane," Caleb said quietly. "I'm

not looking to track down these people to have them starved to death."

"Rather a fastidious attitude for a man of your caliber," Grierson snapped.

The muscles in Caleb's jaw jumped and he took a warning step forward. "What caliber of man do you think I am, Colonel?" he asked quietly.

"A man who kills and enjoys the killing," Grierson said implacably.

Caleb gave no indication that the words hurt him. He eased back and drew a deep breath. "There's killing and then there's killing. I do the one, but not the other."

"That's a fine distinction," Grierson said, with a slight smile. "By all means, make it, if it eases your conscience."

Caleb opened his mouth to reply, then closed it. He wanted to tell the smiling superior officer that his conscience didn't bother him, that he'd done what he had for a reason, a good reason that most men would have accepted. But suddenly he felt sick, too sick to explain, too sick to defend himself. For fourteen years he'd ridden the Comancheria searching out the villages, dealing death to all within, caring little if his bullets found the body of a man or woman, for the Comanche women went into battle as well. Now, standing before this man who had retained his civilized veneer, Caleb felt sickened by himself. Silently, blindly, he made his way from the room, out into the hot air, where dust whorls rose in the square. He rested his hands on the horse rail and leaned forward, fighting back a sudden, inexplicable nausea that had claimed him.

"Caleb!" Margaret Rudd called to him. He raised his

head and watched her approach. "Thank you, Caleb," she said, taking his hand. Her sharp brown eyes studied his face. "Are you all right?"

"I'm fine," he lied. "I have to go. Captain Wright is waiting for me."

"You're going after those Indians that attacked the fort?" Margaret asked.

Caleb nodded.

"Don't go," she said suddenly. "Let someone else do this. You've done enough."

Silently he shook his head.

"You've the look of a man who has a sickness in him, Caleb," Margaret said. "I see it in your eyes."

Roughly he pulled away from her.

"Caleb, I'm sorry if I'm buttin' into your business."

"You are," he said, without looking back at her.

"Have a care, Caleb," she said. Her voice sounded sad. He thought of Ned and turned to face her. The corners of his mouth softened a little.

"Have a care yourself, Margaret," he said, and then was gone, striding across the parade ground with great long steps. Without looking back, he mounted his horse, joined Captain Wright at the head of the file of soldiers, and galloped out of the fort. Margaret watched him go and shook her head, wondering if she'd ever see Caleb Hunter again.

Tracking the Comanche was easier this time. They were shaken by their defeat at Adobe Walls. They carried their dead with them, symbols of the Great Spirit's disfavor. Caleb picked up their trail near the place they'd first encountered Two Wolves and his raiding party. From there he tracked them westward. Some instinct led him onward, even when the trail disappeared, and always he found it again in a careless print of an unshod hoof, in a broken twig or a scrape against stone. He interpreted the signs as clearly as a schoolboy might peruse his reader, and at the end of the fifth day, they were near the unsuspecting village.

The voices of the women and children were raised in howls of grief, all save White Weasel, who sat silent and dry-eyed in her tepee before the dead ashes of her cooking fire. There was no longer a warrior in their tepee, no reason to prepare the venison or tan the hides, no reason to don her prettiest dress and paint her face. Ten Bears had not returned. His body lay far to the east, at a place called Adobe Walls.

Wild Sage had mourned, running to her secret place high above the village and throwing herself on the ground while great sobs tore at her breast. She'd wept until there seemed to be no more tears and her strength was gone. When at last she'd risen and gone back down to the village, it seemed she'd entered a place of lamentations, for in nearly every tepee a warrior had been lost. The slain bodies had been carried to the sacred place in the hills and put to their last rest. The women rent their clothes and gashed themselves, all save White Weasel, who sat without speaking or eating or sleeping. Three days had passed since their warriors had returned carrying their dead. Three days and White Weasel had remained untouched by the world around her, untouched by the wails of grief. She journeyed in a spirit world where no others could reach her.

Wild Sage sat for long hours beside her, wanting to reach through that spirit world to reclaim her mother, yet knowing only the Great Spirit could decide what would become of White Weasel.

Two Wolves had returned with the other warriors, his spirit crushed. Even Quannah, the great Quahadi war chief, had crept away from the white man's bullets at Adobe Walls. There would be no marriage now, if ever, for the village was mourning its losses not only of its strong and brave young men, but of its way of life. If they could not depend on the Great Spirit to give them special powers as Ishatai had predicted, then the Comanche were not strong enough to defeat the white man and his guns.

Wild Sage sat throughout the third night with her mother, unable to rest while she thought of all that this defeat meant. Her dreams as a young Comanche maiden were also ended, she realized. Her life would not be spent on the wide, open prairie, but on a reservation where all dignity and pride would be slowly crushed from her and her people. Now she understood White Weasel's tears the day Red Otter came to them. Now she understood White Weasel's retreat to the spirit world. This was too hard to bear.

Through the night Wild Sage had kept vigil with White Weasel, and now, as the call of a prairie dove echoed in the first gray streaks of dawn, Wild Sage rose and pulled from her parfleche the beautiful wedding dress White Weasel had made for her. It symbolized all the things that would never be now. As if in a dream herself, Wild Sage donned the soft, pale buckskin dress with its ornate beading and fringe. She put on the moccasins, as well, and carefully groomed her hair, covering the part with red paint and perfuming the braids with herbs and sage as she would have done if she were going to her husband this day. When she was finished, she sat beside White Weasel again, waiting, she knew not for what.

Suddenly, on the cold morning air came a flurry of horses' hooves, the sound of gunfire, and the hoarse, terror-filled cries of women and children. Eyes wide with fear, Wild Sage waited. Beside her, White Weasel trembled and whimpered.

"Mother," Wild Sage whispered, gripping her hand.

"The soldiers have come." White Weasel gasped and pulled away from Wild Sage's grasp. Leaping to her feet, she took up Ten Bears's lance and bow.

"No, Mother. You must not," Wild Sage cried, running to White Weasel.

For a moment White Weasel's vision cleared. Her dark eyes regarded this girl she'd taken and loved as a daughter. "I must do this," she whispered urgently. "You do not understand. You were not born a Comanche. They will take you from me—"

"No, I won't let them," Wild Sage cried. This was one fear she had not guessed, that she would be taken from her people. "I am Comanche. We will go to the reservation together, my mother. I will care for you."

White Weasel's eyes were sad. She noted that Wild Sage had donned her wedding dress and she nodded in approval. "I have been proud of you, my daughter," she said. "Now I must go to join Ten Bears." Without hesitation she stepped outside the lodge, the quiver of arrows slung over her shoulder.

"No!" Wild Sage cried, for she knew there was death awaiting her mother. She threw back the tepee flap and paused, taking in the scene of chaos and destruction. Blue-uniformed soldiers rode through the village, their guns blazing. Tepees flared as the morning breeze fanned their flames. Women and children alike ran, looking for safety, but there was none.

Two Wolves and some of the warriors had managed to mount their horses; now they engaged in a more equal battle with the white soldiers. She saw the war chief raise his rifle and take aim, heard his shrill, victorious cry when a soldier fell from the saddle. He spurred away, pursued by several soldiers on horseback. The stench of burning leather and blood assailed Wild Sage's nostrils and reminded her of the danger to White Weasel.

"Mother," she cried, and ran through the chaos searching for her. When she saw White Weasel plunge a lance into the side of a mounted soldier and fall before his galloping steed, she cried out and raced across the village square. White Weasel had regained her feet now and fumbled to notch an arrow to her bow. Her arm was strong, her aim true.

A young soldier's cry ended in a death gurgle as the arrow pierced his throat. Just as quickly as it took him to fall from his horse, White Weasel had another arrow ready, but a man rode forward. He wasn't dressed as the rest of the soldiers, and for a moment Wild Sage felt confusion as to who he was; then she saw him aim his gun at White Weasel and her confusion vanished. He was a white eyes, and he meant to kill her mother.

Wild Sage leapt forward, throwing herself against the

side of his horse. The impact sent her reeling to the ground. The stallion reared in surprise. With a curse the rider brought him back in hand and once again aimed, but White Weasel had moved on. His quarry was lost. With another curse he leveled his gun at the girl on the ground. Wild Sage saw the infinite blackness of the gun's bore and knew this must be the place beyond, where the Great Spirit lived. The man hesitated, and Wild Sage rolled away, drawing up her knees, so when she stopped rolling she was able to spring to her feet. She ran, expecting any moment to feel the impact of a bullet against her back, but death did not come to her.

Instead it claimed White Weasel. Wild Sage saw her fall and sprinted toward her, her cry lost in the scream of a horse. White Weasel was smiling when Wild Sage reached her. Her dark eyes were already clouding with approaching death. Her outflung hand still clutched Ten Bears's bow.

"Mother," Wild Sage whispered, kneeling beside her and taking her free hand. Blood was gushing from White Weasel's breast. Wild Sage tried to stop the flow of life from her mother's body. White Weasel shook her head in denial.

"No, my daughter," she said softly. "It is done. I go to join Ten Bears, which is where I want to be. You see, even now my eyes turn to stare at the sun. Soon I will not see it, but my eyes will go on looking. I will be searching for Ten Bears."

"You cannot leave me behind," Wild Sage cried.

White Weasel's smile dimmed. "You must go to your own destiny, my daughter. For a time it was with us.

Now it is done." White Weasel's hand grew limp in Wild Sage's.

"No!" Wild Sage cried, and rocking her mother in her arms set up a wail of grief.

All around her the battle raged on. Two Wolves and his warriors were being driven from the village by the fierce fighting. Although many soldiers lay dead and dying, the battle was turning against the Comanche. Wild Sage paid little attention to the passage of time or the dwindling battle sounds. The fury was gone. Defeat was at hand. Two Wolves and his few remaining warriors had been forced to abandon the village, driven deeper into the Cross timbers.

Suddenly white soldiers were beside Wild Sage, gripping her shoulders, carrying her away from White Weasel. "No!" she cried out, flailing at them with all her strength. Her foot lashed out, catching one of the soldiers in the crotch. She heard his grunt of pain and one arm was released. Before the other soldier could react, she'd pulled her knife and plunged it into his shoulder.

Spinning free, she ran toward an Indian pony that had lost its rider and was frightened by the noise and confusion. If she could just get to the horse, she'd be free; she knew it, for she was one of the village's best riders, often outbesting even their warriors. She was only a few steps away, her hands already outstretched to clasp the mane, when a body crashed into hers, knocking the wind from her and carrying her to the ground. With a shriek of fury, she rolled, still gripping her knife, aiming it toward the large body that struggled to subdue her. He'd guessed her intentions and ended their rolling struggle with him on top, his weight pinning her slight body while one big hand gripped her wrist in a painful clasp that brought numbness to her fingers.

"Drop it," he muttered near her ear, and even though the words had been uttered in the white man's language, she obeyed. The pain in her wrist lessened. She tried to wrench away from him, but he was not to be taken off-guard as the soldier had been. He gripped both her wrists with one hand and reached for her knife, wiping the soldier's blood from it before sticking it in his boot.

"That's the last white blood that weapon will take," he growled, and getting to his feet jerked her up with him.

Wild Sage lashed out with her foot, barely missing him. His free hand doubled into a fist and landed against her jaw with enough force to nearly break her slender neck. She went limp, sagging to her knees, held erect only by his grip on her wrists. She shook her head slowly, all defiance knocked from her.

"Get up," he said roughly, and jerked her upright. The pressure on her arms was immense. She staggered to her feet and felt the pain lessen. Still swaying with weakness she faced him, her eyes hot and defiant.

Caleb Hunter looked into her gray eyes and started. "You're a white woman," he said in astonishment.

The girl spat at him. "I am Comanche," she said proudly in the Comanche language.

Caleb nodded in grim understanding. "All right, you're Comanche," he said in English.

He tied her wrists behind her back, his touch quick and impatient, denoting disgust, then he twirled her around, his gray eyes hard as granite.

"I don't care how you started out," he said. "You've

gone Comanche, and in my book that makes you one. I'd as soon kill you as look at you, so go ahead and try to escape. That might be just the excuse I'm looking for."

His words were spoken rapidly, from between clenched teeth, so she had difficulty in interpreting them. His hostility seemed to be directed toward her personally. His big hand went to her shoulder and shoved her backward. Wild Sage stumbled and righted herself, staring at him with dread. This was the man known to her people as The Hunter. Imperiously he motioned her toward the pitiful knot of defeated villagers. Subdued at last, she did as he bid. Silently she went to join them.

"Caleb!" a soldier called to the man who had captured Wild Sage. "Ellery's dead. The bitch killed him."

The man called Caleb swung his gaze back to her, his eyes almost black with anger. She wondered if this were the excuse he needed to kill her, but he turned away as a soldier whose uniform bore a different insignia came forward. The officer listened to the man named Caleb, shook his head, then glanced at her. Wild Sage sensed they were talking about her and turned her back on them. She could see White Weasel where she lay, her sightless eyes staring at the rising sun. She has gotten her wish, Wild Sage thought bitterly, but what of me? What am I to do now that I've lost my mother and father and perhaps even the warrior who was to become my husband? She looked around, trying to detect Two Wolves's body among the fallen. He would never allow himself to be taken alive, she guessed.

The surviving women and children had been rounded

up now. There were a few old men among the captives, but none of the warriors, except those that were wounded. Soldiers were going from tepee to tepee, throwing out skins and parfleches and setting the dwellings afire.

The man called Caleb stepped before the captives and spoke to them in Comanche. "You may gather up what supplies and robes you can carry on your horses," he said. "You are each allowed one horse. Do not attempt to run away. We are guarding you and will bring you back." He looked around the circle of defeated faces. "Where is your chief?" he asked. No one answered him.

"Where is your peace chief or someone of his family?" Again his dark eyes held a warning.

Chin high, Wild Sage stepped forward. "Ten Bears, our peace chief, is dead," she said.

Caleb studied her closely. "Were you his wife?"

Wild Sage's chin raised a bit more and she bit the inside of her lips to keep from weeping. Now, of all times, she must not show this weakness.

"His wife, my mother, White Weasel . . . is dead. She lies there, killed by your soldiers."

"Where is your husband?" Caleb asked after a short silence. She'd wanted him to feel guilty that White Weasel was dead, but he displayed no emotion whatsoever. Instead, he demanded more answers.

"I have no husband," Wild Sage said.

"Isn't that a Comanche wedding dress you're wearing?" he demanded.

Her eyes widened in surprise. He knew many things about the Comanche ways. "I do not have a husband," she said stiffly.

Caleb studied the dirty, blood-smeared face with its closed expression. She was a Comanche all right, he thought. She'd had that same stoic air that so many of the Indians used when they didn't want to talk to the whites. Shrugging, he turned away and spoke to the captain.

"What should we do with her?" Wright asked, studying the girl's averted head.

"Leave her with the others," Caleb said flatly. "She's gone Comanche. Remember what happened to Quannah's mother when she was brought back?"

"She had Comanche children and a husband," Wright said. "This girl's young. She can still change."

"Don't count on it, Captain," Caleb said. "At any rate, she'll be easier to handle if you keep her with the other women and children."

Thoughtfully Wright nodded his head in agreement.

The battle had raged throughout the morning. The sun had passed its zenith. Captain Wright wanted to have his soldiers and the Comanche captives far away from this site before the escaped warriors had a chance to rally aid from other villages. When all the women and children were mounted, with their pitiful remaining supplies tied behind them, the soldiers finished firing the village. Then they set about systematically killing the horses.

"Why?" Wild Sage cried, and in her distress was unaware she'd spoken the word in the white man's tongue. The man known as Caleb turned to her, his eyes narrowed, his mouth grim. Slowly he rode his horse beside her.

"So you've remembered your own tongue," he said in English.

"Why?" Wild Sage repeated helplessly, then reverted to Comanche. "Why do your soldiers kill our horses?"

"Without additional horses, your warriors cannot hunt buffalos. They cannot raid or ride to war."

His gaze was pitiless, his mouth twisted as he spoke. She read the contempt in his eyes. His hatred for the Comanche smote her.

"When the horses your escaped warriors now ride are gone, they will be on foot. Then they'll make their way to the reservation."

Tears wet Wild Sage's face. She made no effort to wipe them away. For the first time since being captured by the Indians as a child, she tried to remember her native tongue. "White men take our lands, k-kill our horses and sta-starve our women and ch-children on th-eir res-reservations."

Caleb remained silent while she struggled with the words. There was a poignant kind of dignity in her effort. "Wh-y do th-does the white man th-think he ha-ss this right ov-er the Comanche?" Her voice gained strength as she continued. "The land of the Comancheria bee-longs to Comanche."

"The white father in Washington says it belongs to the white man," Caleb said slowly. "As for the killing, the Comanche have brought this on themselves. They've killed and tortured countless whites, women and children, innocent people who wanted only to make a life for themselves."

"Ev-en if that l-life dess-destroys ours?" she asked.

Caleb felt an impatience with her. Grasping the reins of her horse, he leaned close, his flinty gaze capturing hers.

"You are not Comanche," he said slowly. "No matter how much you may want to be, your blood is white. You're returning now to your true people."

"I am with my people!" In her terror she reverted to the Comanche tongue. "I will not return to the white world. I will stay on the reservation with the other women and children. That is my wish."

Her words were as implacable as his had been. In the distance the gunshots died away. The last of the horses had been killed. Unable to sway her argument to his, Caleb released her horse and turned away. She wasn't his problem. When they got to Fort Sill, Colonel Grierson would take over. Till then, Captain Wright was in charge.

Caleb rode apart from the line of soldiers and captives. His keen eyes automatically studied the ridges for any sign of an enemy, but his thoughts were fourteen years behind him, when he'd first regained consciousness and discovered his mother and father among the ashes of their home. His baby sister lay beneath a tree, her skull crushed. He'd wept bitter tears when he'd seen her tiny body. He remembered her laughter and her tiny hands when she pulled at his pockets to see what surprise he'd brought her. Sometimes it had been a frog he'd found along the creek bed, or a pretty stone, or a piece of candy. He remembered the sound of her laughter and smelled her baby breath when she kissed him. Had she been frightened? Had she cried as the Indian swung her around to bash her against a tree? Then he'd seen the tiny bullet hole in her forehead and had known that at the last moment his father had saved her from such agony.

Such a luxury had not been for his mother. She'd been alive while the savages ravished and tortured her. He'd seen the terror and pain in her dead eyes, and at that moment, hate had been born in him. Caleb glanced at the column of women and children.

Why didn't he feel gleeful, vindicated, comforted by this capture? They'd destroyed another village, captured more Comanche women and children, driven off warriors, taking their horses and leaving them without tepees or robes against the cold nights. Why didn't he feel better? When had the killing become so meaningless for him? From the beginning, he reminded himself. From that first Comanche village he and that posse attacked fourteen years ago, he'd felt no elation at the deaths and destruction. He'd been as untouched then as now.

Only now, was he truly untouched? Margaret said he had the look of sickness on him. And he was sick. Sick of the stench of blood, no matter if white or Indian. Sick of the cries of men dying and women wailing, sick of the smell of burning hides and rotting flesh. He felt as if he were drowning in a sea of blood, Comanche blood, and it hadn't brought back his mother with her beautiful, serene face, or his baby sister with her laughter and baby ways, or even his father, who'd died trying to protect them all. Why had he lived and they had not? The question had tormented him for fourteen years; now he brushed it away and clamped his teeth together. A man couldn't let thoughts like that escape. If they did—if a man examined them too minutely—he might go loco.

Caleb kicked at his horse and rode ahead to examine

a distant ridge and find a safe place for them to camp for the night.

Word had been sounded inside the fort long before they arrived. Colonel Grierson and his officers were lined up waiting for them. Captain Wright led the column of men into the compound. Silently the captives followed and sat with slumped shoulders and stoic expressions as Colonel Grierson looked them over.

"Well done, Captain," Grierson said, nodding approvingly.

"Caleb's the one who found the village, sir," Wright said.

Grierson acknowledged Caleb with a curt nod. His penetrating gaze settled on Wild Sage. "Come inside, Mr. Hunter, and make your report," he said, and Wright and Caleb dismounted and climbed the steps to the colonel's office.

Wild Sage sat on her horse, as did the rest of the women and children. Her heart pounded in her ears. Even the whites called this man The Hunter, she noted miserably. She was surprised at how well she understood the white man's language. She'd listened carefully, hoping to hear something that would help them escape. She'd seen the white officer's keen glance. He'd recognized she was not of Comanche blood. Wild Sage felt a dread building inside her, so she hardly noticed the passage of time as they waited. Soon, the door to the colonel's office opened and the men came out. Colonel Grierson gave some whispered words to an officer standing nearby. The man saluted smartly and nodded to his men. The man known as Caleb glanced at Wild Sage and walked down the steps to grasp her reins.

"The colonel wants to speak to you in his office."

"I wish to stay with my people," Wild Sage said in Comanche. Her heart was beating in her throat. She felt panic rising.

"You must come."

"No!" Wild Sage cried, then again in English, so all would know. Caleb shrugged and turned away; she relaxed her grip on the reins.

Too late she realized this had been but a feint to put her off her guard. His big hands reached for her, grasping her elbow. She swung her riding whip and saw it welt his cheek, but his grip didn't loosen. She was pulled from her horse. She fought, but his strength was greater than hers. He picked her up and carried her up on the porch and into the colonel's office, where he deposited her none too gently into a chair against the wall. It felt hard and strange beneath her. A memory came of climbing onto such a chair once.

The other men had followed them inside and the door was closed, shutting out sunlight and her last vision of the Comanche women and children. Almost at once, the sound of horses moving outside told her the others were being herded away without her.

"I wish to g-go with my people," she cried, trying to get up. Caleb pushed her down again. It was useless, she knew. She could do nothing. She turned to face the colonel, pulling all the dignity about her she could muster.

"You have no right to keep me against my will," she raged, and at the officer's blank look realized she'd spo-

ken in Comanche. "I wish to go wi-th my people," she
said slowly in English.

"Ah, that's good to hear, young lady," the colonel
said, deliberately misinterpreting her words. "That's just
what we intend to do, send you home to your people.
Do you remember the name of your family?"

Wild Sage closed her eyes and took a deep breath. In-
tuitively she knew she must be calm. "I am Wi-ld
S-Sage," she said slowly, fumbling for the right words
in English. "I w-w- I am the dau-ghter of Ten Bears,
peace chief of—of the Kotsoteka Comanche, a-and of
Wh-White Wea-easel. The-ese are m-my people."

"Kotsoteka Comanche?" Grierson looked question-
ingly at Caleb.

"A sector within the Comanche Nation," Caleb answered. "The Kotsoteka and the Quahadi are the last
holdouts."

"I see." He turned his gaze back to the silent girl and
smiled coaxingly. "You said your name is Wild Sage?"
he questioned. She nodded. "Surely you have another
name besides that one." She shook her head.

"Try to remember back to the time before you were
captured by the enemy—the Comanche." Wild Sage
shook her head.

"Somewhere there may be a woman who weeps even
now for her daughter, believing her dead at the hands of
the Comanche," the colonel said slyly. "Think how
happy she might be to know you're alive."

Wild Sage shook her head. "M-My m-mother is
dead," she said softly.

"She was weeping over an Indian woman back at the
village," Caleb said.

Wild Sage raised her head and stared at him, her gaze distracted. "T-Two mothers dead," she said softly, as if looking back a long way.

"You remember your first mother?" Caleb asked, squatting before her. She glanced at him, disliking his close proximity and the white man smell of him. She turned her head away.

"She doesn't seem to like you, Hunter," the colonel said. Wild Sage turned her face back to him, her eyes questioning.

"You are Hunter," she said, poking his chest in distaste.

He nodded. "Caleb Hunter. In Comanche it means—"

"I know," Wild Sage answered, and turned away from him. Sighing he straightened and walked across the room.

"So you've remembered a lot today," Colonel Grierson said coaxingly. "Can you remember your name, your white name, any white name?"

Wild Sage stared at him mutely.

"Try!"

She made no answer.

Grierson gave up and moved behind his desk, assuming his manner of authority as he turned to face the girl. "You will not be allowed to go to the reservation with the Indians." She leapt to her feet. Caleb and Captain Wright sprang forward to restrain her.

"You cannot k-keep me from my people," she cried.

"They are not your people," Grierson said sternly, "and I can keep you from the reservations. They are government run and under my jurisdiction. If I say you may not go there, then you won't."

His glance was without sympathy. Strangely enough, Caleb Hunter's gaze seemed to have softened. Frantically Wild Sage looked around. She needed a friend, but even as she sent a silent appeal to him, his gaze hardened.

Wild Sage felt her knees tremble and sat down quickly on the white man's chair. The stinging behind her lids had begun and she feared she might weep here, in front of the white men.

"Wh-Where am I to go?" she asked stonily.

"I'm not certain for now, but you'll stay at the fort tonight. I'll have one of my officers give you their room. Hunter, stay behind. I want to talk to you." His tone indicated she was dismissed now.

Silently she rose and turned to the door. Captain Wright took hold of her arm and led her out of the office. She would escape, she thought wildly. She would leap on her horse and ride away from here. She would catch up with the women and children going to the reservation and join them, or she would ride back to the village and look for Two Wolves and his warriors who had escaped. But she knew she wouldn't do that. It had taken many days to reach this place. If she tried to go back on her own, she'd be caught. Docilely she followed a soldier to a room and stepped inside. Only after the door had swung shut and she heard the rasp of the lock did she realize the room had no window and she was locked in. She had returned to the white world.

Chapter 4

WILD SAGE ATE no food that night, nor did she sleep on the white man's bed. Instead she huddled on the hard, splintered plank floor and thought of all that had transpired. Ten Bears and White Weasel were dead. Two Wolves was gone. Life as she had known it was ended. She must adjust, be willing to change if she were to survive—and then came the flood of memory, of the time when she first came to the Indian world, when she was made to work hard and endure their taunts.

Those first captors hadn't been Comanche. Only later had she been traded to Ten Bears. She remembered how frightened she'd been of the tall warrior with the fierce, ugly face. Yet he'd been gentle with her, and she soon understood that neither he nor his wife meant her harm. She'd known she must try hard to understand their ways and accept them as her own, and she'd done so. Could she do it again? Could she accept the ways of the white world again?

Lying on that hard wooden floor in the raw government post, she pushed her memory back further, reaching for the time when she'd been in the white world.

Slowly the things came to her, like flashes of light beneath a canopy of leaves, all spangled and unreal. The colonel had asked if she remembered her mother, and suddenly she did. She remembered a woman with long brown hair and gentle eyes, and a dark-haired man with a smiling face. She remembered how he swung her on his shoulders and danced around the yard singing to her.

"Jenny goes a-dancing, a-dancing." She shifted on the hard floor and practiced singing the words. Then she paused, holding the memory and the name fast, so she wouldn't forget it again. Finally she slept.

Caleb Hunter opened the door. He stood in the sunlight watching as she rose from her resting place and blinked against the sudden light. He made no comment about her choice of beds, just waited silently until she left the room and stood beside him.

"We leave in a few minutes," he said gruffly, indicating the two horses and a pack mule, saddled and waiting at the hitching post.

"Wh-Where?" she asked.

"I'm taking you to Kansas—to someone I know up there. I think she'll take care of you and help you find your family."

"J-Jennee," Wild Sage said softly.

"What?"

"Jeennie," she repeated.

"Jenny?" Happily she nodded. "What else do you remember? Any other name? Some family name so we'd know who to look for?"

Wild Sage's smile died. She'd thought he'd be happy with her for remembering that much.

"W-Why y-you?" she asked, frustrated that she couldn't form the white man's words as adroitly as she did the Comanche. He seemed to understand her, though. His eyes took on a cold, distant look she hated to see. It pulled him away, made him a stranger, an enemy.

Sharply she turned away from him, not waiting for an answer, mounting the waiting Indian pony. The saddle was not that of the Comanche with their rawhide-covered wooden frames. The saddle felt too wide and strange beneath her, but she sat still, her shoulders held back in pride as she'd seen her mother ride.

"We won't be alone on this trip," Caleb said, climbing into his saddle and facing her. His glance was impersonal, his lips set in a thin line, as if he weren't happy with this task. "We'll be stopping at Fort Cobb on the way to pick up more white captives."

Wild Sage's glance displayed hope for one brief moment, then she set her expression in stoic lines, revealing nothing of her feelings. Caleb's eyes grew icy as he watched her. She was slight, coming only to his shoulders when standing, but her demeanor was as prepossessing as one of Quannah's warriors.

"Are you ready to go, Jenny?"

She whirled to face him, her gray eyes as dark and stormy as tempest-driven clouds in a prairie cyclone. "I am Wild Sage," she stated firmly, and nudged her mount with her moccasined heel. It sprang forward, galloping out of the fort as if the whole Fourth Cavalry was after him.

With a curse, Caleb spurred his horse and went after her. He might have known she knew how to ride like the rest of the Comanche. He should have expected this and, indeed, he had, but not now, not while they were still in the fort. He leaned forward in his saddle and urged his mount on. She disappeared down a draw— and when the pony scrambled up the other side, the saddle was empty.

Caleb cursed again. Like as not she fell off and broke her silly neck, he thought, and almost felt relieved that he wouldn't have to cart her to Kansas after all. Someone from Fort Cobb could take the rest of the miserable captives back to their families. He slowed his mount, casting a quick glance around the empty draw, looking for a bundle of rawhide and braids, but there was nothing.

His lips set in a grim line; his eyes were dark and dangerous-looking as he guided his mount out the other side. The Indian pony had drawn away a considerable distance now, its saddle still empty, but its gait too driven to be unguided.

Caleb set his own horse to a flat-out gallop. He wouldn't lose her now, if he had to track her for a month, he vowed. She's tricked him, caught him off-guard. That wouldn't happen again. He pushed his mount forward, heedless of the froth at its mouth and the signs of tiring. If his sorrel was tiring, then so must the Indian pony. He pushed on and felt some satisfaction when he drew closer. She was back in the saddle now, glancing over her shoulder, her eyes big, the whites showing. She urged her pony onward, but he was winded. The sorrel was bigger, stronger and faster.

She wouldn't give up. He had to credit her with that. Even when she knew the race was lost, even as he reached for her and she dodged away, so his hand slid from her shoulder, she kept trying to elude him. His big hand gripped a wad of rawhide and yanked, sending her flying from her pony. She hit the ground, hard, but had the presence of mind to keep rolling to minimize the impact. By the time he'd brought her pony to a stop and turned back to her, she was sprawled in the dirt, the dust settling around her, her head thrown back, her gaze directed at the sky. He might have thought her dead, except for the rise and fall of her chest as she fought to draw a breath.

He waited; finally she raised herself up on her elbows and glared at him. The Comanche word she directed at him was not one to be repeated, he figured, so he let her rant while he brought the pony around. When she paused in her tirade to draw a breath, he looked down at her with far more calmness than he felt.

"Now you know that escaping from me is not that easy. By the time we get back to the fort to gather up the pack mules, we will have lost two hours of daylight. Get back in the saddle."

Her eyes were filled with hatred, the same hatred he'd seen in a thousand Comanche faces. She spat at him to show her defiance and remained where she was. Caleb felt the anger rise. Stepping out of his stirrup, he reached for her. She dodged and rolled away, stirring up more dust. He didn't give her a chance to outguess him again. His hand settled on her shoulder—and without regard to any pain he might cause, he yanked her to her feet.

She came up fighting, her feet flailing, aiming for his crotch, her arms landing blows about his shoulders. She was too short to reach higher. For one so little, she was stronger and faster than he'd anticipated. He shook her like a rag doll and held her away, so her blows couldn't reach him. That didn't keep her from trying. Her face was dirty, runnels of sweat and tears cutting through the grime. He could slap her, he thought, and drew back his hand. She saw the movement and flinched, her eyes squinting against the coming blow.

She seemed strangely vulnerable then, and he halted his swing, grabbing her braids and yanking her forward. His mouth settled over hers, grinding and punishing. He meant it to be. He was surprised by the soft sweetness of her mouth. He hadn't expected it. His surprise caused him to soften his kiss. He felt the scrape of her teeth as she tried to bite him. His arms tightened, crushing her to him, holding her prisoner while he let his body experience the rare enjoyment of a womanly body.

She was little, yet fully formed, her curves sweet beneath the soft buckskin dress. His hands went to her rounded buttocks and he pulled her tightly against him, letting her feel his bulging need. She stopped fighting and lay passive in his arms. When he released her mouth and stared down at her, his breath came in gasps.

She tried to pull her face into a dispassionate expression, but her eyes held a flicker of fear. Good, he thought. That was what he'd wanted her to feel. Abruptly he released her, so she staggered and reached out to him to regain her balance. Just as quickly, she jerked her hand away, but he had hold of her shoulders again, gripping the slender bones in an iron grip, his mouth once more a grim, unrelenting line.

"Don't underestimate me, Jenny," he growled. "You

can't get away from me. I'm taking you north—to land where you've never been. You're going to need me to protect you, feed you, and see that you make it alive." He let her go then, shoving her slightly. She bristled and glared at him like a mangy dog that had been kicked one time too many.

"Get on your pony," he ordered.

She hesitated as if she meant to defy him, then her shoulders slumped. Sullenly she climbed onto the pony's back. For a moment she looked down at him, and he read the thoughts that crossed through her mind. He was unmounted, unprepared! She might get away after all. Then she looked into his eyes; he saw defeat grow on her face. She was beginning to understand. Deliberately he turned his back and climbed into his saddle.

No words were spoken as they made the trip back to the fort. They walked the horses to let them rest. When they entered the fort, some of the soldiers grinned and called out to him.

"Whoee, Caleb. Looks like you got a wildcat on your hands."

"Old Caleb knows how to tame her. He's been huntin' wildcats a long time," another called.

The girl's back stiffened and she drew herself up proudly.

"If you need some help, Caleb, I'll come along," a soldier called out. "I ain't tamed me any wildcats in a long time. I've got me a hunger for one."

Colonel Grierson stepped out on the porch; the ribald talk ceased as the soldiers turned away and pretended to be absorbed in some task.

"Any trouble, Hunter?" Grierson called out.

"None to speak of," Caleb said, and, looping the pack mule's reins over his saddle horn, he turned away.

"Tell Major Emory we've nearly got the Comanche licked down here," Grierson called. "We're just mopping up."

Caleb waved a hand without looking back. All this and more had been said in the colonel's office. Caleb had protested this task of hauling the captives back East, but Grierson had been adamant. It was clear he considered this latest victory the ultimate one. They no longer needed Caleb Hunter to guide them into the Cross timbers. They'd attempted to negotiate with Quannah and winter would take care of the rest of the holdouts. Without food, shelter, or horses, it was just a matter of time before the rest of the Comanche came into the reservations. Job accomplished, a man like Caleb Hunter was no longer needed.

Caleb had read the message in the colonel's pale eyes and bland smile. He'd stopped arguing against this trip. Now as he rode out of the fort for the last time, he didn't look back. It hadn't been a home to him—the men hadn't been friends or family. Another part of his life was over; he would simply ride until another part started.

The girl beside him was silent. He didn't know what she was thinking or feeling. He didn't care. The brief moment of pleasure he'd found in kissing her was gone, pushed to some dark forgotten corner of his mind, where he put all such human emotions. He wasn't a man who sought pleasure. He paid no attention to her, except to note that she followed docilely enough.

Only when they'd topped a ridge did he pause and sit gazing down at the valley with the river running through it. For a moment his fierce demeanor relaxed as he took in the peaceful, cleansing power of the view before him. Only at moments like this could he find surcease from that devil that drove him, only here were the bloody images replaced by a quiescent tranquillity, a quiet stillness that bathed him in serenity. The agitation of his memories fell from him and he felt calm within himself.

The girl's pony nudged forward, and his feeling was gone. He turned to her, unaware that his face still held a compassion she hadn't seen there before. Then his eyes seemed to focus on her, and she felt the weight of his contempt.

"Why did you stay with the Comanche?" he asked harshly.

"They are my people," she answered in the white man's tongue.

"They were your enemy. They killed your mother and father and kidnapped you."

"No!" Her eyes were wide and dark. "The Comanche did not. Ten Bears traded for me, from someone else. White Weasel made me her daughter. They were good to me and loved me."

He let it go then. She couldn't remember her last name. Likely she didn't remember who had attacked her family and kidnapped her. Without another word, he led the way down the ridge and into the valley.

Wild Sage watched him go. What a strange man he was, she thought. He frightened her—and yet, at times, like now, when his face had been kind, she thought he might be her friend. She could rely on no one, she thought, except herself. She must remember that . . . and when she had a chance, she would try to escape again. Two days later they reached Fort Cobb.

"Some of these poor souls haven't fared as well as the little girl you brought," Maj. William Emory said, leading Caleb to the building where the white captives were lodged. A soldier stood guard, and at the major's nod, turned to unbar the door. With a start Caleb realized this was the post jail. His lips tightened as he followed the major inside.

The interior of the building was roughly furnished. Extra cots had been set up to accommodate the five women within. It wasn't the building or the sight of the women that caused him to draw in his breath, it was the stench of unwashed bodies and urine. A half-full bucket sat in the corner, the only concession for their needs. Most of the women sat on the floor, staring at the intruders with vacant eyes. Their faces and robes were filthy, streaks of dried blood marking their scratched cheeks. One spat at them, while still another crouched in a corner clutching a rag to her breast as she rocked back and forth, intoning the remnant of a lullaby.

"Like I said, some of these poor things haven't had an easy time of it." The major looked around the bleak surroundings.

"How long have you had them?"

"Three weeks for some of them, a few days for the rest."

"Couldn't you have given them some water to bathe?"

"We did, but they didn't use it—just sat in a huddle, tearing at their clothes and skin."

"They were grieving," Caleb said. "It's their way."

"I figured as much."

"Have they been allowed out to exercise?"

"We tried that, but a couple of them sneaked off before we knew what they were about. By the time my men found them, they were dead from lack of water. It almost seemed they wanted to die."

Caleb nodded. "Have your men bring some water and let's get them cleaned up."

"You mean give them a bath?"

"That's just what I mean," Caleb snapped. "I can't travel with them like that. Bring them some food, and after they've eaten, make them march in the yard."

"They won't eat," the major said. "Some of them haven't eaten a bite since we brought them in."

Caleb looked at the bone-thin women. "We'll force them to eat," he said. "They can't travel in the condition they're in."

"God, Almighty! I hate seeing a thing like this," the major said, shaking his head. "These are white women. We can't just treat them the way you're suggesting."

Caleb studied him. "Right now, they're still Comanche," he said slowly, and stepped outside. The girl had dismounted and stood waiting by her pony, her gray eyes taking in the fort and all its inhabitants. She saw Caleb and ducked her head.

"Jenny, come here," he ordered.

She ignored him, refusing to acknowledge her white name. She wished she'd never told him what she remembered.

"Jenny!" he roared, and she dared not ignore him again. Reluctantly she crossed the yard to him. His face was stern as he looked at her.

"Inside are more of your kind," he said brusquely. "They haven't eaten, they haven't washed themselves. They can't travel the way they are."

"Why don't you release them and let them return to their tribes?" she said, her temper flaring.

He studied her face. The first night they'd paused on their trip north, she'd disappeared toward the creek. He'd just thought of going to search for her when she'd returned with her hair freshly washed and her face scrubbed. He'd been surprised at how pretty she was— and he'd automatically thought of the feel of her small, womanly body against his. He'd watched as she sat on a rock and rebraided her hair. When she was finished, she had looked like a Comanche woman again, and he'd turned away.

Now he noted the slope of her forehead and nose, the small mouth and stubborn chin. She might still think Comanche, but that would work to his advantage now. He took hold of her arm, and she didn't pull away, although she remained stiff and unyielding in his grasp, her eyes going dark in an unspoken warning.

"I need your help," he said. She pulled away from him.

"I will not help you," she stated flatly. "You can force me to go with you to another land, but you can't force me to help you force others as well."

"They need your help," he said softly. "They haven't eaten or bathed themselves. They're still stunned by what's happened to them. Go in and talk to them, reassure them."

She shook her head, denying his request, then just as quickly changed her mind and stepped inside the building with its barred windows and door. What she saw made her head spin dizzily and she gripped the edge of the door, trying to still the outraged trembling of her knees.

These had once been proud women, mothers and daughters and wives. Now they sat in abject misery, their lives destroyed, their pride and hope gone. They'd been torn away from all they'd embraced of life and they sat bewildered, unknowing and uncaring of who or what they were. Wild Sage saw their hopeless despair and felt its echo in her own heart.

Yet she saw something else—and knew this was what Caleb Hunter had seen. They'd lost the will to live, to go on in a world that had become alien to them. They'd adjusted once, embraced a new life. To ask them to repudiate that world and accept yet another was too much, too much. She wanted to sink to her knees and weep with them, but in that way lay defeat and madness. She saw it in their eyes and would not accept it for herself.

The women had not even turned their heads to look at her. In their world, people came and went, but were unacknowledged. Wild Sage walked toward them, stepping around them, trying to catch their eyes. They saw her buckskin dress, her braids, and the Comanche symbols on her clothing, and for a moment a gleam of hope was reborn.

Crouching beside one woman, Wild Sage ran her

hands over the woman's face and shoulders and down her back, soothing and patting, and all the time she whispered in Comanche. The woman raised her head and stared at Wild Sage, a moment of hope breaking through the madness. Wild Sage moved on to the next woman, then the next. Some she reached, some were forever lost.

Two days later Caleb and his entourage set out from Fort Cobb, heading north toward the Kansas prairie towns. Private Billy Moses drove the supply wagon, which also carried the five women from Fort Cobb. Sergeant Butler and Private Theophilus Phillips, affectionately called Teddy or Phil Phillips, rode guard. Wild Sage followed on her Indian pony, sometimes calling out to the women on the wagon. Some called back to her. They were regaining their belief in life. Some would never do so. Wild Sage concentrated on the women who responded to her. They and they alone would help her when the time came.

The journey was not unpleasant. The sun was hot on their heads, but a breeze rippled the grass and cooled their flushed faces. Caleb was surprisingly considerate, stopping at streams and rivers to rest and have a bite to eat. At night he broke for camp early and allowed the women to go far enough away from the wagon and men to attain some measure of privacy. Wild Sage led the women to the streams to bathe themselves, coaxing them to be on their best behavior.

"We must make the white eyes trust us," she whispered to a thin, dark-haired woman named Pretty Shell. "We must bathe ourselves and be agreeable to the white men."

"I will not," Running Deer said. She was a young woman with bitter eyes. "The white eyes have caused the death of my husband. I will not rest until I have shed the blood of the white men."

"Shh. You mustn't talk that way," Wild Sage cautioned. "The one who does not wear a uniform knows our words."

Running Deer cast a skeptical glance over her shoulders. "He does not look our way," she scoffed. "Like most white men, he is unaware of his enemies."

"Do not think little of him," Wild Sage said. "He sees more than he shows." Tired of arguing with Running Deer, she turned back to Pretty Shell. "You must take the food that is offered. It will give you strength, but only eat half of it. Save the rest, so we may have food when we have escaped." She glanced at the intent faces. Three of them were alert and ready for her commands. The fourth stared into the water as if she didn't hear. The fifth woman, Bright Star, sat huddled on the wagon, her food forgotten beside her. For a moment, Wild Sage felt her own despair.

"We must get weapons," she whispered.

"I have a knife," Running Deer said, indicating her laced leggings. "The young soldier was careless and left it beside the river. When he came again to look for it, it was gone." She grimaced, which Wild Sage guessed was supposed to be a smile.

She studied Running Deer for a moment. She was bright and had been quick to take advantage of the enemy's weakness, but she was impatient and would act without thinking. Wild Sage wished she could warn the other woman, but knew any attempt would only anger

Running Deer. Sergeant Butler approached the stream, and Wild Sage made a quieting motion. The women pulled apart and pretended to be absorbed in braiding their hair.

"Howdy, ladies," the officer called out, smiling winningly.

No one made an attempt to answer him, only staring with dark, unreadable eyes. He nodded his head ingratiatingly, filled his canteen with water, and stomped back to the wagon.

"Them women ain't natural," he grumbled, settling beside the campfire and reaching for the coffeepot.

"They shore ain't," Teddy Phillips said. "They jest ignore a man like he ain't even there."

"They know we're there," Private Moses said. "I feel their eyes on my back every hour of the day. I can tell you, if they had a knife, they'd likely—"

"Forget such talk," Caleb snapped. "Just watch your step and your weapons and you'll be fine. The farther we carry them away from Comanche country, the sooner they'll take on their white ways again."

"I hope so," Butler said. "I figured this would be an interesting trip, taking them Comanche ladies back home to their white folks. I figured they'd be real grateful."

Caleb Hunter set down the coffeepot so softly it made no sound at all against the hot rocks.

"Forget any such thoughts," he said evenly.

"Why?" the sergeant challenged. "They been livin' with savages. Don't you suppose they'd be happy to be with a white man again?"

"I'm not supposing anything," Caleb answered. "I'm

just saying leave the ladies alone. If they don't cut your heart out, I will."

"Now look here, Hunter. You ain't in charge of this here trip. You ain't even in the army. I reckon I'm the highest ranking officer . . . and what I say is what counts."

Caleb's gun seemed to appear without him even moving. Its barrel was pointed straight at the officer's thick chest. "I reckon this determines who's in charge, Butler," he said quietly. "I was commissioned by Colonel Grierson out of Fort Sills to take these ladies home and I intend to do that. They're going to arrive there in the same shape as when they started out."

Butler's florid face grew red with anger. He glanced at the other two soldiers, looking for support. They said nothing. Butler shrugged his shoulders and grinned sheepishly. "I reckon what you say goes," he muttered. "I was just thinkin'."

"I know what you were thinking," Caleb said, holstering his gun. "Don't think anymore and you'll stay out of trouble."

"I reckon you can afford to take that attitude," Butler said snidely. "After all, you had several days traveling alone with that pretty little heifer you brought. Reckon you broke her in real good, so's she's almost actin' white now. Me and the boys jest wanted to do the same with the other—"

His words were cut off by the swift movement of Caleb Hunter leaping over the fire and grabbing his shirt collar. Butler was dragged to his feet before he could even close his mouth. He saw the big fist coming at him, but couldn't duck in time. The force of the blow carried him over backward, so he fell against the side of the wagon and lurched to the ground. In the wagon, the woman who'd remained silent, thus far, began screaming, a high-pitched moaning sound that sent a chill up Private Phillips's back. He got to his feet and backed away. Caleb Hunter swung around, glaring at Phillips and Moses.

"Sergeant Butler ain't speakin' for—for me, Mr. Hunter, sir," Phillips stuttered. "I ain't had any such thoughts."

"Me, neither," Moses said from his seat beside the fire.

At the first sound of screaming, Wild Sage had come running from the creek. She hurried to Bright Star and put her arms around her, crooning softly.

"It's all right," she said, rocking the woman back and forth. Bright Star's hands clutched her arms as if she meant never to let go. Once again she lapsed into a blank stare, but her body jerked with suppressed sobs.

Over her head, Wild Sage met Caleb's gaze. "What have you done to her?" she demanded in Comanche, then had to repeat the words haltingly in English.

Caleb shook his head. "No one bothered her. She just grew frightened."

"At white men who fight among themselves," Wild Sage said accusingly. "Can't you keep your anger to yourselves?"

"Put her to bed," Caleb answered. "I'll see she's not frightened anymore tonight."

Wild Sage wanted to berate him further, but the white man's words crowded in her throat and she knew she would only stutter if she tried to give voice to them. Silently she turned away and made up the pallet Bright Star slept on. When she was finished she looked again at the men around the fire. The man known as Sergeant Butler sat before the fire rubbing his jaw. When he felt her gaze, he returned it with a baleful glare of his own. Caleb Hunter glanced at her, then looked away quickly, almost furtively, and in that moment she understood what the fight had been about. They'd fought over her and the other women. Wild Sage shivered and longed to have a knife, as Running Deer had.

That night she rolled herself into her blankets and lay staring up at the black, star-studded night. The smell of the campfire was comforting. The sky was above her, the mother earth at her back. She could close her eyes and almost pretend she was back with Ten Bears and White Weasel and all the rest of her people, but then she heard Bright Star weeping and remembered the tight, hooded gaze of Caleb Hunter; she knew her world was forever changed.

Chapter 5

STEADILY THEY MADE progress across the flat face of
the land. Wild Sage tried to remember signs along
the way that would help her find her way back to the
Comancheria once she'd escaped these white men. But
the land had taken on a sameness that made such land-
marks only a wish. Soon! Tonight, she thought. To go
further would be madness. Even now she might not be
able to find her way back. Wild Sage rode beside the
wagon, her demeanor calm, her behavior sedate and cooperative. Surely by now the men had begun to trust the
women as they had begun to distrust one another. She
saw the angry glances between the men, saw the growing hunger on the faces of Butler and Moses when they
looked at the women.

Even the young soldier seemed troubled—and he
spent too much time watching over Bright Star, as if
he'd made her his personal responsibility. Several times
a day, he rode close to the wagon to extend his canteen.
Surprisingly Bright Star responded to his gentle smile.
Once she even spoke to him, calling him Ta-wah-que-
nah, the Comanche name for the warrior who had been
her husband. She reached out to clasp his hand, then

seeing his pale skin had flung it away while she shrieked in terror.

"Get away from her," Caleb Hunter had shouted, and the young soldier had spurred his horse away. Running Deer had quieted Bright Star's cries, and the wagon had moved on.

They camped near a stream bordered by prairie grass, the tops of which were already turning golden in the summer heat.

Wild Sage sat beside the campfire, seemingly docile and meek, but inside she simmered with anticipation. Tonight! Tonight, they would flee, her Comanche sisters and herself, making their way through the prairie grass until they were well away, then rising to run, fleet of foot, back to the Comancheria. She glanced at Running Deer. The other girl sat with her hand clasping her boot where the stolen knife was hidden, her eyes hard and hostile as she watched the white men move about the campfire.

Wild Sage looked for Caleb Hunter. He sat against a tree, cradling a tin coffee cup between his big hands. She raised her gaze to his face and was disconcerted to find he was watching her as intently as she was him. He knows, Wild Sage thought, her heart thumping with sudden fear. He knows we plan to escape. But how could he? Because he is not an ordinary white man, she reminded herself. He knows too much of our ways. His blank eyes see too much.

Yet as she met his gaze, she saw that his eyes no longer wore the habitual blank expression. The wall had been torn away; she saw something, some need flicker in his eyes. It took her a moment to recognize that need as lust, raw and barely leashed.

She shivered and looked away, then couldn't resist another glance at the big, quiet man. His expression was closed, his eyes unreadable once more. Had she imagined the look in his eyes? Because it was there in the eyes of the other white men, had she imagined it in Caleb Hunter's? She remembered his kiss that first day she tried to run away. It had been savage, undisciplined, and all the more frightening from a man she instinctively knew seldom let his emotions take hold.

She sat puzzling over her captor. He carried himself as one doomed. Had he a *tabebekut*, a curse, placed over him? She turned away and studied the line of ponies and mules staked beyond the wagon. Perhaps they should take the horses instead of trying to flee on foot. There would be more danger of awakening the soldiers than if they went on foot. But would they not need the strength and fleetness of the horses over this vast flatland? She sat mulling her strategy and knew that the thoughts of each of her sisters were the same.

She waited until Caleb had mounted his horse and ridden away from the camp, as was his custom every night. Tense with worry, she watched the other men settling into their beds. This fear was with her every night, for instinctively she knew it was Caleb's presence that kept the men from the women.

Now she watched as the fat sergeant pulled his blankets over his paunch and lapsed almost immediately into a loud snore. The one they called Moses took longer. He sat in his bedroll and watched the wagon where the women slept. Finally sensing her defensive gaze he turned back to Wild Sage, gave her a mocking salute, and laid down. She sensed the young one with the double name, Phil Phillips, at the wagon. She heard his soft murmur and Bright Star's answering murmur. Then he crept back to his side of the campfire and got into his bedroll.

"You have a little luck tonight, Phillips?" Moses sneered. Settling on the hard ground, the young soldier didn't answer. Wild Sage lay back. They were all accounted for. Now she had only to wait until they slept. She glanced at Running Deer and saw the whites of the other woman's eyes. She, too, was waiting. Tonight!

The quarter-moon had reached the high point in the sky, its tiny sliver of light hazy against the black, starless expanse. Wild Sage raised her head and looked at Running Deer. The other woman was ready. They rose as one, moving silently in their moccasins. Wild Sage made her way to the wagon and wakened the other women. They would all go but Bright Star, she had decided. Bright Star's husband was dead. She had no children in the Comanche villages. Her mind was sick and her body too weak to make the journey back with them. As she was once lost to the white world, now she was lost again, this time to the Comanche world.

Stealthily the women joined Wild Sage and Running Deer at the horses. They would not take the saddles of the soldiers; they would ride the animals bareback. With quick, sure motions, the women loosened all the horses and mules, choosing the ones they would ride, and in a sudden flurry of hooves and cries, scattered the remaining remuda to the four winds.

"What the hell?" Sergeant Butler yelled, rolling out of his bedding.

"The horses!" Moses shouted. "The Injuns got the horses!" He pulled his gun and fired shots randomly.

"Put that fool gun away, you idiot!" Butler shouted. "You'll hit someone in the dark!"

"That's what I meant to do!" Moses snapped, gripping his gun while he stared at the retreating horses.

"It's those dad-blamed women," Butler growled, running to the wagon. "They've run off with the horses."

"Bright Star!" Phillips shouted, running to the wagon, his eyes big and scared-looking. When he saw Bright Star's eyes staring back at him, he breathed a sigh of relief and gripped her hand. She didn't reject his touch, simply holding on tightly while she whimpered with fear.

"It's all right, Bright Star," he said soothingly. "Nothing will hurt you while I'm here." Her whimpering stopped, but she still clung to his hand.

Sergeant Butler had been staring in the direction the horses had taken; now, as the sound of their hooves died away, he threw his hat on the ground in rage.

"Dad-blame it," he snarled. "We been coddling them women too much, and look what it got us! If Caleb had just listened to me, I would have put the fear of bejesus in 'em and they'd be grateful just to be allowed to sleep through the night, 'stead of runnin' off."

The sound of an approaching horse dried up his words as all three men tensed and waited. Caleb Hunter rode into camp leading a mule.

"Which way did they go?" he asked. No one had to

tell him what had happened. Sergeant Butler pointed to
the south.

"Two more mules are just over that rise," he shouted.
"Get 'em and saddle up." He rode out of camp at a fast
gallop. No one had to be told he expected them to follow as soon as they had retrieved something to ride.

"In all my born days, I ain't never rode a mule," Sergeant Butler complained. At the same time, he was busy
saddling up the mule Caleb had brought. Swinging into
his saddle he rode out to the ridge Caleb had indicated
and helped retrieve the other mules. In short order, they
were following Caleb.

"Wait!" Wild Sage cried, pulling her pony to a halt.
She slid out of the saddle and placed her ear to the
ground, then rose and leapt back onto her horse.
"Someone's coming after us," she cried. "Let's scatter.
Maybe some of us can escape."

Running Deer immediately turned her horse to the
west, and, with no words of farewell, kicked it to a gallop.

"I will stay with you," Pretty Shell said.

"Then keep up." Wild Sage kicked her own horse
into a gallop, bending low over its neck. The little pony
was valiant and ran swiftly. Foam gathered along his
neck, but he didn't falter. Wild Sage glanced over her
shoulder several times.

At first Pretty Shell followed closely, but eventually
she fell further behind. Wild Sage knew the honorable
thing to do was wait for her companion, but she had no
wish to be recaptured by the hated soldiers. She would
ride back to the Comancheria and find Two Wolves.

She would ride beside him in his raids and defy the
white men until they won the Comancheria back from
their enemies or she lay dead, her sightless eyes staring
at the sun, as White Weasel had done.

She was so caught up in her dream that she wasn't
sure how long a horseman had been trailing her. Slowly
she became aware of the drum of hooves behind her
and whipped her pony to greater speed, but he had
given his best and now he slowed.

"Run swift as the wind, little pony," she cried, and
bent to whisper words of encouragement in his ears.

The little mount tried, but the sorrel was superior in
height and speed. He drew abreast of Wild Sage; she
knew without looking at his face that her pursuer was
Caleb Hunter. She turned her whip on him, and had the
satisfaction of feeling it strike his cheeks and shoulders.
One long arm reached for the whip, wrenching it from
her hand. Then he reached for her.

Wild Sage twisted away, but his hands closed around
her thick braid. Pain seared through her head as his fist
closed over her plaited hair and yanked. She was un-
seated and fell to the ground, fearful at first that she
might fall beneath the thundering steel hooves of his
mount. Then she rolled away. Once again he had bested
her. The last time he had forced his kisses upon her, but
she would not allow him to do so again. Leaping to her
feet, she faced him, weaponless and fearless, her head
held high, her eyes wary.

He'd dismounted by now and walked toward her with
long, angry strides. Wild Sage opened her mouth to rail
at him, but his fist came up and clipped her chin. Blackness rolled over her and she sank to the ground. With-

out preamble, Caleb seized her and threw her over the bare back of her Indian pony. Lashing her hands and feet together beneath the pony's belly, he remounted and headed back toward the campsite. On the way he met Sergeant Butler and the other men. Between them they had recaptured two of the women.

"One got away," Moses called.

"Reckon you won't be so easy on them bitches now," Butler growled. Caleb said nothing. Without further words or recriminations they returned to the wagon.

Wild Sage had regained consciousness long before she saw the dying embers of the campfire. Her jaw felt as if it had been broken and her legs and arms were numb from the tight rawhide straps that bound her. As Caleb dismounted and walked back to her pony, Wild Sage pretended to be unconscious. He might become careless. She might yet escape. Next time she'd take the big sorrel he rode. Nothing could catch her then. She felt his hands at the rope that bound her and remained limp across the saddle. Without ceremony, he dragged her from the saddle and set her on her feet. It was useless to pretend with him.

"Stand up!" he ordered hoarsely, and she struggled to, although the tingling pain of blood returning to her limbs was excruciating. He'd kept her hands bound, and now he jerked on the rope, causing her to stumble. She fought to regain her balance, her eyes widening as she saw what he was about.

"Get in," he said, nodding toward the wagon.

"I—I do not wish to ride in the wagon," she said falteringly, and despised the fact that her voice wavered over the white man's words, making her sound tearful. She would not cry before her enemy.

His face was like stone. "From now on you will ride in the wagon," he said flatly, "as will the other women. Your hands will be bound at all times." He gave her a shove; she fell against the side of the wagon. "Get in," he ordered.

She looked at his face and saw not one shred of kindness. She was frightened by his lack of emotions. He wasn't even angry at their attempt to escape. He was simply insuring they wouldn't do so again. Miserably she obeyed his command, crouching on the wagon bed with her knees pulled up to her chest and her head resting on her knees. Caleb tied her hands to the side of the wagon and turned to the other men, watching silently as they secured the other women.

"There is one woman left," he said when they were finished. "Phillips, you stay here and guard the wagon. Don't untie them for any reason. Butler, Moses ... mount up."

"We can't catch that other one. She's long gone by now. Why don't we leave her? Like as not, she'll be picked up by Grierson's men when they raid the next village."

"We're too far away," Caleb said. "She'll never make it back to the Comancheria. She'll die out there."

"That's too bad for her," Butler said, shaking his head. "I ain't goin'."

"She's a white woman," Caleb said, "and we're responsible for seeing she makes it back to her own kind. Now mount up." Something in his stance was unyielding. Butler saw it, and, with a curse, turned to his horse and mounted.

They returned by noon the next morning with Running Deer riding between them. Her face was gray, her lips parched. When she reached the wagon, she climbed onto it without a word of admonition from the men. Meekly she curled into a ball, refusing to meet the eyes of the other women.

"It is all right," Wild Sage whispered. "We have tried to be free and return to the Comancheria. One day we will succeed." Finally Running Deer raised her head and looked at Wild Sage. Her anger and defiance were gone. Now her eyes held only defeat.

Wild Sage felt her own hope shrivel. Silently the women rode toward the north and the east, toward a destiny they could not guess.

Millbrook could hardly be called a town. It rose from the flat prairie, a pitiful cluster of buildings, a ragged testimony to man's drive to bring his own brand of civilization where there was none. No brook fed the town, so there could never be a mill, but hope springs strong in the hearts of some, and the memory of a life left behind guided the homesteaders in the building and naming of their towns.

Millbrook squatted valiant and ugly against the landscape, boasting roughly-painted signs to delineate the general store from the post office, the hotel from the land office. A small, shoddy church stood as a silent rebuke to those who frequented the saloon that dominated the center of town. Nearby was the stage depot and a livery stable. At the other end of the grassy path serving as the main street was the public well. Rough planks formed unsteady boardwalks and gnarled tree limbs nailed to weathered posts served as hitching rails. As quickly as the town had sprung up, it could be abandoned, if time and conditions dictated. Despite the sweat of brow and muscle, the citizens of the community had achieved, at best, a transient existence. Only by sheer willpower were they making it work.

As Caleb and his group rode into town, people left the dark interiors of the stores and saloon, stepping out onto the plank walks and shading their eyes while they stared with dumbstruck wonder at the motley women riding in the wagon. Wild Sage sat with her head down on her knee, yet couldn't resist studying the town and its citizenry as the wagon rolled past. All too soon they came to the end of the little town and stopped at the livery stable.

"Howdy, stranger," a tall, weather-beaten man with stooped shoulders greeted them. His thin-whiskered jaw worked convulsively on a wad of tobacco.

"Howdy," Caleb said, alighting. "Have you got a sheriff around here?"

"You're lookin' at him, sir," the man said. "Jules Hagen's the name." He held out a thin, weathered hand.

Briefly Caleb grasped it, identifying himself.

"You ain't said what business you're in, sir." The man looked at the women in the wagon. "We ain't got much need for dance hall women, especially Injun ones." He spat between his teeth and hooked his hands in his back pockets, rocking slightly on his heels.

"I don't have dance hall women or Indian squaws," Caleb said, loosening the cinch on his saddle. He came around the sorrel, resting his arm on its flanks while he met Jules Hagen's eyes. "These are white women, captured by the Comanche. We're taking them back to their families, if they got any."

"Well, now. That's all right," Jules said, rubbing his jaw. His glance flickered to the women and back to Caleb. "They look to be in pretty sorry shape. How come you got 'em trussed up like a turkey about to lose his pinfeathers?"

Caleb took a deep breath and looked at the women. His glanced stopped at Wild Sage's bent head. "They don't know yet they're white," he said flatly. "They still think they're Comanche."

"Well, I'll be."

Other people had gathered now and heard Caleb's words. The women clucked in sympathy as they looked at the women huddled on the wagon. The men were silent for the most part, but Caleb saw the question in some of their eyes. What kind of women were these? What good were they now that they'd been with an Indian? Who would want them? Even the women had begun to wonder what atrocities their sisters had known; their fine nostrils quivered in outrage and pity.

A roughly clad man with greasy dark hair and sly, greedy eyes came out on the porch of the saloon with a group of other idlers. "Look at them women," he said, revealing his yellowed teeth in a leering smile. "Reckon on how many bucks they been with."

The men around him shook their heads.

"Right cheer," Hank Radburn shouted gleefully. "Come git your fine ladies. Right this way."

Caleb glanced around and his jaw tightened. "Is there room in the hotel to put them up?" he asked.

"Yes, sir," Jules Hagen affirmed. "There shore is."

The people moved back as Caleb and Sergeant Butler began untying the women. Teddy Phillips was beside Bright Star, reassuring her as she ducked her head in terror.

"You're home now, Mary," he said. "Home! These here are your people, your own kind. They won't hurt you."

"Why do you call her Mary?" Caleb demanded. Phillips flushed and looked away.

"I just figured I'd make up a name for her until she finds out who she really is," he mumbled.

Caleb studied his earnest young face and looked away, his gaze automatically seeking and finding the slender form of Jenny.

"These women won't be much good as wives—you know that, don't you?" he said flatly.

Phillips nodded his head, his blue eyes flashing with denial. "No, sir," he said stiffly. "I don't know that."

Caleb shrugged and turned away from the young soldier. His hands were rough and impatient as they undid the thongs binding Wild Sage. She glanced at him with contempt. His big hand clamped around her arm.

"I know you're the one who led those women to try and escape," he said in a low voice. "Don't try it again. You'll be doing them a disservice. They need time to adjust back to the white world. You might try it yourself. We're not so bad."

Wild Sage jerked her arm from his clasp. "I will never forget my mother dying at the hands of the white eyes," she snapped. "I will pray for a *tabebekut* to be placed on you so that one day you, too, will fall in death and your eyes will stare at the sun without seeing." Gracefully she rose and jumped from the wagon. Her limbs were cramped from the long ride and little exercise, but she would not allow herself to limp or falter. She was a Comanche.

There was a ripple among the onlookers. "Look, they're filthy," one woman said, drawing her skirts aside as if afraid of being soiled.

"The poor things!" another cried. She was an older woman with gray hair and kind gray eyes. Wild Sage caught only a glimpse of her as the crowd parted. She stalked through the aisle they'd made, her gaze fixed straight ahead, but she heard the women's compassionate voice.

"They'll need clothes."

"I have a spare dress."

"I have a petticoat and a pair of boots."

Wild Sage wanted to shout at them that she had no need for charity from the hated white eyes.

The voices raised enthusiastically as the women thought about their wardrobes and wondered what they could spare. "John's got a spare shirt we could part with," another cried, and the women scattered, hurrying back to their homes to gather what they could.

Caleb looked at Margaret Rudd.

"It's a blessing to see you again, Caleb," she said, holding out her arms and embracing the tall man in spite of his unbending stance. A look came over the tracker's face; Margaret guessed he'd not known many hugs in recent years. She stepped back and tilted her head, so she could meet his gaze. Her kind, full face was glowing with a smile.

"I came to ask a favor of you, Margaret," Caleb said,

feeling much as he had fourteen years before when she'd nursed him back to health and he'd stood mumbling his thanks. Asking a favor, even of Margaret Rudd, came hard to him.

"It's for one of the women ... Jenny is the only name she remembers." Uncomfortably he twirled his hat in his big hands.

"The little one who walked so proudly?" Margaret guessed.

Caleb nodded. "That's the one. She doesn't seem to remember any other family. I wondered if—if—since you don't have anyone, either ... ?"

"I'd take her in a minute," Margaret said earnestly, "but I'm not in my own place. I live with my sister, and her soddy is crowded with kids. I may be able to find someone who'd take her in, someone close by so I could keep an eye on her."

"I'd be obliged."

"It's no trouble, Caleb. She must have had a terrible time among the Indians."

Caleb let his breath out and slapped his hat against his leg before settling it on his head. He looked at the hotel where the women had disappeared, at the now empty wagon, and finally back at Margaret.

"She turned Comanche," he said quietly. "She's turned against her own kind."

She saw the bafflement in his eyes. This was a man who'd watched his family murdered and had spent his life seeking revenge. He wouldn't be able to understand how someone like Jenny could adopt the Comanche ways.

"She must have been a young child when she was

captured," Margaret said mildly. "Can you imagine the terror and hardships she endured but survived?"

"It would've been better if she hadn't," Caleb answered. "She took a Comanche for her husband."

"Caleb Hunter, don't you make that kind of judgment about her. She survived. If she were your baby sister, would you blame her for making such a choice if it meant she survived?"

"Yes!" Caleb said flatly, his steely gaze meeting Margaret's head-on. "I would have wanted her to kill herself first. I'm glad my parents put a bullet through her brain if it saved her from some Comanche buck." His words had been spoken in a surprisingly quiet tone, but the veins in his neck bulged with his effort to control the hatred that consumed him.

"Then I'm sorry for you, Caleb Hunter," Margaret said quietly. "Your father should have put a bullet through your head as well. Because you've been a dead soul wanderin' ever since."

She walked away from him, her thoughts in a turmoil. She'd been so happy to see him off the Comancheria. When he asked her to take the girl, she'd known a moment of hope that he might have found someone to ease his loneliness, but now she felt a sense of loss. She'd nursed his body back to health those many years ago, but the wounds on his soul were as raw as ever. Once she reached her sister Sarah's house, she rummaged through her clothes looking for something small enough for the slight figure of a girl who was just as wounded in her own way as Caleb Hunter.

Chapter 6

THE HOTEL ROOM was small and crowded with white men's furniture, a large bed that was too soft, a wooden chest with slide-out portions to store pemmican and feast clothing. But the chest was too large to carry on the back of a horse. Wild Sage scoffed at the impracticality of the white man's things. She approved of the piece of rug on the floor. It was not made of buffalo hide, but of pieces of calico rags twisted together. When she returned to the village, she would try a similar thing as a gift for White Weasel. Then she remembered that White Weasel was dead.

The memory hit her like a blow, so she fell to her knees. She'd been placed in a room with Bright Star, who looked at her curiously but said nothing. Bright Star was eyeing the strange things in this strange room, touching the blankets and pillows, the oil lamp, the rug, as if the memory of them was coming back from a long way. Then she stood before the mirror and stared at her reflection while tears ran down her cheeks. Tearing at her braids and the dirty buckskin dress, she soon stood naked and stared in wonder at her pale skin. Her clasped hands went to her mouth and she shook with silent tears.

"Do not weep, Bright Star," Wild Sage said wearily, her own grief a black cloud that had enfolded her.

"I am not Bright Star," the woman before the mirror said softly. Then her voice gained strength and she repeated the words. "I am Catherine Paris from Loose Creek, Missouri. My daddy is a banker." Her voice took on a faraway wonder. "My mother is the president of the Loose Creek Lady's Society and I have two sisters. We're going to California because Daddy—" Her voice cracked. "Oh, no!" She wept, but they were different from the tears she'd shed before. These were more painful, a sad groping toward a life she'd shut away because she'd thought it lost to her.

Dully Wild Sage stared at Catherine Paris, for such was her name now. On the journey here, she'd thought herself strong and Bright Star weak. Now she saw that Bright Star had begun the journey back to her old life, something Wild Sage could never do, for her memories were too old. She'd been but a child when she was captured. Her indoctrination into the Comanche world had been complete. Yet if she were to survive, she knew she must accept her new life with the whites.

Wearily she pushed up from the floor and crept to the looking glass. Catherine's eyes held wonder as she took in the colors of her eyes and hair. She shrank from Wild Sage's image in the glass and turned to stare at her as if she'd never seen her before.

"I am Jenny," Wild Sage said. "I do not know where I came from or who my white mother and father were. I have been Comanche too long." Tears glistened in her eyes, and suddenly it was Bright Star who was comforting Jenny. The two girls clung to each other and wept for all the fear and loss they'd endured.

"I can't be a white woman." Jenny wept. "I don't know how."

"You will learn," Catherine said softly. "We will both learn."

"I don't want to."

Catherine drew away, looking at Wild Sage with troubled eyes. "Come, little sister," she said. "We will take the first step."

Tubs of water had been brought, and now Catherine helped Wild Sage take off the soft buckskin dress that had been meant as her wedding dress. As if she were a child, Catherine led her to the tub and helped her wash her hair and skin. The soap was strong and smelled bad, but both girls used it to wash away the prairie dirt. When they were finished they dried themselves and wrapped the towels about themselves while they stared at the tumble of hair, lightened now that the oil, dirt, and herbs were washed away. Catherine's hair was dark, with a sheen of red.

"Your hair is like the caramel syrup my mother used to make at Christmas time," Catherine said.

"What is caramel?" Wild Sage asked.

Catherine paused, smiling as she tried to explain a long-forgotten taste and smell. Their chatter was interrupted by a knock at the door. The girls grew hesitant, drawing the old, familiar habits of the Comanche women about themselves.

The door opened, and the kind woman Wild Sage had noticed outside entered. "May I come in?" she asked.

"I'm Margaret Rudd, and I've brought you some clean clothes. They aren't much. Folks around these parts don't have time or place for fancy duds, but they'll cover you decently." She stopped talking and held out a blue dress to Wild Sage.

"You're kind of small, so Sarah and me reckoned some of Louise's clothes might fit you." Wild Sage took the dress without looking at it. Her expression was closed, her eyes downcast, her small chin stubborn and unyielding.

Margaret Rudd turned to the other girl. "Maybe this shirt and skirt will fit you for now," she said. "I brought a belt."

"Thank you," Catherine answered. "I'm grateful for your help." Margaret covered her surprise with a smile. Emboldened, Catherine went on, telling her name and of her family.

"How did you come to be with the Comanche, child? Margaret asked her.

Catherine blinked back tears. "The Comanche attacked our wagon train. The men were all killed and some of the women. The girls were captured. Some of them fought. I saw—" Catherine stopped talking and swallowed against the knot in her throat.

"Don't talk about it now, if it hurts too much," Margaret cautioned.

"I want to say it," Catherine said hoarsely. "I saw one of the warriors raise his tomahawk and bring it down on my sister's head. She was screaming and fighting . . . and then she just went limp. That's how I knew I'd be better off if I stayed still and did everything they told me."

"God love you, child. That was the right thing to do."

"I didn't see my other sister. She was only ten."

"Wait a minute. Did you say Paris is your family name?" Catherine nodded dully. "Seems to me like there was a little girl rescued a few years back and her last name was Paris. They sent her back East to some family."

"Rebecca? Was her name Rebecca?"

"I don't know, child. I may even be wrong about the last name."

Catherine began to cry, great racking sobs that caused her body to jerk in spasms. "I want to go home." She wept. "I want to go home."

"Child, we'll send you back as quick as we can," Margaret Rudd said, patting Catherine's back. Her kind gaze fell on Wild Sage, who hadn't moved while all this transpired. "And what of you, child? Do you know your name?"

Wild Sage made no answer, suddenly tongue-tied at all she'd heard.

"Her name is Jenny." Catherine answered for her. "That's all she remembers. She was just a little girl when she was taken by the Indians."

"You don't remember your papa or mama?" Margaret asked.

Wild Sage raised her chin at the pity in the other woman's voice. "My father was Ten Bears, peace chief of the Kotsoteka Comanche, my mother was White Weasel. Ishatai's dance did not stop the white man's bullets from killing my father. Later, my mother fought, so she would not be taken to the white man's reservation."

"My poor child," Margaret said. "Was your father with Ishatai and Quannah at Adobe Walls?"

"Adobe Walls." Wild Sage repeated the name and slowly shook her head. Her eyes glistened, but she refused to allow the hated tears to stream down her cheeks.

"I was at Adobe Walls," Margaret said softly. "My husband was killed there. It was a terrible fight."

Wild Sage fixed her eyes on the other woman's face. "You were there?"

"Yes, and so was Caleb Hunter."

"Caleb Hunter!" Wild Sage's lips twisted bitterly. Caleb Hunter was at the places where both her parents had died. He'd captured her and brought her here—to this small crowded room with this white woman. Wild Sage clenched her fists. One day, she would avenge the death of her mother and father. She would kill Caleb Hunter!

Margaret saw the dark anger in Wild Sage's face and touched her arm. Wild Sage leapt as if she'd been burned.

"Come, Jenny. Let me help you dress, and then I'll brush your hair."

Wild Sage threw the dress on the floor. "I have no wish to wear the white man's dress, nor do I wish to be called Jenny. My name is Wild Sage. It is the name my mother, White Weasel, gave me."

"It is beautiful," Margaret said. "White Weasel must have been a loving mother to give you such a beautiful name."

Wild Sage's chin raised a little more, but Margaret noted it trembled slightly and the girl's large gray eyes glistened from unshed tears.

"Your clothes are dirty," Margaret said coaxingly. "I'm sure your mother would not wish you to appear in dirty clothes, looking unkempt."

Margaret had struck a nerve, for White Weasel had taken great pride in her appearance and always groomed herself before going among the villagers. Defeated, Wild Sage picked up the hated white man's clothes and tried to pull them over her head. Margaret rose and helped her settle the dress over her shoulders. It was a bit tight across the chest, with no easement for the fullness of a woman's breast. Wild Sage's pert breasts pushed against the soft, oft-washed fabric.

"It will have to do for now," Margaret said thoughtfully. "Ain't many who'll mistake you for a child. Turn 'round and let me tie that belt."

Wild Sage hated the binding seams of the dress. She was used to the loose, flowing lines of the buckskin dresses White Weasel made. Now the bulky bow tied at her back and the swish of too much fabric around her ankles made her nervous about moving for fear of tripping.

Catherine had also slipped into her white clothes, tucking the white man's loose white shirt into the dark linsey-woolsey skirt and tightening the belt at her waist to hold everything up. Then standing before the mirror, she brushed her long dark hair and pinned it up on top of her head. When she turned around, Wild Sage gaped; Bright Star had disappeared—and in her place stood, albeit in bare feet, a white woman. Did she look the same? Wild Sage wondered as Margaret took up the brush and went to work on her tangled hair. When she was finished, Wild Sage crept to the mirror and peered in, fearful of what she might see. She, too, had changed. Her hair had been brushed to a shine and it tumbled nearly to her waist, its pale brown color reflecting lights of gold and red. Margaret had tied her hair back with a blue ribbon to match the dress.

"No!" Wild Sage cried, and tore the ribbon from her hair, then backing into a corner, she proceeded to rebraid her hair in one thick braid to hang down her back. She tied the end with the bit of rawhide she'd worn before and took up the bits of feathers and fur she'd used to decorate her hair. When she was finished she peeked in the mirror. Once again she looked like Wild Sage.

During all this Margaret had wisely said nothing. Now she rose and ushered both girls toward the door. "They wish to meet downstairs," she said. "We must decide how best to help you." She led the two girls downstairs.

Running Deer and Pretty Shell were there as well, freshly bathed and clothed in the castoffs of the white women. Wild Sage looked at Running Deer and saw the curl of her lip. Running Deer was not happy adjusting to the white man's world, either.

The lobby of the hotel was jammed with people. The sheriff was there, along with many of the same people who'd watched their arrival. They were silent now as they looked at the women. A man stood up and banged his gun against the hotel counter.

"Folks, if I can have your attention, please. For those of you who don't know me, my name is Evan Udell, and I'm 'bout the only thing this town has that's near a mayor. Now, we have some young women here who've

undergone a horrible ordeal. It's our Christian duty to
see they get back to their families, if they have families
to go back to, and to give them a home in our community if they ain't." He paused and looked at the five
newcomers. "If any of you have anything to tell us
about your families, we'd be mighty glad to hear it."

Catherine Paris rose at once and told them of her
family in Loose Creek, Missouri. "I want to return there
and see if one of my sisters was saved," she said, and
sat down.

"Well, now, that seems like a reasonable request," the
mayor said. "There's a coach due through here tomorrow morning headin' back East. We'll see you're on it,
Miss Paris, and we'll provide you with an escort."

Immediately Teddy Phillips rose. "I'd like to volun-
teer to see Miss Paris reaches her people," the young
private said.

"Sergeant? Is there any reason why he shouldn't escort Miss Paris back East?"

"No, sir," the burly sergeant said. "As long as he
don't forget to come back."

The roomful of people laughed. There seemed to be
such a feeling of goodwill among them all. Clearly they
saw this as a joyous prayerful event. One by one, they
discussed the lot of the captives. Running Deer was un-
cooperative, and the consensus was that she would be
taken further east and settled into a community there.
They came to Wild Sage, and she sat with her eyes
downcast, her heart pounding. What right had these
white people to determine her life?

"Have you any family you'd like to be returned to,
young woman?" the mayor asked.

Slowly Wild Sage raised her head and met his gaze. "Yes," she said clearly. "I wish to return to my people in the Kotsoteka village in the Cross timbers." The people in the room drew a breath as if one long sigh.

"I'm afraid we can't do that, young woman. You're with your people now." He glanced at the sergeant.

Caleb Hunter stepped forward. "I've asked Margaret Rudd to be responsible for the girl," he said from the back of the room. Wild Sage couldn't see him, but she could feel the strength of his presence. Even now he was dictating what would happen to her. "Miz Rudd has said she'll watch out for the girl, but she lives with her sister and can't take her in. She needs a place to stay."

"Hmm," the mayor said. "Anybody out there got room for one more? I imagine she'd be a big help to someone out there. She's a might small, but looks strong enough."

In the back of the room Hank Radburn got to his feet. "I could use me a good squaw," he said, and grinned, revealing his rotting teeth.

"You don't have a home for yourself." Caleb spoke up quickly. He hadn't brought the girl all this distance to have her end up with the likes of the buffalo hunter.

"That don't make no nevermind," Radburn said. "She's used to livin' in a buffalo hide tent. I'll bet she knows how to tan hides proper like and how to cook a good buffalo rump. My last woman was right helpful in them ways and I took good care of her. She had all the buffalo meat she wanted."

"If you were so good to her, Mr. Radburn, how come she ain't still with you?" the mayor asked. The men around laughed.

Radburn's grin died and his face turned red. With a dirty hand he pushed back strands of unkempt hair. "She took sick. That weren't my fault. I had to trade her off to a tribe of Cheyenne. I didn't git much for her, either."

"We don't propose to send this poor woman back to the life you have in mind, Mr. Radburn," Evan Udall said. "Surely someone else here has extra room. How about you, Frank Walsh?"

The dark-haired man he'd addressed looked around the room and then studied the small figure of Wild Sage. "I'd need her to work," he said. "Faye ain't got strength enough to take care of herself, much less anyone else—and with the kids and all, I've got burden enough."

"What d'you say, little miss?" Evan Udell asked jovially. "Would you be willing to work?"

Wild Sage's chin came up. "I have always worked for my keep," she said stonily. "But I have no wish for white man's charity."

"If you worked it wouldn't be charity," Udell said.

A small, pale woman, seated beside Frank Walsh and large with child, clumsily got to her feet. Her face was heart-shaped, the expression in her dark eyes sweet. A small girl clung to her dress. More children, bearing the same eloquent eyes as their mother, sat silent beside her.

"Please, say you'll come," the woman said, and her voice was clear and sweet as a mountain jack on a spring morning. "I would so love the company. And although the work is hard, we wouldn't be unkind to you."

Something about the thin woman with her ungainly burden touched Wild Sage, as did the small angelic girl beside her. She would never be allowed to return to the Cross timbers villages, Wild Sage thought. If she defied them too much, they would send her further east, as they were Running Deer. Then she could never find her way back to her people. Perhaps here, if she worked hard and cooperated, perhaps one day they would allow her to return to the Real Human Beings.

"Well, girl?" Evan Udell said, taking out his large gold watch and glancing at it. It was nearly time for supper, and he knew Beryl would have his favorite hot dishes ready. Afterward, he would sit in the yard and contemplate the town and how he could make it grow.

"I'll go with them," Wild Sage said.

"Good, good!" The mayor snapped his watch shut with a decisive click and smiled around the room. "It seems we have everyone taken care of. I wish all you women a fine welcome back to your own people and I pray that each of you will find forgiveness in your hearts for the heathens who captured you in the first place. I hope each of you will pray for God's mercy, for the sinful way in which you've been forced to live. But you're back now among civilized folks and we expect you to behave accordingly. Shall we bow our heads and pray?"

Everyone bowed their heads, and the mayor's unctuous voice rolled over them like a benediction from God. Wild Sage and the other women watched this behavior. Catherine Paris had bowed her head, her lips moving in a silent mumble of prayer. The mayor's stomach rumbled with hunger and he drew his prayer to a close. At his amen, everyone prepared to leave.

The pale pregnant woman who'd offered Wild Sage a home came toward her. Her fingers were cold and spidery-feeling on Wild Sage's brown arm. "I'm so glad you're coming," Faye Walsh said. Her smile lit up her face, making it beautiful. Wild Sage had an urge to protect her, to put an arm around her and lead her to a seat, but the woman was stronger than she looked. Bending, she picked up the small girl who whined at her skirts. "Marybeth, this is—" She paused, her smile wide and generous. "I don't know your name."

"Wild Sage," she responded.

"Jenny," Margaret Rudd said at her elbow. She smiled at Wild Sage. "It will be easier for everyone to say."

Wild Sage nodded. "Jenny," she repeated, and felt as if she'd just closed a door on some part of herself.

"May I take Marybeth?" she said, suddenly fearful for the frail woman and the burden of the little girl.

Faye's smile was gentle as she looked at her daughter and smoothed a tear-dampened cheek. "Do you want to go to Jenny?" The little girl hesitated, then held out her chubby arms.

Jenny took hold of her, shifting her to one hip, the better to carry her. The child's hand went out to grab for Jenny's braid and the feathers and furs she'd used to decorate it.

"Pwetty," she said, and grinned, all baby dimples and sweet breath.

Forgetting the curious onlookers, Jenny hugged the

chubby body and felt something inside herself release. She was hungry for a touch of love—and now this little girl's soft hands grazing across her cheek woke that need most poignantly.

"She likes you," Faye said approvingly.

Jenny couldn't hold back the sudden smile. She looked at Faye Walsh, then at Margaret Rudd, and felt something kindle in her heart. She didn't know it was a rebirth of hope.

Frank Walsh was an impatient man. Tall and wide, he towered over his petite wife, almost dwarfing her and his children, a towheaded boy of eight and a girl of ten, with freckles and eyes like her mother's. The combination was enchanting.

"This is Nathan and Hannah." Faye introduced her children. "And you've already met Marybeth."

Frank hustled them all out. "I want to git home before dark," he groused. "I got the cow to milk and the mule to feed."

"Come, children," Faye said softly. Her voice was cultured, with a slight, crisp accent, different from the others here in this prairie town.

Jenny followed them out to the wagon and placed Marybeth on the pallet made for her in the wagon bed. The little girl stuffed a chubby thumb in her mouth and rolled over, her lids already growing drowsy.

A movement at her elbow caused her to whirl. Hank Radburn stood beside her. His gaze was sly, his grin caused a shiver of alarm. Her nose wrinkled at the stench emanating from his clothes.

"If'n you find you're not happy out there with the Walshes, you just remember old Hank Radburn. I'll be around these parts kinda regular like and my offer still holds. I need a spritely little squaw to help me tend my hides."

"I would never go with a man like you," Jenny said. "You are a curse to my people. You take away the buffalo that we need for food and warm robes." She spat on the ground beside his feet. Radburn stopped grinning. His eyes narrowed into angry slits.

"Are you saying you're too good for the likes of me?" he roared, reaching out to grasp her jaw. "You ain't so fine, little lady. There ain't no decent white men goin' to want you now you been livin' among the Comanche."

"Is that why you want me, *tabebah*?" she spat out. "Because you are not decent even among your own people?"

His hand slashed downward across her cheek. His grip around her neck tightened, cutting away her breath. Jenny saw spots dance before her eyes.

Suddenly his grip loosened and he was thrown to one side. Caleb Hunter gave him no time to recover, following his attack against the buffalo hunter with a double-fisted punch to his right jaw and then his left.

Radburn snarled with rage and sprang to his feet. When his hands came up, one of them held a buffalo skinning knife.

Women screamed and backed away from the two men. Radburn lunged, the knife aimed at Caleb's middle. Caleb leapt back and reached Radburn, pulling him forward and off balance. The buffalo hunter sprawled in the dirt. Caleb's booted foot came down on his hand, grinding hard until he released the knife. Quickly Caleb retrieved the weapon and handed it to Jules Hagen.

"I reckon I'll hold on to this until you're ready to leave town," the sheriff told Radburn. "I expect that'll be real soon."

"Not soon enough for me," Radburn sneered, and with a last baleful glance at Caleb, he stalked off.

Silently Caleb bent to retrieve his hat and knocked the dust off against his thigh. He felt Jenny's hostile gaze and turned to her.

"I don't need you to protect me from anybody, Caleb Hunter," she said, her gray eyes hard and unyielding. "If you must protect anyone, protect yourself, because I vow on the lives of my mother and father, I will kill you."

He made no answer, his gaze turning thoughtful as he stared at her, then, placing his hat on his head, he walked away.

"Jenny," Margaret Rudd called to her. Jenny waited as the old woman approached the wagon. "If ever you need anything, you let me know," she said. "I've promised Caleb I'd watch out for you."

"You don't have to," Jenny said. "I can watch out for myself. I've just told Caleb Hunter the same thing."

Margaret's brow furrowed. "I don't know why you don't seem to like Caleb, but he's a good man beneath that hard exterior. There ain't too many people who've touched him like you have. He's suddenly worrying about someone else, instead of closing himself away in that dark cavern of pain he's carryin'. Don't turn your back on him, girl."

"Let's go," Frank Walsh said impatiently from the

front of the wagon. He slapped at his mules, and the wagon lurched forward.

"Frank, don't!" Faye cried, placing her hand over his. Grumbling he pulled on the reins.

"I have to go," Jenny said, grateful for the excuse to get away from Margaret Rudd and her kindness. Jenny hated Caleb Hunter; she didn't want someone trying to talk her out of it.

Seated on the back of the wagon, her bare feet swinging beneath the hated full skirts of the blue dress, Wild Sage, now to be known as Jenny, watched the little town dwindle in size and finally disappear behind the bobbing prairie grass. A meadowlark sent its sweet notes soaring aloft and rose with a flutter of wings. They rode until dusk, and Jenny wondered if they would drive right through the night or camp out, but Frank Walsh turned the wagon away from the straight double ribbon of path and headed northward. Here the lane was barely marked, and she wondered how he knew the way. The prairie grass brushed the bottom and sides of the wagon and tickled her dangling feet. Jenny drew her knees up and listened to the night sounds gathering around them. Once she glanced back at the silent figures of Nathan and Hannah. They sat stiffly watching her. When they met her gaze, Hannah dug her brother sharply with an elbow.

"Did you really live with the Injuns?" he asked, his expression so serious it brought a smile to Jenny's face.

"Yes, I did," she acknowledged.

"Did you become an Injun?" he persisted.

Jenny thought for a long moment. "Yes," she said finally. "I am a Comanche." The little boy's eyes grew wide and he scooted back, closer to his sister.

When nothing more was said, Jenny turned back to her contemplation of the landscape. Here on the prairie, if she closed her eyes, she could pretend she was still with the People, crossing the prairie in search of buffalo. She could smell the sweet prairie grass and feel the evening dew on her face. Then inexorably the memory of Caleb Hunter came to her, the feel of his hard mouth against hers, the moment of awareness that had flared within her—and those eyes, flinty hard, yet at times as vulnerable as Nathan's.

She pushed the memory of the man from her. She didn't want to think of him. She didn't want to remember anything about him. He was her enemy, the enemy of her people. He had been at Adobe Walls, where her father died; his bullets may even have been the ones that pierced her father's body. She could only hate him.

Frank Walsh called out to his mules, slapping their flanks with his whip. The mules strained, hauling the wagon down a slight incline, through a creek, and up to a lonely soddy house sitting in the middle of the vast open land. A cow had been tied to a stake nearby. It mooed plaintively, wanting to be relieved of its milk. Frank Walsh drew the wagon to a halt before the soddy door.

"Nathan, run get the pail," Frank ordered, and the boy leapt out of the back of the wagon. "Hannah, help your mother with the little one."

"Yes, Papa," the girl answered dutifully.

For the first time since they'd left town, Frank Walsh turned his attention to Jenny.

"Well, girl. You'd better git down out of that wagon and help with supper. There's fuel to gather and water to fetch."

Silently Jenny jumped down from the wagon. The loneliness of the place touched her to her very soul. Why did Frank Walsh choose to live out here, so far from other people?

She thought of the Comanche village at dusk, with the campfires lit and people calling to one another. Sometimes there were dances in the village square or the women gathered to gossip or gamble. Here there was no one, only the wind blowing over the prairie, and, somewhere in the distance, the cry of a coyote, as if he, too, felt the lonely silence.

Somewhere behind her a light flared. Jenny turned to the soddy. Inside the dirt walls, a woman had lit a lantern, chasing away shadows and darkness. With her hand on her back to ease the cramp there, she bent over the fire, blowing the embers to life and adding fuel before swinging a kettle over the blaze. Hannah had carried Marybeth in. Faye came to the door of the soddy, a bucket in her hands.

"Nathan, can you fetch some water?"

"He's helping feed the animals. Let the girl do it," Frank Walsh called back. Jenny moved to the door of the soddy and took the bucket.

Faye smiled gently. "Jenny," she called when the girl turned toward the creek.

"Yes, ma'am?" Jenny said in the way she'd heard Hannah answer her mother.

"Welcome," Faye Walsh said.

Jenny turned toward the creek again and she felt a lit-

tle less pain, for she'd seen in Faye's gentle smile the
remnant of White Weasel's spirit. Welcome, Faye had
said, but standing at the creek bed, hearing the moan of
wind and the howl of the coyote, Jenny felt no welcome
in her heart. Instead came the echo of an emptiness felt
long ago—when she was a child like Hannah and she'd
been a captive in a strange land.

Chapter 7

THE SOLITUDE OF the night stayed with Jenny the next morning. At full light she was able to see the pitiful inadequacy of the Walsh homestead. She lay on her pallet taking in the walls of her new prison, for such she felt this to be. Walls, nearly two feet thick, had been built of large blocks of sod cut and placed, one on top of another, with the grass side down. A single window, set in a wooden frame, allowed a glimpse of dawn sky and did nothing to dispel the dark gloom of the cramped room.

An uneven wooden floor, a puncheon floor, Faye had called it last night, was covered with pieces of old carpet. The large bed, where Frank Walsh and his wife slept, and the smaller one, which Jenny shared with Hannah and Marybeth, were made of rough wood and covered with bright patchwork quilts. The mattresses were lumpy, and not as comfortable as the sleeping pads of the Comanche. Nathan slept huddled at the foot of his parent's bed. In the corner a small wooden cradle awaited the birth of Faye's baby.

The snoring from the large bed ceased abruptly, and Jenny clamped her eyes shut. She could hear Frank Walsh rising and shuffling into his clothes.

"Mother," he called to Faye, and stomped out of the room and through the soddy to the front door. Throwing it open, he stood yawning noisily and scratching his buttocks. Then pulling his suspenders over his shoulders, he stepped out into the yard and headed toward the open shed he called a barn.

Faye rose with a cheerful smile on her pale face and called to her children. Jenny sat up and looked at the other woman.

"Good morning," Faye said. "Did you sleep well?"

Jenny nodded, feeling tongue-tied in the presence of these strangers who greeted her so warmly.

"I'm sorry. You'll get used to your bed, Jenny, and to this place and all of us. I know it must be hard for you now." Her face was filled with understanding and sympathy. Jenny blinked against a sudden stinging at the back of her eyelids.

Quickly Faye dressed in the same faded calico she'd worn the day before, then brushed her long, limp dark hair into a severe knot at the back of her head. The style seemed to sharpen her cheekbones and revealed how fragile she really was. Her eyes already showed fatigue, but she cheerfully hurried into the next room, which was a kitchen and sitting room together. She bent over a black cast-iron monster that sat in one corner. Jenny watched in amazement, wondering what the black box was, while she grappled with a fleeting memory of another woman bending over a similar device. The instrument's gaping mouth revealed flames that seemed to gobble up the fuel Faye offered it. Jenny watched as Faye set a pan on its top and placed some ground grain and water in it. Soon the mixture began to bubble and thicken, then Faye added some butter and molasses. Jenny was relieved to see the food was not unlike what she'd eaten at times in the Comanche camp.

"I hope you like grits," Faye said, spooning up a bowl for Jenny. "It's made of corn." Hannah and Nathan were already seated at the table.

"Sometimes, before the soldiers came, we traded with other tribes for corn," Jenny answered, but she stood holding the bowl uncertainly.

"Go ahead. Sit down at the table," Faye said.

Timidly Jenny seated herself at the rough table and benches dominating the middle of the main room. She hadn't joined the Walshes when they ate what they called supper the night before. She still couldn't get used to the fact that the house of dirt had two rooms, one for sleeping and one for eating. This seemed quite unnecessary to her, since the bright sunlight lay just outside the cramped dwelling and one could cook out there and eat there as well. Now she took a deep breath and looked at the bowl of white man's food. Dipping her hands into the grits, she ate a handful. It tasted nothing like what she'd eaten in the Comanche villages, but it was surprisingly good.

"Mama, she's eating with her hands," Nathan called out in a singsong voice that at once alerted Jenny she'd done something wrong.

Faye turned from the stove. "Well, little wonder," she exclaimed gently. "We didn't give her a spoon." She smiled at her son and daughter. "She doesn't know our ways or where things are here. You'll have to help her until she learns."

"But she's an Injun. She said so, last night," Nathan scoffed. "Papa says Injuns are no-account, red-skinned devils."

"Nathan!" Faye's gentle voice took on a steely edge. Jenny drew back in sudden apprehension. "I'll not have you speak in such a way. Jenny is just as white as you and I. She was captured by the Comanche when she was only about your age. She's been very brave, or else she wouldn't have survived."

Nathan eyed Jenny from under his lashes. "How come she don't know how to eat right?" he persisted.

"How would you learn to do things properly if you were taken from your family when you were little?" Faye asked. Her voice was once again gentle, but Jenny remembered the anger and was afraid it would be turned toward her next. She sat with her hands in her lap, the grits forgotten. She no longer had a stomach for them.

Frank Walsh entered the room, his sleeves rolled up, his face and hands freshly washed. "Prayers," he said, and bowed his head. Like the mayor in town, he prayed long and hard, thanking someone called the Lord for the day and the food they were about to eat. Jenny surmised the Lord might be the same Great Spirit the Comanche prayed to. He finished the prayer with the amen that Jenny was coming to recognize and sat silently waiting for his food to be served. Faye hurried to the stove to dish up a bowl of grits and a cup of coffee. A pan of hot bread was brought to the table as well, along with jars of butter and fruit preserves.

Nathan was watching Jenny. "Bet you never had biscuits with the Comanche."

"Nathan!" That warning edge was in Faye's voice.

Again Jenny drew back, fearful she'd caused it. She wanted Faye to like her, for she was already drawn to the woman. However, Nathan seemed unconcerned. He set to eating his grits and a piece of the bread he'd called biscuits, spreading the latter with a generous helping of the fruit stored in the jar.

"You ain't eating?" Frank Walsh said, looking at Jenny from under heavy black brows.

"She's probably not used to our food yet," Faye said, seating herself at the other end of the table.

" 'Waste not, want not,' " Frank said, and his voice sounded like thunder pealing over a mountain. "God don't give us bounty to be wasteful, girl."

"Don't frighten her," Faye rebuked. "Come, Jenny. We mean you no harm." Something in the woman's face and voice reassured her. Faye picked up her spoon and dipped it into the bowl of grits, watching Jenny to see if she followed suit. Jenny did as urged, handling the tool with far more dexterity than Faye might have guessed.

"Do the Comanche have spoons?" Nathan asked.

"We have old spoons made of buffalo bones and new ones of metal traded from the Mexicans," Jenny answered proudly.

Frank Walsh's eyebrows drew together and he glared at his son, then at Jenny. "We'll have no talk of heathen ways in this house," he said. "We don't care how those murderin' devils lived. You're under our roof now, and you'll learn to do things our way. You're not to even think of those savages. You're back with Christian folks, and by God, we'll rid you of those memories. Is that clear?"

Jenny stared back at the man without blinking. Her chin tightened stubbornly. Not to even remember Ten Bears or White Weasel or Two Wolves? This belligerent white man could not control her thoughts or memories.

Frank Walsh took her silence as acquiescence. Now, having completed his meal, he glared around the table. "Prayers!" he ordered, and everyone obediently bowed their heads. His heavy voice offered thanks for his food to the mysterious spirit to which he seemed to have a comfortable acquaintance. He ended his prayer and rose swiftly.

"Work!" he ordered, and the rest of his family scrambled to clear the table.

Jenny sat where she was, uncertain what was expected of her. Frank Walsh stalked past her and paused in the doorway, looking back. Jenny could feel his hard gaze in the middle of her back, but she kept her eyes trained straight ahead, her head high.

"Well?" Frank thundered, and Jenny jumped in spite of herself, glancing over her shoulder to be sure he wasn't about to charge at her. "You have to work for your food, girl," he said. "No more slothful, lazy ways of those heathens you lived with."

"Frank!" Faye begged, but a cutting glance from beneath his heavy brows subdued her.

Anger rose in Jenny's breast. She stood and faced Frank Walsh. "I am ready to work," she said quietly. "I have not yet been told what is expected of me."

"That's right, Frank," Faye said quickly. "I haven't had time yet to show her what I want done."

He looked discomfited at his wife's words. "See she gets busy," he ordered. "The day's wastin' and there's much to do."

"Yes, right away. I—I'll have her help me ... with the wash," Faye said quickly. "Bending over the tub is painful for me right now."

Jenny looked at the woman and felt a surge of protectiveness. "I will bend over the tub for you," she said quickly, although she had no idea what it meant. Both women turned to Frank Walsh. With a final *harumph* of dislike, he stalked from the soddy, calling to his son.

"Don't mind Mr. Walsh," Faye said faintly. "He sounds harsh, but he's a God-fearing, hard-working man."

"Yes, ma'am," Jenny answered, but her dislike for Frank Walsh was already well set.

"Come, we'll go down to the creek and carry up water. "I'll show you how to wash our clothes," Faye said.

In the long hours that followed, Jenny learned how the white men did their wash, hauling water from the creek and heating it over an outdoor fire. Jenny was proud of her ability to quickly build a fire and produce hot coals, but she soon discovered that the white men wasted too much fuel in building their fires. And, she wondered, why not take the clothing to the water instead of bringing the water to the clothes? But when she saw Faye place the clothes into the hot boiling water, she wondered indeed at the white man's strange ways.

In the days that followed Jenny was taught many new

ways to do things. She couldn't help comparing the white man's ways with those of the Comanche.

What reason was there to tear at the tough grass and sow seeds when the mother earth already produced roots and berries for men to eat? Why should they keep such animals as the smelly and troublesome sheep or the demanding chickens when the prairie produced rabbits and prairie hens and buffalo? She reserved judgment about the cow, for she'd come to have a greedy enjoyment of the butter and milk produced by the animal.

But if the white men made work for themselves, Jenny conceded that the lot of women, whether white or Indian, was much the same. Long hours were spent cooking, cleaning the sod hut, sewing clothes, washing, and tending the garden. Jenny worked diligently, striving to prove herself to the ever disapproving Frank Walsh. As patient and kind as his wife was, Frank Walsh seemed intent on proving himself otherwise. Used to the good humor of Ten Bears, she was often dismayed by Frank's sour air. His unhappiness, she surmised, might be the result of his hard labors with the plow and mules. She didn't dare suggest such a thing to him, for in fact she was hard put not to be intimidated by his unrelenting displeasure.

Likewise, his long prayers and impassioned exhortations to this spirit called the Lord left her uneasy, for invariably he included her name in his prayers. When he said the name of his wife and children, his tone held some warmth, but when he uttered Jenny's name, his tone was cold and accusing. She wasn't sure what law of the white man's Great Spirit she'd broken, but she was certain it was bad.

One morning—after a typical breakfast where conversation was held at a minimum and Hannah and Nathan sat staring wide-eyed at their father's stern face—Frank Walsh glanced up and fixed his gaze on Jenny.

"The garden needs hoeing," he said accusingly.

"I—that's my fault, Frank," Faye said quickly. "I've had Jenny so busy with other things, we haven't given a thought to the garden."

"You can't let the weeds take over," he said gruffly. "Nothing you're doing will help us this winter if we run out of food."

"Yes, I know. I—I just wasn't thinking," Faye said. "We'll get onto it right away this morning." Something in her voice drew his gaze to her pale face.

"What's the matter with you, Mother? You feelin' poorly?"

Faye shook her head in denial, but Jenny could see how her hands trembled when she picked up her cup.

Frank Walsh studied her, and for a fleeting moment his expression softened. "You work in the house today, Mother," he said, and his words sounded more like an edict than a consideration for her condition. "The girl here can hoe the garden."

Faye's hands fluttered below the table and settled on her swollen stomach. Slowly she nodded in agreement. Jenny felt a flurry of worry, but she had no time to inquire if Faye would be all right in the house by herself. Frank Walsh pushed his chair back from the table and stalked to the door. Settling his battered, sweat-stained hat on his head he turned a stark, inquiring eye on Jenny.

"You comin', girl?"

Wordlessly she got to her feet and followed him out. Frank was terse in his instructions, handing her a hoe and indicating the rows of green plants in a cleared plot before stalking away. Jenny turned to this new task. The hoe felt heavy in her hands and she wasn't sure how she was to use it. She practiced, chopping at the earth. The hoe skimmed the top of the dirt and hit her in the leg, leaving a light gash. She clamped her hand over the cut until the bleeding had stopped, then moved toward the first row of plants. Frank Walsh seemed to be intent on ridding the mother earth of all plants, and it must be he considered these limp, dust-covered stalks with the trailing vines to be weeds. Carefully she began working along the row of plants, using the hoe to help tear the stubborn roots from the soil. In no time she had one row completed and started another. The sun was hot overhead, burning her back through the thin blue cloth of her dress and bringing beads of moisture to her forehead and upper lip. She was so intent on her task, she didn't at first see the brown toes standing next to the row. When she noticed them, she paused and straightened, wiping her brow on the back of her arm.

"Hello, Nathan," she said breathlessly. The activity in the hot sun was more wearing than she'd expected. "What are you doing?"

The little boy didn't say anything. His blue eyes were accusing as he stared at her. Without a word, he turned and ran away. Jenny shrugged and resumed her toil. She was nearly finished with the second row.

"What in God's holy name are you doing?" a gruff voice cried behind her, and before she could turn, the hoe was wrenched from her hand.

She whirled in time to see a whip swing through the air, then felt its tearing, biting pain across her shoulders and back. She threw up her hands to protect her face as the whip was raised again. It bit into her shoulder and cheek, the pain so intense she crouched in a ball, exposing her back to Frank Walsh's anger. The whip swished through the air again, biting deep into her tender flesh. She heard the rip of cloth, but it was nothing in comparison to the pain and rage she felt. The whip fell again, and despite herself, she fell to her knees in the dirt. The smell of the mother earth filled her nostrils, mingling with the scent of her own blood as the whip continued to fall.

"Frank! For God's sake, what are you doing?" Faye Walsh screamed at her husband. Running across the grassless yard she seized his arm as he raised the whip again. "Frank, stop! You'll kill her!"

"She's been sent here by the devil himself!" Frank cried, his blue eyes terrible with the rage he felt. "She's cutting down the peas, the food you need to put in your children's mouths this winter." His broad chest heaved with indignation and exertion. He jerked his hand, making the whip curl along the ground menacingly. Jenny winced and shut her eyes against another thrust of pain that was not forthcoming.

Faye stared up and down the now denuded rows that once had been peas. Her expression registered surprise and concern, but she knelt beside the shivering girl. The back of the blue gown was torn and blood-soaked. Faye took hold of Jenny's shoulders and raised her to her knees. Though gentle, her touch brought a whimper of pain from Jenny. An ugly gash across one cheek was puckered and bleeding.

"Oh, Lord, Frank," Faye whispered.

"Look at what she was doing!" he cried in outrage. "I should never have brought her here. She's a worthless savage."

"She's little more than a child, Frank. She's trying so hard to do everything we ask of her. Did you show her exactly what you wanted her to do?"

"Of course I did. I gave her the hoe and told her to hoe out the weeds."

"Did you tell her which ones were the weeds?" Faye insisted. Frank looked at her sternly. He wasn't used to having his words questioned.

"Any blamed fool knows what's weeds and what's peas. Nathan himself knew she was cuttin' down the peas. That's how come I caught her. It's a good thing, too, or she would have ruined the whole garden."

"Carry her into the house, Frank," Faye said quietly. Her pale blue eyes held a steely condemnation that only caused his temper to rise.

"I ain't carryin' an Injun into my house like she's royalty!" he shouted. "She can get up and walk in herself."

Faye's eyes were enormous in her thin, pale face. Through her curtain of pain, Jenny could see the cords in her neck work convulsively.

"I can walk," she said quickly, and ignoring the nearly unbearable pain got to her feet.

"See, I told you," Frank bellowed. "She was playin' on your sympathy. You have to be stern with her or you'll be taking care of her instead of the other way round."

Angrily Faye got to her feet, her mouth opened to refute his accusations, but her body betrayed her. The sudden movements brought a spasm of pain to her face and she doubled over, gripping her stomach.

"Frank!" she cried out, a thin hand reaching toward Jenny for support. Ignoring the pain to her shoulders, Jenny grabbed her waist and gave her support to the woman who had become her friend.

"What's the matter now?" Frank snarled, whirling around to face his wife. When he saw Faye's face he rushed forward, shoving Jenny aside before swooping his wife up in his arms.

"Faye! Faye!" he mumbled, carrying her into the house.

Jenny stood in the garden, the hoe and freshly cut pea vines at her feet, and wondered what she was supposed to do. She didn't have to wonder long. Frank Walsh was back at the soddy door.

"Get in here, girl," he bellowed. "She needs you."

Jenny ran toward the soddy, sidled around his menacing figure, and hurried in to see Faye. Her eyes brimmed with tears as she knelt beside the woman. She hadn't wept while Frank whipped her, but now with Faye lying so pale and helpless against the gay patchwork quilt, she fought back the sting of tears.

"Faye, *kaku*," she whispered.

Faye's eyes opened. They were dark with pain.
"Make some sassafras tea and bring some water—and
bathe my forehead, Jenny," she said softly. One hand
gripped Jenny's. "I'm sorry you were whipped. Frank is
not a bad man. He just works so hard—and he worries
about us starving out here in the winter."

"I didn't mean to cut down the pea vines," Jenny
whispered. "I didn't know what they were."

"I know, I know," Faye said, patting her arm softly.
"Now, get the tea."

"Don't apologize for me, Mother," Frank said as
Jenny left the room, but his voice no longer held the
belligerent tone it had earlier. When Jenny returned
with a cup of tea, a bowl of tepid water, and a rag to
bathe Faye's brow, Frank was kneeling at his wife's
bedside. Her thin hand was nearly lost in his big, callused clasp. Nervously eyeing Frank Walsh, Jenny knelt
and wrung out the rag.

"Here, let me do this," Frank said, impatiently taking
up the cup of sassafras tea. Carefully he raised his
wife's head and held the cup to her pale lips. Faye
sipped weakly, then seemed to take strength from the
hot brew. Patiently Frank waited, urging her to drink
more when she would have pushed the cup away.

Standing against the wall, uncertain of what was expected of her and trying to ignore the wretched pain in
her own shoulders and back, Jenny noted how the big
man tended his wife. Hannah and Nathan stood in the
doorway of the other room, their eyes big and scared-
looking as they observed their mother. When Frank
wrung out the rag and gently pressed it against Faye's
brow, Jenny turned toward the children.

"Come on," she said, motioning them away. Meekly they followed her outdoors and down to the creek.

"I'm sorry I got you in trouble, Jenny," Nathan sniffed. "I didn't mean for Papa to whip you."

"It doesn't matter," Jenny said, searching along the creek bed for the right leaves. When she found them she smashed them between two rocks until a green paste had formed. Taking some up on her finger she smeared it along the gashes on her cheek and shoulders. She looked at Nathan and motioned him away, then pulled the blue dress up and over her head, so she was bare from the waist up.

"What are you doing?" Hannah inquired.

"I've made a salve," Jenny answered, "but I can't put it on my back. Will you help, Hannah?"

The little girl had drawn away as if she'd been asked to touch a snake.

"Hannah, won't you help me?" Jenny asked quietly.

"Is that Injun medicine?" the girl asked.

"It's good medicine. It will make my wounds better."

"Papa wouldn't want us to use Injun medicine," she said, and turned back toward the soddy. "Come on, Nathan," she called to her brother. Wordlessly Jenny watched them leave, her shoulders sagging in defeat at their condemnation of her, too.

"I'll help you," a voice said from somewhere behind her.

Jenny jumped and whirled, the front of her dress pressed to her bare bosom. Caleb Hunter stood on the other side of the creek, his wide-brimmed hat pulled low over his steely gaze, but Jenny shivered anyway. Here was the man she'd vowed to hate and to avenge her parents' deaths on, yet she stood mute and vulnerable before him.

Caleb seemed to take her silence as permission for him to cross the creek. When he stood before her, his eyes took in everything about her: the golden brown hair with its feathery tendrils blown free by the prairie wind; the gray eyes, still luminous from unshed tears; the welts on her cheek and shoulders. His expression was unreadable as he reached forward and turned her, his hands surprisingly warm and gentle on her bare shoulders. Jenny gritted her teeth at his touch. He was her enemy.

Caleb was silent for a long moment as he looked at the ugly welt and dried blood marring the slender back. Finally he bent toward the rocks where she'd crushed the leaves, and, taking some of the concoction up on his finger, spread it over the red stripes. Jenny winced, then biting her lips stood still beneath his ministrations. When he was finished, he stepped back and stared at her. Jenny faced him, her chin high and proud, her eyes defiant.

"Who did this to you?" he asked quietly.

"It doesn't matter," she answered. "It is white man's justice."

"It's nothing of the sort," he said, gripping her shoulder. "This shouldn't have happened to you."

"Oh? Perhaps he should have taken his gun and shot me," she flared. " 'The only good Indian is a dead one.' Isn't that what some of the white soldiers said back at Fort Sill?"

"You're not an Indian, Jenny. You're a white woman," Caleb said sternly.

"Frank Walsh thinks I'm an Indian," she said. "He tells his children I'm no-account and lazy and heathen." She was breathing hard, her voice rising in suppressed anger. "He whipped me because I cut down the peas. He whipped me as if I were less than a dog. No one has ever done that to me." She was crying now, the hated tears flowing down her cheeks, her lips trembling, her eyes filled with pain—the pain of living in a world where she didn't belong and could never fit. He saw her pride . . . and how it had been offended in some deep part of her that determined who and what she was.

"Jenny," he said, gripping her bare shoulders, wanting somehow to give her back that lost pride, wanting her to believe in herself no matter what others said, but this time, the warm, smooth touch of her skin beneath his fingers took all words from his mind. He became lost in her eyes. He saw the expression in them change from anger to alarm, felt the warm gasp of her breath against his cheek, then his mouth claimed hers. Her lips were warm and sweet beneath his.

Unlike that first time, when he'd sought to scare and punish her, he took time to know her, to feel the texture of her lips, the small, sharp teeth beyond and the darting tongue. She tried to hold herself stiff in his embrace, even to push away from him, but something in her had changed; she melted against him, her hands no longer gripping the front of her dress. Her arms had crept up and around his neck, and he felt her lift herself, standing on her tiptoes to better accommodate her mouth to his. His arms swept around her waist, melding her to him. He felt heady with the taste and feel of her. Vaguely he was aware the front of the dress had slipped; his hands slid around to cup her bare breasts. Their pert nipples brushed against his shirt, and he moaned.

Jenny wanted to turn away from him, to tear herself from his embrace. This man was her enemy. He'd fought in the battles that had taken her parents' lives; he'd brought her here to an alien land and people—yet all that was forgotten in the blaze of the fire he'd ignited within her. Her arms went about his neck and she felt the unyielding breadth of his shoulders, the muscular back. Her aching breasts were crushed against his hard chest, then his hands cupped her soft flesh, his thumbs brushed against her sensitive nipples, and unnamed desires swept through her. The barrier of innocence melted beneath his touch; she pressed against him.

Caleb felt her longing, her giving of herself, and his blood roared in his ears. Then he remembered the Comanche wedding dress she'd been wearing when he captured her. She'd given herself to a Comanche warrior. An unreasonable hatred shook him, so he thrust her away from him. Her hand flew to her mouth, her gaze, wide and startled, met his—and she read in his eyes the same condemnation she'd seen in Frank Walsh's eyes. The shame he had brought her with his whipping was nothing compared to what she found in Caleb's eyes. What tattered bit of pride remained she pulled about herself like a blanket, taking on an air of stoic dignity as she readjusted her clothing.

Caleb saw the emotions flitting across her face and knew he'd hurt her further. He hadn't meant to, God help him, but he couldn't bury his own past, the hatred and bitter hostility that had ruled his life since his parents' deaths. He ran his hands through dusty dark hair and stared at her, perplexed.

"I am Comanche," she whispered, then repeated it louder. "I am proud of my heritage."

"A heritage of bloodshed and thievery," he rasped. "A noble heritage, indeed."

"You don't know the Comanche."

"I know their work," he said. "I've followed their trail for fifteen years. I've seen the bloodied bodies of men, women, and children, people who wanted nothing more than a piece of land for themselves."

"Comanche land. Do you blame us that we fight to keep what is ours?"

"I blame you for giving yourself heart and soul to murderers."

"Is that why you cannot take me although you desire me?" Her demand to know was less forceful than she'd meant it.

"It isn't that, Jenny," he answered quickly, too quickly to have fooled her. He saw the curl of her lip and knew she despised him.

"It is well you feel this way," she said calmly. "You are my enemy. You fought at Adobe Walls, where my father, Ten Bears, was killed. You killed the people of my village. Perhaps your bullet even struck my mother, White Weasel. You have brought me to this land where the white eyes pretend to be kind but despise me, even as you do. For this reason, you are my enemy. So I tell you, Caleb Hunter. One day I will kill you, and then I will return to my people."

Whirling she stalked away from the creek, heading

toward the soddy sitting in isolated splendor against the
vast prairie. Caleb felt that loneliness. Perhaps he'd
been wrong to bring her here, he thought.

Hunkering down by the creek bed, he thought of the
small woman he'd held just moments before. She'd
been yielding and pliant in his arms; her desire had
matched his own. Now she'd declared a hatred for him.
Could he blame her? He thought of the raw welts on her
back. He couldn't take back all that happened between
them, but he could make sure her future here on the
Walsh homestead was free of such punishment.

He waited until she'd returned to the soddy, then
mounted his horse and made his way around, so he approached from a different angle. When he alighted in
front of the cabin, a distracted Frank Walsh greeted
him, explaining his wife had taken bad for a while but
seemed to be resting easy now.

Through the low door of the soddy Caleb could see
the blue swirl of Jenny's skirt as she crossed from the
table to the stove and back again, preparing the midday
meal. She never looked up once, although he was sure
she'd heard his arrival. Originally he'd thought to take
a meal with the Walshes, but now he declined Frank's
grudging invitation. Drawing from his saddlebag the extra clothes Margaret had sent out for Jenny, Caleb laid
them on the doorsill, so she could see them, then led
Frank away for a little man-to-man chat. When he rode
away from the homestead, he was confident Frank
Walsh would never use the whip on Jenny again. That
was the only comfort he could find on the long ride
back to town.

Chapter 8

THE WEARY DAYS that followed melted one into another. Faye, pale and weak with the pressure of carrying her child these final days, depended more and more on Jenny. Jenny was grateful for the extra work, so she had no time to remember Caleb Hunter and the kiss they'd shared by the creek. But at night, when she lay in the small bed beside Hannah and Marybeth, she couldn't keep her thoughts from that moment—and the wild sweet longings he'd awakened.

Instinctively she knew if she'd been back in the Comanche village with White Weasel, they would have talked about it. Such feelings would have been natural and good. She could never remember feeling this way about Two Wolves. That she felt this way about a white man, her sworn enemy, was the unnatural thing.

She forced herself to sleep, forced herself to rise and think only of the tasks she must accomplish, to care only about the children and the woman who needed her. Caleb Hunter was forgotten, or so she told herself, yet every day as she bent over a scrub board or worked in the garden or toted water up from the creek, she

couldn't help casting a glance toward the overgrown
path leading back to the main road.

If Frank Walsh had not come to accept Jenny with
more graciousness, at least he took more time to explain
what he wanted from her, and if she misunderstood and
did the wrong thing, he did not bring out the whip. With
scowling face he would show her again. But Jenny
hadn't forgotten that earlier whipping, and she always
grew nervous at such times and could not always concentrate on what he said.

"Bah!" he would exclaim at such times, rewarding
her with another dark look before stalking away.

Jenny was sure he considered her stupid and unteach-
able, as he did all Indian heathens. Usually she went to
Faye or even to Nathan and Hannah, who took an espe-
cial delight in instructing her. An uneasy friendship was
forming between Jenny and the children. In return she
told them many things about the Comanche. Nathan especially wondered about the weapons and the skills of
warriors.

"One day, I'm going to fight the Comanche the way
Caleb Hunter does," the small boy said, and leapt to his
feet, using a stick as a pretend spear while he galloped
around the clearing slaying "red devil Injuns." Jenny sat
for a long moment watching him, feeling saddened that
such lack of understanding occurred even in the very
young.

"Don't feel bad about Nathan," Hannah said, seated
Indian-fashion beside Jenny. She was busily involved in
pretending to tan a hide.

"It's the way of men and boys to think about war,"
Jenny said, remembering how the Comanche boys and

girls would use small bows and arrows and pretend to raid against their enemies.

"Do you pray, Jenny?" Hannah asked, using a stone to scrape an old piece of leather.

"Yes, I do," Jenny answered. She'd just finished shelling a basket of early peas, the rest of the same peas that she'd nearly cut down a few weeks before. They smelled sweet and fresh. Occasionally she and Hannah chewed on a handful of the raw peas.

"Who do you pray to?" Hannah persisted.

Jenny set aside her basket and tweaked the little girl's butternut braid. "We pray to the Great Spirit, who is over all things."

"Is he like Jesus?" Hannah asked, trying to comprehend.

Jenny thought for a long moment, remembering Frank Walsh's stark prayers. "Yes, I believe he is," she answered.

"How do you pray to the Great Spirit?" Hannah asked earnestly, so Jenny told her how they fasted and sometimes went into the mountains or prairies, so they could be alone with the Great Spirit.

"Sometimes, he gives us a vision quest or sends an animal or bird that gives us much good medicine to keep us safe and make us strong."

Hannah listened intently, asking many questions—until Jenny grew tired of answering and lay back in the grass. Her chores were done for the moment and she was enjoying this respite. They sat in the shade of the soddy, and the slight prairie wind, though hot, was not unpleasant against her cheeks. Jenny stared at the cloudless blue sky. She thought of the Comanche village where she'd once lived. Where were all the villagers now? Had they been sent to a reservation? Where was Two Wolves? Suddenly she sat up, thinking about the warrior. She must ask Caleb Hunter, if she ever saw him again, if Two Wolves had been captured.

"What is wrong?" Hannah asked. "What are you thinking?"

"It doesn't matter," Jenny answered, and, getting to her feet, gathered up the basket of peas. "I must begin supper."

Faye and Marybeth had napped through the heat of the afternoon. Now as Jenny moved around the kitchen mixing up a batch of corn bread, as Faye had shown her, and putting the peas to cook, she heard Marybeth stir and cry out. Quickly shoving the pan of bread into the oven, she hurried to the bedroom. If she carried Marybeth outside, Faye might be able to rest awhile longer, she thought. But the little girl was curled on her stomach, her chubby thumb shoved in her mouth. Perplexed, Jenny gazed at the little girl. The cry came again, and Jenny turned to the big bed where Faye slept. Her eyes were open and her hands pushed at her stomach as if to rid herself of the painful burden of her unborn child.

"Faye?" Jenny whispered, creeping closer to the bed.

The woman turned wide, anguished eyes toward the girl. Her sweaty hair was plastered against her brow and cheeks. "I think it's time for the baby to come," Faye gasped. "Get Frank."

Wordlessly Jenny backed out of the room. She remembered the times in the village when Comanche women gave birth. There was much mystery and secrecy attached to the event. Only the medicine woman and her aides were allowed to enter the tepee. The husbands were never allowed in. Yet Faye had asked for Frank. Jenny turned and ran from the soddy. She could see the silhouette of man and mule in a distant patch of field.

"Hannah, run get your father," she called to the girl, who still sat in the shade of the soddy, playing with her rag doll. "Tell him Mama needs him."

"Is Mama ill?" Hannah asked, getting to her feet. The freckles stood out on her nose and her eyes were wide with fear.

"Just get your papa," Jenny ordered, and turned back to the soddy. What must she do? she wondered hazily.

"Jenny!" Faye called weakly. Jenny hurried to the bedroom. Faye's face was paler than usual, but her eyes, though dark with pain, were alive with anticipation. "Is Frank coming?"

"Yes," Jenny said, just as Frank Walsh ran into the soddy.

"Mother," he called, and ran to her bedside.

"It's time, Frank," Faye whispered.

"Are you in much pain?" he demanded hoarsely, desperately looking her over as if he might find some other reason for her discomfort, something that he could do something about.

"Not much," she said, placing a cold, white hand against his cheek. "But you must ride to Millbrook for Sarah McKinsey."

"Sarah McKinsey?" he asked blankly.

Faye smothered a smile. "The midwife," she reminded him gently.

"Oh!" Vacantly Frank got to his feet and looked around the room, his gaze settling on Jenny. "I'll send the girl," he said.

"She doesn't know the way," Faye answered weakly, her voice thin from the onset of another pain. "Go quickly. Hurry!"

Frank cast a last desperate glance at his wife and stumbled toward the door. His glare settled on Jenny and he pointed one big, callused finger. "You watch her, help her. Get her whatever she needs."

"I will," Jenny said, nodding fervently.

"Hurry, Frank," Faye called from the bed.

Jenny remained by the wall, uncertain what to do. Through the small window, she saw Frank Walsh unhitch the plow from the mule and fling himself on its bare back. Cursing and shouting at the poor beast, he turned it toward the main road, kicking it into an ungainly gallop. When the sound of man and mule disappeared, the soddy seemed unnaturally quiet.

"Jenny," Faye whispered, but the sound seemed like a shout to Jenny, who jumped and hurried forward. Faye clasped her hand. "Here's what you must do."

"Yes, *kaku*," Jenny answered, dropping to her knees beside the bed and taking Faye's ice-cold hand.

The other woman smiled weakly. "I've heard you call me *kaku* before," she said mildly. "What does it mean?"

"It is meant in respect," Jenny said, suddenly afraid she'd offended this woman. "It is what I called White Weasel."

"White Weasel was your mother?"

Jenny nodded.

Faye's grip tightened briefly. "I'm honored," she

whispered. She fell silent then, her pale lids closed, so Jenny could see the faint spidery tracing of veins in her translucent skin.

"What did you wish me to do?" she asked, suddenly fearful Faye had lost consciousness, but the pale lids lifted and a smile wafted across her features.

"You must draw a bucket of fresh water from the creek and put it on to boil. Bring the scissors from the sewing basket and that piece of soft blanket I've been saving."

"Yes, ma'am." Jenny rose.

"The baby clothes are in that chest under my mother's quilt. And Jenny"—she paused, smiling fondly at the girl—"don't forget the bread in the oven."

Jenny nodded. She'd forgotten all about the preparation of food.

"This will take some time," Faye said quietly. "When you have time, feed the children. Frank can eat when he gets back."

"Yes ma'am," Jenny answered, and hurried off to do as Faye had requested.

Absentmindedly she fed the children, but they had little appetite. Their small faces were pinched with worry. Sensing something was wrong with her mother, Marybeth, normally a cheerful little girl, began to whine.

"I'll take her," Hannah said, pushing back her chair.

"But you haven't eaten," Jenny admonished.

"I'm fasting," Hannah said, lifting the little girl in her arms. "Come on, Nathan," she called. "We'll play outside."

Jenny was grateful for Hannah's cooperation, for it

was becoming clear—even to her inexperienced eyes—
that Faye's baby was about to make its appearance long
before Sarah McKinsey could be brought. Jenny was
uncertain of what to do, then a calmness enveloped her
and she remembered a time on the trail when a woman
had given birth to her child. The women had gathered
around her, taking her from her horse and walking her
until it was time. Faye should not be lying in that bed,
she thought, and hurried into the room.

"Faye, you must get up," she said, pulling the covers
aside. "You must walk. It will help the baby make his
passage into the world."

"I don't think I can," Faye said, panting against the
pain.

"I will help you." Jenny leaned her slight body
against Faye's for support, and together they paced
around the room. The pains were coming faster now,
running one into the other.

"Walking helps," Faye gasped. Her face was moist
with sweat and alarmingly pallid. "I think the baby is
about to come now."

"Then you must squat here beside the bed," Jenny instructed. "Hold on to this post."

"I can't. My baby will be hurt," Faye said.

"Trust me, *kaku*," Jenny said. "Your baby will make
its journey without harm." She prayed it was so. She
knelt behind Faye and reached beneath the woman, the
piece of blanket, soft from repeated washings, spread to
catch the emerging infant.

Faye's scream could be heard beyond the soddy. The
cords in her neck stood out as she pushed her child
from her womb.

"It's coming," Jenny cried, half laughing, half crying. Faye took a breath and pushed again.

Vaguely Jenny was aware of voices outside the soddy and running feet across the puncheon floor, then the room was filled with people. Faye gave a final cry of distress; the baby, fat and slippery, dropped into Jenny's blanketed hands.

"God in heaven!" someone behind them cried, but Jenny paid no attention. Automatically she began to work on the baby while Faye clung to the bedpost, still squatting in a pool of blood.

"You're killing her," Frank Walsh roared, but Sarah McKinsey and Margaret Rudd ushered him out of the room.

Jenny took no time to look up. The baby had made no sound. Now she gripped the corner of the blanket and swabbed the mucus from his mouth, then held him aloft, upside down, and pounded his back gently. The baby coughed and remained silent.

"My baby," Faye cried, still clinging to the bedpost and peering over her shoulder.

Frantically Jenny lowered the child to her knees, and bending, blew into his mouth—once, twice, three times. He coughed again, then set up a lusty wailing. At the same time, Faye's grip on the post tightened and she, too, cried out. Frank Walsh pounded at the door.

"Let me in!" he bellowed. "If that heathen harmed my wife and baby, by all that's holy, I'll take her life!"

"Shhh," Margaret Rudd said, opening the door a crack. "Don't blaspheme the Lord's name. Your wife and son are healthy. Sarah's just going to clean them up a wee bit and you'll see them."

"A son?" Frank Walsh repeated numbly.

Margaret nodded in satisfaction. "A big, strapping son that looks just like you. Now let me help your wife; you can come in soon."

Dazed and reassured Frank Walsh wandered out to the front yard. His tear-filled eyes turned automatically to the sky as he praised his God. Finally a mumble of sounds came to him and he followed its source to the back of the soddy. There he saw his three children, their faces smeared with patches of mud, their arms outstretched to the sky.

"What are you doing?" he thundered. Hannah and Nathan turned to their father, their eyes wide and scared-looking. Marybeth stuck her finger in her mouth and began to cry. "I said what are you doing?" Frank Walsh asked, making a conscious effort to soften his voice. Hadn't he just prayed to God himself?

"We're prayin' to the Great Spirit, Papa," Nathan answered. Frank Walsh's figure stiffened.

"The Great Spirit?" he repeated.

Hannah nodded. "We prayed for good medicine for Jenny, so she could help Mama until you got back."

"Where did you learn this heresy?" Frank demanded, although he was sure he already knew the culprit.

"Jenny told us how she and her people pray for strong medicine—" Hannah began.

"No more," Frank Walsh thundered, pointing at them with the finger of doom. The children quaked. "Go to the creek and wash that mud from your faces at once."

"Yes, Papa." The two older children ran toward the creek. Marybeth took one last glance at her father and ran after her brother and sister. Frank fairly ran back to the front door of his soddy.

"Where's that heathen?" he shouted, lunging inside.

"Shhh!" Margaret Rudd hushed him.

Frank Walsh shook his finger at her. "Don't you shush me," he ordered. "I saw what that godless creature was doing to my wife and baby."

"That godless creature, as you would call her, Mr. Walsh, helped your wife during her birthing—and if not for her quick action, your new son would now be dead. If she did it in the only way she knew, you must not condemn her for it, but praise the Lord that she was here today. And as for you shakin' a finger at me, Frank Walsh," Margaret went on, "don't you ever think to do it again. I might just forget I'm a God-fearing woman and bite it off." With a whirl of calico skirts she entered the sickroom, closing the door firmly behind her.

Perplexed, Frank Walsh wandered outside again and sat on a stump, where he ran his fingers through his hair numerous times and called upon God's assistance and wisdom in how he was to rid his home of these signs of the devil's work.

By the time Sarah McKinsey and Margaret Rudd had left the soddy and climbed into their buggy for the trip back to town, he still had no answer.

"Your wife and son are just fine," Sarah said, with a firm smile. "With Jenny to care for them, they'll recover quickly."

"Thank you for comin', Miz McKinsey, Miz Rudd," he mumbled.

"By the way, Mr. Walsh," Margaret said, leaning forward, so she could fix him with a stern eye, "have you heard we have a traveling preacher stopping in Millbrook for a few weeks? When your wife's better, you might want to bring her to town for a church meeting."

A light went on in Frank's head and he nodded with more enthusiasm. "I'd be right happy to do that, ma'am," he said. "Did the preacher say what denomination he is?"

"Nope. We figure the word of the Lord is just fine—no matter who's givin' it to us," Margaret said, and slapped the reins against her mule's rump. "See you Sunday mornin', Mr. Walsh. There'll be a picnic after."

"Thank you, ma'am. Much obliged," Frank said, waving them off. He turned back to his soddy, feeling reassured. He'd prayed earnestly for an answer to his problem and the Lord had surely answered. He'd set the new preacher onto Jenny and her pagan beliefs. Maybe between the two of them her heathen soul would be saved. Frank went into his soddy to see his new son and wife; he didn't even growl at the slender girl who scurried around tending to everyone's needs.

In the days that followed, Jenny and Faye seemed to grow closer together. Hannah and Nathan were unusually subdued and Marybeth was grappling with the dismaying thought of a usurper of her mother's affections. She began to whine over the slightest thing and reverted to wetting herself. Jenny gave her extra attention and often brought her in to Faye, who cuddled the girl and reassured her she was still loved and could now be a big sister, too.

The baby wailed lustily when hungry and slept when his stomach was full, but Jenny noticed the pallor of

Faye's cheeks hadn't lessened, nor did her strength return as it should have. Jenny prepared extra dishes, rich stews and beef broths that should have added color to her cheeks but didn't.

When Sunday came and Frank revealed he planned to take the family to Millbrook to meet the new minister, he was disappointed to find his wife unable to make the trip. All week he'd planned on this outing.

"Take the children and go," Faye urged him. "I'll stay behind with the baby. I'll be all right. Jenny can stay with me."

Frank thought for a long moment, then finally shrugged in agreement. Perhaps it would be best this way, he thought. He could speak to the preacher in privacy and inquire how best to handle this thing. Jenny helped get the children ready to go and couldn't restrain a surge of disappointment that she wasn't going, too. She would have liked seeing Margaret Rudd again, for the woman had been friendly. Perhaps Caleb Hunter would have been there.

The thought made her halt her task and stand trying to justify the unbidden wish. She wanted only to keep track of her enemy, she told herself, so one day she could carry out her vow. There was no other reason to be concerned about him, but inside herself, where lies couldn't live, she knew her thoughts had betrayed her. Now she was grateful she wasn't going with the Walsh family. She waved them good-bye and turned back to the lonely soddy, grateful for the piercing cry of the littlest Walsh, who occupied so much of her time. When the little one had been diapered anew and settled beside his mother to nurse greedily, Jenny took up a piece of mending and sat beside them.

"You've learned much of our ways, Jenny," Faye said, smiling at the younger woman's bent head. "Are you happy with us now?"

Jenny paused in her mending and looked out the window, wondering how best to answer. Sometimes, when she thought of Ten Bears and White Weasel, her grief was as sharp and overwhelming as that first day she saw her mother fall in battle.

"I still do not understand the white man's ways," she said at last. "Why do you not take the clothes to the creek? Why do you not use prairie grass to diaper the baby instead of these clothes, which must always be washed? Why do you eat inside this small, dark soddy when the sunshine and open prairie are beyond the door? Why do you tear at the mother earth instead of collecting her bounty? Why—?" She paused and shrugged.

"There are many things I do not understand. Why do you live here, so far from the village and the rest of the people?" She glanced from under her lashes. "Why do you wish me to be happy here, when you are not?"

Faye looked surprised, then leaned against the pillow, cuddling her son as she gazed at the ceiling. "I am not unhappy here," she said, "but like you, sometimes I wonder why I'm here—so far away from Papa and Mama and my sisters and the life I once knew. Frank was a clerk in a mercantile back in Kentucky, but he wasn't satisfied. He wanted to have land of his own. When he heard about the government giving land to anyone willing to work it, he was like a different man.

All he could talk about was coming out here." She was quiet for a time, and Jenny thought she might have fallen asleep. Then she continued in a faraway voice.

"My parents didn't want me to come. They didn't like Frank. They didn't think he could take care of me."

"But you came anyway."

"Oh, Jenny. I was sorely tempted to stay behind. If you'd seen my parent's house, you would have understood my hesitation. It was three stories high, with pear trees that reached the windowsills of that top floor. Mama always had starched white curtains in the windows, and in the winter, when the leaves were off the trees, you could see all the town and the countryside beyond. There were gentle rolling hills for sledding in the winter and fields of emerald green in the summer, not all parched and brown like it is here.

"And there were people, women like me, women I went to school with—and children for Hannah and Nathan to play with. We used to have Sunday picnics and dances and afternoon teas. I can remember the smell of my mother's peach cobbler wafting on the breeze. We'd sit on the porch swing, talking with Papa until Mama brought out hot cobbler with rich cream on top." She stopped. "I've forgotten how peach cobbler tastes," she said, and began to weep silently.

"I'm sorry I asked if it makes you cry," Jenny said contritely.

"I want to talk. It feels good to remember. I just miss Mama so, and dear Papa. He hated to see us leave. Hannah was just a baby and I was pregnant with Nathan. He was so worried." She sighed. "When we got here, the prairie was beautiful, green with hundreds of wildflowers. I began to believe Frank when he said we'd come to paradise. I stayed at the hotel in town until he got our house built. When I came out and saw it, I wept. I was so ashamed of my weakness, but I couldn't seem to stop. Poor Frank, he promised he'd build me something better as soon as he could and I know he will." She chuckled. "There I was, weeping like a spoiled rich man's daughter, and Frank was trying to tell me how superior this home was to any other kind. He said it was cool in the summer and warm in the winter—and fireproof from prairie fires and Indian arrows."

"Indian arrows?" Jenny asked intently. "Are there Indians out here?"

"There used to be," Faye said. "I remember the first time a bunch of them came here. I was so frightened I just cowered in the corner with Hannah. Frank was gone and I was alone. The Indians snooped into everything and finally took my best cooking pot and all my rice and flour. By the time Frank got back I was still in the corner, crying my eyes out. I guess I was pretty lucky. They just stole from me, but they scalped our neighbor and killed his wife. He went back East, poor man, but he never regained his mind."

"What tribe were they?" Jenny persisted.

Faye seemed to sense something in her tone. Her dark eyes stared at Jenny. "They were Comanche," she said quietly.

Jenny looked away. Faye glanced at her son. So many questions crowded her mind, but she was afraid to ask them. Now she seized the opportunity to change the subject.

"He's very strong, isn't he?" she said, tracing her son's cheek.

"Yes, he is," Jenny agreed, "especially when it's time to eat."

"I'll think I'll call him Samson," Faye said.

"Samson?" Jenny repeated blankly.

"He was a very strong and a very righteous man in the Bible," Faye explained, "and I think this little one will have to be both in order to live here on this prairie."

"What if he does not wish to remain here?" Jenny asked, and was immediately sorry. Faye's face had become drawn again.

"Then he will be allowed to leave here," she said lightly. "No one should become a prisoner here." She flushed and looked at Jenny. "You aren't happy here, are you?" she stated flatly.

"I do not belong here," Jenny replied. "I do not know where I belong now."

"You poor child," Faye said, suddenly reaching out to grip her hand. "How confused you must feel by all this."

Jenny made no answer, and Faye lay back. Her son had finished suckling and now slept, his pink lips moist with milk.

"Take him back to his cradle," Faye ordered dispassionately. "I want to sleep for a while."

Jenny did as Faye ordered and left the room, going to sit outside, her hands idle now, her thoughts a jumble of confusion. The afternoon heat waned and finally, in the distance, she could catch a glimpse of familiar forms moving among the waving grasses. She stood up and shielded her eyes while she watched the travelers approach. Soon the farm wagon and mule took shape. She could see Hannah and Nathan and Marybeth in the back and Frank Walsh's burly figure on the wagon seat. Besides that there was a rider on horseback. Her heart gave a lurch as she thought of Caleb Hunter, but as the rider came closer, she saw it was a stranger. A sense of foreboding possessed her and she lowered her hand and went into the dark interior of the soddy, not reemerging until the wagon had rolled into the yard and Frank Walsh called out to her. Hesitantly she went to the door.

"Girl, we got company," Frank called, indicating the stranger. "Brother Nestor has come to stay with us a few days."

The man doffed his hat to Jenny and spoke a pleasant greeting. His pale eyes ran over her figure and came back to her face. "You must be Jenny," he said. "I've heard much about you." He dismounted and turned to her, smiling blandly. He was tall, with a sleekness to his figure that belied the kind of work men like Frank Walsh did. He wore a suitcoat, but Jenny saw it was worn in several places and his breeches were shiny at the seat and knees.

"Ain't you goin' to welcome him?" Frank said, having climbed down out of the wagon and come to stand beside the preacher. He slapped him on the shoulder with familiarity. "Right this way, Brother," he said, ushering the man toward the soddy. "Nathan, unhitch the mule. Hannah, help him." He glanced at Jenny. "Come on in, girl," he ordered, "and make up a pot of coffee for our visitor."

Jenny gripped her hands together tightly to still their

trembling, then pulling the stoic Comanche air around herself, she entered the soddy and moved to the stove. She could feel Brother Nestor's pale eyes watching her and suddenly she understood. Frank Walsh had indeed called a curse down on her head—and somehow it was in the form of this stranger with the easy smile and calculating eyes.

Chapter 9

"**I** DO NOT wish to learn of your Lord," Jenny said adamantly, facing the two men on the other side of the table. Brother Nestor sighed and looked at Frank, who pounded the table with his fist and rose to tower over her.

"You've brought your heathen ways to my family for the last time," Frank said. "You led my wife into methods of birthing that were ungodlike and shameful, and you taught my children to pray to this Great Spirit of yours. You will study with Brother Nestor every day he's here. He'll rid you of those evil notions and bring you back to God."

"Why is the Great Spirit wrong and your Lord right?" Jenny demanded.

Frank's face turned red in disbelief. "Do you see what I mean, Brother Nestor?" he asked. "It's a wonder God don't smite her where she sits."

"Now, now, Brother Frank," Owen Nestor said quietly. "She's been led astray, there's no doubt about that, but it's up to us to bring all of God's sheep into the fold, especially the black ones. We'll teach her the rightness of things—and once she knows, she'll not turn her back on God again. We'll begin easily, with Bible praying and reading every morning and every night . . . and during the day if I see fit for it."

Frank Walsh sat down. "I'm much obliged to you, Brother Nestor."

"Now, now," the preacher said. "This is likely the reason the good Lord led me here. He knew how badly I was needed."

Jenny stared at the smiling man and wondered if he knew why *she'd* been sent here, but she didn't ask, sensing she'd shock their righteous convictions.

In the week that followed, Owen Nestor was not an unpleasant guest in the Walsh home. He seemed to spend a lot of time in prayer down by the creek with a fishing pole and Bible reading at the rough table between meals. Jenny wondered how he could concentrate when all around people lent their shoulders to one task or another, even Hannah and Nathan. Even Marybeth had been given the task of running small errands for her mother, who despite her continuing weakness was determined to rise from her sickbed and recommence her duties.

In the evenings after supper, Brother Nestor sat beside Jenny on the hard stools and read to her from the Bible, explaining the difference in the God he worshiped and the heathen one she'd been led to. So forcefully did he speak of this God called Jehovah and Lord and other perplexing names, that Jenny began to believe that he had far more power than the Great Spirit of the Comanche. With tales of fire and damnation ringing in her ears, she would creep, shivering and confused, into her bed beside Hannah and Marybeth, while Brother Nestor bedded down on the table in the other room. By the time the following Sunday came and they climbed into the wagon for the trip to Millbrook for church, Jenny wasn't certain what she believed.

Faye and little Samson were going as well. A picnic basket had been filled with fresh corn bread and a dish of beans and ham hock. But more importantly, Faye had instructed Jenny in the making of a green tomato pie. It rested in golden-crusted splendor beneath a clean towel—and even Brother Nestor had said the smell of it had driven the thought of God right out of his mind. Jenny couldn't help looking around to see if God would punish the preacher for his trite words. Apparently holy men had special dispensations with their Gods.

There was an air of festivity as they loaded onto the wagon and started out. Frank Walsh, in a freshly washed and well-mended shirt, flipped his whip at the mules, urging them up out of the creek bottom and onto the path toward the main road. Jenny sat at the back of the wagon swinging her bare feet, much as she had when she first came to the homestead. This time, though, she wore one of the faded calico dresses Margaret Rudd had sent out by Caleb Hunter. She'd washed her hair and carefully braided it halfway down her back, leaving the ends free to curl in the wind. Now she wondered how she looked—and if Caleb Hunter would be in town. She swung her legs and sighed.

"Don't look so down, Sister Jenny," Brother Nestor called from his horse. "You're on your way to meet the Lord, and you should be rejoicing."

Jenny forced a smile because it would please him. She was learning what was expected of her and had found it was easier to respond as the white people expected. Now she noticed Brother Nestor's gaze fixed on her bare legs beneath the hem of her dress. Quickly she pulled her skirts in place, nearly covering her feet.

Brother Nestor smiled. "The Lord loves a modest woman, Sister," he called heartily, and nudged his horse forward, so despite the thigh-high grass he could ride beside the wagon and talk to Frank Walsh.

She was surprised at her sense of familiarity when the wagon pulled into the little town. Though she'd only seen it once, when she'd first been brought to Millbrook, she remembered many of the details. Now she watched, wide-eyed, as the wagon rolled through town toward the little sod church at the other end. Her heart gave a lurch as she noted a familiar figure slouched against the saloon porch.

Other farm wagons and buggies and saddle horses were gathered in front of the church, and people milled about on the trampled yard waiting for the circuit preacher's return.

"Howdy, Preacher," they called as Brother Nestor nudged his horse forward and greeted them all by removing his hat and holding it aloft. Jenny could not help think his bravado was equal to the Comanche warriors when they returned from a successful raid and entered the village with their latest trophies held aloft. Brother Nestor alighted from his horse and walked to the little church.

"Come in, come in, one and all," he invited.

Frank Walsh had pulled his wagon to a halt and driven a stake to tie off his horses. Jenny leapt off the back of the wagon and hurried around to take Samson while Faye climbed down. Taking her newborn son,

Faye walked toward the makeshift church, her face glowing with anticipation. Jenny helped Marybeth off the wagon and halted in the middle of setting the girl on her feet, for a rider had come forward and sat staring down at her.

Jenny looked up at Caleb Hunter and felt her cheeks redden. The sun was full in her face and his hat brim was pulled low as usual, so she couldn't see his expression, but she felt the unswerving strength of him from where she stood. She remained silent, while emotions swept through her, shifting, bothersome emotions she couldn't name.

Caleb looked at her for a long minute, then touched the rim of his hat and nodded. "Ma'am," he said, and his voice was low and deep, as she remembered. It caused a chill to race up her spine. She had no chance to answer, for he kicked at his horse and moved on.

Jenny turned sharply away from him, placed Marybeth on her feet, and, taking the chubby hand in hers, hurried toward the church.

There was not enough room for everyone to crowd inside the small, dark building—and those who managed to get in, soon found themselves sweating and gasping for air. Margaret Rudd and some of the other ladies had brought fans made of prairie grass, which they waved back and forth before their faces. The men took off their hats and stood in stoic discomfort, ignoring the runnels of sweat that poured down their temples and brows.

Brother Nestor looked out over his congregation and led them in a well-known hymn. When everyone had finished singing, Brother Nestor picked up his worn Bible and began his sermon. If Frank Walsh had seemed to have a special ear for his God, Brother Nestor seemed to sit at his right hand. He spoke with great authority on what the Lord expected of all of them, entreating them not to spend their lives in storing up possessions and losing sight of their responsibilities to God and church. Then he passed a basket; meager coins were dropped into it by the hard-working people. Eagerly Brother Nestor counted the money, then fixed his eye on the congregation.

"Maybe I haven't made myself clear, folks," he said. "Millbrook needs a church, a real church where God can hear our prayers. Now I urge you to dig deep into your pockets and find an extra tithing for the Lord."

Once again the basket went around. Jenny saw the troubled faces of the men and women as they took more money from their meager fare. When the basket went back to the preacher, Margaret Rudd stepped forward.

"I've been thinking, Brother Nestor," she said, "ever since you spoke to us last week about this new church, that we ladies could contribute to it."

"How's that, Sister?" Brother Nestor asked eagerly.

"We could hold a fair or a raffle. Our ladies' sewing circle could make a quilt to be raffled off, something that folks need in exchange for their money."

"Why, Sister . . . that sounds right fine. I'm sure the good Lord will bless each of you for your labors." The women smiled at one another, a final hymn was sung, and the congregation happily forfeited the small, dank building for the blinding sunshine outside.

Quickly everyone got back into their wagons and carriages and headed outside of town to a spot already deemed suitable for a picnic. Jenny helped the children onto the wagon, glancing around for a final glimpse of Caleb Hunter. He was not to be seen. Disappointed, she jumped up on the wagon as Frank Walsh followed the others.

If the churchgoers were somber in their religion and daily work, they were not afraid to let down their hair and relax on this, the Lord's day. Horseshoes were brought out and stakes driven into the ground. Men in rolled-up shirtsleeves lined up to play, while others sat in quiet groups, talking about their crops as they waited for the food to be set out.

A flat wagon bed had been covered with several starched white tablecloths. Amid much talk and laughter, the women put out the dishes they'd brought, exclaiming over the others' talents and exchanging recipes. When all was ready, the men were called to fill their plates, then the women and children crowded up to eat. Within a short while, everyone was replete and settled on the grass to let their stomachs settle, all save the children who ran hither and yon in games of hide-and-seek and turkeys and geese.

Restless, Jenny wandered away from the others. Marybeth and Samson were napping. Faye was happily engaged in conversation with the other women. Jenny had never seen her so animated and happy. She wandered far out into the waving grass, until only the shrill cries of the children could be heard, and sat down. Here she could no longer see or be seen. She sat with her eyes closed, pretending for a little while that she was back in her village with her people and that it was White Weasel and Ten Bears who sat chatting with their friends. A sudden noise startled her, so she opened her eyes.

Caleb Hunter stood staring down at her. He held his hat and the wind blew his dark hair across his brow. His gray eyes were direct. She felt the color rise in her cheeks.

"What do you want?" she demanded.

"I came to talk to you."

"We have nothing to say."

"I think we have."

She fell silent. He studied her a moment longer, then settled himself beside her in the grass.

"I'm sorry I haven't been out to see you in some time."

"I didn't expect you," she said truthfully.

He grimaced. "I took your friend, Running Deer, back to Missouri."

"To a place she does not wish to go."

"She didn't object. In fact, I have a feeling she was kind of interested in finding out something about her own people again. She was sixteen when she was taken, plenty old enough to remember."

"What is that to me?" Jenny inquired. "I have no such memories, and my life here with the white eyes is not what I want."

"I'm sorry to hear that," Caleb said, and his voice did sound sorrowful. She glanced at him swiftly, but his head was turned and he sat staring out over the waving grass. She felt anger rise within her.

"Are you sorry enough to take me back to my people?" she demanded.

He looked at her then, taking in the rich molasses

color of her hair, the clear gray eyes and straight nose and chin. What was there about her, he wondered, that had made her stay in his thoughts these many weeks? He'd seen other women as pretty. His gaze dropped to her drawn-up knees and the bare brown toes peeking from beneath the hem of her skirt.

"Has Frank Walsh whipped you anymore?" he asked.

"He has decided that Brother Nestor must pray for my soul and convert me to this mysterious Jehovah."

"Is it so hard for you to give up your belief in the Great Spirit?"

She shrugged. "I think they are the same," she said. "But I can't say that to Frank or Brother Nestor. They call me a heretic." She turned to Caleb with a puzzled look. "What is a heretic and why is it so bad?"

Caleb hid a smile that played at the corners of his mouth. "A heretic is someone who doesn't believe in their God."

"Does that make *them* heretics, since they don't believe in mine?"

"It doesn't work that way," he said, hedging, "but you may be right about the two gods being the same. They'd never believe you, though."

"You mean because I'm a woman or because I'm a heathen?"

"Both, I guess." He sighed.

"Will I ever be anything else in the white man's world?" she asked, and her lips tightened bitterly.

He glanced at her sideways, taking in the sedate profile with its small nose and stubborn chin. In profile she looked more like a child—until you took into account the fullness of her bosom and the slimness of her waist beneath the faded, ugly calico.

"What you become, depends on you, Jenny," he said, and his use of her white name made her pause.

"I am not Jenny," she whispered. "I am Wild Sage." There were tears on her cheek. "I am part of the prairie and sky. I am not meant to live in a dirt house and dig into the breast of the mother earth. I am a Comanche." Her words carried more significance than if she'd shouted them. With shaking hands, she wiped away the tears.

Unaccountably he wanted to take her in his arms and coddle her, but the memory of such gentle things between a man and woman was long buried. He took a deep breath and slowly let it out.

"What would you do if Two Wolves came for you?" he asked stonily. He knew her answer before she gave it.

"I'd go with him," she said, then raised her face to his. He saw the flare of hope as she studied him. "He's coming for me, isn't he?"

Caleb's gaze was unwavering, but he made no answer. She didn't need one. A smile spread across her face and she raised her eyes toward the sky. "Two Wolves is coming for me. He will take me back to my people."

"He'll only bring death to you and to his own people."

"No." She was cat-quick in facing him now, her voice jubilant. "Two Wolves is a good warrior, a war chief."

"He's a murderer," Caleb said implacably. "He kills women and children."

Her smile faded. "You lie."

"He's already killed homesteaders in Texas. He captured Sergeant Butler and Private Moses on their return to Fort Sill. He tortured them. I saw them. There wasn't much left of them. Colonel Grierson figures they told Two Wolves where you were before they died. I've been sent back here to take you somewhere else if you want to go."

"No!" She backed away from him. "I'll stay here until Two Wolves comes for me, then I'll go back to the Comancheria with him, as his wife. I belong to him."

Caleb had his answer. He got to his feet and stared down at her. "When he comes, he'll kill the Walsh family."

"No, he won't," she answered, facing him. "I won't let him."

"You can't stop him."

"I will. He'll listen to me when I tell him how they fed and sheltered me. We Comanche do not kill our friends, only our enemies."

"Two Wolves is killing and burning everything in his path," Caleb said. "I've been sent back here to stop him."

"No, Caleb!" She sprang forward, placing her hand on his arm in a silent appeal. He saw the fear in her eyes. Was it for him or for Two Wolves? Then she spoke, and he knew.

"You are a brave warrior. In our village we called you The Hunter . . . and many braves feared you. They believed you had stronger medicine than they. You were at the place where my father died, and again where my mother was killed. I do not know if it was your medi-

cine that took their lives, but you must not take Two
Wolves's. He's all I have left of my old life. You must
give it back to me."

He studied her pleading eyes. She saw the flicker of
care in his own and stepped forward, rubbing herself
against him.

"You want me, Caleb Hunter," she whispered. "I
have seen it in your eyes. Many white hunters take Indian women. There is no shame in this. I give myself to
you, if you will give me this in return. Do not stop Two
Wolves."

"And let him murder innocent people?"

"Then take me to him. I will be yours until we reach
him, then I will tell him how you helped me. He will be
grateful. He'll return to the Comancheria and no one
else will be killed." She was bargaining with the only
thing she had to offer. Now she leaned against him, letting him feel the heat of her body through the thin calico. She saw a muscle flicker in his jaw, saw the
darkening of his eyes, and pressed herself closer, melding her slender body to his. His hands grasped her arms
as if he meant to push her away, but she clung to him,
her voice husky.

"Take me here in the grass," she whispered. "No one
will know or see us, and you will know I mean what I
say." He groaned low in his throat and his mouth
claimed hers.

The kiss was hard and punishing, crushing her tender
lips against her teeth until she yielded; he invaded her
mouth. Her knees trembled and she sank to the ground,
fell back into the soft, fragrant grass. Without relinquishing his claim on her mouth, he followed, the full

length of him covering her. She felt his weight and the answering fire in her own loins. Caleb's knees pressed against her thighs, and she opened to him. Impatiently he tugged up her skirt until it was rumpled at her waist, then his hands explored her sleek legs and flat stomach, grasping her small, round buttocks to lift her and ground her tender mound against the hard bulge of his arousal. A fire burned through her, consuming her, and she no longer thought of Two Wolves or of the Comancheria, only of this man who held her and awakened such passion within her. The hot sun burned down on them, further igniting their hot blood. Cicadael called to one another in the hot grass, their high-pitched sound a special music in the lovers' ears.

Caleb released her mouth and buried his face against her throat, breathing in the sweet, musky smell of her. Some part of him knew he couldn't take her like this. He could never give her what she bargained for, the freedom to return to Two Wolves. He knew something that he could never tell her. Two Wolves must die— and he, Caleb Hunter, would see to it. Now he lay cradling her against his body, wanting to weep with his need of her and trying to control his passions. As if from a long way off came a call.

"Jenny!" Other voices had joined the cry.

Caleb drew back from her. She lay with her arms thrown above her head, her eyes heavy-lidded and bright with passion. Her lips were moist and parted and her long legs sprawled wide, nestling him in the sweet, hot vee of her body.

"Someone's calling you," he said, his voice so heavy he could hardly speak. At first she didn't seem to hear him, then slowly her eyes refocused on his face. With a start she turned away, staring at the sky and the edge of grass that defined their world.

"They're looking for me," she said, and leapt up, smoothing her skirt around her.

"I'm here," she cried, waving to someone in the distance.

"Where were you?" Frank Walsh called. "It's time to go."

"I—I fell asleep in the grass," she said. "I'll be right there." She squatted and looked at Caleb. Her eyes studied him, taking in the long body, and she felt a shiver of desire even now. "Take me to Two Wolves," she whispered. "We made a bargain." Then she was gone, running through the tall grass.

"Jenny," he called softly, but she didn't turn back. He stayed where he was, waiting until he heard wagons moving out and men calling to stubborn mules, then he rose and made his way to his own mount.

As he rode back to town, the feel and smell of Jenny clung to him. She belonged to Two Wolves, she'd said, and Caleb knew the meaning of that. Yet she would have given herself to him just now—and he knew her hunger had been as great as his. Was she so wanton then, or had it all been an act, a part of the bargain she thought she was making to return to the Comanche warrior?

Caleb rode into town in time to see the Walsh wagon heading toward their homestead. Jenny sat in the back holding a little girl on her lap and the circuit preacher rode alongside. When she saw Caleb, she made no effort to wave, but her eyes watched him until the road turned and they disappeared beyond the last building. Wearily Caleb dismounted and went into the saloon. Tonight he was going to drink until he couldn't remember the taste and feel of a slender girl with pleading gray eyes—and tomorrow he was going out to find Two Wolves and kill him.

Chapter 10

Two Wolves was coming for her. She thought of little else on the ride home. Seated in the back of the Walsh's farm wagon, with a drowsy Marybeth cuddled against her, she thought of Caleb's words and felt her heart quicken with elation. Soon she'd be back with her own people on the Comancheria. This time the white man would be forgotten, left behind her forever. She belonged to Two Wolves. He would take her as his wife and they would go to live on the white man's reservations, but they would be among the other Real Human Beings and life would be bearable.

Marybeth stirred against her. Jenny shifted, and the little girl's arms tightened around her neck. Jenny's elation was tempered now with the thought of how much she would miss the Walsh children. Although Frank Walsh had remained a harsh, unforgiving man during her weeks with them, Faye had become her friend, and Hannah and Nathan looked to her, and Marybeth . . . Jenny's arm tightened around the warm, chubby body. Marybeth's blond curls were damp and stuck to her rosy cheeks and neck. Jenny placed her lips against one flushed cheek. Marybeth smelled of baby sweat and hot prairie sun and earth. She sprawled in abandoned slumber and innocent trust against Jenny. Suddenly Jenny had an image of a Comanche knife slicing the fine, silky hair from the sweet head. Her arms tightened convulsively, and Marybeth cried out fretfully.

"Shh. I'm sorry, Marybeth," Jenny whispered against her cheek. The little girl settled at once.

Faye Walsh looked over her shoulder. "She probably has a stomachache from eating too much watermelon."

"She's all right now," Jenny said, blinking rapidly.

Nathan studied her intently. "Mama, Jenny's crying."

"What?" Faye swiveled on the seat, adjusting her hold on her baby son.

"I just got a bug in my eye," Jenny said quickly.

"Close your eyes," Faye suggested.

They were silent for the rest of the ride home. Nathan and Hannah fell asleep. Marybeth slumbered on. Samson woke and cried out, but Faye quickly parted her dress and nursed him, modestly turning, so her bare breast would not be exposed to Brother Nestor, who rode alongside the wagon. Even the preacher had remained strangely silent on the ride home. Perhaps he'd preached himself out that morning and had nothing more to say. The only sounds were the steady clopping of the mules' hooves against the hard prairie earth and the *ping* of insects in the parched grass.

Jenny was left to the turmoil of her thoughts, remembering the feel of Caleb's hands on her body, the demanding heat of his mouth against hers. She'd bargained with her body for his help in returning to Two Wolves, but she hadn't been immune to the passion that flared between them. If Caleb Hunter were to

take her up on her offer, she would return to Two
Wolves less than the bride she'd hoped to take to his
tent, for not only would she no longer be a virgin, but
her heart would have been ravished as well.

She was glad to see the creek and the small soddy
crouching in the late afternoon sun. Frank Walsh drew
the wagon to a stop before the front door. Without help,
Faye alighted and went inside. Jenny gently roused the
older children, then carried a still sleeping Marybeth indoors and put her to bed. A quiet peacefulness lay over
the homestead, a feeling of coming home.

Wandering outside she watched the fading glow in
the west as the sun sank below the flat horizon line of
prairie grass. Somewhere out there were mountains.
Somewhere out there was Two Wolves and his warriors,
making his way here to her. She'd never thought the
surly war chief was that caring of her. He'd always
seemed to take her presence for granted, but now he
was proving his love by braving the white soldiers' bullets to rescue her.

Yet her earlier elation had faded as she thought of
Caleb Hunter's words. He'd called Two Wolves a murderer, claiming the war chief had killed innocent
women and children on their journey north. Was that so
much worse than what the white soldiers had done at
the Indian villages? Hearing the sounds of people behind her, of Frank Walsh feeding his animals and the
children chasing a hen down by the creek and Faye's
voice on the evening air as she called them to bed,
Jenny felt her heart turn.

She remembered Frank Walsh's tenderness toward his
wife. He was a hard man, but he worked feverishly to

take care of his family and he was fervent in his belief
of his God. In the Comanche village he would have
been looked upon favorably.

Ignoring the danger of rattlers that could be hiding in
the bushes at this time of day, Jenny walked back toward the creek. A hushed stillness had fallen over the
land, while the western sky flared with layers of orange,
pink, and mauve. The last rays of light disappeared into
gray dusk. Jenny stood staring at the sunset, but her
thoughts were on the hot prairie grass at midday and the
feel of a man's body pressing her to the earth. She'd
never felt so alive, so much a part of the prairie, so
much a part of a man as she had at that moment. Now
she stood wondering why Caleb Hunter, with his
haunted eyes and bitter mouth, should claim her more
completely than Two Wolves had ever done.

"Please, send Two Wolves for me soon," she whispered, and wasn't certain to which God she'd prayed.

She turned back to the house and started as she
caught sight of a figure watching her.

"Two Wolves?" she called, her voice wavering between fear and joy that her prayer had been answered so
quickly. Then the figure moved, and she made out the
figure of Brother Nestor in the gathering gloom.

"I ain't a wolf, Sister Jenny," he said, stepping toward her softly. "There's no cause for alarm."

"I'm not alarmed," Jenny said, shivering in the evening chill.

"You're cold," Brother Nestor said, putting an arm
about her and pulling her close. "Funny how hot the
days can be here in the prairie and the nights get so
cold."

Jenny tried pulling away from him without offending him. "I'd better get up to the house. Faye likely needs me."

He had hold of her arm and wouldn't let go.

"You don't need to rush back just yet, Sister," Brother Nestor said. His voice was meant to be soothing. His touch was soft on her bare arm, slithering across her skin like a rattlesnake.

"I—I promised to tell Marybeth a bedtime story."

"She's sound asleep," Brother Nestor persisted. His hold on her arm tightened.

Alarm swept through Jenny. "I'm tired, Brother Nestor. I reckon I'll go to bed." She jerked away from him and turned toward the soddy.

"You weren't tired this afternoon."

His words caused her to freeze in her tracks. Her back to him, she waited for him to go on.

"I saw you in the grass this afternoon, sister." He'd moved closer, standing right behind her. His breath came in quick gasps, disturbing the tendrils of hair at her neck.

"I was sleeping," she said.

"You weren't alone, Sister Jenny," he said, and stepped around her, shoving his face close to hers. "I'm beginnin' to believe what Brother Frank says about you. You're actin' in a mighty heathen way."

Jenny drew a breath. Someone had seen Caleb Hunter and her in the grass! She felt ashamed and angry.

"We're goin' to have to pray for you, Sister," Brother Nestor was saying. "Yes, ma'am. Pray mighty hard that the good Lord looks down on your heathenish ways and takes them out of you. We're going to have to read His words and study over them and hope that God leads your footsteps away from the devil. Otherwise, you'll be dragged down to the fiery pit of hell and all your mortal flesh burned off you. You'll scream and cry out in anguish, but there'll be no one to hear you, no one to save you, Sister, except me, Brother Nestor." He'd taken her arm again, and now he ran his fingers over her wrist and up the inside of her elbow.

"You've got to turn to me, Sister." He lowered his voice, whispering her name. "Only I can save you from hell's damnation."

He touched her hair, smoothing it down as if she were a child, then slid his hand around to her cheek and throat. His touch was unpleasant. His eyes glittered in the rising moon. Jenny's breasts rose and fell with the terror he'd awakened in her. Suddenly, overcome by her aversion to this man breathing fire and brimstone, she jerked away from him and ran toward the soddy.

"Wait, Jenny! Sister Jenny," he called, running after her. "You can't run away from me and the word of the Lord or the curse of the devil. He runs right at your back—and I'll be there, too, Sister . . . right behind you, tryin' to fight off the devil that would claim your heathen soul." He caught her at the soddy door.

"Sister!" he exclaimed, holding her captive beneath his hard grip. His watery pale eyes bored into hers. "You're a sinner, Sister. I know about you. I saw you in the grass. But I ain't lettin' the devil have you, Sister. I'm fightin' for you."

The door behind Jenny gave way. With a sense of relief she fell backward into the soddy.

"My goodness, Jenny . . . Brother Nestor. You startled me," Faye Walsh exclaimed.

"I'm mighty sorry, Sister Faye," Brother Nestor said piously. "I was just telling Sister Jenny that she needs to spend more hours at her Bible readin' and prayin'. I intend to help her, so when we baptize our new church, we'll be baptizing Sister Jenny in her new life as a Christian."

"Oh, Jenny! How wonderful and appropriate," Faye cried.

Jenny cast a furtive glance at the preacher. Why had he lied to Faye? Why hadn't he revealed what he'd seen in the grass that afternoon? Quietly Jenny crept to bed, grateful for Brother Nestor's discretion about what he'd seen, but deeply disturbed at his words about this burning place called hell. It sounded fearsome.

In the days that followed, Brother Nestor did indeed work with Jenny, reading the Bible and praying with her. Kneeling on the hard, uneven plank floor until her knees ached, Jenny listened to the preacher's entreaties on her behalf. Sometimes, at the height of his exhortations, he reached out to take her hand and lift it to the ceiling. Once he'd done so, he continued to hold her hand throughout the long prayers. She could feel the sweat grow between their palms and longed to pull away, but she was frightened of further offending the preacher and his God. She'd known all along the feelings she'd had for Caleb Hunter were wrong. He was her enemy, the enemy of her people, the Comanche. To lie in the grass and offer her body was sinful to the white man's God. No wonder Caleb's face had held

scorn that day by the creek. He'd known she was heathen as well. She felt further dishonored.

During the rest of the time, Jenny went about her
chores, troubled and uncertain. She seldom stopped to
play along the creek bed with Hannah and Nathan, or to
take them picking wildflowers or berries.

"Are you mad at us, Jenny?" Nathan asked wistfully.
She'd just shooed him away, claiming she was too busy.

"I'm not mad," she said, smiling at his solemn face. "I
just have to get this cream churned so we can have some
butter tonight."

"Come play with us for a while. Please?" Hannah
said, tugging at Jenny's skirts.

With a final glance around, she considered. Marybeth
and Samson were napping. Faye had walked out to the
field to take Frank some cool water. Brother Nestor and
his everlasting prayers about hell and damnation was
blessedly not to be seen for the moment.

"Come on, Jenny," Nathan begged.

"Okay, I'll go down to the creek for a little while,"
Jenny agreed.

With a gleeful shout, Nathan took off at a run with
Hannah and Jenny following close behind. For the first
time in days, she felt the weight of her sins lift from her
shoulders. At the creek, they settled their bare feet in
the cold running water and wriggled their toes.

Nathan, unable to sit still for long, prowled along the
edge looking for pretty rocks.

"Look at this one!" he cried each time he picked one
up. Finally tiring of that pastime, he brought them to
the bank and dumped them in Jenny's lap. Idly she
picked them up, studying their colors and shape.

"This one looks like an arrowhead," she said idly.

"Let me see," Nathan cried, running back up the bank and grabbing the rock. He studied its shape, turning it this way and that. "Do you mean I could make a real arrow with this?"

"Well, sort of," Jenny said. "Real arrows are made by warriors who have special medicine. They know how to make the arrows strong and straight and they give some of their special medicine to each arrow, so it will fly true and kill our enemies."

"Can you make one for me?" he demanded.

"I can make a play one for you, the kind that Comanche boys and girls play with. We'll have to find some sticks."

Eagerly the children hunted along the creek until they found some reasonably straight sticks, then using dried prairie grass Jenny tied the pointed rocks to the sticks and plaited grass to form a bowstring. If it wasn't resilient enough to propel an arrow, Nathan was nonetheless happy and ran off to play.

"I'm a girl. There's nothing for me," Hannah said, pouting.

"You must make a tepee and cooking pots," Jenny said.

Retrieving a worn-out buffalo hide, now being used as a piece of carpeting in the soddy, Jenny showed Hannah how to use sticks to form a frame and wrap the hide around them. Then they set about making play cooking pots and spoons from the clay along the creek bed. For a while Jenny forgot her worries, forgot about Two Wolves and Caleb Hunter and Brother Nestor's prayers. She thought about those times when she was a

child in the Comanche village. The other children had
shunned her because she was white, and she'd watched
them from a distance, longing to join in, longing to belong. She paused now, staring at the tumbling creek water, troubled by this new revelation. She had never
really felt she belonged to the Comanche world, either.

"I'm an Indian brave and I'm coming to tear down
your village and capture you," Nathan shouted, and
with a bloodcurdling scream launched himself into the
middle of Hannah's tent. The frame collapsed, and Hannah screamed and pelted him with mud. Jenny laughed
and sat back, so she wouldn't be hit as the children continued to pelt each other.

"Nathan! Hannah!" Faye and Frank Walsh raced toward the creek bed and came to a sharp stop, gasping
for breath as they stared, wide-eyed, at their youngsters.

"You're not hurt!" Frank said, his words more like an
accusation than concern. "What in tarnation are you
screaming about?"

"Frank, don't swear. Brother Nestor might hear you,"
Faye said.

"Well?" Frank Walsh stared down at his children. Nathan quivered with fear and dropped his bow and arrow.

"He knocked my tepee over." Hannah sobbed.

"What is this, boy?" Frank asked, picking up the bow
and arrow. Without waiting for an answer, he glared at
Jenny. "What heathen things have you been teachin' my
boy now?" he demanded.

"Maybe no harm was done," Faye said, but Frank's
chilling glance quieted her. He turned back to his children.

"Git up to the house!" he thundered. "Take out the Bible and read—about heathens!"

Nathan and Hannah ran toward the soddy. Frank turned back to Jenny. She'd gotten to her feet now and backed away from him. Her palms were wet and she felt a shudder of dread. Somehow, once again she'd done something wrong.

"Frank, don't whip her. You promised Caleb Hunter you wouldn't."

"I won't break a promise made to any man, but I won't let this deed go unpunished. He glanced up as Brother Nestor rode into view. He had his fishing pole in one hand and his Bible in the other. "Brother Nestor," Frank called.

"Hello, Brother Frank. I've been up the creek a-fishin' and talkin' to the Lord. I got so busy talkin' to the Lord, I forgot to look at my line and I lost the biggest fish you ever did see. Whooee, Sister Faye. We'd have had a mighty fine supper if I hadn't been listenin' to the—"

"Brother Nestor, we need you," Frank said, without taking his eyes off Jenny. Sensing the tension in the air between the three of them, Brother Nestor swung down off his horse, carefully propped his fishing pole against a bush, and joined them.

"What can I do for you, Brother Frank?" the preacher asked.

Frank Walsh pointed to the scattered playthings. "There you are, Preacher. Proof of what I've been telling you she's done to my children."

Brother Nestor looked at the broken sticks, mud pots, and buffalo hide and shook his head. "This is a sad thing, Brother Frank," he said. "I see what you mean." His eyes glittered as he looked up at Jenny.

"I've promised the man who brought her here that I'd not raise a whip to her again, and I won't go back on my word."

"But I ain't promised, Brother Frank," the preacher said. "You and Sister Faye just go on up to the house and I'll deal with this."

"Brother Nestor," Faye said, gripping his sleeve. "She's little more than a child. She tries hard to be good; she just doesn't understand our ways yet."

"Yes, ma'am, I'll keep that in mind," Brother Nestor said, patting her hand. "You just go up to the house and I'll take care of this."

"Come on, Faye," Frank said, and took hold of her arm to urge her up the bank.

When they were gone, the preacher turned to Jenny. She'd stood mute all this time. Now she stared at the preacher with wary eyes.

Slowly he shook his head. "It makes me sad to have to do this, Sister Jenny," he said. Taking out a knife he cut a green branch from one of the bushes.

"What are you going to do?" she asked warily.

"Well, now. You heard Brother Frank. He don't want you teachin' his children how to be heathens." Slowly, one by one, he cut away the leaves from the limber stick.

"We were just playing," Jenny said, edging away from him.

"I know you were, Sister," he answered. The leaves were all gone now; he swished the stick through the air a few times as if to test its strength and flexibility. It made a sharp, swishing sound. Satisfied, he met Jenny's gaze and smiled. "There are certain kinds of play you mustn't do, Jenny," he said gently.

He took a few steps toward her. "I'm sorry I'm going to have to hurt you, girl," he said, reaching out a hand to slide along her arm.

"Don't whip me," she said, trembling in spite of herself. She remembered the feel of Frank Walsh's whip across her back and the humiliation she'd felt.

"I have to, Jenny. They expect me to. I have to make you humble and respectful of our ways. 'Course, you could plead with me a little. It might help." He was standing close to her now. She could smell his breath and feel the heat of his body. "Beg me, Jenny," he whispered. His hand continued to brush against her arm, scant inches from her breasts. He seemed excited, for he was breathing heavily. His eyes watched hers and he smiled as if anticipating her fear. He wanted her to be afraid. He wanted to see her beg, she thought hazily, and drew back from him, raising her chin determinedly. He saw her defiance and his grin widened.

"Turn around, girl," he ordered, hitting the palm of his hand with the switch. "Bend over!"

She obeyed . . . and felt the heartbeat of a moment as the switch was drawn back, then fell across her buttocks. She jumped at the pain, then clenched her fists and bit her lip to remain silent. The switch fell again and again, cutting through the thin calico skirts as if they weren't there. Despite her resolve not to cry, tears filled Jenny's eyes and rolled down her cheeks. It seemed he might never stop. The switch fell with a rhythmic motion against her backside, then finally stopped. Jenny remained as she was, bent over. Brother Nestor stood gasping in air.

"Come here," he ordered, and Jenny straightened and turned toward him. "Here!" he said, pointing with the switch.

Jenny crept closer, her head down so he wouldn't see her tear-streaked cheeks, but when she was close enough, he grabbed hold of her and pulled her against him. At the contact of their bodies, her head came up in protest. His soft hands had hold of her, one twisting her chin up, so he could look at her face. He smiled in satisfaction at her tears.

"I'm glad to see I've had some impact on you, Sister Jenny," he said, his voice breathy and heavy.

She pushed against him, hating the feel of his soft body. His grip on her jaw tightened painfully. His free hand grasped her arm, jerking it back against him, then slid down her arm until he gripped her hand and carried it forward. She realized a moment too late where he was taking her hand and tried to jerk away, but he was surprisingly strong. He rubbed her fingers against his bulging manhood, his eyes hot with lust. Jenny couldn't avert her face, but she lowered her eyes and willed herself to remain passive.

"Feel that?" he said. "Did that man in the grass show you that? Did he pleasure you? Did he pull up your dress and lay something like this against you? I'll bet you liked it, didn't you?" His grip on her had become more frantic and he increased the friction against his crotch. At the same time he opened his mouth and tried to kiss her, swirling his tongue over her tightly closed lips and down her cheek to her neck.

"You want it, don't you, Jenny? I know you do. You been with the Injuns—and they don't think nothing about lyin' with any buck that comes along. Just touch me, Jenny," he begged, bucking his hips against her. "Just touch me. You'll like it, you'll see." He loosened his hold on her, reaching for her skirts, sliding them up her hips.

With all her strength Jenny brought her bare foot up, felt it connect with the preacher's bulging crotch. With a howl of pain, he doubled over, clutching himself. Jenny whirled and ran up the creek bank. Without looking back she bolted to the soddy and pounded on the door.

"Faye, let me in. Faye!" she cried.

The door was flung open, and Faye was there, taking her in her arms and patting her head. Wide-eyed and pale, Nathan and Hannah sat at the table, the Bible open before them.

"I'm sorry, Jenny," Faye whispered. "I know you shouldn't have been whipped, just like last time—"

"Not like last time," Jenny gasped, wiping at the tears that wet her cheeks. She shook her head so violently that tendrils came loose and fell across her face. "He—he made me—" Hannah was watching and listening.

"What, Jenny?" Faye asked in alarm.

"I made her repent her heathen ways, Sister Faye," Nestor said from the doorway. "And she fought me."

"Brother Nestor, are you all right?" Faye hurried toward the man. Jenny stood forgotten and accused. Frank

Walsh came in from feeding his animals. Brother Nestor sank into a chair.

"I've done all I can do with her," the preacher said. "I will continue to pray for her soul, but she tried to tempt me, Brother, like Salome and the seven veils, throwin' herself at me and fightin' me. I've done the best I could, Brother Frank, Sister Faye. But I hope you'll understand when I tell you I must go elsewhere. The devil is here in this girl and I can't fight him alone. I'll go to Brother Gilkenson's family. Although he's got all those daughters and it might be unseemly for me to stay there, I'm safer there than here."

"I'm sorry you feel you have to leave, Brother Nestor," Faye said, wringing her hands and looking from Jenny to the preacher and back again.

"I understand, Preacher," Frank Walsh said, holding out his hand and shaking Nestor's. "We're sorry to see you leave us."

"I'll be in church on Sunday, Brother Frank," Nestor said, pushing back his hair and settling his hat on his head. He never once glanced at Jenny. "I hope you and Sister Faye will be there, too. I'll be prayin' for your family."

"Thank you, Brother Nestor. That's right fine of you. And I thank you for trying to take care of our problems."

Frank stepped outdoors with the preacher to see him off, and Faye turned back to Jenny. "What did you do to him?" Faye asked.

Jenny glanced at the children and turned to the bedroom, settling on the edge of the bed she shared with

Hannah. Gripping her waist, she bent over, trying to still the chills that shook her.

"Jenny, what happened down there?" Faye demanded, kneeling before her. "Tell me or you'll just have to tell Frank when he comes in."

"No!" Jenny cried, and rocked back and forth.

Faye was silent for a moment, studying the girl. Jenny's head was bowed, so Faye couldn't see her face, but she sensed the girl was crying.

"He didn't want to whip you, Jenny," she began reasonably.

Jenny's head snapped up. "Yes, he did!" she flared.

"Why? What do you mean?"

"He liked it."

"What are you saying? This is sinful." Faye edged away, then halted when she looked into Jenny's eyes.

"What did he do?" Something in her tone had changed. Some unspoken understanding that exists between two women made her reach out a hand to Jenny.

"When he switched me, he grew hard," Jenny whispered.

"How do you know?"

"He made me touch him."

"No!"

"Good night, Brother Nestor," Frank Walsh called outside the window. "Godspeed."

The house grew quiet. Faye and Jenny stared at each other, waiting, although for what, neither of them were certain. Frank Walsh opened the outer door to the soddy. His footsteps were heavy as he crossed the room to the bedroom. Hannah and Nathan had remained silent throughout. Marybeth and Samson still slept. Pausing in the doorway, Frank looked at his wife, where she still crouched in front of Jenny.

"What does she have to say for herself?" he demanded.

"Shhh!" Faye said, rising and crossing to the door. "The babies are sleeping. Come outside."

Jenny heard their footsteps crossing to the door, then all was silent. From outside came the stout denial of an angry male, then all was silent again. Exhausted by all that had transpired, Jenny fell back on the bed, careful to roll on one hip to lessen the pain of her stinging buttocks.

Later came the aroma of corn bread baking and beans, but she made no effort to rise and go to the table. She couldn't bear to see the accusations in Frank's eyes. Perhaps Faye believed her, but he never would. The sounds of supper died away. Marybeth rose and was fed and shadows crept into the room through the tiny glass window. Jenny watched the growing darkness and never felt more alone. Later, though, when all was quiet save the murmur of voices from the other room, Faye came with a lamp and a pail of cool water. Raising Jenny's skirts, she applied cool cloths to her stinging flesh and smoothed the hair back from her forehead.

"We've not done well by you, Jenny," she whispered. "But we've tried our best. I'm sorry we don't understand your ways better. We keep making you change to our ways—and when our ways fail us all, we still blame you." Her hand was gentle on Jenny's head, and, for a moment, Jenny could believe it was White Weasel soothing away her pain.

After a while she slept, and never knew when Faye withdrew and went to sit before the fire, her thin fingers busy with darning her husband's socks, while her mind was busy trying to find a way to mend Jenny's life.

Chapter 11

*N*OW WHEN THE Walshes went into Millbrook to attend church, Jenny no longer went with them. Her life had narrowed to the small soddy in the middle of a prairie, her hope had narrowed to Two Wolves coming to rescue her.

The third Sunday after Brother Nestor left the Walsh homestead, a rider came to the soddy. Jenny had just washed her hair and sat in the sunshine letting it dry. It spread around her shoulders like a curtain as she contemplated the bland sky and willed Two Wolves and his warriors to ride into the yard. If they came now, there would be no danger of the Walshes being injured by the Comanche. She would just climb on the back of Two Wolves's horse, and they would ride with the wind until they returned to the Comancheria.

So deeply did she wish all this that when she first heard the hoofbeats, she believed her vision was about to happen, then she realized there was but a single rider and there was no urgency in his approach. Disappointed, she lowered her gaze and recognized the broad, straight figure of Caleb Hunter. She stayed where she was seated on the ground, letting him come to her. He halted his horse, mere inches away, and stared down at her. Neither spoke, and finally Caleb shrugged, knowing the ways of the Comanche and that she would never acknowledge him first.

"You haven't been coming into church with the Walshes," he said, slouching in his saddle, one knee thrown over his saddle horn. He pushed his hat back, so she could see his eyes if she cared to look. She told herself she didn't and kept her profile turned to him.

"I do not wish to go to church," she replied.

"Why not?" Caleb asked.

She remained silent. Sighing, he slid out of his saddle and crouched beside her. Now his gaze was level with hers, but she maintained her steadfast watch on some distant object.

"There's talk in town."

"I do not understand."

"There's talk you offered yourself to the preacher."

At last she looked at him, outrage in her clear gray eyes and in the line of her mouth.

"I would not give myself to this man. He is dishonest. He talks about his God being stronger than our Great Spirit, yet he is a bad man. If the white man's God is that strong, why does he choose such a man to speak for him?"

"I expect that question has been asked a time or two by the white men!" Caleb couldn't repress a grin. It did strange, wonderful things to his face. His eyes sparkled with light. Tiny crinkles formed at the corners and his mouth lost its bitter line. He looked younger, lighthearted, like one of the young Comanche boys who'd just succeeded in playing a prank on one of the old grandfathers. Before she could adjust to it, the grin was gone and his face settled back into its stern lines.

"The people are trying to raise money for a new church."

"I know," Jenny answered.

Caleb hesitated, then plunged. "They're having a dance to raise money. Are you coming to it?"

"No!"

"Why not?"

She thought about not answering him. He had no right to ask such questions of her.

"I have no wish to go to a white man's dance."

Caleb pulled in a deep breath, then let it out slowly. "You know, things would be a damn sight better for you if you'd try to be a little friendly with folks."

"What folks? The ones who are talking about the preacher and me?" She'd gone back to studying the pure sky.

"Some aren't talking."

"The ones who aren't talking will only stare at me as if I'm a bad spirit."

"Maybe they're staring because you're a pretty girl."

She glanced at Caleb's face, surprised that he found her pleasing to look at, but he seemed intent on something in the creek. Silently she studied him, his broad shoulders, the stern mouth that could be surprisingly tender or passionately demanding. She shivered, remembering how their last two encounters had ended. She had no need for that to happen again, unless . . . She turned to him.

"Did you find Two Wolves?"

He glanced up, startled by the abruptness of her question. "Not yet," he said finally. "He and his warriors have hidden in the hills out yonder someplace. Right now they're staying quiet."

"You mean he isn't coming after me?" Disappointment burned through her.

"He may never come, Jenny. You can't bury yourself out here waiting for him to find you. Come to town, to church and the dance. Let folks see that you're not so different from them." His hand barely touched a windswept lock of her freshly washed hair. "Wear your hair down like this instead of braided like an Indian; you'll have every single man in the territory trying to dance with you."

"I don't want men to dance with me," she said, leaping to her feet. "Then there will be more talk in town about me."

He heard the pain in her voice and wondered at her cause.

"Folks only talk because they don't know any better."

"They talk because they listen to Brother Nestor and believe his words. I did not offer him my body. He tried to take what I would not give."

Caleb stared up at her, his eyes going dark as he thought about what she'd said. Slowly he got to his feet. "Are you saying the preacher got familiar with you?"

"What do you mean, 'familiar'?" Jenny demanded, striding away from him. In her anxiety she had to move. Caleb followed.

"Tell me what happened," he demanded.

"There is nothing to tell. I told Frank and Faye and they did not believe me. Now I will not tell anyone again."

His hands on her shoulders brought her to an abrupt halt. She was turned to face him, even shaken a little.

"You will tell me," he said softly, but his mouth and eyes were hard. She knew he wouldn't release her until she talked. She lowered her lashes over her eyes.

"He saw us in the grass that day of the picnic."

"Damn!" Caleb swore under his breath.

"He tried to make me behave as I did with you."

"And did you?"

She glared at him. Before he could move, one small brown fist drew back and landed smartly against his jaw. Whirling, she made her way toward the creek.

"I'm sorry," he yelped, hurrying after her. "I just meant—"

"Even a Comanche heathen understands what you meant," she snapped. "It may be the way of my people for a warrior to offer his wife to a guest, but my father, Ten Bears, never shared White Weasel, and I—I also will know only my husband."

"Wait a minute," Caleb said. "What was I to think? You offered yourself to me."

"Only if you would return me to Two Wolves." She whirled to face him. A prairie wind had sprung up and bellowed her skirts. Her rich golden brown hair feathered against her cheek and down her back. Her clear gaze never wavered as it met his. "That offer is still meant." She held his gaze, waiting for his answer.

Suddenly he wanted to reach for her, to taste again the sweetness of her mouth, to feel her slender body against his. As if she'd read his mind, she backed away, her eyes suddenly distrustful. Striving for control, Caleb took a step away from her and the moment passed.

"I can't take you to Two Wolves," he said quietly. "When I see him, I'm going to kill him." He turned back toward his horse.

"He may kill you first," she called. When he made no answer she ran after him. "Two Wolves is a brave warrior. His medicine is strong. You can't kill him."

Caleb stopped and jerked her toward him, shoving his face close to hers. Her hair blew around and between them like silken strands of prairie grass.

"I know Two Wolves very well," he said through clenched teeth. "I know how brave he is. The first raid he went on as a boy, he came to my parents' home. I saw him lift my baby sister's body; he bashed her head against a tree."

"No!" Jenny cried, placing her hands over her ears so she couldn't hear, but Caleb pried them away and went on talking.

"He took her scalp—and that of my father and mother. They hang on his scalp pole. They hang in the lodge you shared with him. You made love to him within sight of my mother's scalp. Don't tell me how brave Two Wolves is. Just know this. When I see him, I'll kill him." He released her hands and stood staring at her for a moment more.

"I came out here today because I think of you as a victim of the Comanche, just like my mother and sister. Now, tell me if you can go back to that murderin' coward."

"Yes," she hissed. "Because although my skin is white, my blood is Comanche. And I, too, have seen the dishonor of my enemies. They ride into our villages and kill our men and innocent children. They rape our women, and, when they are through, they tear their bellies open with their long knives. The Comanche are not the only savages here on the plains."

Her words were too honest, too pain-filled to be swept aside. He wanted to forget them, wanted only to remember his own pain, wanted to hold only the memory of his butchered family and his hate for the Comanche. But this slender girl with the clear, far-seeing eyes made him look at new truths he didn't want to see. Without another word he climbed into his saddle and rode away. He didn't look back, but he knew she was still standing there, watching him go, her glorious hair blowing about her face, the calico dress molded to her figure by the wind. She touched parts of him long buried, parts too battle-scarred and pain-riddled to be brought to life again. He set his spurs to his horse's flanks and galloped away over the prairie.

Jenny watched him go, wanting to call him back, wanting to tell him they could share their pain and take comfort in each other. At the same time she fervently prayed he would leave Millbrook and never return.

Wearily she returned to the soddy; when the Walshes returned, her hair was tidily braided and no trace of the hated tears remained.

Faye seemed in high spirits as they unpacked the picnic basket and settled the tired children in their beds.

"They've got the frame in place for the church and some of the walls up," she chattered happily. "Maudie St. John came to church today and stood up after hymn singing and declared that if Brother Nestor was going to raise money for the new church by having a dance, she was going to spend the whole night on her knees praying for a windstorm to come and carry the walls to the four corners."

"Why would she pray for that?" Jenny asked, perplexed.

"Why, she thinks the church ought'n to raise money for a new building with a dance."

"If she has that much power, why doesn't she just ask the Lord to give the money they need to finish the church?"

Faye laughed. "I swear, Jenny. Sometimes I think you make more sense than any of us." Frank Walsh paused in the doorway, then, seeing Jenny, walked back outside. Faye looked at Jenny's downcast face.

"Frank is troubled," Faye whispered. "Today, Brother Gilkenson talked to him about the preacher. Seems there's been some problems with the preacher and his daughters." Impulsively she took hold of Jenny's hand. "He's beginning to think he wronged you by not believing what you said about the preacher."

Jenny said nothing, but she wondered what would happen if Brother Nestor had attempted to molest one of Eldon Gilkenson's daughters. Would anyone dare doubt her word, or would they still believe the preacher?

In the days that followed, Jenny was too busy to ponder over Brother Nestor's credibility, Caleb Hunter's anger, or even the chance that Two Wolves would show up. The labor on the garden had come to fruitation as Brother Frank called it in his morning prayers. There had been no rain and the ground was hard and small cracks appeared. Frank fumed over his fields of corn and wheat. Water was hauled up from the creek for the vegetable garden, but even its plentiful supply seemed to be dwindling.

As soon as the vegetables were ready, Faye, Jenny, and even the children were busy harvesting and preserving the food, putting it out to dry or storing it in the dirt storm cellar Frank had built against prairie cyclones. They canned and dried and put up food in every shape and form. Cabbages and potatoes were stored on shelves in the underground storm cellar. Some of the heads of cabbage were kept back and chopped into fine strips for sauerkraut. This was pickled with vinegar and spices and stored in large clay pots. Inverted plates, weighted down with rocks, acted as lids. The crocks wouldn't be opened until winter, when the sauerkraut would be properly aged.

The cornstalks dried in the hot summer wind, which blew unceasingly. Faye fretted over the condition of the corn, for it would be their mainstay throughout the long, lean winter months. With ground corn they could make breads and pancakes or grits. In the end, it was the crop that would sustain life. The wheat was also a necessary ingredient to their meager food supplies. It could be boiled plain or baked into biscuits and flapjacks. But wheat was a more uncertain crop, more susceptible to the vagaries of the elements. Frank had planted it only in the hope of adding variety to his family's table and of bringing in a meager supply of money for things they couldn't grow on the homestead.

Now Jenny understood the depth of Frank's anger over the lost rows of peas she'd chopped down. To compensate she took the children out into the prairie in search of wild gooseberries, wild grapes, wild crab apples, and hazelnuts. Each time they managed to return with their gunnysacks filled with something. Once, along a line of bluffs, they even found some plums, which made Faye clap her hands and immediately set about making a plum pudding. That night at supper everyone seemed lighter hearted, almost festive. Even Frank smiled and praised the children. Then his fierce blue gaze turned to Jenny.

"You did a good job, girl," he said.

She flushed with pleasure. For a moment it didn't matter that he never called her by her name.

In the days that followed she redoubled her efforts, showing the children where to find pawpaws and globe apples. While they chattered and collected this new fruit, Jenny noticed Mullen plants growing nearby and picked some. She knew it was used by the medicine man in the winter. She also gathered horsemint and catnip for Faye to make teas.

"Jenny, you've got company," Faye called as they made their way back to the house.

She paused, thinking of Caleb Hunter. She glanced at her dirty dress and poked at her hair, which had fallen loose from its braid and was filled with grass seeds and cockleburrs.

"Come on, Jenny," Nathan said. "You got comp'ny."

Squinting her eyes against the sun, Hannah watched Jenny's attempts to tidy herself. "Jenny, have you got a beau?"

"What is a beau?" Jenny asked, puzzled, then memory of the word returned. "Don't answer, I know!" She picked up her gunnysack and continued toward the soddy.

"Well, do you?" Hannah insisted.

"No!" Jenny snapped. "How could I have out here? There's no one else around."

"Brother Nestor used to like you."

Jenny halted and stared at the little girl. "How do you know that?"

"He used to watch you when you worked. He had a funny look on his face . . . and I don't think he was thinking about his prayers then."

"I do not like Brother Nestor," Jenny snapped. "He's a bad man."

"That's what Mama told Daddy." Hannah walked along quietly. "Then there's Mr. Hunter."

"What about him?" Jenny refused to slow down or acknowledge her interest as other than the most casual.

"Every Sunday we go to church he takes off his hat to Mama and asks about you."

"I don't care," Jenny said, but inside she felt elated that he had inquired about her so often. His trip out to the soddy on Sunday hadn't been an accident.

By the time she got to the soddy, Jenny was fairly running, but when she saw the buggy and horse sitting in the yard, her heart slowed in disappointment.

"Jenny, Margaret Rudd has come to see you."

"Hello, ma'am," Jenny said, bobbing her head. She placed the sack near the door.

"Why, what have you found today?" Faye cried in anticipation. "Jenny has gathered many things for us from the prairie."

Margaret Rudd was studying the girl's face. "You're lucky to have Jenny, Faye," she observed. At her kind words Jenny glanced up, her expression brighter.

How beautiful she is, Margaret thought. No wonder Caleb Hunter keeps thinking about her. She could be the salvation of him yet. But what about her? Is she happy living here among her own kind? Caleb says she still wants to go back to Two Wolves. Silently she watched as the girl lifted the bag onto the fresh-scrubbed table and pulled out the bounty they'd gathered.

"Them's globe apples," Margaret said, nodding toward a small knotty-looking fruit. "It makes up into preserves, and you can always find them out on the prairie, even when you can't find other fruit."

"Oh, Jenny's very good at finding things on the prairie. She's gathered berries and nuts and wild grapes— and Margaret"—Faye placed a lean hand on Margaret's arm as if sharing a wonderful knowledge—"she even found some plums. Let me give you a jar to take home."

"I couldn't take your preserves."

"I insist," Faye said, bringing a small jar of her precious horde. She was inordinately pleased that she could offer something so fine to a neighbor. When the pleasantries were over concerning the gift, Margaret turned back to the wilted leaves on the table.

"That there's a Mullen plant," she said. "You can make it into a hard candy for the children so they won't get colds come winter. I'll give you the recipe, if you need it."

"I'd be much obliged," Faye said, pouring out a cup of tea for her visitor.

Margaret sat down and looked around the snug soddy approvingly. At last her gaze turned back to Jenny.

"How are you, child?"

"I'm well," Jenny replied blandly. "Thank you for sending out the dresses for me."

"I brought you another one today," Margaret said, holding out a folded bundle. "Go on. Take a look at it and see if you like it."

Tentatively Jenny shook out the bundle. The dress had been worn before, but was in good shape. Of a pale yellow muslin, someone had adorned the dress with fine embroidery around the square-cut neckline and down the front. The work reminded Jenny of the fine dresses White Weasel had made for her. Despite herself, she crumpled the dress to her chest and fought back the tears.

Margaret clucked her tongue with embarrassment and sympathy. "You can wear that dress to the dance next Saturday night," she said. "You folks are planning to come, aren't you?"

"Why, I don't know," Faye said. "Frank's been working so hard."

"Looks to me like you all have," Margaret observed. "It'll do you some good to come visit with folks. You and the baby can stay with my sister's family. Frank and Jenny and the kids can stay in the wagon."

"Oh, I don't know. Your sister has such a big family. I wouldn't want to put them out."

"You won't," Margaret said firmly. "We'll send Ozzie and the older children out to sleep on the back of your wagon with Frank."

"My, you have it all worked out," Faye said.

Margaret turned her gaze back to Jenny. "You'll be there, won't you, Jenny?"

Having recovered herself, Jenny glanced at Faye. "Of course she will," Faye said. "We'll all be there."

"Don't you have to ask Frank, first?" Jenny asked.

Faye grinned. "Sometimes, I get to make a decision," she said. "We'll be there, Miz Rudd. You thank your sister for her offer. We'll come to her house after the dance."

"Good." Margaret nodded and rose. "I'd best be on my way then." She looked at Jenny. "Why don't you wear your hair down, honey?" she said. "It's a mighty pretty color."

Jenny stood in the doorway watching the old woman climb into the buggy and pick up the rein. Her hands played with her hair. Maybe she would wear it down. Caleb had said she should. Would he be there at the dance? Was he the reason Margaret had driven all this way out here? Suddenly she knew Caleb had talked to Margaret. Between them they'd contrived a way to get Jenny and the Walshes into town.

Faye was nearly as excited as Jenny about attending the dance, so Frank could scarcely refuse to go. Although he'd planned to avoid Brother Nestor, his dance, and the controversy it had occasioned, the brightness of Faye's eyes reminded him of the first time he'd seen her at a dance and he agreed to go. He had little to give her, but he could give her this night.

The rest of the week was a flurry of washing and ironing every stitch of clothes they possessed, as well as their bedding and the bright patchwork quilts Faye's mother had given her. The bedding would be folded and stored in the back of the wagon. The children could sit on it during the ride to town, and that night, after the dance, beds would be made in the back of the wagons. Faye was determined that the other women would see what a fine housekeeper she was. By Saturday noon the level of excitement could barely be contained. Faye had baked a cake with the last of her supplies of flour and sugar. It sat clothed in boiled icing, and everyone's eyes went to it time and again as they hurried about. Pans of corn bread and fried salt pork were ready to go as well. They'd stop just before they got to town and eat something, so they wouldn't grow hungry during the dance. The cake, of course, would be taken to the dance and set on the table with the other desserts to be served later.

Jenny and Hannah hauled water for the bathtub, then slipped away to the creek to take a hurried cold-water bath themselves. Frank quit his work in the fields and came in to bathe behind his son and wife. With a fresh, stiffly starched shirt and sharply ironed work pants, he looked almost handsome, even to Jenny. When the children were all dressed, Faye and Jenny smiled at each other, then hurried to don their own dresses. Faye wore the pale cream, lace-trimmed dress she'd been married in. It hung on her now, for hard work and childbearing had left her nearly gaunt, but she tightened the silk belt at her waist and turned to fasten Jenny's dress.

"You look beautiful, Faye," Jenny said.

"Once I was," Faye said. "Once, I looked like you, with blooming cheeks and rounded arms. You're the beautiful one now, Jenny."

Jenny blushed and looked away. It had been a long time since she'd considered herself pretty. Now, even in the white man's dress, she sensed she looked better than she had in a long time. Her spirits lifted considerably and she reached for her hair to wind it into a braid.

"Don't do that," Faye said quickly. "Let me fix your hair."

Jenny hesitated, then acquiesced, sitting on the edge of the bed while Faye picked up the brush and went to work on the rich strands.

"Faye, let's go," Frank called impatiently.

"Just a minute. We're nearly ready," she called, her nimble fingers putting the last touch to Jenny's hair. "There, it's finished," she cried, putting aside the brush and stepping back. She held up the small looking glass she'd brought from the East. Jenny gazed into the mirror. The sides of her hair had been pulled up on top of her head and twisted into a smooth knot, held with a narrow yellow ribbon. The back of her hair flowed down her back in rippling waves. "Do you like it?" Faye asked.

Slowly Jenny nodded.

"Faye!" Frank bellowed.

"We're coming." Taking Jenny's hand, Faye threw open the door and walked outside the soddy.

Frank had already packed everything, including Samson, who was nestled in a bed of his mother's quilts. Seated on the wagon seat, Frank turned toward them impatiently and gaped. His gaze went from his wife to Jenny and back again. Wordlessly he got down from the wagon and held out his hand.

"You're beautiful," he said, and his gaze was nearly worshipful.

If Jenny had ever wondered about the feelings between these two very different people, she would wonder no more. The love on Frank's face transformed him—and suddenly Jenny understood what made Faye travel so far from her family to live here in a dirt soddy. She thought of her own life. Would she be able to make such an adjustment for the man she loved? It didn't matter, for Two Wolves was coming for her. He'd take her back to her people. Then the thought of Caleb Hunter erased all images of Two Wolves from her mind. She felt confused.

Faye and Frank had finished embracing, now they turned to Jenny.

"Oooh, Jenny's pretty," Nathan and Hannah cried from the wagon. Frank studied the girl and slowly nodded.

"You are pretty, girl," he said.

"My name is Jenny," she answered.

"You look mighty pretty, Jenny," he said, and held out his hand. "Do you need some help up on the wagon?" Faye squeezed his arm. With an unaccustomed grin, Frank swung Jenny onto the back of the wagon, then went back to help his wife up.

All the way into town they sat close together on the wagon seat, their voices low and intimate as they talked. A sense of well-being had settled over them all. Forgotten for the moment was the drought, crops, and every other hardship they coped with every day. Just outside of town, they stopped to eat the meager cold supper they'd brought.

Dusk was just falling as they pulled into town. Jenny couldn't help glancing around, looking for any sign of Caleb Hunter. Frank pulled the wagon straight through town to the other end. Jenny was surprised to see a half-finished building lighted with lanterns. In a few short weeks Brother Nestor had indeed accomplished a lot in gathering funds for a church and finding volunteers to raise the roof and walls. Frank pulled the wagon into place beside the other wagons and climbed down to unhitch the mules and stake them out beyond the town buildings. Other men and women milled around outside the half-finished church. Jenny and Faye climbed down from the wagon and gathered up the baby and Marybeth.

"Stay nearby, you hear?" Faye called to Hannah and Nathan as they hurried off to join the other children.

"Howdy," Viola Porter called, and hurried over to talk to Faye. "You might want to keep an eye out for that Maudie St. John," she confided. "Some folks are startin' to say she's tetched in the head."

"Why's that?" Faye asked, taking down her basket of food for the dance.

"Why, she's been going around town all week sayin' how she's been prayin' for the good Lord to blow the building down rather than have money raised for it with a dance."

Jenny glanced at the sky. "Doesn't look like much of a chance of that," she observed.

Viola laughed, a hearty sound, and ushered Marybeth into the half-finished building after her mother. "My, my. Is that a real cake?" she asked when Faye set out her dishes. She glanced at Jenny. "You're lookin' right pretty tonight. You don't look at all like you lived with the Injuns."

"Jenny's a pretty girl," Faye was quick to say, smiling to soften any hurt Viola's thoughtless remark might have caused.

"We got us a schoolteacher now, did you hear?" Viola said, nodding toward a strange young woman who'd entered the building with some other women. "Her name's Rachel Tyler. Ain't she just the prettiest thing you ever seen? We're going to have us a real school in the old soddy we're using as a church. In the meantime, she's going to teach there through the week and Brother Nestor'll use it on Sundays."

"Is Brother Nestor going to stay with us?" Faye asked. Jenny's expression had grown dark just at the mention of his name.

"I reckon he is, despite what that horrid Stella Gilkenson tried to say about him. He's such a God-fearing man—and so lovin' to his congregation—she just misunderstood what the good preacher was about."

Faye exchanged a glance with Jenny and said nothing, but Jenny could see she looked troubled. The other women joined them, all of them talking. Rachel Tyler was introduced all around and welcomed to the community. As the women drifted into talk about their gardens and the weather, Jenny wandered to the unfinished door and peered outside. Caleb Hunter had just ridden up and was tying off his horse. Jenny felt her heart leap.

"Who is that man?" a voice said from behind her, and Jenny turned to find Rachel Tyler peering over her shoulder. The schoolteacher was taller than Jenny by nearly a head and her pale hair was piled high on her head, which gave her an added sense of height. Her blue eyes were bright with interest as she gazed over Jenny's shoulder.

"Do you mean Brother Nestor?" Jenny asked innocently.

"Goodness no," Rachel replied. "I mean that tall, good-looking man over there." She pointed toward Caleb Hunter.

Jenny could find no excuse not to tell the schoolteacher his name, but it was no sooner out of her mouth than Rachel swept past her and crossed the trampled grass to Caleb. She paused, said something to him, then laughed gaily. Jenny saw Caleb push his hat back from his face. His mouth twisted in a grin and laughter, deep and masculine, mingled with Rachel's.

Jenny felt anger course through her. He'd never laughed around her. He'd always been stern and commanding.

Seizing the opportunity, Rachel struck up a conversation with him, tilting her head prettily as she gazed up at him. Jenny thought she looked rather silly—since she stood nearly as tall as Caleb!

"Rachel," one of the ladies near the food table called. "Why, my goodness. Where could she have gone?"

"I'll get her," Jenny called, with a little too much enthusiasm, and hurried toward the couple.

Caleb's head was tilted closer to Rachel's as he listened to something she said. The corners of his eyes were crinkled, as if he were ready to laugh at anything she said, amusing or not.

"Miz Walters wants you, Rachel," Jenny said loudly at her elbow. Annoyed, the schoolteacher glanced over her shoulder.

"Don't you know it's rude to interrupt when adults are talking," she reprimanded.

"Miz Walters wants you," Jenny repeated, staring back at the beautiful young woman.

"Tell her I'll be there directly," Rachel said, with some exasperation.

"She wants you now," Jenny insisted.

Angry color crept up Rachel's pale cheeks and her eyes flickered with annoyance. "Oh, all right. I'll come now," she said. "You will be staying for the dancing, won't you, Caleb?" she asked prettily.

"Yes, ma'am. I will," he said.

"I hope you'll ask me to dance." Rachel touched his sleeve lightly.

"Miz Walters's waiting!" Jenny snapped.

"I'd be honored if you'd dance with me later, Miss Tyler," Caleb said.

With a final smile, Rachel Tyler made her way across the yard to the church building. Her walk was such that her bustle swished back and forth just the tiniest bit. Jenny glanced at Caleb and saw he was watching that bustle for all he was worth.

" 'I hope you'll ask me to dance,' " Jenny mimicked, twitching her own slim, unbustled hips.

Caleb glanced at her, a gleam of amusement in his eyes. "Why, yes, ma'am. I intended to do just that. I hope you'll do me the honor of a dance."

"I don't dance!" Jenny snapped, and flounced away.

She heard Caleb's laughter behind her and wanted to fly back and box his ears. How dare he? He finally was laughing at something she'd said, but it wasn't the same as the laughter he'd shared with Rachel Tyler.

Why should she care anyway? she thought. But as she sat on a makeshift bench and watched the fiddlers set up and people gather for the dance, she acknowledged she did care what Caleb Hunter thought. She cared far more than she wanted to.

Chapter 12

No MATTER HOW harsh life was for the prairie settlers, they threw themselves wholeheartedly into
the dance. Brother Nestor appeared and thanked everyone for their contributions and for coming. With the
money from the dance, he was certain they now had
enough to finish the church. He prayed, calling the
blessings of a higher power down on their dance, then
ended it abruptly and called to the fiddler to begin.
From her seat on the sidelines, Jenny was able to ob-
serve everything. The men and women danced reels and
rollicking square dances and sedate waltzes. When they
were hot and thirsty, they stopped for chilled horsemint
tea and rested around the sidelines or outdoors, where
the men lit pipes and talked crops.

When the fiddlers stopped for a rest, Maudie St. John
appeared and walked to the middle of the dance floor.
She was a gray-haired woman, nearly sixty years old,
yet her body had remained blessedly free of arthritis
and other disabling afflictions, so she still moved with
the vigor of a much younger woman. Now she waited
until everyone in the building had ceased talking and
was watching her.

"The Lord says, 'Whatsoever you ask it shall be, do we ask in faith, believing.' "

"Go home, Maudie," Viola yelled at her.

"Shame on you, Viola Porter," Maudie declared. "You should go down on your knees right now and ask the Lord to forgive all of you for this sacrilege. Have a care, for I'm going home now—and I'll be on my knees asking the Lord to blow this building down."

She stomped out of the building and disappeared into the night.

"Strike up the fiddles, boys," Brother Nestor called, and the dancing began again.

Margaret Rudd walked by where Jenny sat holding Samson. Marybeth clung to her skirt with one hand and sucked on the thumb of the other.

"What are you doing here, child?" Margaret declared. "You should be out with the young folks, dancing and visiting."

"I don't mind watching the babies," Jenny said quickly. "Faye's enjoying herself so much—and besides, I don't dance."

"You don't dance? Why, everybody dances. Here, you let me have that baby." The big woman took Samson from Jenny's arms. "Caleb," she called, and Jenny felt the blood suffuse her cheeks. "Caleb, come show Jenny how to dance."

Caleb approached, his eyes nearly dark when he looked at Jenny. "I don't know much about dancing myself," he said.

"That's not what you said to Rachel Tyler!" Jenny snapped.

Caleb's grin was enigmatic. Margaret looked from

one to the other, noting Jenny's heightened color and Caleb's grin. She'd seldom seen the boy grin!

"You two can learn together," Margaret said firmly, and pushed Jenny toward him. "Go, dance and be like other young folks."

Tentatively Jenny held out her hand as she'd seen the other women do. Caleb took one hand in his and placed his arm around her waist. Jenny's cheeks grew hot. It wasn't as if he hadn't touched her in such a way before, but this time there were the standards of others guiding them, limiting what they could say and do. Caleb took a step out onto the floor, dragging Jenny with him. She lurched and stepped on his polished boot.

"Pardon me," she stuttered, and stepped on his foot again.

He kept moving her around the floor, simply by his sheer strength, and finally she began to feel the rhythm of the steps and how they fit to the music and how his body moved to it. She began to relax and she moved better. They became one person, gliding smoothly to a waltz, acquainting themselves to the flow of the other's body.

"You wore your hair down," he murmured. "You look beautiful, Jenny."

At first she'd fixed her gaze on his shoulder, but now she felt the heat of his gaze and slowly raised her eyes to his. Suddenly the voices and movements in the room lost all meaning to her. She was locked in a special world where only Caleb and she moved, a world that was warm and inviting and dangerous and exciting. The music stopped, and they halted, his arm still about her, their eyes still locked.

"Oh, there you are, Caleb. I've saved you this dance," a voice called gaily. Caleb and Jenny broke apart, shaking themselves as if waking from a long dream.

"Thank you for the dance, Jenny," he said, and his voice sounded shaky. "You dance well."

"I'd better get back to the children. They—they may need me," she stammered.

"My goodness, Mr. Hunter. You seem to have made a conquest. I do believe that little girl fancies you," Rachel said in a voice loud enough for Jenny and several others to hear. Jenny's lips set tightly.

"What are you looking so angry about?" Margaret asked when she saw Jenny's face. "Did you and Caleb have a spat?"

Jenny shook her head.

"Where is he then?" Margaret demanded gently, then she caught sight of the couples on the dance floor. "Oh, I see the new schoolteacher's got her eyes set on him, too."

"I don't have my eyes set on Caleb," Jenny snapped. "And I don't fancy him. He's—he's the man who captured me and brought me here. How could I fancy him?"

"He didn't capture you, child," Margaret said gently. "He rescued you and you just don't recognize it yet."

"You don't understand," Jenny said dully. "I didn't want to be rescued, to be brought back to this—a world that's alien to me, a world that can't accept me as I truly am."

Margaret was unaccustomedly silent for a moment,

then she nodded her head. "It's done now, Jenny. You have to make the best of it."

"No. I'm going back as soon as—"

"As soon as what?"

"Never mind."

"Tell me, child," she insisted.

"A storm's comin'," someone yelled. A man ran into the building, pushing his way through the dancers. "It looks bad. Get to safety. A storm's comin'. Run!"

People stared at him without comprehension for a moment; some even wondered if this man had been sent by Maudie St. John to break up their dance. The fiddlers had quit playing; in the prevailing silence, the high whine of wind reached them.

"Cyclone!" a woman screamed.

The walls of the unfinished building began to shake. Women screamed, children cried, and men cursed. Faye made her way to Jenny and Margaret, snatching up Samson.

"Come with me," Margaret called. "Ozzie's got some room in his storm cellar." She began pushing her way toward the door.

"Jenny, bring Marybeth," Faye cried. When they reached the door, she looked around wildly for her husband. "Hannah, Nathan," she screamed, but the wind tore the words from her mouth and flung them away unheard.

Marybeth was screaming, and Jenny picked her up in her arms. The little girl was getting bigger and was harder to carry. Now, in her terror, she fought against Jenny, sobbing for her mother. In the pushing crowd, Jenny lost sight of Margaret and Faye.

Outside the church, people were running helter-skelter. The men were trying to secure their horses, so they wouldn't panic and run away, others were ushering their families under their wagon or beds or toward the soddy that had served as a church till now. Bits of twigs and debris were airborne, striking any unsuspecting soul across the face. Jenny tried to shield Marybeth's face and look around for Faye.

"Faye!" she screamed. "Miss Rudd."

"Jenny!" Caleb was beside her, taking a sobbing Marybeth into his own arms. "Where are the rest?"

"Margaret was taking them to her sister's storm cellar. I don't know which way to go."

"Too far away now," Caleb shouted above the whine of the wind. "Head for the soddy."

He put an arm around her, guiding her, protecting her as best he could with his own big body. They reached the soddy and stumbled inside. Other people were already huddled there. Caleb closed the door and pulled a table in front to insure it stayed closed, then he sat on the floor beside Jenny.

No one spoke. Several pairs of eyes stared fearfully at the bucking door. It seemed the wind intended to come right inside. For hours they crouched, waiting for the wind to subside. Then came the sound of fury against the roof and door.

"It's hailing," someone cried, and crept over to peer out the crack in the door. When it stopped the silence was more ominous than the noise had been. Wide-eyed, the people in the soddy looked at one another.

"Reckon it's over?" Zeph Norris asked.

"Let's open the door and take a look," Caleb said, getting to his feet.

"Be careful," Jenny cried, standing up. Marybeth whimpered and clung to her.

The table was moved, and the door swung open.

"God Almighty. Them ice balls are pert' near as big as an apple!" one of the men cried.

"Don't take the Lord's name in vain!" Viola Porter snapped from her corner.

"Here comes the rain, boys," said someone, and the men hustled back into the soddy just as the roar of water hit them. It pounded against the earth like a punishment, blotting out sight and sound of anything but its own wrath.

Caleb settled down beside Jenny and Marybeth and took the little girl on his lap. "Look what fell outside," he said. "Hold out your hand." Marybeth stopped whimpering long enough to do as he bid, and he placed a large ball of ice in her hand. She giggled and dropped it, wiping her hand against her dress. Caleb picked it up and showed it to Jenny.

"This is going to carry on for most of the night," he said, nodding at the roof. "We might as well try to get some sleep."

Jenny thought she'd never be able to sleep, but the steady drumming of the rain soon made her drowsy. Marybeth was already sound asleep, her head in Jenny's lap.

"Lean against me, if you want to sleep," Caleb offered.

"No, thank you," Jenny said stiffly, but before long

she was nodding, her head rolling on her slender neck like that of a drunken man.

Caleb reached for her, pulling her against him and settling her head against his shoulder. He felt so warm and steady, she couldn't force herself to push away from him. Gratefully she closed her eyes.

Caleb watched the brush of silken lashes against her flushed cheeks and tightened his arm around her shoulders. What was there about this girl that made him feel so protective? he wondered. Her loosened, silken hair brushed against his cheek; he drew in the clean scent of it. She'd used some kind of herb to perfume it.

What had been her Comanche name? Wild Sage. It suited her. She was wild and tough, like the prairie plants that grew despite the sun and rain, like the flowers that showed the world their beauty in the fertile greenness of spring, a beauty that hid the tenacious strength and will to survive.

Somehow he wanted to help her, so she would never be hurt again, and in that desire to protect, he recognized the beginnings of an emotion he'd not felt since the year he was fifteen, before the Comanche attacked their spread and killed his family. He could love this small, stubborn girl, he acknowledged, and felt a shudder of fear, for he could never stand the pain of losing someone again. Easier to push her away, easier not to love, not to need. But he didn't push her away. He sat holding her throughout the night—and knew when the sun rose again, he would leave and never look back at her. Her medicine was stronger than his.

* * *

By morning the rain had stopped. The sun rose with the same intensity it had shown before. Those who'd spent an uneasy night in the storm cellars and soddies crept out of their muddy holes to stare about at the town. Millbrook's lone tree had been uprooted. It sprawled in its death throes, no longer able to offer that bit of shade to those who'd gratefully sought it. The buildings were undamaged, all save the new church. Its walls were gone, its frame collapsed in on itself. The boards that once had made up the walls were scattered across the prairie. People stood staring at the mangled remains of what had been their proud dream, shaking their heads in disbelief.

Faye and Margaret Rudd came from the direction of the McKinsey house. Hannah and Nathan were beside their mother. When Faye saw Jenny and Marybeth she ran forward.

"Oh, my baby," she cried, grabbing Marybeth and hugging her tightly. With tearful eyes she looked at Jenny. "I was so afraid you'd been caught in the storm. I tried to come back and look for you, but Margaret wouldn't let me. She said she saw you go toward the soddy with Caleb."

"Yes, I didn't know where you'd gone, so he helped Marybeth and me." Jenny didn't tell Faye how she'd huddled against Caleb through the night, warm and safe in his arms. Now she blushed and glanced at Caleb, who stood with the other men discussing the damage to the church. He sensed her gaze and looked up. Their eyes held for a moment.

"Didn't I warn you?" Maudie St. John called from her buggy. Her bonnet was askew and her mule was winded as if she'd ridden hard to get back to town. "Didn't I tell you I was going to pray for just this to happen?"

"Shame on you, Maudie St. John," Viola cried, "that you'd even want to harm God's tabernacle!"

"It's wasn't a tabernacle. It was a dance hall," Maudie cried.

The argument between the two women was joined by others—and might have gotten out of hand completely, except that a farm wagon was driven headlong into town, bouncing over the rough street before being brought to a stop before the assembled crowd.

"Where is he?" Eldon Gilkenson shouted. "Where is that godless, no good preacher?"

"What's wrong, Eldon?" one of the men called.

"My daughter—Stella—didn't come home last night."

"She may have been caught in the storm. Many a family stayed in storm cellars last night."

"Not mine!" Eldon bellowed. "I smelled the storm in the air, so I took 'em home early. Stella was with the rest of the girls, but this morning she was gone. She sneaked out sometime during the night."

"What makes you think she's with Brother Nestor?" Viola asked curiously.

"'Cause I watched her and him a makin' eyes at each other," the distraught man snapped. "I kept thinkin' he'd do the right thing by her, him treatin' her so special-like, but I don't like this one bit."

"We ain't seen the preacher around here since—well, since the dance started last night come to think of it," Shep Wilson said.

"I saw him ridin' out of town afore the storm hit," someone called. "I reckon he was headed out to your place, Eldon."

"He never showed up," Eldon growled.

"Brother Nestor's got the money for the church," Minnie Campbell said. She looked around at the faces turned toward her. "Well, he said it'd be safer for him to take care of it."

Uneasily the people looked at one another. They didn't want to admit the thoughts going through their heads. Their church was destroyed and the preacher and their money were missing, not to mention one of the parishioner's young daughters.

Eldon Gilkenson stood up in his wagon. "Well, he took your money as well as my daughter. Are you going to help me track him down now?"

"I reckon we better have a look," Ozzie McKinsey agreed. "I'll help you look for him, Eldon."

"Me, too," said Shep Wilson.

Other men offered their help. Jenny glanced at Caleb. He'd also agreed to look for the missing preacher.

Frank Walsh came over to Faye and Jenny. "Can you stay here in town for the day, Mother, while I help them search for the preacher?"

"We'll stay with Miz Rudd and her sister," Faye said. "You go on."

The women watched as the men saddled up their mules and horses and followed Eldon out of town. Jenny watched until she could no longer see the men. Caleb hadn't turned around to look at her. Slowly she made her way to the cleared wooden platform that had once been the church. The boards laid across sawhorses that had served as a table had been blown over. The tablecloths lay out on the prairie. Broken dishes lay on the ground. Nathan sat nearby weeping.

"What's wrong, Nathan?" Jenny asked, sitting down beside the little boy. "Were you frightened by the storm? It's all over now."

"I wasn't 'fraid of no storm," he scoffed.

"Then why are you cryin' like a baby?" Hannah demanded. She'd been standing to one side watching her brother. Now, at her challenge, he raised his head and glared at her.

"I didn't get any of Mama's cake," he wailed. "She promised I could have the biggest piece and the storm blowed it away."

Jenny couldn't repress a chuckle. Nathan glared at her.

"I'm sorry I laughed," she said quickly. She drew her brows down in a frown and pressed her fingers against her lips to control her giggles. "I was just so relieved you weren't hurt or anything. We'll save up flour and sugar and make another cake. And this one we'll have just at home and we won't share it with anyone."

"Promise?"

"I promise," Jenny said. "Come on now, we're going to spend the day with the McKinseys. I'll bet there'll be some special things to eat and you can play with their kids."

Nathan got up and wiped his face, already eager for what the day would bring. Jenny watched him and Hannah as they ran to join the other children. How quickly they forgot their hurts, she thought. It got harder when you got older and the hurts were deeper.

The day seemed to drag for Jenny. Although she stayed busy caring for the younger children and listening to the ladies' idle gossip and speculation about Stella Gilkenson, Jenny felt restless. She wished she could have ridden off across the prairie the way the men had. She missed that old freedom she'd once had in the Comanche camp.

The sun reached its zenith, burning down on the beaten earth, quickly drying the precious moisture received from the storm. The women fed the children and settled the younger ones down for a nap. Jenny was left to watch over the children while the women visited the general store and a few of the other shops in the small town. She didn't mind not going herself, for she had no money and had no need to buy white man's things.

Late in the afternoon, the men rode back into town, their expressions glum, their mouths tight-lipped. They led a horse, over which was placed a man's body. The women watched silently. Eldon Gilkenson brought up the rear, his face grim-set, his daughter's body at rest in the back of his wagon. Without acknowledging anyone, even the men who'd helped him, he continued on through town and headed out toward his homestead.

"What happened?" Margaret Rudd asked when the men had dismounted and stood around as if uncertain of what to do.

"They got caught in the storm," Shep Wilson said. "They took shelter under a tree. Lightening struck 'em."

"Did you find any of the church money?"

"No, their belongings were blown to the four winds."

"Just like Maudie prayed for," Viola said.

"It's like a sign from God," Maudie said in awe.

She'd remained silent throughout the day, but she'd kept watch with the other women.

Now they heard her words and nodded in sad agreement. Brother Nestor had made them believe they could have a church out here on the prairie, that they could begin to build a community not unlike the ones they'd left behind when they came here. Now the dream was gone. They'd been too proud of their new church; they hadn't listened to the truth about Brother Nestor before it was too late.

Silently Frank motioned to Faye to get the children and prepare for the ride home, then he went off to hitch his mules back to the wagon. Jenny looked around the circle of men for a now familiar face, but Caleb Hunter was not among them. She longed to ask about him, but held back. Stoically she helped gather their damp belongings and settle the children back on the wagon.

"Where's Caleb Hunter?" she heard Margaret Rudd demand, and couldn't stop herself from pausing to listen to the answer.

"After we found the bodies, he lit out," Ozzie told his sister-in-law. "Said he had some unfinished business to attend to."

Jenny's heart gave a lurch. He was going to look for Two Wolves again. She knew it as surely as if he'd told her himself. How could he hold her so tenderly one moment and set out to murder the one man who could rescue her the next? Did he have so low a regard for her?

Wordlessly she climbed into the Walsh wagon to begin the long ride back to the little soddy. Everyone was silent, lost in their own thoughts. The smaller children slept, worn out by the excitement. The visit, which had started with such high festivities, had ended in death and betrayal. The town of Millbrook wouldn't have a church—and now it didn't have a preacher.

Furthermore, Frank had spent all day worrying about the damage the storm might have brought to his own homestead. His face wore the same stern look it normally did, but this time, it didn't intimidate Jenny so much. She was beginning to understand the weight of his responsibility and how much the rest of them depended on him for their very lives.

The damage from the storm was evident before they reached the soddy. Driving past the fields of wheat, Faye cried out and Frank's face became more sternly set. The hail had flattened the stalks; the rain had buried them in mud; the hot sun had baked the mud into a hard shell.

"Oh, Frank!" Faye sobbed.

He didn't pause, whipping the mules on to cross the creek and bring the wagon to a stop before the soddy. Everyone sat where they were, staring at the cornfields beyond, the stalks that had stood like dry, rattling sentinels were now broken and bent. Faye lowered her face into her hands and began to weep quietly. Nathan and Hannah heard their mother and sat up, their eyes still sleepy and vague.

"What's wrong?" Hannah asked, creeping closer to Jenny.

"Nothing is wrong," Jenny said. "We're home again . . . and Mama's glad to see her soddy still standing."

"Yes," Faye said, digging out a handkerchief and wiping at her eyes. "That's just it. The Lord didn't take our home and we should count our blessings over that."

With a determined air, she climbed down out of the wagon and smiled back up at her husband. "It's good to be back home, Frank," she said gently.

Frank Walsh looked at his wife, who still wore her wedding dress. Now it was torn and dirty and her hair was uncurled from its customary knot and hung down past her ear on one side. But her pale, thin face was shining with love and loyalty and determination. Jenny heard a sound, hoarse and rending in its pain. Frank Walsh jumped down from the wagon and gathered Faye into his arms. His dark head was bowed on her thin shoulder and his body jerked. Jenny knew he wept and she turned away. Comanche men did not weep, even at death. To do so was considered a weakness. Yet Frank Walsh was not a weak man.

Finally he raised his head from his wife's shoulder and wiped at his cheeks with the palm of his hand. Then taking Faye's face in his big hands, he gently kissed her as if he cherished her above all things. They embraced again, and over Frank's shoulder, Jenny could see that Faye's face was radiant.

Did love do that to a woman? she wondered. Did it give her strength and lend this special light that glowed from within? White Weasel had looked like that when she was with Ten Bears, but Jenny could never feel that way about Two Wolves. Why hadn't she? He was a mighty warrior, a leader, a war chief. She should have felt pride in him and the same loyalty and generosity as Faye and White Weasel.

The answer came to her unbidden. Frank needed Faye as Ten Bears had White Weasel, but Two Wolves needed no one. He was untouched by those around him, going his own way, taking what he wanted. He hadn't needed Wild Sage, he'd merely wanted her as his wife for the prestige she brought as Ten Bears's daughter. He had considered her worthy of his own sense of greatness.

She thought of Caleb Hunter and her responses to him. She sensed his vulnerabilities. He was a strong man, but like Frank Walsh, his needs were great—and hidden from the eyes that didn't want to see them. When he took a woman as his own, she would be as cherished as Faye and White Weasel. These startling new thoughts spiraled through Jenny's mind, bringing a better understanding of herself as a woman.

Faye led Frank into the soddy; Jenny unhitched the mules and fed them, tending to the other animals, too. Silently Hannah and Nathan helped her. It was dusk by the time they finished and turned toward the soddy. Jenny paused, looking at the low, ugly building. Faye had lit a lamp and was busy at the stove, making a hot supper for them. Jenny could see the flickering shadows as she moved about. The lamp lent a rich, welcoming glow to the windows and doors.

"Come on, Jenny," Nathan said, tugging at her hand. "Let's go in. Supper's ready."

Jenny let him lead her toward the soddy—and for the first time since she'd arrived here, she felt at home.

Chapter 13

JENNY SAT IN the shade of the soddy plaiting seven strands of prairie grass into a long rope. When she had enough, she would sew the braids together to form a straw hat with a wide enough brim to shade her face while she worked in the fields. She glanced out over the flat prairie. She was at rest now, but she'd spent long hours with Frank, gleaning the cornstalks for any ears that might be saved. The stalks themselves would be used as feed for the hog until butchering time. They were stacked beneath a makeshift shed Frank had devised of stunted, twisted tree trunks as corner posts and overlapping boards for the roof. Nothing must be wasted. This was an attitude Jenny understood, for thus did the Comanche women manage to survive and feed and clothe their families.

Frank had already ploughed up the wheat field and replanted it. They'd done without butter for weeks now, ever since the dance, so Frank could take it into town and sell it in exchange for seeds and the things they needed.

Faye had been busy sewing, making dresses for Hannah and Marybeth from old sheets redyed with goldenrod and walnut bark into soft yellows and dark brown. Faye had also set about making trousers for Frank from old grain sacks. In the evening, after supper dishes were washed and put away on the shelves Frank had built her, she sat before the fire, her thin fingers fairly flying over her needles as she knitted woolen mittens and mufflers while she talked of having their own sheep next year. At first Frank was glum and unresponsive, but Faye's constant optimism began to have its effect on him, so now he sat figuring what it would cost to keep a small bunch of sheep.

Faye fussed over the coats sent from back East several years before. The children had outgrown them.

"Marybeth can wear Nathan's old coat. It's a little big on her, but she can grow into it. Nathan can wear Hannah's, and I can cut my coat down to fit Hannah." She glanced at Jenny. "I don't know what I'm going to do about you. Maybe Frank has an extra coat you can borrow."

"I will make my coat from animal skins," Jenny said.

"You know how?" Faye exclaimed.

Solemnly Jenny nodded. "I can make moccasins, too."

After that admission, Faye set about with new vigor, checking all the furs they'd acquired from Frank's hunting. Some of them were poorly tanned and not nearly as supple as those finished by the Comanche women, but they would do. Jenny showed Faye how to cut and punch holes with awls, so the pieces could be sewn together. Frank sat at the table reading his Bible, now and then glancing up at them. Jenny was afraid he might berate her for reverting to her heathen ways, but he said nothing. At last, he seemed to understand that some of the Indian ways were valuable in surviving the unforgiving prairie.

In return, Faye showed Jenny how to make soap, using fat she'd saved and the lye she'd made herself from the ashes of their fires. After the grease had been boiled and reboiled in lye, Jenny carefully ladled the foul-smelling mixture into a wooden tub to cool. Later, Faye stored the soft mixture in a small wooden barrel. Afterward, Jenny rested on the creek bank and thought of how the Comanche women gathered a special plant whose split stalks yielded a sweet-smelling soap. The white women did things in a strange manner.

Invariably at idle moments, Jenny's thoughts turned to Caleb Hunter. He'd not returned since the dance. Now that they no longer traveled to town on Sunday for church meetings, she had no way of asking about him. Then one day Margaret Rudd's buggy could be seen across the creek and she rode into the yard.

"I thought I'd drive out and tell you folks. We got us another preacher!" she shouted even before stepping down. Faye glanced at Jenny.

"I'm not certain we're up to another Brother Nestor," she murmured.

"Bosh, Faye! That's not like you to judge all by the misbehavings of one. This man and his family are in need of a place to stay. We gave him the old soddy we were using as a church."

"What about your school?" Faye exclaimed.

"The men went out and found what they could of the church walls and carried it back. We decided maybe we should build a school first. The new preacher will use it on Sundays as a church."

"How exciting!" Faye cried. "A real school. I expect Miss Tyler's excited about it."

"Hmm, I expect she will be if she gets her mind set on it. Right now, the kids are helping their folks on their homesteads, so this ain't no time for school. Miss Tyler's kept herself busy looking over the eligible bachelors."

Jenny heard her words and flushed to the roots of her hair as she thought about Caleb Hunter. Was that why he hadn't been out to see her? Had he returned to town and set about wooing Rachel Tyler? She longed to ask Margaret but didn't. Instead, she sat listening, hoping she'd hear something about him, but nothing was said. Finally Margaret lumbered back toward the carriage; Jenny could contain herself no longer. Running over as if to assist their visitor into her carriage, she took a deep breath.

"How's Caleb been?" she asked timidly.

Margaret paused in the act of hoisting herself into the carriage and stared at Jenny. "I thought you knew, child," she said. "He's left these parts. Someone said he headed back to Texas."

"Oh!" Jenny stepped back, her disappointment worse than she'd expected. Then she remembered something else. "Did he say why he was going back to Texas? I mean . . . was he looking for anyone in particular?"

"I don't know, child," Margaret said, heaving herself up on the seat and taking up the reins. "I'm afraid he may have gone back to killin' Comanche. I don't know what he'll do when the last one's dead. Who will he hate then?" She slapped the reins against the back of her horse, and the carriage rolled out of the yard.

"Good-bye," Faye called from the door of the soddy. "We'll be to church come Sunday." Margaret's hand fluttered in a farewell.

The following Sunday morning, Frank hitched the mule to the farm wagon, and they all piled in to make the long trek into town. No one wondered aloud what the new preacher would be like, but the thoughts of each were on this new man of God. Would he prove to have feet of clay as Brother Nestor had?

For all his charisma, Brother Nestor had never truly possessed the qualities of a dedicated minister. Now Rev. John Crane stood outdoors welcoming his congregation. His wife, dressed in the same sturdy calico dress as the other women, stood at his side, her stern, tight-lipped demeanor a further reassurance of the good reverend's devotion to all that was right. His children stood, wide-eyed, staring at the other children in the gathering crowd, and when one of the girls stuck a tongue out at the minister's children, the youngest daughter didn't hesitate to retaliate in kind. The result was a smiling truce between the two girls, and after church they became fast friends.

If Brother Nestor had held them in awe with his sermons of brimstone and damnation, Reverend Crane gave them a gentler sermon and a loving God. Folks left feeling that God was indeed watching over them and found their industry good. Jenny had listened closely to what the timid minister had said about the white man's God and felt much eased by this new vision.

Once again picnic baskets were brought out, a make-shift table covered with starched white cloths, and special dishes shared with neighbors. The betrayal by Brother Nestor hadn't daunted their faith in God and themselves. Jenny sat on a blanket spread on the grass and watched the laughing faces, weathered by sun and aged by hard work, and she saw the basic goodness of these people. They were not so different than the women of her village had been. Why then was there this hatred of Indians and their ways? Was it born of fear, as hers had been?

"Hello. Your name is Jenny, isn't it?" A clear, bright voice broke through Jenny's reverie. She looked up to see Rachel Tyler standing over her. The schoolteacher wore a lovely yellow silk dress trimmed with brown velvet ribbons and a drape of bustle in a yellow-and-brown-striped silk. Her pale blond hair was pulled high in an intricate swirl of curls and ringlets. Jenny looked down at her own home-dyed dress of yellow and recognized the difference. Rachel looked like a beautiful butterfly, while Jenny looked like a grubby caterpillar.

"You can talk, as I remember," Rachel said crisply, her lovely brows dipping over her blue eyes.

"Yes, my name is Jenny."

"I thought so," Rachel replied. "You *are* that little Indian girl that Caleb Hunter brought in back last spring."

"I'm not an Indian!" Jenny snapped, then stopped, confused that she would deny what she'd so vehemently claimed before.

"No, you were just raised among them," Rachel replied, and fidgeted for a moment. "Have you heard anything from Mr. Hunter recently?"

Jenny met the woman's gaze and a gleam of humor lit her gray eyes. Rachel saw it and jerked her head up sharply, like a nervous filly that's not been well broken. Jenny felt elation at Rachel's question. If Caleb had made no effort to say good-bye to Jenny, then neither had he the beautiful schoolmistress. Getting to her feet and drawing herself up, Jenny faced Rachel.

"Haven't you heard?" she asked lightly. "Caleb's gone back to Texas."

Rachel's cheeks stained red at Jenny's supercilious tone and at the information. "Has he gone back for good?"

"That's what he said," Jenny replied, without revealing the words had been said to Margaret Rudd and not to her.

"Then you aren't likely to see him, either, are you?" Rachel asked sweetly.

Jenny arched an eyebrow and studied a broken thumbnail. "I expect I will, in time," she answered smugly.

Rachel stared at her a moment more, then unfurled a tiny silk parasol that matched her dress and marched away. Jenny watched her go—and suddenly she longed for silk dresses and matching parasols. Then ashamed of her conversion to anything of the white world, she turned away and slumped on the pallet.

The ride home was uneventful. Jenny stared out over the brown prairie, wondering where Caleb Hunter was and if he gave any thought to her, or even to Rachel Tyler. Summer was passing quickly; soon it would be fall. Faye had said they would butcher the hog and Frank would go hunting with the other men for elk and

deer and even buffalo. Somehow none of it seemed real
to Jenny. She couldn't imagine herself spending the
winter in the dirt soddy. She thought of the winter just
past. White Weasel and Ten Bears had been alive then.
She felt sad, abandoned, alone again. The friendship
she'd formed with the Walsh family faded in her melan-
cholia.

The wagon rolled down the bank and through the
creek, then something out in the prairie, through which
they'd just traveled, gained Jenny's attention. Startled
she looked around. Had it been a deer coming to the
creek to drink? Uneasily she studied the trail behind
them.

The wagon crossed to the other side of the bank and
into the yard. Faye climbed down from the wagon.
"Come on, Hannah, Nathan. I need you to fetch some
water."

Some dread was building in Jenny. "I'll fetch it for
you," she said, jumping out of the wagon and taking the
buckets from their hands. She couldn't repress a glance
around. "Go on inside," she said, without looking at the
children. "It'll be dark soon." Her voice sounded hol-
low and far away even to her own ears. The children
sensed her tension.

"What's the matter, Jenny? Why are you lookin' out
there like that?"

"Nothing. Don't be silly," Jenny replied, giving him
a shove. "Go on inside like I told you." When he only
stared at her, she swatted his backside. "Go on. Git!"

The children hurried inside the door, then turned to
stare after Jenny. "Mama," Nathan called over his
shoulder. "Something's wrong with Jenny."

"What?" Faye said, coming from the stove to peer over their shoulders. "Why, there's nothing wrong with her. She's just going down to the creek to get water." She turned back to the black kettle in which she was heating beans for their supper.

Jenny stopped along the creek bed and looked around. A cry of a coyote came from nearby, making her jump and drop the bucket. Crouching to pick it up, she stared at the thick grass. Was someone hiding there? Had Two Wolves come? The thought should have given her joy, but suddenly she was thinking of all the things Caleb had told her about the homesteaders Two Wolves and his warriors had killed.

What if Two Wolves was out there, just waiting for the right moment to attack the Walshes? Frank wouldn't have a chance against them. He had a lone rifle, which he was careless about loading. She didn't want them to die.

She thought of Marybeth's sweet chubby body pressed against hers in sleep. Marybeth trusted Jenny to take care of her, and what of Samson, only a few months old and already smiling and gurgling and trying to sit up? He was a happy baby, never giving any trouble. Would his sweet round head be bashed against a tree like Caleb's sister?

The cry of the coyote came again, a call that demanded an answer. She couldn't. Her mouth was dry, yet every moment she remained here, undecided, Two Wolves's warriors might be circling the soddy, ready to attack. Numbly she knelt to dip the buckets into the creek when she heard the swish of dried grass and looked up. Two Wolves stood staring down at her, his face twisted into a bitter mask of hatred.

"I have come for you," he said in the Comanche language.

Slowly Jenny stood up, her eyes wide and dark with fear. "I'm ready to go with you," she answered in kind.

Two Wolves nodded as if he'd known she would answer thus and looked toward the soddy. "How many white eyes are there?"

"No, Two Wolves! You must not hurt them. They have been my friends." She was unaware she'd reverted back to the tongue of the white men. Two Wolves's face grimaced in anger.

"They were your captors," he replied. "They will be punished."

"No! I can't let you hurt them. They're innocent, good-hearted people. They fed me and clothed me and had me in their home."

Silently Two Wolves studied her. "You have changed."

"I am the same," she answered, with greater calmness than she felt. "A Comanche does not murder those who have offered their hospitality."

"No true Comanche would take the hospitality of the white eyes," Two Wolves retorted.

Jenny saw her pleas were to no avail. Whirling she ran back up the bank. Two Wolves came after her. She could see Frank Walsh just walking to the soddy.

"Indians!" she screamed, running toward him.

Frank stopped as if stunned, then, seeing the fear on her face and the pursuing Indian, he ran toward the soddy. Jenny's cry had already drawn Faye to the door;

now, seeing what was transpiring, she pulled Nathan and Hannah away from the door, shoving them down on the floor while she ran to the pegs that held Frank's rifle.

Jenny saw all this as if looking at a still picture captured by one of the photographers traveling the prairies. She saw, and reached for the soddy and the warmth and safety it had offered her, but she felt Two Wolves's hands gripping her hair and jerking her backward. She stumbled and fell, but she could still see the soddy and the frightened people within. Frank had reached the doorway; Faye was there with his rifle. He raised it and aimed at Two Wolves. The bullet went wide, but was warning enough to the war chief. He let out a bloodcurdling scream and turned toward the soddy. Other warriors had crept up from the creek banks, gliding out of the grass, as insidious and deadly as a winter fog.

"Get inside!" Jenny screamed, and Frank ran into the soddy and began swinging the heavy wooden door closed. Faye caught it, trying to hold it open.

"No, Frank. Jenny's out there," she cried.

"It's too late for her," Frank shouted, and knocked her aside. The soddy door closed just as Two Wolves's tomahawk hit the thick wood.

"Jenny! Jenny!" Faye screamed from inside.

Tears formed in Jenny's eyes at the sound of her friend's cries. Faye had cared about her and wanted to save her. Now came the tinkle of broken glass as Frank knocked out a pane of one of Faye's windows and took aim. He fired, and one warrior cried out and fell to the ground.

Two Wolves looked about him, then ran to Jenny,

and, grabbing hold of her long, unbound hair, dragged her back toward the creek bank. When they were out of range of Frank's bullets, he released her, shoving her back on the ground and pinning her there with one knee in her stomach. Jenny fought against the pain as he yanked her hair, bringing her face closer to his.

"You are no Comanche," he snarled. "You have become a white eyes."

"Please, Two Wolves," she pleaded. "I will return with you. I want to. I've waited for you to come for me. But please don't raise your weapons against these people. You bring dishonor to me, if you do."

"Bah! You bring dishonor to yourself," he spat out, and released her hair. Jenny curled on the ground while he conversed with his warriors. One of them was badly wounded and they blamed Jenny for warning the white eyes. After some time, Two Wolves came back to Jenny, gripping her hair and yanking her up.

"You will go to the soddy and tell the white eyes that we will not harm them. We wish only for food and supplies so we may travel back to the Comancheria."

"They have no extra food, Two Wolves," she said. "The drought has taken most of their crops."

"You will go tell them what I said," he ordered. "Tell the white man to put down his gun and we will not harm them. We do not kill women and children. You will tell him this."

Jenny looked into his face and saw the same hard madness Two Wolves always wore when he went on a raid or returned from one with fresh scalps. She had little doubt he would kill her if she refused his request.

Shakily she got to her feet and climbed the bank. When she drew closer to the soddy, the door was thrown open.

"Jenny. Thank God," Faye called. "Thank God you're all right."

They drew her into the warmth and smallness of the soddy, into the sturdy homeyness of it. She caught familiar whiffs of cooking and people she'd come to appreciate and even love. Now, Faye threw her arms around Jenny while Hannah and Nathan clung to her skirt.

"We thought they killed you," Hannah bawled. Even Marybeth had to be held and reassured. When the children quieted down, Jenny turned back to Faye and Frank.

"They sent me here to give you a message," she said wearily. She looked at their dear faces and couldn't go on. Then she raised her head and set her mind as she had when she was a Comanche. "They say they wish only to have food—some flour and cornmeal, some meat—and they'll leave. They say they won't harm you."

Frank cursed and turned away from her. Faye was silent, studying Jenny's face. "They're going to kill us, aren't they?" she asked softly.

Jenny couldn't maintain her rigid control. Her eyes filled with tears and she turned toward Frank. "They won't if you give up your gun as they've asked. Give me a little food and I'll take it to them."

"No!"

"I must, Faye. I'm the reason they're here. I was pledged to become Two Wolves's wife the day Caleb

and the soldiers attacked our village. He has come to retrieve what belongs to him."

"You can't go," Faye said. "We won't let you.
Frank?"

"If I don't go back out there, they won't leave.
They'll keep fighting until they wear you down. You're
one man, they are many. They wouldn't stop until we
were all dead. If I go with them, Two Wolves will make
war on you through the night, but by dawn he will want
to be gone, to cover his tracks. He wants to return to the
Comancheria with me at his side. He wants to show the
other warriors that he is invincible against the whites."

"Do you want to go?" Faye asked.

"I must. I have no choice." Jenny looked at Faye; the
two women embraced. "I'm sorry to have brought this
on you." Jenny wept.

"We won't let you go. We'll fight, won't we, Frank?"
Faye pulled away and looked at her husband. Frank's
eyes were sad but resigned.

"Give her some flour and grits," Frank said, "and a
jar of that plum preserve you're so proud about."

"No!" Faye cried out.

"Faye, listen," Jenny said in a low voice. "It has to
be this way. Get the food before they get tired of waiting and attack."

Sobbing quietly, Faye filled a gunnysack with some
food supplies and handed them to Jenny. Her eyes were
dark in her pale, thin face. "This isn't right," she whispered. "We shouldn't let this happen to you."

"You can't stop it," Jenny said. "Good-bye, Faye."
Jenny turned toward the door. Frank waited until she
was ready, his hand on the wooden bolt.

"I never told you, gi—Jenny, how sorry I was that day I used the whip on you."

Jenny touched his arm in silent forgiveness and nodded. Frank drew back the bolt, and Jenny hurried out.

"Jenny!" Faye called at the last minute, as if beseeching her to stay.

Jenny closed her heart to the sound and walked across the clearing and down to the creek. Two Wolves was crouched by the water. Now he stood up and strode over to her, snatching the sack from her hands.

"What is this?" he demanded.

"They've sent us food," she answered.

"They were supposed to come out to us."

"They won't do that, Two Wolves. They've heard how you've killed other settlers and their families."

His chest swelled with pride at her words. "The name of Two Wolves is to be feared among the white eyes," he bragged, looking around at his warriors. Now, with a wild yell, he leapt up the creek bank and disappeared through the grass. Some of the warriors followed him. Jenny was pushed down on the ground and made to wait for nearly an hour without knowing what was to happen. She thought about Faye and Frank in the little soddy. How much worse the tension must be for them, wondering if they could save the lives of their children.

Then, as the night deepened and the shadows grew black, unlit by the moon, Two Wolves and his men returned. Jenny could tell by the sounds coming from the grass that they'd moved their horses nearer. Her heart leapt with hope. Perhaps they would simply ride away and leave the Walshes unharmed. But Two Wolves and his warriors made themselves comfortable in the grass and fell asleep. For long hours, Jenny strained to see through the dark, wondering if she might get away, yet knowing there was no place for her to go. Besides, if she escaped, Two Wolves would just take out his anger on the inhabitants of the soddy.

At last, light streaked the eastern horizon. Two Wolves and his warriors rose, drank from the creek, and mounted their horses. Glaring down at her, Two Wolves held out his hand. Jenny took hold of it and was pulled up on the back of his horse. With a silent nod to his warriors they galloped up the creek bank and into the clearing, their voices raised in shrill cries. Round and round the soddy they galloped, shooting into the windows. Torches were thrown up on the soddy roof, but the sod roof wouldn't burn. Two Wolves seemed to delight in riding close to the front of the soddy, taunting the man within. Jenny realized he carried her on the back of his horse as a shield for himself.

She heard the scream of the mules and the squeal of a pig. Chickens clucked in terror and ran every which way to avoid the galloping hooves. The warriors rode through the garden, squashing melons and pumpkins under their mounts' hooves. The supply of cornstalks was torched, then blazed up in a quick-burning inferno. The washtub and heavy black kettles where they did the wash were overturned and every manner of order wrought into disorder. Jenny clung to Two Wolves's waist and thought of all the hard work it would take to right everything.

Frank's rifle had made an impact on the warriors. Two of them were badly wounded now, barely able to stay on their horses. Two Wolves waved to his men and they pulled away from the soddy, galloping out on the prairie as if the wind itself drew them. Jenny offered no resistance. Once again life had changed for her; she must begin to adjust if she were to survive.

All day they traveled westward, pushing across the prairie. At night, Two Wolves and his warriors made camp. No fires were lighted. They chewed on dried jerky. Going through the gunnysack Jenny had brought, Two Wolves discovered the jar of preserves and held it up to the fading light.

"Open it and eat some," he ordered Jenny.

Silently she did as he bid, taking a portion of the preserves onto her finger and popping it into her mouth. Two Wolves studied her face for a while, then snatched the jar and sat down to finish it himself. Jenny heartily wished it might give him a bellyache, but he seemed untouched by its richness. Instead, he rolled into his robe and soon was snoring. All around, his warriors were doing the same. No offer of a warm robe had been made to Jenny. She shivered in the evening chill, then crept close to Two Wolves's back and tried to sleep. It was long in coming—and the last thought she had was for Caleb Hunter. Where was he now? she wondered.

Chapter 14

CALEB HUNTER RODE into the clearing and studied the soddy. The doors were closed and the place looked abandoned. A fire smoldered in what once had been an open barn. To one side lay the carcasses of mules and a pig. Chickens pecked nervously at the ground and fluttered away at the slightest movement. The homestead was ominously silent.

Drawing his gun, Caleb dismounted and ran toward the soddy door. Whatever had caused this mayhem without, the soddy was still the safest place if the attackers were still around. He hit the door with a sharp thud, pushing against it, but it held, locked from within. His heart beat heavily. He tapped against the heavy wood with the butt of his gun.

"Is anyone there?"

"Who's there?" a man's voice demanded from inside. If he'd wanted to he could have fired right through the door and killed Caleb, but he hadn't. Caleb recognized Frank Walsh's voice and identified himself. The door swung inward.

"Are you folks all right?" Caleb asked, looking around.

A boy and girl he'd seen with Jenny stood wide-eyed and silent. The little girl he'd carried to safety in the storm clung to her mother's skirts sobbing. Impatiently Faye Walsh picked her up.

"We're fine, Caleb, but they took Jenny."

"They took her against her will?"

Mutely Faye nodded. "She did it to save us. The Indians' leader tried to trick us into coming out, but she warned us they'd kill us. Then she took a little bit of food and went with them. She didn't want to go. I could tell."

"How long ago did they leave?"

"Sunrise."

Caleb swore. The sun was already riding high. "You didn't happen to see the way they went?"

"East," Frank said.

Caleb thought and shook his head. "They weren't headed east, that's for sure. They must have doubled back and headed west. Now that they have Jenny, they're going to head for the Comancheria as fast as they can."

"Where are you going?" Frank asked, following Caleb outside the soddy.

Faye came out, too, looking around fearfully. "Are you sure they've left?"

"Yes, ma'am. Like I said, now that they've got Jenny, they won't take a chance of getting caught around here." He crossed to his horse and pack mule and began shifting his supplies.

"I'm heading out after him," he said to Frank Walsh. "You take my mule and ride back to Millbrook. Tell them what happened—and wait until they form a posse, then bring them dead west, you understand?"

"Yes, but how do you know—?"

"I know," Caleb said, tightening his cinch. "I've been hunting Comanche a long time. Hurry now.

"Ma'am, you and your children stay locked in the soddy until someone comes out here to stay with you."

"All—all right," Faye said. "Frank, be careful."

"I will. You take the rifle."

"No, the kids and I will be just fine. You'll need it, especially if you go with the posse."

"Get going, Walsh," Caleb said, and raised his hat to Faye. "You'll be safe enough, ma'am. Just do like I said."

"Be careful. Try to bring her back alive."

"I will."

Caleb dug his spurs into his horse, and it sprinted away. He was hard put not to keep it at that pace for the rest of the day, but he knew better. He slowed the horse to a reasonable gait and set about studying the terrain, looking for any sign of Comanche. When darkness stopped him, he still hadn't picked up their trail. He forced himself to rest. He'd need his strength when he caught up with Two Wolves.

They'd been riding for two days now, a forced march without hot food or proper rest. Now they came over a rise and saw a cattle spread below. The house was a soddy much like the Walshes', but corrals had been built around it and cattle grazed in the distance. Two Wolves and his braves conferred out of earshot of Jenny, then, having agreed on a course of action, settled down to wait for darkness. Jenny's stomach quivered with anxiety. Below she heard a voice calling to someone and thought of Faye and her family at twilight as they finished their chores and gathered for supper.

She couldn't sit by while Two Wolves and his warriors prepared to attack these people. More blood would be shed. Needless blood. She shifted, and instantly, Two Wolves was beside her, his knife raised.

"You will not warn the white eyes," he warned, the Comanche words heavy and guttural.

"I wasn't going to," she lied. "But Two Wolves, why do we wait here in the dark like coyotes skulking toward a kill? These people have done nothing to us. Let us go now to the Comancheria and join our people."

Two Wolves's tone was derisive as he answered her. "We will not return to the Comancheria empty-handed. We will take many horses and scalps of the white men."

"These are not warriors we face," Jenny said desperately. "They are a family, a mother and her children."

"A man with a rifle and a hunger for Indian land," Two Wolves answered. "See how he has fenced off parts of the prairie! Does he ask us if we wish this? He is our enemy; we will take his horses and his scalp and those of his woman and children. All white eyes must die."

"No!" Jenny cried, and tried to stand, but he grabbed hold of her arm, yanking her down beside him. His grip bit into her arms, making her wince and cry out.

"Silence!" he hissed, pushing her down on the ground. His face was an ugly mask of hatred. Fearfully she struggled against him and saw the impatience mirrored in his eyes before he raised his fist and struck her. Blackness closed over her.

When she regained consciousness, she was alone. All around her was silence, but from the valley came an orange-red glow of light. Feeling sick from the blow to her head, she crawled through the grass until she could peer down on the scene below. The flames of the burning sheds and barns cast flickering, menacing shadows over all. Two Wolves and his mounted warriors had already gathered the horses from the corrals and were now engaged in further acts of destruction against the homestead. Two Wolves himself sat on his white stallion directly in line with the soddy door. Big Elk waited beside him. Two Wolves raised his hand; all around him the warriors fell silent. Jenny leaned forward, straining to hear what he said.

"You have no more bullets," he called. "You cannot kill us, and we have no wish to kill you. We only wanted your horses and some food. Send out your woman and children. We will not harm them. They may go free."

All was silent from within the soddy. Jenny leaned forward, her body tense, her throat muscles locked in some silent scream of denial. Don't believe him, she wanted to cry, but the words wouldn't come—and even as she tried to cry a warning, the soddy door opened and a man stepped out on the porch, his hands held above his head. Behind him came his wife and three small children. At once Two Wolves's warriors sprang into action. Now the sound came from Jenny's throat, high-pitched and tearing in its anguish, but it was swallowed up in the terrible, triumphant shrieks of Two

Wolves and his men. Like hounds of the devil they converged on the trembling family.

Their weapons held high, they slashed at the man and his wife, cutting them to shreds. The man stumbled into the yard as if trying to lead them away from his family. His wife had turned back toward her children, striving in her last moments of life to protect them. Shots rang out, thudding against the soddy wall. A small girl, the age of Marybeth, fell to the ground, sprawling in the abandonment of a child asleep. The older boy pushed at his brother, urging him to run. The bullets caught both children, so they stumbled and fell. Instantly warriors dismounted and began scalping the victims. A child screamed. Jenny wasn't sure which one, but a warrior, known once as Gentle Calf, raised the butt of his rifle and brought it down on the child's head. With a cry of triumph, he bent over the still body, then rose, gripping his bloody trophy.

Sickened, Jenny turned away. She could watch no more. Bile rose in her throat and she lay weeping for the mother and children below. At last, she lay empty of tears and feelings, her body exhausted, her mind numb. These were the fine deeds of Two Wolves and his warriors. This was the man she'd been willing to give herself to. Now the thought of him touching her was repulsive, so she gagged and knelt huddled over, her body jerking and heaving, though nothing came to relieve her misery. At last, her body stilled and she glanced at the scene below. The first rays of sun were painting the landscape in sepia tones. The soddy windows shone flickering orange from the fire inside. Two Wolves's warriors were done with their looting and destruction. Now they'd remounted and were prepared to ride away. Jenny saw Two Wolves turn his horse toward the rise where she waited.

"No!" she cried, and leaping to her feet sped away in the opposite direction.

She could hear the pounding hooves as he pursued her. She redoubled her efforts, gasping in air as she raced across the prairie. But he was there, his white pony knocking her flat. She sprawled facedown in the grass, smelling the goodness of the earth, and prayed for Two Wolves to deliver her a death blow.

She felt his rough touch at her neck as he grasped her hair and jerked her up and onto his horse.

"Leave me!" she pleaded.

"You belong to the Comanche," he grunted, and kicked his horse into a gallop after his men. Behind them they left death, sprawling and obscene, awesome in its ungodliness.

Caleb Hunter came upon the homestead late the third day out. Topping the rise, he drew his mount to a halt and stared down at the devastation. His stomach roiled at the sight; memories—sickening and as real as yesterday—clutched at him. He'd lost valuable time finding Two Wolves's trail. Since finding it, he'd pushed his horse and himself almost beyond endurance. He figured the posse couldn't be far behind. Two Wolves hadn't taken time to rest or build a campfire to mark his trail. He'd moved fast, traveled hard, not even stopping to raid until now. The renegade Indian must have considered himself well beyond any danger of pursuit.

Slowly Caleb rode into the yard and counted the bodies of the children. Deliberately he stared at the bloodied heads, waiting for the familiar rage and hatred to build. For years he'd carried it within himself, poisoned himself with it, prayed to have it leave him, but now he welcomed the fury and wrath that calmed his shaking and sharpened his vision.

Automatically he looked for clues to tell him something about the raiders, looked for signs they might have left behind in their careless need for blood and vengeance. He studied the hoofprints that circled the half-burned soddy, found the prints of Two Wolves pursuing and those of a small woman in Indian moccasins fleeing before this carnage.

Caleb studied the trampled grass where Jenny had struggled against Two Wolves, pleading for him to leave her behind. His eyes narrowed as he pictured what had happened. She wouldn't have wanted to be with this man who wrought terror and murder. He thought of the gentleness she'd shown the little girl the night of the storm, the concern on her face when she spoke of Faye and the others, and he remembered the heat of her body against his, the passionate sweetness revealed in her kisses.

He could have taken her by the creek that day and later as they lay hidden in the prairie grass, could have known her passion then, but had backed away, somehow afraid of giving any woman a hold on him, especially one who'd lived among the Comanche. Yet now he saw in the crushed grass the symbol of all that Jenny was, proud and intuitive in her giving of herself, open and resilient. She'd survived more ably than most because of those qualities.

He thought of the light in her gray eyes, those eyes that had claimed his attention from the first moment he'd captured her at the Comanche village. Uttering a trail of profanity, he rose and swung into his saddle. His horse whinnied a protest, reminding Caleb he'd earned the right to a rest and food and water, but Caleb booted his belly; the valiant animal pushed off across the prairie, away from all those animal comforts.

Wearily Jenny sat on a log and stared into the flames of their campfire. Since the raid on the homestead and the capture of horses and scalps, Two Wolves and his men were less wary, as if certain they'd left all danger behind them. Late in this fifth day, they'd even taken time out to hunt and set up a camp along a stream. Jenny had been cuffed about the head and put to work cooking the game. Rabbits and prairie hens sizzled on makeshift spits over the open flames. Carefully she turned them, not wishing to burn them and thus bring Two Wolves's wrath down on her again.

Absently she rubbed at her wrists, still sore and bruised from the tight rawhide ties he used on her as they traveled. The skin around one eye was purple and swollen and the corner of her lower lip cruelly cut and dark with dried blood. Two Wolves's fists were swift and merciless in exacting punishment. She'd finally learned it was best not to defy him. Still, she remained watchful. The time might come when he and his men were careless and she could creep away.

Two Wolves kicked the log where she sat, and Jenny

jumped, automatically raising her arms to protect her face. With a grunt and an impatient gesture, the war chief indicated she was to serve him some meat, even though it was not yet cooked through. Without protest, Jenny removed the spit from the fire and held it for him to slice away the back haunch of a rabbit. Immediately he raised the bloody meat to his mouth and wolfed down a bite. His eyes gleamed as he watched her replace the spit over the fire. Jenny refused to meet his gaze. Once, she would have done so, would have challenged him for his arrogance, but now she recognized she was at his mercy, of which he had little. Despite her resolve not to show emotion, she shivered and heard Two Wolves's snicker.

She was afraid of him, afraid he'd claim her as his woman, and he sensed her reluctance. Now, like an Indian dog playing with its quarry, he left her guessing when he might make such a claim. Jenny couldn't help glancing at him and shuddering at the cruel, thin mouth slick with grease and the blood of the half-cooked rabbit. Quickly she turned away; his sneer turned to laughter, a hard, unmelodious sound that carried no resemblance to humor or joy.

"Soon we will be back on the Comancheria," he said, sitting on the ground across from her and tossing the bone into the fire. With the back of his hand he wiped at his mouth and belched. "You will be Two Wolves's woman."

"Why do you want me as your woman?" she heard herself asking in a low voice. "My blood is not that of the Comanche. It is the blood of your enemy, the white man."

"Have you become a white eyes, Wild Sage?" he demanded.

She could not answer him. She thought of her parents and the Comanche village of her childhood. She'd known happiness and love there. But that Comanche village no longer existed. Ten Bears and White Weasel were gone from her. She thought of Faye and Frank and their children, of Margaret Rudd and Caleb Hunter, and her cheeks grew hot.

"Have you become a white eyes?" Two Wolves demanded, leaping up to tower over her.

"I do not know," she whispered. "I didn't want to be part of the killing you and your warriors did at that homestead. Now I want to go somewhere and live in peace . . . forget the smell of blood in my nostrils."

"Bah! There is no such place for the Comanche," Two Wolves scoffed. "Always we have fought against our enemies, the Cheyenne, the Apache, and now the white eyes. The Comanche warrior does not seek peace like old women weeping over their campfires. We are men, warriors of Ishatai and Quannah. We will once again win his protection by fighting and killing all white eyes until they are gone from our land."

"Don't you understand, Two Wolves? This will never happen. There are too many white eyes. We must learn to live with them in peace or we Comanche will all die."

His fierce, hard gaze fixed on her; with a quick movement he pushed her backward, so she fell over the log and landed heavily on the ground. Two Wolves crouched over her.

"You are not Comanche. You are white eyes. You are an enemy."

"Then let me go, Two Wolves," she pleaded. "If you have no use for me, let me go back to the white world."

"I have a use for you," he said, and smiled down at her. "This man called The Hunter—"

"Caleb?"

"This is what the white eyes call him." Two Wolves nodded. "He follows us."

Jenny started and looked around as if to penetrate the dark shadows and thus catch a glimpse of Caleb.

"He follows us for you," Two Wolves said. "You have become his woman."

"I am no man's woman," Jenny said, suddenly fearful for Caleb. Two Wolves would set a trap for him. He would allow no man to take what was once his—and Jenny had been promised in marriage.

"We will set a trap for him," Two Wolves said slowly. "We will capture him and watch him as he dies slowly."

"You have no need of vengeance against him, Two Wolves. He helped me, took me to the Walshes."

"He kidnapped Two Wolves's woman, and for this, he will pay."

Jenny studied his face. "This has nothing to do with me," she whispered. "You wish to kill him because you fear him."

Two Wolves's fist was swift. It landed against her jaw, bringing an explosion of pain. Jenny fell back against the ground and curled into a ball. She made no outcry. To do so would only bring more retribution.

Two Wolves crouched over her a moment longer, then rose and stalked away.

Jenny waited until she was sure he was well away, then slowly rose and reseated herself on the log. The rabbits were roasted a golden brown now. Carefully, for her hands trembled, she removed them from the fire and set them to one side, then sat staring into the flames. Her jaw ached as if it had been broken, but she made no move to bathe it. The ache in her heart was much worse. Caleb Hunter was coming for her . . . and Two Wolves would kill him. So be it, she whispered fiercely. Why should she care? But she did care. She cared for the white eyes more than she did her own people. Eyes brilliant with unshed tears, she tried to pray for Caleb Hunter and the Comanche, and for herself, but she was no longer sure to which God she must pray.

Chapter 15

CALEB SHIFTED SLIGHTLY, so the rocky gravel no longer bit into his hip, and refocused his attention to the valley below. He was close enough to Two Wolves's camp to smell the ashes of their fire. The flames had died down to gleaming coals, barely lighting the mounds of warriors as they lay sleeping. Caleb strained, trying to pick out the slighter form of a woman, but the darkness defeated him. He wasn't in the mood to be thwarted. He'd pushed long and hard to catch up with Two Wolves and his band. Now, once and for all, he meant to exact the final vengeance against the man who'd killed his family, but he didn't want Jenny to be hurt. He'd have to rescue her from the camp before fighting started.

Impatiently he glanced back the way he'd come. The possee was back there, scant miles away. He'd left a sign for them, which surely they would have found by now. If they pushed, they'd be here by dawn. Caleb had to believe they would be. The time had come for him to make his move, to creep down this rocky embankment and release Jenny. Taking a last cautious look at the sleeping Indian camp, he crawled forward on his elbows

261

and belly, pausing every now and then to be sure he hadn't wakened anyone. When he reached the edge of the flat valley where they camped, he got to his feet and stood crouching, taking in the sleeping forms. At last he found her, huddled against a log, her knees drawn up to her chest, a thin blanket clutched about herself against the night chill. Automatically his eyes searched for and found the long, hulking form of Two Wolves. He slept closer to the fire, his face turned away from Jenny.

Stealthily Caleb crept around the camp. A warrior moved restlessly and mumbled in his dreams. Caleb froze and waited long, interminable minutes until the warrior settled down again, then slowly he lowered himself behind the log where Jenny slept. So far, so good! Reaching over the log, he clamped one hand over her mouth. At once, she went rigid, her hands going up to tear at his. Quickly he brought his face close to her ear.

"It's Caleb," he whispered, and felt her body go limp. Casting a quick glance at the still forms by the fire, he motioned her over the log.

Silently she slid over and settled near him, her body fitting easily between the log and him. He felt her softness and warmth, caught a whiff of spice and sage that was so much a part of her scent, longed to wrap his arms around her and just hold her, but their position was too dangerous.

His gaze sought hers in the flickering light and he placed a finger against his lips, signifying silence. Her breath was warm against his cheek as she nodded in understanding. Cautiously he turned away from her and crawled toward some bushes. She waited until he was out of sight, then followed, staying low on her belly, as he had done. When they had reached cover, he crouched, gave a final glance over his shoulder, and led the way back up the incline. They'd no sooner reached his horse when he heard a cry from the camp below.

"They've discovered I'm gone," Jenny whispered. "They'll find us."

Caleb leapt astride his horse and held out a hand for her. "Come on!"

"We'll never be able to outrun them riding double."

"Come on! Time's wasting," he growled, and yanked her up behind him. "Hang on," he admonished, and set his heels to his horse's flanks.

Jenny wrapped her arms around his hard middle and rested her head against his back. She could feel the ripple of muscles of the mount as he strove to do his master's bidding, but the animal was tired. Now and then he faltered, then regained his footing and pressed on. Jenny could hear the shrieks of Two Wolves and his men, the pounding of their ponies' hooves as they gave chase. Caleb turned toward the prairie, racing through the flat grassland. Two Wolves and his warriors followed.

Suddenly the sound of gunshots punctured the prairie stillness. Jenny strained to look back. Even from there she could recognize Frank Walsh and some of the other men from Millbrook as they bore down on Two Wolves's warriors. At once the renegades left off their pursuit of Caleb and Jenny and turned to meet this new challenge, all save one lone horseman. Two Wolves still pursued them.

"He's still coming after us," she shouted to Caleb, who whipped his pony's flanks and bent low over his foam-lathered neck. They rode till the sound of gunfire and fighting diminished, and still the steady drumming of Two Wolves's horse followed them. They came to a stream; Caleb reined the sorrel to a sliding halt.

"Get down," he shouted. "Hide yourself along the creek bank."

Automatically she did as she was told, sliding over the horse's rump. Caleb handed her a weapon. "Take this," he ordered. "Use it if you have to."

"Wait, Caleb. Let me help you." Her words were lost in the staccato of hoofbeats as he veered away from the creek and rode out to meet Two Wolves head-on.

Jenny crouched behind some low bushes, straining to see the two horsemen as they rode toward each other. Caleb had his rifle out, sighting along its barrel. His first shot missed Two Wolves, but the second spun him from his saddle. The war chief tumbled head over heels in the prairie grass and got to his feet, his knife at the ready, his feet spread, as he waited for Caleb's next attack.

"No, Caleb!" Jenny cried as he rode toward Two Wolves. Too many times she'd seen Two Wolves's prowess with a knife. No man had walked away from him in hand-to-hand combat.

Caleb didn't slow his horse as he neared the Comanche, simply flinging himself out of the saddle and into Two Wolves. The two figures rolled across the ground, carried by the momentum of Caleb's leap. When they finally rolled to a stop and sprang apart, Two Wolves still held his knife and Caleb crouched across from him, his own blade at the ready. The two men sprang at each other, their bodies straining in an effort to best each other. Two Wolves's arm swung up and arced down with deadly intent.

"Caleb!" Jenny screamed, and raced up from the creek bed. She couldn't wait in safety while he fought for their lives.

She sped across the ground, halting as she neared the entwined figures. With shaking hands she raised the pistol Caleb had given her, cocking the hammer. Her chest rose and fell with each gasp of breath. Caleb pushed away from Two Wolves and took a tottering step backward, then slowly collapsed, facedown. Instantly Two Wolves sprang forward, his knife held high to finish the kill and claim the most coveted scalp of all, that of The Hunter.

"Caleb!" Jenny cried, and Two Wolves straightened and stared at her.

Slowly she squeezed the trigger. Dirt kicked up near Two Wolves. Desperately she recocked the gun and aimed again. With a hideous shriek he sprang away from Caleb and ran toward her. The gun fell from Jenny's nerveless fingers and she knelt, her hands frantically brushing across the ground in search of the gun, her terror-filled gaze pinned on the approaching Comanche. She read death in Two Wolves's eyes, death for her and for Caleb. She gave up the search for the gun and took flight, beating her way through the grass and shrub, back toward the creek. At any moment she expected to feel the pain of his knife in her back.

Two Wolves shrieked again; Jenny glanced over her shoulder and came to a stop. At first she couldn't see the warrior. He seemed to have vanished from the face of the earth, but she heard his shout. Hesitantly she made her way back, guided by the sound of his voice.

"Wild Sage!" he shouted, and she paused, staring down into a bottomless black pit, an abandoned well left by some settler who'd given up and left this land.

Cautiously Jenny leaned over the black hole and recoiled, for Two Wolves's head was just below the edge; he clung desperately to the stubborn grass roots. Every movement he made sent clods of dirt and roots plummeting and he slid a little further down the well. His moccasined feet scrabbled at the sides, looking for a toehold that was not there. His black eyes held fear as they fastened on her face. The whites were yellowed and bloodshot.

"Wild Sage, bring my rawhide rope," he ordered. When she made no move to do as he bid, his lips drew back from his teeth in a feral snarl. "I will kill you if you do not do as I say."

Slowly Jenny shook her head, denying his request, and backed away from the well.

"Wild Sage!" Two Wolves called.

She heard him scrambling at the well's edge, tearing at the roots and grass until his head rose out of the dark pit. His hate-filled gaze settled on her as he clawed for a better hold. Her heart beat furiously. Her breath came in gasps as she waited for him to climb out of the well pit and exact his terrible revenge upon her and then Caleb. Jenny sobbed, shaking her head in denial, her terrified gaze pinned on Two Wolves. He would kill them both, slowly and tortuously, taking great pleasure in his revenge. She stumbled against something and almost fell to the ground. Her distraught gaze fell on the pistol she'd dropped earlier. Frantically she picked it up and aimed it at Two Wolves. His head and shoulders were above the lip of the well. He needed only one more heave upward and he would be free of the pit. His terrible eyes held triumph and rage as he glared at her, then he saw the gun. His gaze was startled, then held the sudden recognition that there was no help for him.

"Wild Sage!" he shouted hoarsely.

Swiftly she brought the pistol up and pulled the trigger. A circle of blood bloomed on his bare chest. For a moment he teetered on the edge of the pit, his glare that of a maddened beast, then slowly he let go of the grass roots. He wavered and slowly began to slide backward into the pit. Breathlessly Jenny watched until his head disappeared. She heard his cry of terror and defiance echoing for long, drawn-out moments, then silence.

With a last gulping cry, Jenny dropped the pistol and ran back to Caleb. He was crawling toward her, trying to regain his footing. One hand was clamped to his bleeding shoulder.

"Jenny," he called with relief, when he saw her, then he sank to his knees. "Where's Two Wolves?"

"Dead!" she said, running to kneel beside him. With gentle hands she tore away his shirt and studied the deep gash. "You are lucky," she said. "His knife has not brought death." Tearing away a piece of her gown, she brought a tuft of grass and placed it over the wound and tied it in place. "Come, we must go," she whispered. "Soon Big Elk and the others will come looking for Two Wolves. Hurry, I will help you onto your horse." She placed a shoulder beneath his arm and lent her weight, so he might stumble back to his horse.

"Can you ride?" she asked, and was relieved when he nodded.

She helped him into the saddle and climbed up behind him to hold him in place. Though they would make better time if she rode Two Wolves's horse, she had no wish to take anything that once had belonged to the murderous war chief. Half holding Caleb in the saddle she guided his horse north, away from the battle between Two Wolves's men and the posse.

She made no stop until darkness fell, when she knew they were well away from the place where Two Wolves had died, well away from the place where his warriors fought the white eyes. Taking shelter in the sandy bank of a creek, she built a fire, set a hook to catch fish, and made a comfortable bed of grass for Caleb. He lay watching her as she went about her chores. When she had a pot of coffee perked, she brought him a cup, resting his head against her shoulder, so he could drink. When he was finished and she lowered him back to his grass pallet, his hands reached for her, gathering her close. His eyes were dark with unnamed emotions that stirred her own and made her breathing shallow. She pulled away from him and crossed back to the fire. His gaze followed her, hot and troubling.

Silently she prepared a meal for them and banked the fire, then, still feeling the lick of his gaze, she rose and turned toward him. Few words had been exchanged between them as she'd tended him, redressing the wound, bringing him food, seeing to his comfort. Now, as she saw the raw hunger in his gaze, she knew it was echoed in her own heart.

Without words, she stripped away the calico dress,

hearing the raspy intake of his breath as she stood before him, her small, virginal breasts jutting proudly, her slender body outlined in the fire's glow. Turning away from him, she stepped into the cold running water of the stream and knelt and bathed herself, then rising, she sluiced the water from her limbs and breasts and walked back to him. He was waiting for her, his hands reaching for her, pulling her down to him, his mouth hungry and demanding as it claimed hers.

She melted against him, feeling the heat of his body dry her limbs. His chin was stubbled, brushing against her skin, leaving a trail of tingling sensation as he covered her face and throat with hot, passionate kisses. His head dipped, his stubble brushed against her swollen nipples, causing her to start, then his hot, moist mouth was there, suckling, his teeth gently nipping, awakening a fire within her. She moaned and moved against him and felt his big, warm hand brush down her body as if melding her to him. He rose on his elbow, grimaced at the pain of his injured shoulder, then ignored it as he swept her beneath his big body. His hands touched, explored, awakened, then in one impatient move, he threw aside his clothes. She could see the hard ridge of his arousal, felt its hot smoothness against her thigh, then he was gently spreading her legs, lowering himself over her, thrusting himself into the moist, womanly center of her. She felt his onslaught on her maidenhead and made no outcry. He was the one who groaned as if in pain and halted above her.

"I didn't know," he whispered in her ear. "I thought you belonged to Two Wolves."

"Not in this way," she answered and suddenly she

was pleased she'd come to him still intact, for white men placed much value in such innocence.

She wound her legs about his waist, urging him down to her again, and felt him begin the sweeping, thrusting rhythm she'd once glimpsed Ten Bears use with White Weasel. Then she'd been a child and had been only curious; now she was a woman, understanding these special movements, instinctively fitting her own rhythm to his, arching upward, so he might better reach that secret, hidden place within herself, which she so freely opened to him.

He moved against her, each stroke reaching for that core of her, reaching until she gasped with anticipation and her muscles quivered against him. One final thrust and he was there, his hot seed spewing against her. She cried out, her voice echoing across the quiet prairie, her legs and arms cradling this man who carried love and pain and passion within him, this man who fought for her, who followed Two Wolves to rescue her—and who finally had claimed her as his own. She gave herself willingly, and gloried in the giving. She was never meant to be Two Wolves's woman, she recognized now. She was Caleb's; she could never belong to another.

The hard edge of passion slowly ebbed from their bodies and they lay together, quiet now, until the need rose between them again. Jenny wrapped her arms and legs around Caleb, claiming him even in repose, and his big hand rested on her breast, cupping it, feeling the heat of her nipple against the palm of his hand.

At last, when the heat of their passion had been fed and they lay beneath a blanket, Caleb turned to her.

"Why were you never claimed by Two Wolves?" he

asked. "You wore a wedding dress when I captured you."

"We knew your soldiers were coming to the village," she replied, without rancor. "I thought I would never be a bride, and so I donned the dress as my burial dress."

Caleb's arms tightened around her. Far into the night they talked, revealing parts of themselves they'd never shown another before. Jenny had few memories of her early life with her white parents, but she told him of White Weasel's kindness and love and of how Ten Bears had rescued her from another tribe that had treated her cruelly. He listened, then marveled that she'd been able to survive, that all the goodness and fineness that was Jenny had survived her ordeals.

During the night, he took her again, slowly, sweetly—patiently waking the virginal body to the raptures of passion—and in the doing, finding new depths within himself.

When the sun rose over the prairie, Caleb was awake, staring at the golden, rippling water and wondering where he must go from here. He thought of Frank Walsh and the homestead he worked so hard. Could he, Caleb, stay in one place, tearing at the soil in the vain hope it would sustain life for himself and Jenny for another year? He glanced at her, sleeping beside him. Her face was smooth in repose, her dark lashes hiding the luminous gray eyes. She deserved better than he could give her, and though she might think she could forget the anger and hatred she'd once felt for him, the time would come when she remembered how he'd killed her adopted people and the hate would return. He couldn't bear to see her eyes reflect that loathing again.

Grimacing against the pain of his shoulder, he rose and knelt beside the still-warm coals. Blowing on them until they flared to life, he quickly added dried stems and finally twisted hunks of grass until a small, hot fire was going. By the time Jenny woke, coffee was made and salt pork was sizzling in a fry pan.

"Umm." She purred contentedly, one bare arm resting behind her head. "Comanche men do not make food for their women. I like the ways of the white eyes."

There was no responding grin from him. His face was stern as he concentrated on flipping the meat. The smile died in Jenny's eyes and slowly she sat up. The blanket fell away from her smooth breasts. She made no effort to cover up.

"Is something wrong, Caleb?" she asked softly.

He glanced at her, then back at the fire. "We have to get started back to Millbrook," he said gruffly. "If the posse managed to run off Two Wolves's men, Frank and the others will be searching for you. We'd better let someone know."

Hiding her hurt, Jenny pulled on the calico dress she'd discarded last night and moved to the fire. Caleb handed her a cup of coffee and a tin plate with hard biscuits and salt pork. He still hadn't met her gaze. Settling back on his haunches, he ate out of the frying pan.

Unable to eat, Jenny set the food aside. "What have I done to displease you, Caleb?" she asked quietly. Her gaze was steady on him.

He looked at her in stony silence. His expression was troubled, his profile stubbornly set as he gazed off across the prairie.

"Are you still unable to forget I was raised among the Comanche?" she asked flatly.

He nodded. "I'm not the man for you, Jenny," he said at last. "Your life has been too filled with sadness and upheaval. You want a steady home, a place to call your own—with a man you can depend on. A man like Frank Walsh who'll farm and work to feed his family. I don't think I could do that." She made no protest, only waited quietly while he went on.

"I don't know what it's like to have a family, some-one to care about and be responsible for. I've been on my own too long."

"We'll learn together, Caleb," Jenny cried then, see-ing the joy she'd known so briefly slipping away from her.

Slowly he shook his head. "I don't know how to do anything but kill Comanche, while you know only love for them."

"That isn't true," she said. "I killed Two Wolves to save you. I have never killed a man before."

"I know and I'm grateful, but you and me—it just wouldn't work."

"Why not, Caleb? Why can't we try?" She stood close beside him now, her skirts swishing against his boots. He could smell the sweet sage scent of her, and if he wished to turn and lean forward, he could bury his head against her breasts.

"We're not anything alike, you and me. We were raised different; we don't see things the same way."

"What difference does that make?" Jenny de-manded. "Faye and Frank are not alike, but they love each other. I love you and you love me." She paused. "Don't you, Caleb?"

He saw the pain in her eyes, but knew if he let her hold on to a dream that included him, the pain would be worse later. He had nothing to give her, except pain.

"I never said I did, Jenny," he answered quietly. "I've never had a hankering for a Comanche squaw."

"But I was—" She floundered, searching for the white words to describe her purity.

"It doesn't matter," he said roughly. "I don't want to spend my life with you, Jenny. I just came to rescue you from Two Wolves because I felt I owed you that, but now my obligation to you is finished."

She was silent, so he thought she hadn't heard his words. When he looked at her he saw she had. He saw the pain; he saw the dawning outrage. Good. Let her be angry with him. It would help her to regain her pride and walk away from him.

"A Comanche warrior would not have treated me with such disrespect," she said in a low voice. "If he had, Ten Bears would have killed him."

"Do you wish to kill me, Jenny?" he asked wearily.

"Yes," she whispered, and sprang at him, her hands balled into tiny fists that were hardly felt by him. She pummeled him about the shoulders and face, and he made no move to protect himself. At last she tired and drew away from him. Tears rolled down her face and dripped, unchecked, from her stubborn little chin.

"You do not mean these words," she said, with sad wisdom. "You love me, but you are afraid. I am not afraid, Caleb Hunter. I belong to you now."

He couldn't deny her then. Cursing himself he

reached for her, snatching her into his arms, pressing her sweet form to his. Her head lay against his chest and he heard her weeping, but her strong, young arms were wound about his waist, holding him as if she meant never to let him go. Some dam burst within Caleb then, and he laid his cheek against her sun-warmed head and wept. His body jerked with each hoarse, guttural sob. Jenny stood still in his embrace. She'd seldom heard a man weep before—and she wondered that she didn't find it a sign of weakness. But these were not tears of weakness, rather they were the breaking of a wall that had held a man prisoner.

Her arms tightened around him and she raised her face to him, kissing his cheeks, tasting the salt of his tears, sharing the despair and glorying in the joy that would follow. In her young wisdom, she sensed some defense had been breeched, and, though she had no understanding of how it had come about, she sensed she'd been a part of it—just as she would be a part of the rebuilding Caleb would do as a new man. Her lips parted in a smile of joy and she stroked his bowed head. The weight of him bore her down to the prairie, and they sat for a long hour saying nothing, silently pledging themselves to each other.

At last his grief abated and he sat up, rubbing at his eyes with the heels of his hands, an endearing gesture that touched Jenny's heart. Silently she waited. She could be as patient as necessary now. Briefly she wished White Weasel could be here to see her newfound patience and meet Caleb. White Weasel would understand her love for this man and she would appróve; Jenny was sure of it. At last, Caleb raised his head and looked at her.

"We belong to each other," he acknowledged, taking her hand. "You will be my wife and I will call you Wild Sage." Her heart swelled with love.

"That is not necessary," she said, squeezing his hand and carrying it to her heart. "I am not unhappy with the white man's name . . . as long as I have you at my side."

"Are you sure, Jenny?" he whispered. "Are you sure this is what you want? Life with me won't be easy."

"Life is never easy. Death is easy," she answered. "I choose a life with you over death without you."

Caleb's answering smile was filled with all the love and reassurance she could ever ask for. Then a noise made him start and look around. "We'd better hurry, if we're to meet the posse."

They kicked at the smoldering embers of their campfire and repacked and saddled the horses. Jenny stood on the creek bank looking around. She would always remember this place and the things they'd discovered here.

"It's time to go," Caleb called softly, and she turned and made her way to him.

Her gray gaze was soft and filled with happiness as she climbed up behind him on the back of the sorrel. Settling her hands at his waist, she sat proud and straight as they moved across the prairie in search of the posse.

Chapter 16

JENNY AND CALEB caught up with the posse well before they reached Millbrook. Jubilantly the men greeted them, expressing their relief that Jenny was alive. Proudly they told of their triumph over the Indians.

"We routed them," the sheriff declared as Caleb rode close. "You should have seen it, Hunter. It was a sight to behold. We sent those miserable devils back to Texas, where they belong."

But as the men rode back to their families, their triumphant mood had passed. They'd met the Comanche renegades, driven them away, and now their thoughts turned back to crops, the drought, and the families they'd left alone. They tried not to look at the radiant, silent girl who rode among them. Frank Walsh had told them little of what had transpired, except that Two Wolves had come to kidnap her and take her back to the Comanche tribes. With her stoic air, she reminded them too readily of the Indians who had threatened them. They thought of the homesteader and his family who'd died. Had it been because of this silent girl? Some believed so, and felt a rising distaste for her presence among them.

They rode hard and reached Millbrook in three days' time. As the posse rode in, women gathered along the streets, straining to catch a glimpse of their husbands or sons among the riders. Faye Walsh was there and she waved energetically, tears sliding down her cheeks. When the riders drew to a stop in the middle of the street, Faye was the first one to dart forward and hug Jenny.

"Thank God, you're safe!" she cried. "I've prayed so hard for your deliverance from those savages."

Other women crowded around her, hugging her or touching her hair. "Faye told us of the sacrifice you made for her family," they cried. "What a brave thing to do."

"You poor child," Maude St. John said. "I told the Lord he'd best give you back into our hands. We needed the likes of you, and those murderin' devils didn't."

"Welcome back," Margaret Rudd said, hugging Jenny. "You made a difficult choice back there, and we're all grateful. You saved the lives of the Walsh family."

"I love them," Jenny said simply. "I couldn't see them harmed." She glanced at Caleb, proud that he was seeing how the white women accepted her.

In consternation the men watched the women hugging the girl in dirty calico and wondered at the vagaries of women—until their wives began to drift toward them and revealed the things Faye had told them about Jenny's brave actions. The posse had been formed so hastily, the men had heard none of this. Now, touched by the bravery of the young girl they'd saved, they dismounted and milled about, feeling even better about the outcome of their skirmish with the Comanche.

Then Caleb stepped forward and dispelled their euphoria with a few words. They had no guarantee the renegade Indians had returned to Texas. How could they be sure the murdering devils weren't holed up in the hills north of the territory, waiting to lull them all into a false sense of security before sweeping down on them again? As Jenny heard him speak, she felt a curl of pain begin in her stomach. She had little doubt about what Caleb would say next.

"There's no need for all of you to go out," Caleb said. "I just need a few good men to act as scouts."

"Caleb, no," Jenny cried, running forward and throwing her arms around him in front of everyone. Astonished, he steadied himself against her onslaught and looked down at her.

"Don't go," she pleaded. "You've been wounded. Haven't you done enough? Next time you might be killed." There was a murmur of concern among the other women. None of them wanted their husbands exposed to more danger. They were needed at home for crops and chores and just being husbands and fathers.

"We won't be fighting, Jenny, I promise," Caleb said, his eyes crinkling at the corners with tenderness. "We'll act only as scouts. If we find any evidence the renegades are still in the territory, we'll report it to Fort Mann and let the army take care of it. At any rate, we need to let the army know what's happened here."

Jenny pulled away from him, gazing into his eyes.

'Do you promise you won't fight the Comanche if you see them?" she whispered.

"I promise," he said, gazing into her eyes. Not a man or woman there but knew that Jenny and Caleb were a couple now. No one noticed Rachel Tyler slip away from the crowd.

Three men volunteered to go with Caleb. They hurried off with their wives to restock their supplies and say good-bye to their children once again. People stayed in town to watch the scouting party ride out again, some men shuffling from side to side in their boots, feeling guilty that they hadn't volunteered themselves, mentioning crops and family shamefacedly.

"Hurry back soon," Jenny whispered, and kissed Caleb before the whole town, then stood back, her head raised proudly as he swung into his saddle, and, with a final salute, rode out again. The other scouts did likewise.

The onlookers were silent as they watched them ride out of sight, then one by one they gathered up their children and hitched tired mules to farm wagons and headed back toward their homesteads. They had farm animals to attend to. Frank Walsh watched them go, thanking each of them for coming to Jenny's rescue and thinking he had little to return to on his own homestead. His crops were burned, his livestock killed. He would need a miracle to feed his family through the coming winter. Then he glanced at Faye and Jenny talking with their heads close together, their faces smiling. It could have been much worse, he thought, and with renewed determination and joy in his family, lifted his children into the wagon, then turned to Jenny.

"Do you need a hand, girl?" he asked, and though his tone was gruff as always—and he hadn't used her name—Jenny sensed a new softness about him. Something within her responded to his awkward truce. Although she'd jumped up in the wagon a hundred times by herself, she now smiled.

"I'd be much obliged," she said lightly, and took his proferred hand.

When she was seated on the back of the wagon bed, with her moccasined feet dangling, Frank grinned at her and nodded his head in approval, then he turned toward Faye and helped her into the wagon. Handing up their baby son, he clambered up beside her and took up the reins. His shoulders were set with a new lift, a new pride. His family had been threatened by one of the deadliest foes on the prairie, but he'd kept them intact. His other problems seemed small by comparison.

Riding down the lane toward the soddy had a sobering effect on them all. Jenny stared at the creek bank, where only a few days before Two Wolves had stood, his knife at her throat, his eyes filled with hatred. How close to death they'd all been, she realized now, then shivered. She was grateful Two Wolves was dead, happy that he'd met his fate at the hands of some unknown settler who'd left behind an open well pit. His warriors, wounded and shamed by their defeat, would slink back to the Comancheria without ever having found their leader's body. That was Jenny's revenge for the homesteaders they'd murdered.

Yet she grieved for the choice she'd made, for now she could never return to the land of the Comancheria, never return to the tepees of her adopted people, and the

thought saddened her greatly. As much as she'd come to
love Faye and her family, as much as she loved Caleb
Hunter and looked forward to being his wife, she had
never thought herself capable of turning her back on the
Comanche. And she hadn't. She'd only rejected the hideous vengeance and death dealt by Two Wolves and his
men.

The wagon had come to a halt now; everyone sat still
remembering the terror they'd known here. Hannah
crept closer to Jenny and clung to her sleeve. Vultures
lazily circled over the cleared fields, having taken their
fill of the mule and pork flesh. The stench of the decay-
ing bodies reached the people in the wagon, so Frank
Walsh threw down the reins and resolutely climbed
down out of the wagon.

"Well, Mother. Looks like we have a lot of work to
do," he said loudly.

Faye had been silent, dread building in her heart at
the sights before her. Now, at the command in her husband's voice, she nodded in agreement.

"We won't get it done sitting here," she said crisply.
"Come, Hannah, Nathan, Jenny. Let's get started."

Her words seemed to galvanize them all into action.
Jenny went around to take the baby from his mother's
arms and carry him inside. Marybeth was weeping,
whether from fear or fatigue, Jenny wasn't sure. She
hugged the little girl and tucked her into bed for her
nap, then looked around the soddy. The roof needed re-
pairing. Boards had broken through under the weight of
Two Wolves's warriors looking for a way in. Clods of
dirt had fallen to the floor below. Broken dishes littered

the table. Abandoned arrows protruded from the walls. Hannah stood staring at one, her eyes enormous.

"Here, we might as well get rid of these," Jenny said, stepping over to the wall and tugging the arrow free. Disdainfully she threw it into the fireplace. Immediately Hannah looked relieved.

"Those old Indians didn't hurt us," she said, laughing a little.

"The Great Spirit was with—I mean, the Lord was with us," Jenny said.

"Weren't you afraid, Jenny?" Hannah asked, coming to clasp her hand affectionately.

"Now, don't be bothering Jenny about this," Faye remonstrated. "She'll tell us all about it when she's ready."

"There's little to tell," Jenny said, thinking of the murdered homesteader family. She would never speak of that to anyone, she vowed. She would try to forget. "But I was afraid," she said, and smiled at Hannah.

The girl threw her arms around Jenny. "I was afraid, too," she said. "I was afraid you'd never come back."

Jenny returned her hug, smoothing Hannah's fair curls from her freckled brow. "I'm back."

Her smile faded as she thought of Caleb Hunter, traveling somewhere out there on this vast prairie, putting himself in danger to protect others. Then she thought of the way he'd wept and clung to her, the things they'd talked about, and her sadness disappeared. The man who'd ridden out of Millbrook this day was not the same embittered, wounded man he'd been before. She would take comfort in that during his absence. She shouldn't have let him go, she thought, but she'd had little choice.

Like any great warrior, Caleb was a man who acted without the say-so of any man or woman.

The rest of the day was spent in righting the soddy and gathering what was left of the garden. Frank and Nathan buried the carcasses of the dead animals and spread fresh earth over the place where they'd lain. A prairie wind carried away the last taint of death and decay. The dry grasses rattled plaintively. Faye went to stand beside her husband as he stared at his shriveled fields and the mounds that held his livestock.

"I don't know what will keep us from starving this winter," he said in a low voice, and Faye flinched at the defeated note in his voice.

"We'll make it somehow," she whispered.

"How? What more does God expect from me? I try to be grateful that we're all alive, that we survived the Indian attack, but Two Wolves and his warriors may have killed us anyway. Only this death will be slower and more painful."

"Shh. Don't talk like that," Faye whispered, putting her arms around her husband. His shoulders shook under the weight of his sobs.

"I should never have married you, Faye," he said, wiping at his wet face. "I brought you here—and put you to live in a shanty made out of dirt and prairie grass in the middle of nowhere. We're living like animals, and our children—what kind of life am I giving them?"

"You're teaching them to be independent, hardworking, fearless men and women." He raised his head and met her warm gaze. "I'm proud of you, Frank," she whispered. "I'm proud of what we're achieving here in a wilderness, where no white man has been before. You and me, Frank, and our children, building something from scratch. We haven't inherited this from our forefathers, and what we pass on to our children will be of greater value than a brick house or money in the bank. Oh, Frank. Don't you see how happy I am with you, how much I love you?"

"Faye. Dearest, dearest Faye," he said, clamping his arms around her thin figure and holding her tight. His face was like a prayer, so much love and wonder did it hold.

Standing at the corner of the soddy, Jenny had heard their words and meant to move away, so she didn't intrude on their privacy, but something in the beauty of their words and dreams caught at her and she stood in wonder, wishing Caleb had been here, so he could see what love between a man and woman was all about. This was the way she and Caleb would love each other over the years. If he didn't know how, then she would teach him.

Walking down to the creek to fetch water, she thought about the man whose soul had been sick, whose heart had been afraid to feel, whose courage had lain in the taking of another man's life, not in the taking of a woman's love. Now he was none of those things. He was healing. Squatting beside the creek, she bowed her head on her knees and wept for Caleb Hunter and for herself. Two incomplete beings, half formed because of their pasts, yet miraculously they'd found each other . . . and together they would grow whole again.

A sound on the path made her raise her head and wipe away her tears. Riders were approaching, and a fear, intuitive and without reason, made her race back up the bank toward the soddy.

"Indians!" she screamed, her heart pounding.

From where he and Faye stood, Frank whirled, his eyes searching the landscape, his hands already pushing Faye toward the soddy. Horses galloped toward the soddy and a voice called out.

"Frank. It's me! Walt St. John . . . and Ben Morley." The men brought their horses to a halt in the yard. Jenny stopped running. Frank and Faye stood as if carved of salt.

"I don't blame you folks for being extra cautious," St. John said approvingly. He was a big man with graying hair and kindly blue eyes. He smiled benevolently at Faye. "Ma'am, I brought them hogs you inquired about."

"I'll get my mother's quilts." Faye turned toward the house.

"Faye, what are you talking about?" Frank demanded.

"I offered Maudie St. John my mother's quilt in exchange for two of their hogs. She was kind enough to agree. She's always coveted those quilts."

Walt St. John laughed. "Yes, ma'am. That's a fact. She does, but she said to me that she doesn't have much need for them right now and she'd just as soon you kept them awhile longer. She'll get in touch with you if ever she needs 'em."

"I can't accept charity," Faye said.

"No, ma'am. It ain't charity. It's folks helpin' out folks. Ben here has brought a couple of extra mules."

Ben Morley, a thin, dark-haired man with a quiet air

about himself, nodded. "I figure you can pay me back by helping me take in my crops come harvest time."

"I'm much obliged," Frank said gratefully.

"My grandson, Jonathan, back there," St. John said, "is pulling a wagon with some other goods you folks might need until you get back on your feet. Extra things from folks' gardens, things they ain't never going to have time to preserve for the winter. They thought you might could use it. Likewise, my wife sent some of her canned peas and whatnot. She remembers how generous you were with your canned preserves earlier this summer."

Faye was speechless as she moved along the side of the wagon looking at all the goods sent by her friends. Her eyes were shiny with tears when she turned back to Frank.

"We're mighty obliged to everyone," she said. Her voice trembled. St. John nodded in satisfaction and climbed down off his horse and started unloading.

Jenny and Faye set about immediately sorting out what must be canned at once and what would be best dried or stored in the cellar. Frank took the men off to see the damage to his crops and his burned shed. By the time the men had toured the tiny homestead, they seemed impressed by Frank's handiwork.

"You're a hardworking, God-fearing man, Walsh," they said. "We need people like you to help keep this land settled. We hope you aren't discouraged by all that's befallen you this summer."

"Not at all," Frank said.

"And if we had been, the generosity of all our neighbors would have given us heart again," Faye said, coming to stand beside her husband. "We thank you and the others."

"Well"— St. John climbed into his saddle and looked down at them—"we figured this misfortune wouldn't have befallen you if you hadn't taken in the girl. You tried to do your Christian duty and got repaid by the devil. We just wanted you to know we're behind you."

Standing near the soddy, Jenny heard Walt St. John's words and hung her head, saddened at the thought she'd brought so much misery to the Walsh family. She shouldn't have come back here. Like Caleb, she should have just ridden away into the prairie until she could no longer be seen. But common sense said she couldn't have done that. The men in the posse wouldn't have let her leave. Caleb wouldn't have allowed it. She was a woman who must depend on others to stay alive. Even in the Comanche village this was so. When the winter snows swept across the prairie, the People huddled together in their tepees, happy for the company and presence of one another in the long, silent, bitter winter.

With a final salute, Walt St. John and Ben Morley galloped out of the yard, heading back toward town. The empty wagon bounced along behind the mule Jonathan St. John drove. The expressions on their faces and the set of their shoulders showed the pride they held about themselves for the good deeds they'd done. The Walsh family had been helped to overcome the inconvenience of taking in a Comanche foundling, a stray, a castoff. At this moment she'd never felt so much like an outcast in the white man's world.

Faye turned and saw her face. "Why, Jenny. What's

wrong? Weren't you pleased by all the food and supplies our neighbors sent?"

"Yes, of course I am," Jenny said. "It's just that you wouldn't have needed them if not for me." She turned away and ran down to the creek. Helplessly Faye looked at Frank.

"I'd better go to her."

"No, Mother. Let me go this time."

"Frank, don't say anything to hurt her further."

"I don't intend to, Mother," he said.

Jenny sat on the creek bank scrubbing at her eyes to hold back the hated tears, but just as they fell unchecked when she was a girl, now she could not stop their flow, either. She was aware someone approached her from behind and expected to hear Faye's gentle voice, but the footfall grew heavy and the hand against her shoulder was rough and calloused from work. Startled, she looked up and saw Frank Walsh's stern gaze. At once she stiffened her back and raised her chin, not wanting him to see her weeping. He sat down beside her and remained silent until she had her tears under control.

"Thank you," he said when the weeping had stopped and her face was once again stoic.

"For what?" she half whispered.

"For everything," Frank said, then paused, swallowing, so his Adam's apple bobbled. "I'm not much good at words, not like some folks," he said. "All I know how to do to show my feelings is to work with these hands." He held them out before him. "I've been afraid, thinking I was all alone out here and that feedin' my family and carin' for them depended solely on me. I'm not a brave man."

"I think you're as brave as any man I know," Jenny said quietly.

"When it comes to somebody I love, I can be," Frank said. "What I'm tryin' to say is that I learned something by all this. I learned I'm not alone. I'm part of a group of people—men and women just like Faye and me—who are trying to do something. Knowing I'm not alone gives me courage and comfort. Then I sit here and I think about you."

"What about me?" Jenny asked, and held her breath. He was going to order her to leave.

"Well, seems to me, you're alone here. You act like you don't think you belong to anyone. I remember how scary that feeling is, so I just wanted to say . . . you belong to us, Jenny. I'd like it a heap if you'd call yourself by our name, Walsh. That's about all we, Faye and I, can give you is our name."

Jenny sat dumbfounded. "Jenny Walsh," she whispered. "Jenny Walsh!" She turned toward Frank. "Do you mean it?"

"Of course I do. You're family . . . as much as if you were born to us."

"And you don't hold it against me because Two Wolves came here?"

"You couldn't help that, and you tried to stop him."

"He'll never come again, Frank. He's dead."

"Are you sure?"

"He fell down a well. I saw him."

Frank's brow wrinkled in consternation, then glancing at Jenny, he forced a smile—or what passed for a smile—on his otherwise somber face. "Then we can both forget about him," he said, getting to his feet. "Come on, Jenny Walsh," he said, holding out a hand. "Faye's waiting supper for us."

Jenny took hold of his hand and was pulled to her feet. Her heart felt so joyful at his words, she didn't hesitate to fling her arms around him in a tight hug.

"Thank you. Oh, thank you!" she cried, and spun away to run up the bank. "Faye! Faye!" she called, bursting through the door. Faye and the children turned questioning eyes toward her.

"My name is Jenny Walsh," she gasped.

Frank had come up behind her; Faye looked at his face, then back at Jenny's. Tearfully she rose from the table and ran to hug Jenny. Hannah and the other children were not to be outdone.

"Does this mean you're my sister?" Hannah demanded.

"Your aunt," Jenny acknowledged.

Standing in the midst of their happy cries and warm embraces, Jenny forgot the sting of Walt St. John's words.

Supper was a festive affair. Again and again Faye's bright gaze moved to her husband's face. She was eternally grateful for his gesture. She thought of the lovely three-storied house she'd left behind, the servants and the ease she would have known. None of it seemed real to her, not compared to this cramped dirt room and the man seated at the head of the table. Samson cried out; Faye lifted him from his cradle and nursed him, while all around her the talk flowed.

Jenny watched the faces of her new family and

thought she hadn't felt this happy since before Ten
Bears had gone off to fight the white eyes, secure in the
belief that the Great Spirit had given them a special
power against the white man's bullets. She'd known
much grief since then, but at last she'd come to this, to
belonging to a family again. If only Caleb were here,
sharing the lamp glow and the food and laughter. If
only he could feel the circle of love present around this
table. She had to believe he'd be back soon. She would
think of him every night and pray to the Great Spirit—
and to the white man's Lord—that they watch over him
and bring him back safely.

At last the excited chatter slowed, eyelids grew
heavy, and Faye sent the children off to bed. Jenny prepared to follow.

"Good night, dear Jenny . . . my sweet sister," Faye
said softly.

Jenny went off to bed with the warmth of her new
family's love enfolding her. But once she was snuggled
beside the girls, beneath Faye's family quilts, she found
herself too restless to sleep. Finally she rose and made
her way to the bedroom door. She didn't mean to eaves-
drop, but something in the hushed tones beyond the
door and the sound of her name made her pause.

"It can't be," Faye was saying. "Surely he's dead as
Jenny claims."

"I hope to God he is dead," Frank answered, "but if
he was still alive when he fell down that well, he could
have climbed out."

"Do you think he'll come here again?"

"He might," Frank said quietly.

"He will!" Jenny whispered, and with trembling

knees moved back to the bed and huddled under the covers.

She could remember the sight of Two Wolves's face as he slid down the well. It had been filled with hate and the promise of revenge. In spite of his wounds, he could still be alive. If he managed to crawl from the well, he would kill her and anyone who'd given her aid. Jenny's body was numb with terror and fear. Caleb, she thought. Oh, God! Don't let Two Wolves find Caleb and the scouts. The maddened Indian would surely kill them. She knew what she must do; she lay waiting for Faye and Frank to come to bed, so she could leave this house, this tiny soddy so filled with love. She would travel across the prairie and surrender herself to Two Wolves. Perhaps, then, when she lay dead at his feet, he would forget Caleb and the Walshes and return to the Comancheria.

Chapter 17

WHY WAS HE still out here on the prairie? Why wasn't he back in Millbrook with Jenny? Caleb Hunter reined the sorrel to a halt and sat looking out over the sweeping flatland. Zeph Norris and Hatch Murphy sat watching him. He had his head up, as if he could sniff out the Comanche. Both men had gained tremendous respect for Caleb on this trip.

They'd caught no glimpse of the renegades, seen no evidence that they were still in the territory, yet Caleb continued to search among the hills and ridges, following the trail of unshod hoofprints until Zeph thought he meant to go all the way back to Texas.

The memory of Jenny had haunted him since he'd ridden away from her. The thought of her, warm and trusting in his arms, the passion of her, the silken womanliness, pushed all thoughts of vengeance from his mind. Yet the memory of her, smiling and waving to him as he rode away, awakened a fear of the Comanche warriors he'd never known before.

What had happened to him that he couldn't just ride away and forget her? He'd had other women. But Jenny wasn't like other women. She stayed in a man's mind, clung to his senses, haunted his sleep, so he longed to turn the sorrel and ride it hell-bent until he was back in her arms. Why had he left her again? he wondered. Other men could have come scouting the renegades. He could have stayed behind. His wounds would have been excuse enough, but he knew he could never rest easy with Jenny until he was sure of their safety. Two Wolves was dead. He'd not come seeking Jenny again, so why this nagging worry?

They'd come out of the plains, into the hills and valleys. The Rockies lay like a smudge on the distant horizon. Caleb felt the loneliness of the place. Once he would have wandered like a ghost across a land that had defeated him after all. Long ago, this land and the devils that lived on it had taken his family and he'd ceased to be a whole person. One small woman had changed all that. He had to protect her.

"Let's search along that ridge," he said, and sent the men in different directions while he rode directly forward. He topped a crest and found himself gazing down into a beautiful valley. Trees grew in clumps along a narrow river and meadows of lush grass stretched away on either side.

He could never be a farmer, Caleb thought, studying the landscape. He could never chain himself to the soil as Frank Walsh had done, trying to tear a living from it. But he could raise cattle. In a place like this he could ranch, starting small and building as his father had done. He had money in a bank back at the fort, money for guiding the troops to the Cross timbers, blood money that had meant nothing to him before, but now offered him an answer, an alternative for his life.

Would Jenny like a place like this? Would she help
him raise cattle and give him sons to help as well? He
could picture it all, a neat ranch house nestled in the
valley not too far from the water and corrals and barns,
cattle dotting the fields beyond. He could see Jenny
standing at the corral gate below, a smile lighting her
gray eyes, her laughter filling the air as she waited for
him. He blinked and the vision was gone, but the valley
was there with all its promise, with all its hope.

Long shadows lay across the landscape. The sun
streaked the sky with brilliant colors. The day passed
into the gray dusk of evening, but not without a final
banner that proclaimed a new day would come. Caleb
wanted to kick the sorrel into a headlong gallop back
toward Millbrook, toward Jenny, but he knew he
couldn't. Men didn't survive out here with such heedless actions. Instead he signaled to the other men and
led the way down to the river, where they built a fire
and cooked supper. Then he lay back in his bedroll and
studied the starry sky, thinking of Jenny. If his thoughts
could only fly across the empty prairie to her, he
mused, she would know how much he loved her and
needed her. She would know he was coming back to
her—and this time there would be no good-byes. Never
again.

Jenny waited until the house was still, then carefully
slid out of bed, taking care to cover Hannah and
Marybeth. Frank sighed in his sleep and turned. Jenny
froze, waiting until his breathing deepened, and then
she crept from the soddy. The moonlight was pale, ob-
scured by clouds. A wind had picked up, chilly and

menacing in its promise of a winter that was just around the corner. Jenny made her way to the patch of field where Frank had set up a makeshift corral for the mules. She hated to take one of his new mules, but without it, she wouldn't get very far. In the long run, it would be worth the loss of a mule to save his family's life. She slipped a harness over the mule's head and prepared to mount, then took a final look around.

How she'd hated this place when she first came here. The ways of the white men had seemed strange and meaningless to her, but she'd come to understand them and they her. They had given her the greatest gift of all. They'd given her their name. She would carry it with her and cherish it until the day she died. The thought jerked her back to reality. Death was not so far away, once she found Two Wolves. She shivered and leapt onto the back of the mule. Tears coursed down her cheeks as she rode away. She would never see Faye or Frank or the children again, but the memory of their love gave her the courage for this final deed.

She walked the mule at first, not wanting to alert Frank, and when they were far enough away from the soddy, she kicked it into an ungainly gallop. She rode throughout the night, using whatever stars and moonlight shone between the clouds. She grew tired but dared not rest. She must go far away, so no one would find her. What if she missed Two Wolves and his men on this vast prairie? she wondered. She couldn't think of it. The Great Spirit, in all his mercy, wouldn't let that happen.

When the sun rose, she pushed onward, thirsty and hungry and tired. She'd brought no water or food, think-

ing only of getting away to meet Two Wolves. Now she
saw how ill prepared she was. By noon she'd found the
creek where the men in the posse had camped on their
way home, just scant days before. That had seemed like
a lifetime then, a dream time when all fear from Two
Wolves was gone. Jenny watered the mule, then staked
him to a scraggly bush while she sought along the creek
for fish. The creek was too shallow, but she startled a
rabbit—and in her chase of it, found a nesting prairie
hen. She took the eggs and carefully tied them into a
bundle from a torn patch of her skirt. Cleaning the hen
for roasting was difficult without a knife, but she found
a sharp stone and did the best she could. When it was
browned, she tore off a portion and ate it, then carefully
packed the rest for her supper.

There was an odd kind of reluctance to leave this
place, this last reminder of Caleb and the posse who'd
rescued her, but Two Wolves might even now be out
there, gathering his warriors, preparing his vengeance
against Frank and his family. Climbing onto the mule,
she started out again.

It was easy to follow the trail the posse had used
coming and going. The old things White Weasel and
Ten Bears had taught her came back automatically. She
looked for mule droppings and sites of campfires and
was strangely comforted by them. If she'd found her
way here, she could find her way back. But there would
be no going back for her. Her course was set, her destiny fixed.

She went first to the well where Two Wolves had
fallen. If he were still there, she would return to

Millbrook. If not, her resolve was made. She would find
him.

Her heart beat loudly as she neared the place where
Caleb and Two Wolves had fought. Warily she glanced
around, as if expecting the war chief to leap out of hiding and ride her down.

His war pony was gone. An ominous sign! The pony
had been well trained; he would not leave his master.
Dismounting, Jenny approached the well site.

The trampled, torn grass told its story. Somehow,
Two Wolves had made his way out. Unshod hoofprints
showed how he'd called to his pony to help him those
final feet. Kneeling, Jenny studied the ground. Two
Wolves had been bleeding badly. His injuries had
stopped him from riding to the homestead right away.
She looked around. He was out there somewhere with
his men, waiting until his wounds healed. Then he
would be back. She had to warn Caleb. But how could
she find him on this vast prairie? Perhaps it would be
better if she found Two Wolves, after all, and tried to
stop him herself.

Wearily she climbed back on the mule. Which way
would the injured warrior go? she wondered. Westward
and south to the Comancheria? Resolutely she turned
her mule in that direction. Distracted as she'd been, she
hadn't noticed the mules anchored down by the stream
or the man who lay against the bank watching her.
When she'd gone, he loaded his mules and set out after
her.

Weariness made her pause for the night. There was
no stream for water, but she started a small fire and
huddled near it for warmth. Somewhere off on the prai-

rie, a coyote howled. Jenny shivered, aware of her solitude. She'd never really been without someone nearby before. In the Comanche camp, they all drew together for safety. Even when Caleb had captured her and brought her north, there had been others about. Now she was alone on the prairie and the prospect frightened her. Finally she lay back in the grass and closed her eyes.

Something in the night woke her, some small noise. She rolled over and sat up, then gaped wordlessly at the man seated across the fire from her. He'd added hanks of grass and buffalo dung, so the fire blazed, and a coffeepot was boiling. A pan of salt back was frying. Jenny's stomach cramped with hunger, but she strained to make out the face of the intruder. He sat in shadows.

"Who are you?" she demanded, although the sudden stench of his clothes told her before he moved into the light and spoke.

"Why, you remember me, don't you, girlie? Hank Radburn's the name. We met back in Millbrook. I seen you out here on the prairie by myself and I said to myself, Hank, I said, that there girlie's lost and she ain't got no food or beddin'. She needs you, Hank Radburn, I says. So I just come on over to your camp, real neighborly like, to offer you my hospitality."

"That's very kind of you," Jenny said, looking around warily. "Is there anyone else with you?"

"Nope, just me and my mules." He turned the meat in the frying pan and held it out to her. "I believe this here's done. I reckon you're starvin'. Go on. Take it and eat."

Hesitantly Jenny took the food he offered and ate. When he passed over his canteen, she wiped the mouth

and drank her fill. Hank Radburn said little as he
watched her, only chuckling now and then as if enjoying a rare joke.

"Thank you," Jenny said when she'd finished. She
felt much better now. She couldn't hold back a yawn.
Furtively she covered her mouth.

"That's all right, little lady. I'll bet you're plenty tired
after riding all day. You'll sleep better now, with your
belly full." He rose and crossed to one of his mules, returning with a musty-smelling buffalo robe. "Here, you
just wrap yourself up in this. It'll keep you warm for
the night."

"I couldn't take your robe," Jenny protested, feeling
alarmed at his generosity.

"I got me another one," he said, and dropped the robe
near her before seating himself back on the other side of
the fire.

Jenny couldn't resist the warmth it promised. Ignoring the musty smell, she wrapped it around herself.

"There now, that's better," Radburn said. His stubbled jaws wobbled in a semblance of a smile. "Are you
out here by yourself?" He didn't look at her directly as
he waited for her answer. There was a certain slyness
about him that worried Jenny.

"I'm on my way to meet Two Wolves," she said
gruffly. Like as not, he'd take back his robe now, she
thought.

"Two Wolves! I thought he was dead, killed by the
posse!"

"No, he escaped," Jenny said, "and I'm looking for
him. He's looking for me, too."

"You don't say." Radburn nodded his head as if

thinking something profound, then got to his feet to retrieve another buffalo robe. "I tell you what, girlie. I'll
just bed down here with you tonight, just to see no coyotes bother you."

Jenny said nothing, just stared at the grinning man.
She wished she had a weapon. She could only hope her
story about Two Wolves would scare Radburn away
from her. She lay back in the grass and pulled the
smelly robe up to her chin. For a long time she waited,
tense and edgy, until she heard Hank Radburn's snores.
No man could snore like that and not be asleep, she rea-
soned, and finally closed her own eyes.

She woke in the morning with a start. Hank Radburn
stood over her, his eyes hard and calculating.

"Time to wake up, girlie," he said. "Time to get moving."

Jenny sprang up and faced him, holding out his robe.
"Thank you for the use of the robe and for the food,"
she said firmly. "I'll be on my way now."

"Just a minute, girlie," Hank said, his glittering eyes
narrowing slightly. "I took care of you. You belong to
me. I been wantin' me a squaw to help me with my
trade. You was too uppity when you was first brought to
live with white folks, but I figure you ain't so choosy
now, if you're trying to get back to the Injuns. Now me,
I'll treat you fair and square. You work for me, tan my
hides, cook my meals, and—" he paused, giggling a
little—"warm my bedroll, and I'll treat you real nice."

Jenny's eyes widened in alarm. She whirled to run
from him, but his big hand closed around her arm, dragging her back. He hit her without warning, a blow that
knocked her to her knees. She made no outcry, simply

knelt, shaking her head, trying to still the whirling prairie. Hank towered over her, his tone satisfied.

"You got the idee now?" He grunted. "Life can be hard on you or easy. Any way you want it, girlie. Now git up on that mule of yours and we'll git goin'."

Numbly Jenny did as he ordered. Her head was still spinning. Hank Radburn mounted and rode up beside her.

"See that there prairie chick a-takin' flight out there?" he said, pulling a huge wicked-looking rifle from its leather sheath. With ease he took aim and fired. The ungainly bird exploded in midair, bits of feather and meat falling back to earth. Jenny turned her head away, but Radburn reached over and twisted her face around to him.

"You see old Betsy here?" he said, lovingly stroking the gun. "She can drop a buffalo bull at two hundred yards without the cows a-knowin' what happened. If you try to git away from me, I'll have to put a bullet in the middle of that pretty back of yourn." He let go of her then, sheathed his rifle, and, grabbing the reins of his pack mule, started off.

He didn't look back to see if she followed. He didn't have to worry. He'd made his point, and she had no choices left to her. Jenny followed the buffalo hunter, wondering where Caleb was, wondering what would happen to Frank and Faye if she didn't find Two Wolves and stop him.

"I believe they're gone," Zeph was saying. "We've sure covered a lot of territory, and not one sign of the renegades. I say let's head for home."

"I'm for that," Hatch Murphy said. "How about you, Caleb?"

Caleb nodded his head in agreement. "You men ride on ahead. I'll catch up directly." He was loathe to leave this valley.

He sat by the fire long after the other men had saddled and ridden out thinking about what he was going to do. He'd made up his mind. He was going after Jenny and bringing her here to this valley. He'd show her how the mauve shadows turned silvery white as the sun rose in the east and how the birds flitted along the riverbank looking for insects. He'd tell her about his dream of building a ranch here. It would only start out as a soddy to begin with, but eventually, he'd build her a real house with wooden floors and a wide porch for them to sit on evenings, the kind his pa had built his mother.

He paused, remembering his mother's pleasure. For the first time, he could remember such things without the pain of their loss. The healing was beginning. He'd tell Jenny that, too. He'd tell her of the lonely lost years, years without hope or dreams, and he'd tell her of all the dreams that crowded into his mind now, each one of them built around her.

He grinned thinking of her. A little girl, not much bigger than a scrap, but her impact on his life had been monumental. He'd make her see the wonder of that. He'd hold her and they'd talk for days and nights. So many things he'd closed away inside himself without sharing them; now they pushed at him, wanting to be released.

He'd been a happy boy, he remembered, always teasing his mother and father. He'd made his mother laugh at him and found pleasure in the sound. His father had thought him a fine lad. Pa used to say it that way, clamping him on his shoulder. "You're a fine lad, son." Caleb paused in tightening his cinch. "A fine lad!"

"I tried, Pa!" he whispered. "I tried."

Now it was time to go on with life. Swinging into the saddle, he cast one last glance around the green valley.

"I'll be back," he promised, and turned his horse east, following the other men. He was going to collect his woman.

Chapter 18

WARILY JENNY WATCHED as Hank Radburn settled himself against a log and aimed his gun at a small herd of buffalo. She wanted to stop him, but was afraid to try. For the past two days they'd sparred with each other—she trying to hold him off from his intent to share her bed, and he, enjoying the cat-and-mouse game he seemed certain of winning. She'd come to recognize what a cruel, insensitive man he was. This was the white eyes who destroyed the buffalo herds her people needed for food and clothing.

Radburn squeezed the trigger of his rifle, and the sound echoed across the prairie. In the distance, a bull quietly fell to his knees as if about to pray, while the cows around him kept feeding.

Radburn cackled gleefully and cast a glance back at Jenny. "See that?" he cried. "They're so dumb, they don't even know what's about to happen to 'em." Tears stung Jenny's eyes as she thought of the Comanche people and their dependence on the buffalo herds. There were few buffalo left—and yet evil men like this still slaughtered them for their hides.

Radburn squeezed off another shot, and a cow fell.

306

Jenny turned away, unable to watch, and her glance settled on Radburn's packhorse with the large knife used
for skinning buffalo. Furtively she edged closer, until
the knife was within reach. Suddenly there was a thunder of hooves and the buffalo herd took flight, moving
like a wave across the prairie toward them. Radburn
jumped up.

"Something's spooked 'em. They're headed this
way," he yelled, and hastily swung into his saddle.
Without looking back to see if Jenny followed, he set
off at a wild lope, away from the stampeding buffalo.

Distracted as she was by the thought of obtaining a
weapon, it took Jenny precious moments to act. Fear
spiraled through her as she looked at the black cloud of
dust veering toward her. She knew about buffalo stam-
pedes. As a girl, she'd seen the care her people used in
approaching the herds and the death found beneath the
thundering hooves. Heart in her throat, she leapt astride
the mule, who was straining to get away. Giving the
mule its head, she headed after Radburn, climbing a
slight embankment.

From his perch, Radburn was waving his hat and
cackling like a man who'd lost all reason. Jenny
glanced at him, then turned to watch the herd thunder
by. For a moment the swaying sea of buffalo were lost
to her in the billowing dust, then they were gone,
sweeping away across the prairie.

"Whoee! Ain't that som'pin!" Radburn exclaimed. "I
remember when there used to be big herds out here.
Used to take them pert' near a day to pass by you.
Reckon the buffalo's goin' the way of the beaver." He
shook his head in sorrow and seemed not to equate the

demise of the buffalo with his own evil pursuits. Now he glanced at Jenny.

"Come on now, girlie," he said. "Let's see what your Comanche mama taught you 'bout skinnin' buffalo." He led the way back down the embankment to the silent mounds left behind on the prairies.

"Can't figure what spooked 'em," he said, looking around, "less'n it was a coyote." He took out a knife and handed it to Jenny, his glittering gaze holding hers.

"I seen you eyeing this knife, girlie," he hissed, his bad breath escaping between his gaping teeth. "I know what you had in your mind, but it ain't going to happen. Old Radburn's way ahead of you. You just take one wrong step while you're using this knife and you'll be dead." He patted the pistol strapped to his hip. "I'm just as good with this here pistol as I am with old Betsy. Understand me?"

Silently Jenny nodded, and, taking the knife, set about skinning the buffalo hides from the carcasses. It was hard work. She'd often seen White Weasel and the other women at such work and she'd been used to helping with the lighter tasks. Now, with the burden fallen all on her shoulders, she soon tired.

"Get busy," Radburn would yell when she tried to pause and rest. The sun sat straight up from them, its hot rays adding to her discomfort. Through the afternoon she worked beside Radburn, skinning the buffalo, and as the sun slipped to the western horizon the interminable day came to an end.

"Cut away some fresh steaks and cook 'em up for supper," Radburn ordered, and Jenny was only too happy to do as he ordered. He's said nothing about the knife she was using. Maybe he'd forgotten about it.

She carried the meat down to the small creek, well away from the dead buffalo. The abandoned carcasses would soon bring wild animals intent on an easy meal. She built a fire and put the meat on sharp-pointed sticks over the coals to roast. Then seeing her bloodied calico gown, she placed the precious knife on a rock and waded into the creek, where she scrubbed away the stench of her day's work. When she climbed out, Radburn was waiting on the side of the creek, idly tossing the knife against a small scrub tree. At once his eyes flickered to her wet bodice and the dark aureoles of her breasts, which showed clearly through the wet material. A leering grin appeared.

"You worked good today," he said, without moving his gaze from her breasts, "real good." He licked his lips. Jenny crossed her arms over her chest and turned to the fire.

"I have to tend to the meat," she said, and was surprised to find she could barely force the words from between her stiff lips. Hank Radburn's intentions were very clear. He would try to claim her tonight—and he'd regained the only weapon she had against him. She could have cursed herself for her foolishness. Better to have worn the bloody gown forever than render herself helpless against such a man.

The meat was nearly done, but Jenny's appetite was gone. She moved away from the fire, into the shadows, and sat on the ground, sunk in misery, her head on her updrawn knees. She could hear Radburn eating, smacking, and belching. He sounded like an animal himself.

She wanted to scream, to leap up and run wildly across the prairie rather than submit to his rutting, but she thought of Frank and Faye Walsh and the reason she'd traveled to this lonely part of the prairie. She must get free of this man and find Two Wolves. Even now, he might have passed her on the prairie. Desperately she prayed to the Great Spirit, then for good measure she prayed to the white man's God as well.

"Hello the camp!" a voice called.

Hank Radburn flung aside the meat he'd been chewing on and reached for his gun. "Who's there?" he called, wiping at his greasy mouth.

"Caleb Hunter," the voice called back.

Jenny's head jerked up. "Caleb," she breathed, and the word was like a prayer. Radburn motioned her to stay still.

"What do you want, Hunter?" he called back.

"That's not real hospitable of you," Caleb's voice said. He was closer now. Through the haze of smoke, Jenny could see him just on the edge of light.

"Have you got an extra cup of coffee or a bit of meat to spare a traveler?" He walked to the fire.

"I reckon not," Radburn said. "Besides, you and me ain't friends enough to share anything, much less a cup of coffee."

Caleb was studying the meat roasting at the fire. "Seems you're the one who was shooting buffalo earlier today."

"What of it?" Radburn asked belligerently. "I ain't south of the Arkansas River now, Hunter. You can't stop me from doing my business."

"No, I guess I can't." Caleb sighed and squatted beside the fire. "From the number of humps out there, looks like you didn't have much luck today."

Despite his earlier declaration, Radburn filled a tin cup with coffee and passed it over to Caleb. "Something spooked 'em," he mumbled.

"You don't say?" Caleb replied.

His hat was pulled low over his face, but Jenny heard the quirk of laughter in his voice. He'd been the one to spook the herd. Had he been out there all day watching them? He hadn't once glanced at her. Did he know she was here?

"I reckon I could spare you some grub," Radburn was saying. "My woman here turned squeamish and she ain't eatin'."

For the first time, Caleb's eyes turned to her, and she read the rage in them. Was he angry with her? she wondered. Did he believe she would willingly go with such a man as Hank Radburn?

Hank Radburn had seen the exchange of looks between them and eased his gun from its holster. "She's my woman now, Hunter," he snarled. "I found her wanderin' around on the prairie and I took her. You can't take her back."

"Does she want to be with you, Radburn?" Caleb asked quietly.

"No!" Jenny said vehemently.

"She ain't got no choice," Radburn whined. "I rescued her. She's mine."

"She's a human being, Radburn. She has rights. You can't treat her like one of your mules."

"She's an Injun squaw. She ain't got no rights. You took her to a white settlement and they tried to tame her, but it didn't work. She run away from 'em. She don't want to live back there. She's wild like all them other savages."

"That's not true! I didn't run away!" Jenny cried.

"Seems like the lady doesn't agree with your version of the tale," Caleb observed. He'd pushed his hat back, so the firelight shone on his face.

"She's just mad 'cause I made her work today," Radburn was saying. "Anyway, she's mine. I've already claimed her. She's right good in the bedroll." Radburn didn't see the muscle jump in Caleb's cheek.

"That's a lie!" Jenny cried, getting to her feet.

Radburn's face grew ugly. "Now you jest set yourself back down there and be quiet!" he bellowed.

Caleb's hot coffee hit him full in the face. Radburn yelped, his hands going to his face. When he looked up, Caleb was facing him with a pistol in each fist. Radburn grabbed for his holster, but it was empty.

"I've got it right here, Radburn," he said, waving one of the pistols. "If I remember correctly, you always have a hair trigger on your gun."

"B-Be careful," Radburn said as the pistol wobbled at him.

"Let's have a little talk, Radburn," Caleb said. "Tell me again how you rescued Jenny."

"I did! I did, I tell you! She was out here all alone, without any food or water. She'd 'ave died if I hadn't come along and took her under my wing." He paused, studying Caleb's face. "I—I wasn't goin' to do nothin' to her. I—I was takin' her back to Millbrook just as soon as I got me some buffalo hides to make my trip worthwhile."

"That was mighty nice, Hank," Caleb said. "But now the lady has to go—and you won't mind a bit, will you?"

"N-No, no," Radburn said. "I don't want no squaw who don't want to stay with me. Go on. Git outa here."

Jenny grinned and stepped toward the fire. "You won't mind if we take some of this extra grub, will you, Mr. Radburn?"

"Take it all. I don't care," he cried. "There's plenty more where that come from. Help yourself."

Jenny rolled up a packet of the cooked meat, bent to retrieve the skinning knife, and hurried to her mule. Caleb continued to hold the pistols on Hank Radburn. When she was mounted, she looked back at Caleb.

"Take off," he yelled.

"What about you?"

"I'll follow you."

"You aren't going to kill him?"

"I haven't decided." Caleb's fist tightened on the pistols.

"No, no. I ain't givin' you no trouble. I ain't even going to try to follow you."

Caleb grinned at the buffalo hunter. "Ride out," he told Jenny, and this time she obeyed, kicking against the mule's sides with her moccasined feet.

The little mule seemed to know lives depended on him and he lit out across the prairie. In no time, Jenny could hear hoofbeats behind her and looked back to reassure herself it was Caleb.

Once again he'd found her on this vast prairie. They

were together again. Then she remembered Two Wolves and her need to go to him and her elation died. They rode for some time, putting distance between themselves and the buffalo hunter. Finally Caleb motioned her to a halt and looked around.

"I think we're safe enough here, even if he did work up the courage to follow us."

"Are you sure he won't follow?"

Caleb nodded. "Men like him don't do well alone—unless they hold all the cards." He slid off his horse and came around to her, reaching up to help her off the mule. His big hands settled at her waist, lifting her, cradling her, bringing her to rest against his own body. Wordlessly Jenny gazed up at him, then his head blotted out the star-spangled prairie sky and his lips claimed hers. Finally he broke away.

"What in God's name are you doing out here?" he demanded.

"I can explain,"she said, with some desperation.

"You'd better. Hold on." He turned to the horses. Jenny helped stable the mounts and spread out his bedroll. At last, when they were seated side by side, he turned to her.

"Now tell me what excuse you could possibly have for riding back out on the prairie? Don't tell me you've changed your mind and want to go back home with the renegades?" His voice held a tremor of uncertainty, so she told him of Two Wolves escaping from the well pit and her fear that he would once again seek revenge on the Walshes.

"I came here to stop him," she said somberly, "by

giving myself to him. Perhaps when I am dead, he'll be satisfied."

"You know that won't stop him," Caleb said. "He's become a renegade. He'll kill anyone who crosses his path. The only way to stop him is to kill him."

"But we tried and he lived," Jenny cried. "His medicine is stronger."

"Is it? Is that the real reason you were willing to sacrifice yourself a second time, to save me?"

"If you fight him, he'll kill you."

"Don't you know, Jenny, that if he killed you, I wouldn't want to live, either?" Caleb whispered, taking her into his arms. "I couldn't bear another loss like that. I need you. Remember what you said? We belong to each other now. You can't make a decision like that without me."

"Caleb!" She couldn't help the tears that streamed down her face—tears of weakness she'd always thought them, but now they were tears of joy. Caleb's hungry mouth found hers and she gave herself to the glory of his kiss. He pulled her back against the soft bedroll and his kiss became more insistent. His big hands skimmed over her body, soothing, arousing, awaking that passion they'd shared before.

"I love you, Jenny," he whispered, and his voice caught as if he were unused to saying such things. She wound her arms around his neck, pressing him closer.

"I love you, Caleb," she said, and felt all the anguish her heart had suffered lifted from her. They were together again. They belonged to each other.

Their lovemaking was gentle, languid, as if they had their lifetime to enjoy each other, to lie together and

discover. Jenny caressed Caleb's lean, hard body, mar-
veling at the beauty of it. His skin, she discovered, was
very white beneath his clothes, like hers. That made her
feel they were the same.

He unbraided her hair and spread it out around her
like a fan for her sweet face, then he took away the now
dry calico and kissed her in places that made her blush
with shyness and excitement.

"I never thought much about pleasuring a woman,"
he said softly. "You'll have to help me, Jenny."

She laughed, a soft, guttural sound, deep in her
throat. Her face blazed with joy. "You are doing just as
you should," she reassured him, then showed him what
pleased her by her gasps of delight.

Caleb was lost in the wonder of it, in the sensual
beauty of her face when his movements aroused her.
Bathed in moonlight, her every thought and response
was open to him, so he touched and explored and
aroused until he himself was ready to explode. Only
then, when he was certain his woman was ready for
him, did he sheath himself in her silken flesh and begin
the rhythmic motions that would carry them to a place
neither had ever been before.

Jenny's fingernails bit into his shoulder as she
strained against him. He felt her release, felt the tightening of silken muscles and flesh, felt his own response,
throbbing and earth-shattering. For a moment the prairie
shook, and dimly he wondered if a herd of buffalo were
stampeding toward them, then the sensation passed and
he knew it was something he would experience time
and again with this woman.

They lay beside each other, bathing in the afterglow

of their lovemaking. Jenny stroked his bare shoulders and hips, running her fingers lightly over his flesh, petting, loving, giving him some profound sense of being loved that he'd known only as a boy at his mother's knee. But Jenny was not his mother. She was his lover, teaching him the ways between men and women.

He smiled thinking that she, this untried, virginal girl, raised among the Indians, should know more of love than all the women he'd paid. He rested, breathing in her scent, learning the wonder of sleeping beside a loved one, twining his legs around her slender thighs, and, finally, driven to new desires, he took her again. She laughed, a joyous sound, and gave as willingly as before, and, when he lay on the pallet beside her, spent and tired, she bent over him, dropping light kisses on his eyes and brow.

"I have something to tell you, Jenny," he murmured sleepily.

"Tell me tomorrow," she whispered.

"It's important." He sighed.

"Tomorrow," she crooned.

"About a valley, a beautiful valley—and you and me and our ranch . . ." His words drifted away.

Jenny lay beside him long into the night; when a rim of gray light lay on the black perimeter, she rose and quietly dressed. She had deliberately staked out the mule away from their camp. Now she eased toward it and fumbled in the dark with the stake. At last the reins were free, and she hurried to the mule's side, preparing to mount.

A hand came out of the blackness and gripped hers

across the mule's back. She gasped and fought to free herself, but without success. The mule stomped the ground impatiently and tried to shimmy away. Hank Radburn had found them, Jenny thought frantically. Then she heard the familiar voice.

"Caleb!" she cried out.

His laughter came to her out of the darkness and he leaned across the mule, his hand still gripping hers. He stared into her eyes and his face sobered.

"Have you forgotten so soon what we pledged to each other?" he asked softly. "We're not alone anymore, Jenny. We have each other for always."

Tears clotted Jenny's throat. "I can't let Two Wolves kill you," she cried. "I love you too much."

Without relinquishing his hold on her, he slapped the mule, startling it away from them, then he pulled her into his arms.

"Whatever happens from now on," he said, "it happens to both of us."

She searched his face for any doubt or fear. There was none. Silently she went into his arms. He held her close, his head bowed, so his lips were against her hair.

"Don't you know I fear no man as much as I fear losing you? Don't leave me, Jenny. I need you. I'm not a man without you."

His words woke music in her heart. Her arms went around his broad shoulder and it was she who held him now, cradling him, loving him. He was a strong man, she knew, but he wasn't afraid to reveal his need for her. She had never felt so fulfilled. Silently she followed him back to their pallet and cuddled beside him and finally slept—a deep, restful, dreamless sleep—and when the morning dawned, they rose and faced it together.

Chapter 19

"W E MUST WAIT until your wounds heal, Two Wolves," Big Elk admonished his war chief. "We cannot ride against our enemies if you die."

"I will not die." Two Wolves grunted, pushing up from his pallet. Sweat stood out on his brow. His normally brown cheeks were gray. "I have lived for one reason only, to kill this man known as The Hunter and the white eyes woman who shared our campfires and called herself Wild Sage."

"We will take our revenge on them someday for their betrayal," Big Elk said. "First you must heal."

Two Wolves fell back and clasped his friend's arm. "You must promise me this," he said through gritted teeth. The stench of death was upon him. "If I am not able to take the lives of my enemies, you will do it for me. You will revenge my death."

"You will not die," Big Elk lied. "We will yet triumph over your enemies." He alone had stayed behind when the rest of the renegade band had returned to the Comancheria. Faithfully he'd searched until he'd found the place where Two Wolves and the man called Hunter had fought; there he'd found Two Wolves's horse and had lowered himself into the well to rescue his friend and leader. He glanced at the mangled leg and bound chest of Two Wolves. Many men would have already died of the injuries he'd sustained. Two Wolves's medicine was strong, but not strong enough.

"Tomorrow!" Two Wolves cried, and struggled to rise from his pallet. His dark eyes wore a milky haze, as if even now he gazed upon his friend from behind a nether veil. He was too weak to rise by himself. He fell back, sweating and gasping with pain. Big Elk held a cup of water to his lips, but Two Wolves made no effort to sip from it. "Tomorrow, we will ride!" he whispered.

"Tomorrow we will ride and claim the scalps of Hunter and Wild Sage," Big Elk said.

Two Wolves snarled, drawing his lips away from his teeth like a wolf. For a moment, Big Elk felt fear, then awe at his brother warrior's predatory spirit. Then he heard the death rattle in Two Wolves's throat. Two Wolves's fierce gaze held his, even after his spirit had fled his body.

Sitting beside the dead warrior, Big Elk raised his voice in a death chant. He was alone now, here in enemy land, land that had once belonged to his people. He must take the body of his war chief home to the Comancheria. When the chant was finished, Big Elk extinguished the fire and loaded Two Wolves's body on his faithful war pony. Flinging himself on the back of his own horse, Big Elk led the way on his southward journey. He could travel far under the safety of darkness; soon he would be among his people again. He thought of the things Two Wolves had told him of Wild

Sage—about her betrayal, of how she had fired a bullet into his chest, causing him to fall into the well pit.

Once Big Elk himself had thought of taking the fragile white Indian girl for his wife, but when Two Wolves courted her, Big Elk had withdrawn, not wishing to compete against his friend. Now he remembered Wild Sage's gentle ways and wondered how she could have changed so drastically. Yet he'd seen it himself in the way she'd warned the white eyes and the way she'd tried to run away from the warriors who'd come to reclaim her. She'd forgotten she was Comanche. She was now their enemy. So be it. One day, he, Big Elk, would seek out the traitorous Wild Sage and carry her scalp home to their people.

The sight of slain buffalo made him pause in his journey. In the distance he saw the pale light of a campfire. Big Elk's nose twitched at the sweet, rotting smell of death and he sensed an enemy was near. Drawing back his lips as Two Wolves had done, he moved silently toward the riverbank, where a dirty, foul-smelling white man, a buffalo hunter, lay snoring loudly, an empty bottle and empty dreams his last companions in life. . . .

"We'll head back to the fort and request soldiers to go to Millbrook to protect us until we know Two Wolves is gone," Caleb said, saddling his horse.

"Do you think Two Wolves has gone to Millbrook yet?" Jenny asked anxiously.

Caleb glanced up, studying the land and sky, looking for an answer to her fears. "I don't know," he said finally, "but the fact he didn't retaliate at once leads me to believe he was injured in that fall and he's holed up somewhere trying to mend. At any rate, the sooner we get to Millbrook, the better for us all. We'll round up another posse and prepare the outlying homesteaders against an attack."

When they were ready, they set out across the prairie, retracing the path they'd taken the night before. When they came to the valley where buffalo carcasses lay rotting, she turned her head away.

"Do you think Hank is still here?" she asked faintly.

"Not if he's smart." Caleb appeared preoccupied as he studied the vultures circling the carcasses. "Look there," he said, pointing toward the creek where the camp had been. Vultures made a slow, lazy circle.

"What does it mean?" Jenny asked.

"We'd better find out," Caleb said. "Stay here."

"Out in the open, alone?" she cried. "I'm not a child."

He grinned at her. "I remember," he said briefly, then his expression hardened as he contemplated the creek. Pulling his gun he kneed the sorrel into a light gallop. Jenny followed close behind.

When they reached the creek, Caleb motioned her to fall behind. Feeling safe this close to him, she complied and waited while he dismounted and walked down the embankment to where she had built the campfire. Hank's mules were gone. He must have packed up and left by now, leaving some unwanted meat behind, she thought idly. Then she caught sight of Caleb standing rigid as he stared down at something.

"What is it?" she called, starting to dismount.

"Stay there," he ordered harshly, and again she did as

he commanded. He came back to his pack mule and looked at her.

"What's wrong?" she demanded.

Caleb paused, looking up at her. "Comanche!" he said.

"Two Wolves!" she cried, looking around in terror. There was no sign of anyone on the vast prairie. "He's on his way to Millbrook."

"Maybe, maybe not," Caleb said, studying the ground for signs. He saw hoofprints and squatted to study them before following them.

Jenny didn't wait. Jerking the reins, she kicked at the mule's sides and set off across the prairie.

"Come back here, Jenny," Caleb shouted. "Don't go off half-cocked. You'll get yourself killed."

The mule didn't slow.

Cursing, Caleb leapt on his horse. Spurring his mount after Jenny, he thought of how stubborn and independent she was. She didn't mind a man's word at all. Was he ready for this? he wondered, then remembered her sweetness and her loyalty toward those she loved; he urged the sorrel on until he overtook the mule.

"Dad blame it, don't you know better than to go galloping off by yourself?" he shouted at her when he finally caught her.

"Two Wolves has a head start on us."

"We may be panicking for nothing," Caleb snapped. "There was only one set of moccasin prints back there and two horses, one loaded heavier than the other, as if it carried a burden. Think, Jenny."

"I don't know what all this means."

"It means that one man killed Hank Radburn and he

was leading an Indian pony. Why would one of your braves do that?"

Jenny stared at him in puzzlement, then her face cleared. "If a warrior falls in battle, his friend takes his body back to his people. But who?"

"You and I both shot Two Wolves before he fell down that well. He must be dead and one of his men is taking his body back to the Comancheria."

"Big Elk," Jenny said. "He would risk his life to save Two Wolves—and he would never abandon his body."

Caleb nodded. "From the direction he took, I'd say he's heading back to his people."

"How can you be sure? Maybe someone else killed Radburn," Jenny cried, afraid to hope.

"Those were Indian ponies back there. Their hooves were unshod and I saw the print of an Indian moccasin in the mud along the creek bed, and last,"— he glanced at her—"whoever killed Hank Radburn took his scalp."

"Then you think the danger is over?"

"It might be. But we won't take chances. We'll ride to the fort as we planned, then return to Millbrook."

Jenny nodded. She let him take the lead and set the pace, following docilely behind. When he stopped to water the animals, she stopped. When they halted for the night, she sat tense and uneasy until he pulled her down on the bedroll beside him, reassuring her just with his presence. There was no attempt to make love. They simply lent their support and strength to each other. Lying together, their arms wrapped around each other, they learned another facet of the love they shared.

Jenny slept fitfully and rose as soon as Caleb indicated they should move on. The prairie was gray with early light, unwarmed yet by the morning sun. It mattered little to Jenny. She didn't see the beauty. She thought only of the people she loved back in Millbrook and the death that might await them if Caleb were wrong. They traveled first to Fort Mann, where they told their story and were reassured by Major Egan, who sent a detail of soldiers out to search for Big Elk.

"I'll send soldiers to Millbrook at once," he said, shaking hands with Caleb. Though puzzled by Jenny's part in all this, he nevertheless took her at face value. She was a white woman caught in an untenable position.

"We're much obliged for your help," Caleb told the young officer before taking Jenny's arm and turning toward the door.

"Why don't you stay and ride back with my men? You'd be a lot safer," the major offered.

Caleb glanced at Jenny and shook his head. "We're in a hurry, Major. Thanks anyway."

Gratefully Jenny followed him to the horses. The specter of the buffalo hunter's scalped head haunted her, driving her on toward the little soddy that held people she'd come to love. Caleb said nothing, seeming to sense her urgency.

Late in the afternoon, they paused for a rest. They weren't far from the Walsh homestead now. They'd make it before nightfall. Jenny felt an easing of the tightness in her chest. Maybe Caleb was right. Maybe the danger was over. She even managed a smile for him when he brought her a tin cup of water from the creek. . . .

* * *

He'd avoided the soldiers all day. Now he lay on the ground peering over a ridge, watching them pass by below. From the direction they were headed, he knew they were searching for him. He'd never slip past their tight guard. Big Elk lay thinking, staring to the east. There, less than a day's journey away, lay Millbrook and the traitor Wild Sage. To think of it made his heart thunder within his breast. What honor he could bring to himself if he brought home the scalp of the woman who had caused Two Wolves's death. If he were alive, Two Wolves would go east and fight or be killed in his seeking of revenge.

But Big Elk was not Two Wolves. He thought of his mother and father back on the Comancheria and of his comrades who'd already left, driven southward by the soldiers. No, he was not Two Wolves with a singular purpose. He would return to his people and fight the white eyes another time. But how was he to get past the soldiers?

A west wind had come up, blowing hot and dry, and suddenly he remembered a time of his childhood when the hot winds had brought fire and destruction to the prairie and his people had broken their tepees and fled. He looked to the east again. Such a fire could have a twofold effect, drawing the soldiers away and posing a final act of revenge to Wild Sage and the people of Millbrook.

Crouching low, Big Elk made his way back to his horses and searched among his pouches until he found the pieces of flint for which he searched.

When the small soddy came into view on the distant horizon, Jenny could contain herself no longer. With a quick glance at Caleb, as if seeking his approval but unable to wait for it, she kicked her mule into a gallop. Frank heard her coming and hurried up the creek. Faye stepped out of the soddy, herding her children inside. The memory of that night of terror had made them cautious. When they saw Jenny, they cried out a welcome and ran forward as she brought the mule to a stop and leapt off.

"Jenny, thank God. We thought you were dead!" Faye cried, throwing her arms around her.

Hannah and Nathan came running to crowd up for hugs as well. Feeling left out, Marybeth set up a howl until Jenny picked her up and settled her on one slim hip.

"What happened to you, girl?" Frank ask when some of the pandemonium had let up. "Why did you go off like that? Did we do something to offend you?"

By this time Caleb had ridden into the yard. Jenny glanced at him and turned to face Frank. "I'm sorry I worried you," she began, "and I'm mighty sorry I took one of your mules."

"That's not important," Frank said dismissively. "It was you we cared about."

Tears sprang to Jenny's eyes.

"Jenny's cwying." Marybeth gulped and started bawling. Faye took the little girl and cradled her head against her shoulder.

"Obviously, we can't talk out here," Faye said. "Come on in and I'll get us all some cold sassafras tea." She led the way into the cool darkness of the soddy. Caleb dismounted and followed them.

Jenny settled Marybeth for her nap, singing her a lullaby until her lashes fluttered against her flushed cheeks. She felt as if she'd been away for months and was finally home again. She looked around the familiar, cramped room. This was no longer home, she thought idly. When all this trouble was over, she was going off with Caleb. He would be her home now. Dropping a last kiss on the sleeping girl's brow, Jenny rose and went back to the table.

"Why did you leave?" Faye asked in her quiet way.

Jenny lowered her head and studied her clasped hands. "I overheard you and Frank talking about Two Wolves, and suddenly I feared he might be alive after all—and if he were alive, I knew he'd come looking for me. As long as I was here, you were in danger, so I thought I would find him and . . ." Her voice trailed off.

"And let Two Wolves kill her, because that was what he would have done," Caleb said from the doorway, where he'd been standing and studying the prairie.

"Jenny, you couldn't have done that," Faye said. "We wouldn't have let you make such a sacrifice."

"I thought you understood when we gave you our name," Frank said, "that we were making you family. That means we would have fought Two Wolves together."

"Apparently, togetherness is something she doesn't understand," Caleb said from the doorway. "She tried to sneak away from me as well." He scowled at her.

"I love you all," she said, blinking back the tears that stung her lids. "I lost Ten Bears and White Weasel. I couldn't bear to lose anyone else."

"You won't," Frank said, scowling. "By God, I

bought me an extra gun and ammunition. We're keeping water and food nearby, so if we ever get attacked by the Comanche or any other varmint, we can withstand a siege."

"Caleb thinks Two Wolves is dead," Jenny said, feeling as if it might be true after all. "He—we think Big Elk has taken his body home."

Caleb stepped forward, nodding his head in confirmation. "Major Egan has sent out a detail of soldiers to search for Big Elk. The renegade band has already passed through on their way to Texas. If Big Elk is returning to the Comancheria, he likely won't return."

"Then it's over," Faye said, with obvious relief.

"Thank God, the murdering bastards are gone," Frank echoed.

"Frank!" Faye exclaimed. Her eyes were round with surprise. Frank Walsh had never been known to use a curse word in his life—and especially never around women.

"I wasn't going to be run off my own land," he said, "not by a no-good, red-skinned—'scuse me, Jenny—renegade who didn't know nothing better than killing. Yet, I wasn't looking forward to killing a man, not even a red heathen like Two Wolves."

"We've had a narrow escape," Caleb said, coming to the table and looking around the circle of faces. "Two Wolves had no boundaries, no sense of how far is humanly right and what goes against God's laws."

"He wasn't even bound by Comanche honor," Jenny said. "He truly was a renegade. He'd cast away all laws but his own."

Frank was silent in the face of their words. Faye's

face was pale, her lips trembling as she thought of how close they'd come to death. Then she glanced at the slender girl standing beside her. She alone had sensed the magnitude of Two Wolves's evil—and she'd been willing to sacrifice herself for them. She clasped Jenny's hand.

"Thank you, Jenny," she said, tears streaming down her face. The two women embraced. Hannah and Nathan began to bawl. Faye drew away. "Goodness, look at me, weeping and carrying on," she said, wiping at her eyes. "Hannah and Nathan, that's enough now. We're all safe—and we're going to be might hungry in a little bit here. Come on. Help me get supper. Nathan, you get the water. Hannah, you gather wood."

The two children rose and went to do their chores. Faye began bustling around the kitchen, lifting pots and bowls, organizing herself. Jenny smiled. How familiar and dear all this was. She grinned at Caleb, and he saw that her eyes sparkled with renewed tears—this time tears of happiness.

Nathan entered the cabin and looked around, his eyes overly large in his pale face. "Pa, could I see you outside?" he asked.

"Sure, son," Frank said broadly. "Come on, Caleb. Let's go on out and give the womenfolks room to work." The two men followed the boy out of the cabin.

"Wonder what that was about?" Faye said indulgently. Her smile was serene and tolerant of any male shenanigans the three might come up with.

Jenny felt a prick of unease, then pushed it aside. It was time to stop worrying, time to accept the normal everyday events of life. But instinct told her this was not one of those times. "Something's wrong," she said going to the door. Faye was right behind her.

Everything outside looked the same. The chickens pecked nervously around the soddy. The hog wallowed in the trough, waiting to be fed. The mule Jenny had ridden, and the sorrel, were still in the yard, still saddled. The other mule stood patiently waiting in the field, still hitched to the plow. The men were nowhere in sight.

"Where did they go?" Jenny whispered, and edged out into the yard.

Faye motioned Hannah to the house. Wordlessly the girl lay aside the armload of wood and did as her mother bid. The events of the past few days had given them a new discipline.

Carefully Jenny rounded the corner of the soddy and halted. The men stood staring off at the horizon. Jenny looked but could see nothing except a lazy swirl of smoke.

"Prairie fire!" Faye cried beside her. Jenny looked at her. Faye's eyes were dark with fear, her face pale.

"Mother, get the children and get the wagon," Frank ordered.

"It's too late now," Caleb said. "They'd never be able to outrun the fire with the wind blowing in this direction. We'll have to make a firebreak."

Frank nodded. "Mother, get Hannah and Nathan. Fill buckets and pour it on the roof. Caleb, we'll have to set a backfire. I've got furrows plowed around the house, but with this wind the fire may jump it."

"Jenny, grab some sacks and tie them around the

hoes. Set up buckets of water down by the furrows. Wet down the haystack by the barn."

Everyone took off running. Buckets of water were carted up the hill to the house and poured over the rooftop, then more water was carried to the new open shed Frank had built. He'd just brought in his baled hay and stacked it around it for walls. The whole mass had been contrived to provide shelter for the cow and mules for the coming winter, but now, standing so close to the soddy, it provided a fire hazard.

Caleb and Frank set a backfire, working furiously to control it. Faye worked beside them with a hoe and wet sacks. Jenny and the children carried pails of water until they were ready to drop from exhaustion, and still they worked. Dusk was settling over the land before they were finished, so they slipped and fell up the creek bank with their watery burden.

At last it seemed they'd done all they could. All that was left for them was to wait. The fire had roared closer, flaring in the darkness like some exotic flower, its beauty eerie and menacing. Tiny jets of flame shot skyward, like fireworks on the Fourth of July. Through the night they watched, fascinated and repelled at the same time.

They slumped against the soddy walls, their heads on their knees as they sought brief rest. The children were huddled inside, frightened and unable to sleep, but forced there by Faye, who couldn't deal with their fears and her own.

"Get ready; the flame's getting closer," Frank said finally, and they pushed themselves to their weary feet, wiped at their sooty faces, and took up a stance against their fiery enemy.

Would the backfire work? Would the plowed furrows around the soddy turn the fire away from them or would they all perish in the flames? Staunchly they stood waiting, and when the fire sent out its deadly fingers, seeking an inroad into their scanty defenses, they ran forward with wet sacks and hoes to beat out the flames.

Jenny's arms had long since lost feeling when Frank shouted, "It's turning away from us. Mother, we're safe."

"Oh, Frank." Faye sobbed, falling into his arms. He embraced her, laughing and crying at the same time, their teeth and the whites of their eyes gleaming in their soot-covered faces.

Jenny stood watching her friends express the joy and love they shared and looked at Caleb. His gaze was fixed on them; then he turned to Jenny, and she saw the hunger in his eyes—not the physical hunger they'd shared already, but a hunger for the deeper love and commitment he saw between Frank and Faye. He held out his arms to Jenny, and she ran to him, throwing herself into his arms, feeling the strength of this man flow through her. He had been right. It was better to join with others rather than fight alone. It was a lesson he'd learned well, and now he'd taught her. They belonged to each other and to their friends. They were part of all men and women, not isolated souls struggling to find themselves. With this same sense of belonging they turned and joined hands with their friends.

Chapter 20

"**W**E'VE BEAT IT," Frank said. Tears made runnels through the black soot, and Jenny giggled at him. Faye's laughter joined hers, and they stood with their arms around one another, bent over in glee.

"You ladies don't look so good, either," Caleb said, and Jenny put a hand to her face. She could feel the slippery blackness covering her features. Hastily both women hurried to the washbasin and put the lye soap to good use. When they rejoined the men, Caleb and Frank were talking in low voices.

"The fire's turned away from the town," they were saying, "but we'd best go see if anyone else needs our help."

Caleb nodded. All the old habits of his father and life on the ranch were coming back to him. Neighbors helped neighbors. "We'd better take the women and children to Millbrook. I hate to leave them out here alone."

Frank nodded. "I expect you're right. I'll tell Faye to get the kids ready."

Dread washed through Jenny.

"Why do we have to leave now?" she asked. Her voice was trembling. "The fire's gone past us."

The men turned to look at the two women. Frank took Faye's arm. "Mother, there's still a danger to us here if the wind shifts."

"You don't think that Two Wolves . . .?" Jenny's voice trailed off. Mutely she looked at Caleb. "Did he cause this fire?"

"Two Wolves is dead, Jenny," Caleb said. "You have to start believing that."

"Big Elk then!"

He couldn't lie to her. "Maybe."

Her eyes widened in terror. "He's here then."

"Jenny!" Caleb took her into his arms. "Have faith, Jenny. A prairie fire can be started by many things."

"Big Elk could have started it."

"Yes, he could have. But I don't think he's here, Jenny. Now, go on and help Faye get the kids packed up in the wagon. We'll take you into Millbrook, then Frank and I will go help whatever neighbors need help from the fire."

Silently she nodded and went to help Faye, but her face held all the fear and guilt she could carry.

"Now don't you start blaming yourself for this, Jenny Walsh," Faye said. "Sometimes God just visits disasters on a person's head to try his faith. Let's just do what we have to do and thank the good Lord we're alive." She nodded as if all was said and done. "We'd best get our belongings together. No telling how long we'll have to stay in town." She turned toward the soddy; Jenny stayed where she was, sunk in misery.

"Go help her, Sister," Frank said, and his kind words

brought tears to Jenny's eyes. Biting her lip, she raised her chin and brushed away the tears.

Caleb was watching her, his expression sympathetic and loving. "We're all in this together, Jenny," he said gently. Jenny nodded, and, forcing a grin for him, she went off to help Faye.

In no time they had the wagon filled with food and clothing and bedding. All that was needed was to bring the sleeping children. Suddenly hoofbeats sounded in the distance, and both men sprang up to grab their rifles.

"Get back in the house," Caleb shouted, and Jenny and Faye ran to the soddy.

"Frank Walsh!" a voice shouted, and the men lowered their guns. "Ben Morley here."

"Come on in," Frank shouted, and the small, dark man who'd brought them new mules just days before rode into the yard with a handful of other men.

"Looks like we got here too late," Ben said. "We were out fighting fires at Jacob Wilson's place."

"Did he get burned out?" Frank asked.

Ben nodded. "He's alive, though. Bracken Bell was killed, overcome by smoke. Damn fool wouldn't give up fighting the fire."

"Poor Miz Bell," Faye lamented. "To see her husband fight so hard and then die like that. How is she bearing up?"

"As well as can be expected, ma'am," Ben said. "We took her and her baby on into town. Reckon she could use her friends right now."

"Of course, we were just going in," Faye said. "Frank, you want to bring the children?"

"We'll be along as soon as we get our family safely to town," Frank told Ben. "Is the road to town clear of the fire?"

"It was when we passed," Morley said. "The fire hadn't reached it yet. With the shift in the wind, we figured the fire's headed down to the Hack place. The other men rode on down that way, while we came by to see about you folks. We'll be going on if you don't need us."

"I'll ride back with you," Caleb said. "Frank can drive the women and children into town." Frank nodded in agreement and hurried into the soddy and began carrying out his children.

Jenny overheard their plans and felt her heart squeeze tightly. Caleb came to help her up on the back of the wagon, then he took hold of her cold hands. "You'll be all right now," he said, gazing up at her.

She smiled sheepishly. "I know. Be careful. I couldn't bear to lose you now."

"I'm coming back, Jenny," he said somberly. "There's going to be a wedding, and we're going to our own place—that is, if you can leave Faye and Frank. I found a pretty little valley north of here. We can raise horses and cattle. There's a pretty little stream and . . . I'll build you a cabin." He paused. "There aren't any other settlers up there yet," he said. "It'd be lonely on a woman."

"If you were there, I'd never feel lonely," she said. A smile lit his features.

"I love you, Wild Sage," he cried, squeezing her hand.

He left her then, leaping astride his horse and follow-

ing the rest of the men. At the creek, he turned back to
wave at her. Jenny watched him leave, her heart filled
with love and happiness.

The wagon pulled out of the clearing as it had a hundred times before and took the path toward town. Off in
the distance the fire glowed, creeping through the buffalo grass and flaring up in the redtop bunch grass. At
times the fire burned too close. They could feel the intense heat of the flames. At times they had to leave the
road, driving well around the encroaching flames. The
smoke was thick, clogging their breathing. Cinders flew
out, so they were constantly slapping at their clothes.

The town had barely been spared. Some of the buildings bore the blackened reminders of just how close the
fire had come. Their arrival in Millbrook seemed somehow anticlimactic after the harrowing ride to get there.

The townspeople were strangely calm. Homesteaders
had brought their families to town in the hope of finding safety from the fire. They'd left behind their soddies
and livestock, their crops and fields. If all were destroyed, they'd build again. Now they sought only to
preserve life. No one had given in to panic. Women and
children milled about the streets talking about all that
had happened. Some of them had been driven in from
homesteads already burned out. But they were alive and
their spirits were undaunted.

Frank parked the wagon among the others at the
church, and, unhitching the mule, saddled it and left for
the Hack homestead. Women surged to the wagon to
talk to Faye and Jenny, eager for fresh news about the
fire.

"Thank God you're all safe," Maudie St. John said,

hugging Faye. "We've been praying for the well-being of all the outlying homesteaders."

"Did they all make it into town?" Faye asked.

"You and your family were the last ones," Viola Porter replied.

"You look exhausted," one of the women observed.

Faye gripped the wagon wheel, her knuckles white. "We spent all night fighting the fire."

"Did you save your place?" a chorus of women asked.

Faye nodded. "All except the crops—and the drought followed by that hailstorm just about took care of that."

"Ain't that the way of it?" Viola Porter spoke up. "Sometimes I wonder if the Lord's even listening to us puny humans down here."

"Hush your mouth, Viola Porter," Maudie said. "Don't you blaspheme the Lord."

"I only said—"

"I know what you said. You ought to be down on your knees this minute beggin' the Lord to forgive you."

"You ain't the only one with a noddin' acquaintance with the Lord, Maudie St. John," Viola snapped. "I'll be down on my knees praying when I think the time is right, not when you tell me."

"Ladies, ladies," Margaret Rudd said sternly. She'd come to put her arms around Jenny shoulders in unspoken support. When she had everyone's attention, she went on. "These poor people have been on their feet all night long. I reckon we ought to get them to bed."

There was a chorus of agreement. Viola and Maudie

cast a last angry glance at each other, then reached out to clasp hands in mute apology.

"The children can continue to sleep in the wagon. Faye, you and the baby and Jenny can come sleep in my sister's beds." Margaret looked around at the other ladies.

"As for the rest of us, folks'll be needin' something to eat. I expect we'd better get some food to cookin'."

The women nodded in agreement and hurried back to other tasks. Now that they were sure the Walsh family was safe, their thoughts turned back to their own plights and their voices rang with false bravado. They would not be defeated, Jenny thought in wonder. She remembered how she'd hated them in the beginning with all their strange, stubborn ways. She imagined her white mother and father had come from such stock. She took courage from them, picturing the beautiful valley Caleb had told her about and the hardships they would face in the years ahead. Could she be all he needed her to be? Her heart swelled with love and confidence. For such a man as Caleb Hunter, she could be anything.

She thought of her white parents and wished she'd known them—and that they had met White Weasel and Ten Bears. They would have liked one another if they could have put aside the hostilities and distrust that separated the two races. But it wasn't as simple as that, she knew. Once the Comancheria had belonged to a mighty nation, the True Human Beings, the Comanche. Now it belonged to the white men because they had been stronger, their numbers and their weapons greater than that of the Comanche. Such was the way of things, but the lesson was a bitter one.

One day when she had children, she would tell them of her Comanche family, of their kindness and wisdom and bravery, but she would also tell them of these people, of their perseverance and their love for one another.

Margaret took Faye's and Jenny's arms and guided them toward Sarah McKinsey's house.

"Sarah's down helping the doctor with Miz Bell," Margaret said, ushering them indoors. "She won't mind a bit having company. You just make yourselves at home."

Jenny had never been in the McKinsey house before. Now she glanced around the small frame building. Though larger than the Walsh soddy, it was scattered with the clothing and belongings of too many people confined to too small a space. Jenny felt closed in, as she had the first night with the Walshes. She'd never be able to relax and rest here, but when her head hit the pillow, her eyes closed immediately and she was soon fast asleep.

"Poor child," Margaret said, placing a cup of coffee in front of Faye.

"You don't know the all of it," Faye replied, taking her baby son onto her lap and opening her bodice to nurse him. Greedily his gums clamped onto her swollen nipple and he relaxed against his mother. Patiently Margaret waited until Faye had taken a few sips of coffee and begun to relax. A sense of peace and everyday events had settled over them. The noise and unrest of the town was kept outside the sturdy little house.

"She tried to save us from all this," Faye began, and told Margaret everything Jenny had related to her.

"So Hank Radburn finally met his end," Margaret

said. "I could have told you he'd come to it in some violent way. He was a coarse, evil man."

Faye nodded in agreement and continued her story. "The one good thing that seems to have come of this," she observed, "is that Caleb seems to care about her an awful lot."

Margaret nodded in satisfaction. She could have told Faye about that as well, but she remained silent, sensing the special bond between Faye and Jenny.

Having filled his tummy and been reassured in his mother's arms, Samson was fast asleep. Faye yawned, and Margaret stood up.

"Time to get you to bed," she said, and led Faye to a cot.

When Faye was asleep, with her baby son curled against her side, Margaret tiptoed out and checked on the children in the wagon. Their smudged faces were angelic in slumber. Margaret nodded her head in satisfaction and went off to inform her sister of their guests and to check on the progress of Claire Marie Bell.

Three days later, Caleb and Jenny were married. The wedding, coming so hard on the heels of the fire, had done much to lift spirits. Major Egan and a detachment of soldiers had ridden to Millbrook to see that all was in order and to inform Caleb that Big Elk had been found. He'd been caught in the prairie fire. Knowing her former kinsmen were indeed dead put Jenny's fears to rest.

The day of the wedding, people strolled down to the church for the ceremony. Afterward, there would be a dinner and dancing at the schoolhouse. Jenny and Faye were at Sarah McKinsey's house preparing for the wedding. Caleb was already at the church, his clothes freshly brushed and cleaned.

Reverend Crane was in attendance, as was his family. When the guests were all in the schoolhouse, Jenny opened the door and walked up the aisle. She wore Rachel Tyler's dress of yellow silk, which had been hastily cut down to fit her. The schoolteacher had been surprisingly generous and friendly to Jenny. Perhaps, like Jenny, she'd learned special lessons here among these people. Rachel smiled as Jenny passed by.

Faye was weeping, and Hannah stared at Jenny as if awestruck. But it was Caleb's face Jenny watched. She saw the love and pride as he met her gaze. She'd gathered her hair into a loose knot on top of her head and tied a yellow ribbon around it. She carried a bouquet of scorched prairie flowers, and he thought he'd never seen a more beautiful bride.

Jenny came to a stop beside him; Reverend Crane beamed down on them. The wedding vows were repeated. Caleb's gaze was steady as he listened to the words and made the proper answers without hesitation. Jenny's voice was firm and clear as she made her pledges. And then they were man and wife, standing before the homesteaders, who were beaming. Their sadness had been put aside to help Jenny and Caleb celebrate this moment in their lives. Reverend Crane raised his hands.

"It must be the will of the Lord," he said, "that in the midst of hardships comes a renewal of faith by two young people. Jenny Walsh and Caleb Hunter have pledged themselves to each other. Now they will journey away from us and go to a place where they'll start their own home. We know they'll love and cherish each other in the years ahead and we will miss them."

Caleb's lips were firm and warm on hers. She heard Hannah giggle. Then they were walking down the aisle and out of the schoolhouse. People were kissing them and throwing little handfuls of rice. Jenny knew it was rice they could ill afford. The winter ahead would be hard on all of them.

"Won't you stay the winter with us?" Faye asked later, when the festivities were over and Jenny was preparing to leave. "We can share what we have with you."

"We'll go on to our own place," Jenny said, nodding gently. She'd taken off the beautiful wedding dress and carefully packed it. Once again she was dressed in a calico gown, ready to travel. She didn't say so to Faye, but as soon as they arrived in the valley and Caleb had brought in some deer, she intended to make them both warm buckskins for the winter.

"How will Caleb have time to build you a house before the snows fall?" Faye asked, truly troubled about her friend.

"He may not," Jenny answered serenely. "We may spend our first winter in a tepee."

"You'll freeze to death."

"We'll survive," Jenny answered, suddenly serious. She touched Faye's cheek. "I have many skills at my disposal, my dear friend—those of my Comanche family and those you have taught me."

Faye put aside her worries and hugged the slight girl. Once she had reassured her mother in such a manner. "May God go with you," she whispered.

"Both of them," Jenny said solemnly.

Frank and Faye and the rest of the homesteaders gathered to see Caleb and Jenny off. They had between them two horses and two pack mules, loaded with supplies that would have to see them through the winter. Jenny's demeanor was serene as she waved good-bye to all her friends.

"We'll be back come spring," she cried.

They rode out of the town and headed north, across the vast prairie. For nearly an hour they did not speak. Finally Jenny nudged her horse forward, so she rode side by side with Caleb.

"I'll miss them all," she said.

"I know, but you're my woman now, Jenny. I'll be there for you." She smiled, secure in his love, and sighed contentedly.

In five days they came to their valley and paused on a hill to look down at the green, fertile meadows and sparkling water. Like Caleb had done before her, Jenny pictured their home here—and their children riding across the valley. Neither of them spoke. Their minds and hearts were too full. Caleb reached for Jenny's hand, and, side by side, they walked down to the river.